CAPITAL MURDER

ARCANE CASEBOOK 7

DAN WILLIS

Print Edition – 2021

This version copyright © 2021 by Dan Willis.

All rights reserved. No part of this book may be reproduced or transmitted in any form or by any electronic or mechanical means, including photocopying, recording or by any information storage and retrieval system, without the express written permission of the copyright holder, except where permitted by law.

This novel is a work of fiction. Names, characters, places and incidents are either the product of the author's imagination, or, if real, used fictitiously.

Edited by Stephanie Osborn
Supplemental Edits by Barbara Davis

Cover by Mihaela Voicu

Published by

Runeblade Entertainment
Spanish Fork, Utah.

1

THE HARD WAY

Gary Symms was a mountain of a man, six feet tall and two hundred and twenty pounds of solid muscle. He worked as a foreman on the south side docks, overseeing several gangs of rough men who manhandled cargo off ships, into warehouses, and then onto trucks for distribution. He wasn't a particularly educated man, but he had an innate cleverness that ran toward cruelty. It was that, plus his prodigious size and strength, that landed him the job of foreman. Gary was smart enough to get his work done well and strong enough to keep his men in line.

He was also a murderer.

Alex Lockerby didn't have any proof of that last one, but he had innate skills too. As he watched Gary stride off the shipyard grounds as the shift whistle blew, those instincts were telling him that Gary Symms had killed his wife.

It had been almost a week since Julia Sark had come into his office. She was a plain woman with round features, an overly large nose, and dirty blonde hair that tended toward the color of mud. When she entered Alex's office, she also had a black eye.

Gary had given her that.

Alex clenched his fist inside the pocket of his overcoat as the man in question crossed the street and headed north, toward the capital. Most of the men who worked on the docks lived in the various slums that surrounded it, but not Gary. His position afforded him a decent income and he'd married very well, so Gary lived in a brownstone several blocks past the low-rent district.

Julia had told Alex the story, how her sister, Millie, had fallen for Gary and married him. When Julia and Millie's father died, Gary and Millie had just moved into the brownstone, claiming it for their own. Julia hadn't minded; she worked as a legal secretary in Trenton and only came to the city to visit her sister.

At first everything seemed fine, idyllic even, but then Julia began to notice changes in her sister. Millie would only invite Julia over during the day when Gary was at work. Several times she had bruises that she blamed on her own clumsiness. Julia became suspicious of her brother-in-law, but every time she pressed Millie on the subject, Millie would assure her everything was fine.

Then last week, Millie had called Julia during the day. She declared that she wouldn't spend another night in the brownstone and told Julia to meet her at the ferry. Julia went, but Millie never showed. Concerned, Julia crossed the river and took a cab to the brownstone, but when she got there, Gary was home. He demanded to know where Millie had gone, but Julia knew that for the lie it was. She wanted to come in and search for Millie, but Gary refused. When she tried to push past him, he'd given her the black eye.

Julia had come to Alex the next day.

He'd tried using a finding rune, of course, but links to dead bodies were much weaker than those with the living. This case would require Alex to do things the old-fashioned way.

Alex's first step had been to call the police. They questioned Gary, but he claimed that his wife had run out on him, just as he'd implied to Julia. He even told the cops that she was probably with her sister in Jersey. The cops had searched the house, but found no evidence of foul play, so they let the matter drop.

Alex had been following Gary for five days now. He watched the man go to and from work, stopping at a five-and-dime for breakfast, then going to his favorite bar for dinner and a drink on his way home.

The previous night, he'd even stayed out drinking with a gang of his friends. It definitely wasn't the behavior of a grieving husband whose wife had disappeared.

Alex sighed as he followed Gary through the south-side slums. It was early December, and the sun was already down. Dingy street lights cast pools of sickly yellow light onto the dirt streets, supplemented by the occasional fire barrel surrounded by forgotten men and women the depression had cast aside.

Gary walked as if he were on a brightly lit street in a good part of town. None of these ragged people would bother him and he knew it. Alex kept him in view as the slums gave way to seedy businesses. Another two blocks and Gary would reach Finn's Bar, his favorite dinner spot and watering hole.

Up ahead, Gary turned the corner of the block and Alex quickened his steps to keep up. He'd just turned the corner by a pawn shop when he was grabbed by the lapels of his overcoat and slammed into the side of the building. Alex grunted as the air was forced from his lungs.

"Why are you following me?" Gary demanded, leaning in to use his body weight to press Alex against the brick wall. A man like him was used to being bigger than everyone else, but Alex had him by at least an inch, though he wasn't as bulky. "You think I didn't see you back there?" Gary went on, trying to cow Alex with his glare. "What do you want?"

Alex gave Gary a friendly smile and pulled his hand out of his overcoat pocket.

"Alex Lockerby," he said, holding one of his business cards up where Gary could see it. "Private investigator. Your sister-in-law hired me to find out where you dumped your wife's body."

It took a moment for Gary to process what Alex had said; clearly it wasn't what he'd been expecting. When he finally put it together, he let go of Alex's overcoat, then doubled up his fist and slugged Alex in the gut.

The air wooshed out of Alex's lungs again and he staggered back into the wall to keep from falling to his knees.

"I'm going to teach you not to spy on your betters," Gary growled, raising his hands into a boxer's stance. "Then I'm going to deal with that busybody."

"Julia," Alex gasped, giving Gary a grin. "Her name is Julia."

Gary just shook his head in astonishment.

"I'm going to enjoy this," he growled, moving in toward Alex.

"What's all this about?" a new voice interrupted.

Gary sprung back as if he'd been hit, though Alex hadn't moved. A uniformed policemen in a blue winter overcoat had just rounded the corner. He wasn't as tall as Alex or Gary, but he had big hands and a nose that had obviously been broken more than once.

"This fella is following me," Gary growled, jerking his thumb at Alex. "Figured he was up to no good."

The policeman cast an appraising eye over Alex, noting his expensive coat and shoes.

"Bill collector?" the cop said.

"Private Detective," Alex replied, holding out another of his business cards.

The cop took the card and glanced at it before handing it back.

"I heard of you," the cop said in an unamused voice. "You're that hotshot that's always in the paper, the runewright detective. Supposed to use finding magic to solve your cases."

Alex chuckled as the cop handed back his card.

"Something like that," he said.

"Well we don't need any help keeping the peace around here," the cop said, giving Alex a hard look. "You'd best be on your way."

"All right," Alex said, holding up his hands in acquiescence. "My finding rune is almost done anyway," he cast a knowing look at Gary. "Then I won't need you to find Millie."

Gary's eyes hardened and the side of his lip curled in a snarl. Alex was certain that if the policeman hadn't been there, the man would have tried to murder him. Alex gave him a grin, then turned and went back around the corner the way he came.

Five minutes later, Alex opened the door from his vault to his office and walked down the narrow hall that led to his waiting room. Three doors occupied the left side of the hallway as he went. The first was to his private office, the second was a makeshift rune-writing room where his employee, Mike Fitzgerald, practiced his craft, and the last was Alex's map room.

Opening the door to the map room, Alex found three people already gathered around the table where his enormous map of Manhattan had been permanently mounted.

"Hi'ya boss," Sherry Knox said, giving him a sly grin. "I had a feeling you'd get it done tonight."

Alex chuckled but didn't respond. Sherry was a very special magical practitioner, the only one of her kind in North America, maybe even the world. She was an Auger, someone gifted with the ability to see the future.

Sometimes — when whatever power she had decided it wanted to play ball. Apparently today was one of her good days...magically speaking.

"How did it go?" the taller of the two men asked. He was several inches shorter than Alex with tan skin, dark hair, and almond-shaped eyes. He was also one of Alex's oldest friends and his primary contact with the New York Police Department.

"You should'a seen this guy, Danny," Alex laughed. The motion sent a twinge through his abdomen where Gary had slugged him, and he cut the laugh short with a wince. "I moved up my tail to less than half a block and I'm still surprised he made me."

"But you planted the stone on him, right?" Mike Fitzgerald asked.

Alex looked down at the map. The table was empty except for two items, a cheap tin compass and a small, black stone. The compass was more or less in the center of the table, but the red-painted side of its needle didn't point north, it was indicating the black rock. The stone was round and flat. Alex guessed it had come from a river somewhere, but since he bought it off a notions vender on Runewright Row, he had no way to verify that. It was one of two, a matched set that were magically linked to each other. Alex had several of the sets and had used them in the past to follow cheating husbands. All he had to do was slip one stone into the pocket of his quarry, and use a finding rune to link the second stone to a map. After that he could follow the first stone wherever it went.

"I got slugged in the gut for my trouble," Alex said, "but I dropped it in his coat pocket." He nodded at Danny. "Officer Hodgkins played his part perfectly. Be sure to thank him for me."

"You got the stone on him," Danny Pak said, indicating the map, "but did he take the bait?"

Alex grinned and waggled his eyebrows at his friend.

"Of course he did."

"Then how come he's having dinner in a pub?" Mike asked. "If that stone is right, he's at Michael's Pub, like he hasn't a care in the world."

"He can't do anything yet," Danny said. "Too many people might see him moving a body at this hour."

"Unless he already dumped her in the harbor," Sherry offered.

"Even in the dead of night, someone would have noticed him carrying a body eight blocks," Alex said. "No, he hid Milli somewhere close to his brownstone. Probably buried her, or my finding rune would have connected with her body."

"So we just wait?" Mike said, sounding a bit let down.

"Welcome to detective work," Danny said with a chuckle, then he looked at Sherry. "You think Marnie's still downstairs?"

Alex's secretary gave Danny a glowing smile and pulled a heavy thermos from under the table.

"I like to come prepared," she said, reaching down for a stack of paper cups.

"Did you bring some sandwiches, too?" Alex asked. "I'm starving."

"Iggy thought of that," Sherry said, indicating a wicker basket on the sideboard that sat against the wall.

"Bless that old man," Alex said, moving to the basket and helping himself.

The chairs that normally went with the heavy map table were kept out of the way, pushed against the back wall of the room so Alex could walk freely around the table. He grabbed one and dragged it with him as he returned to the table.

Over the next few hours, they finished off the coffee and the sandwiches while they watched the black stone. As Gary Symms moved around, the stone followed him, creeping slowly across the map.

After dinner, Gary went back to his house and remained there till well after ten. Alex was starting to worry that he hadn't put the fear of capture into Gary, but eventually the stone moved away from the brownstone, inching along to the east.

"Looks like he's headed toward the Capital Building," Danny said. "That doesn't seem a very likely hiding place for a corpse."

"Still, you'd better get your boys moving," Alex said, nodding at the candlestick phone sitting next to the now empty sandwich basket.

Danny stood and moved to the phone.

"Dispatch," he said once his call went through. "This is Lieutenant Pak. I need you to contact radio car twelve. Tell them that the subject is moving east from home base in the direction of the Capital. They're to get ready to move but hold position until I give the word."

There was a long pause while Danny just stood with the earpiece pressed to his head, then he nodded.

"Understood," he said, then he hung up. "We're ready," he reported as he set the phone down. "Any idea where he's headed?"

Alex stared intently at the map. He wasn't terribly familiar with that part of town, but he did recognize a large building on a corner half a block from Gary Symms' current location.

"Isn't this a church?" he said, indicating the space.

Danny stared at it and shrugged.

"What are you thinking?"

"What better place to hide a body than a churchyard," Alex noted.

"Wouldn't people notice if you dug up a cemetery?" Mike asked.

"Not if there was a fresh grave there already," Alex pointed out.

Danny nodded along.

"He'd just have to dig a few feet down. Only enough to cover the body."

"Don't look now, boys," Sherry said, pointing at the map. "But the stone just stopped at the church."

Danny stood up, a wide smile splitting his face.

"I'll call the boys and have them move in."

"Give Gary ten minutes," Alex said, rising and moving to the sideboard. He opened the bottom of the cabinet and pulled out a bottle of Scotch and a stack of shot glasses. "That way, when the cops get there, he'll already have most of the digging done."

"A fine idea," Mike said with a nod.

"I believe I'll drink to that," Danny said, accepting a tumbler full of amber liquid from Alex.

Alex arrived at his office sharp at nine the next morning. The previous night's operation had gone according to plan: Gary had been apprehended by the police literally standing over poor Millie's corpse. By the time Alex had gone to bed it was almost midnight, but he knew he'd have to telephone Julia first thing and he didn't want to keep her waiting. The news had been expected, but she still burst into tears when Alex told her the news. At least her brother-in-law would get the chair for his crime.

Thank God for small favors.

The rest of Alex's morning was taken up with bookkeeping. Mike had been taking on more involved cases using Alex's finding rune, and Sherry had a lost engagement ring and a stolen fur coat that needed to be picked up by their rightful owners. While the others saw to the tasks that kept his agency running, Alex sat at his desk filling out the reports on a new typewriter with agonizing slowness. If the city hadn't started requiring official forms be typewritten, Alex wouldn't have bothered with the newfangled device. Unfortunately, he did enough business with the Central Office of Police that it was a necessity.

"Got a minute, boss?" Sherry asked.

Alex looked up from his work to find her leaning against the frame of his open door. She wore a blue blouse with a black skirt and a fuzzy white sweater. Sherry didn't have Leslie's beauty queen figure, but in the sweater she could turn heads. As distracting as her pose was, Alex focused on her face. She had a strange, pensive look.

"What's the matter?" he asked.

She held up her deck of tarot cards and shook them. Apparently her gift was still working from last night.

"Uh-oh," he said with a bit of trepidation. "What now?"

Sherry's card readings were almost never good news.

"You sure you want to know?" she asked.

Alex indicated his mostly clean desk top and she crossed from the door. Without commentary, she dealt out one card face down.

"Don't you usually use more than that?" he asked.

"I use as many as are necessary," she said. "This is you." She tapped the back of the card, then turned it over. The card depicted a man walking with a long stride. He had a knapsack thrown over his shoulder like Charlie Chaplin in *The Tramp*. The figure stood on the edge of a cliff with one foot over the edge as if he were about to fall, while he looked up at the sky without a care.

"The Fool," Sherry said.

"Well, you did say it was me," Alex said with an amused look.

"The Fool can mean a journey," Sherry explained. "Sometimes literally, sometimes it's a new beginning."

"I'm getting a new secretary," he guessed.

Sherry gave him a hard look.

"I thought you said you wanted me to do this."

Alex held up his hands in a placating gesture and she drew another card.

"The Magician," she said, putting down a card with a man in a flowing robe on its face.

"Inverted," Alex said, noting that from Sherry's perspective, he was upside down.

She nodded in acknowledgement.

"The inverted magician is a trickster," she said. "He deals in falsehood and illusion."

"Wonderful," Alex said without enthusiasm. He had enough lying cheats in his life without a new one adding to the list.

"Temperance," Sherry said, ignoring him and turning over another card. This one had a large chalice on it.

"Prohibition's coming back?" Alex guessed. "I hope it's not telling me to give up drinking."

"It could mean that," she admitted, "It could also mean alcohol will be important to you."

"Like I'm going to meet someone in a bar?"

Sherry shrugged.

"Possibly, but in this case I think it means to avoid extremes, to take the middle path."

Alex wasn't sure what to make of that, so he just nodded as she drew another card.

"The Two of Swords," she said, her brow furrowing as she set it down. The card depicted two crossed swords.

"Indecision," she said, then shook her head. "Maybe a stalemate or something that has two parts. That's all I can see."

"So I'm going on a trip with new beginnings where I'll meet someone in a bar who wants to fool or trick me, and I should indecisively avoid extremes."

"Don't make fun," Sherry said, annoyed. "My visions are serious."

Alex sighed, looking at the cards on his desk. Sherry's visions usually didn't make much sense, but this made less sense than usual.

"Do you ever have specific visions that could actually warn me of trouble before I'm neck deep in it?" he asked.

"As a matter of fact I do," she said, looking in the direction of the waiting room. "Miss Kincaid just arrived."

2

DISTANCE

Alex sighed, glancing in the direction of his waiting room. It wasn't quite eleven, which meant Sorsha hadn't come for an impromptu lunch date. Sherry was right, that was a bad sign.

"You want me to run interference," she asked, picking up on his mood without the necessity of foresight.

Alex shook his head and rose from his desk.

"Wait here a minute, would you."

"Fight fair," Sherry said, patting him on the shoulder as he passed her.

It only took a moment for Alex to move along the short hall to the door that separated the hall from his waiting area. Without hesitation, he grabbed the door handle and turned it smartly.

"Alex," Sorsha said as he stepped into the room. As usual, she was dressed impeccably in a white button-up shirt with black cuffs and a black collar offset by an ice blue scarf and a form-fitting skirt. She was standing in front of Sherry's desk as if waiting for her to return. The Sorceress knew very well that she could simply go back to Alex's office, for she'd done it on many previous occasions. The fact that she was hesitating confirmed Alex's fears.

"You can't make it tonight," he said. His tone conveyed that the statement wasn't a guess.

A look of chagrin played across Sorsha's porcelain features and she looked away, turning so the A-line of her hair hid her face.

"I'm sorry," she said.

Alex knew she meant it.

She always meant it.

It was her resigned sincerity that galled him. They'd been officially going out for almost four months and in that time they'd managed to get together twice, not counting the time Nazi spies had tried to abduct her from the Rainbow Room. The first time they'd gone out for lunch, but they both had afternoon appointments and couldn't linger. The second time they'd gone to a nightclub, but Sorsha had been called away by her FBI lackeys before their hors d'oeuvres had arrived.

Since then it had been one broken date after another.

To be fair, Alex had broken a few of their appointments himself, but Sorsha outstripped him by far. He'd even tried meeting her for a cup of coffee at Empire Terminal ten floors below his office, but she hadn't even managed to make that. It was clear, at least to Alex, that whatever he thought they had together simply wasn't a priority to the sorceress.

"What is it this time?" Alex pressed, his voice making it abundantly clear that he would consider any answer inadequate.

"The Bureau is sending me out of town on a case," she said, her voice uncharacteristically small.

"And naturally you can't tell me anything about it," he pressed. "No doubt it's a matter of National Security or some such."

She still wouldn't look at him.

"Something like that."

"Well I guess that takes precedence over your social life." Alex knew he was twisting the knife of her guilt, but he did it anyway.

With a gasp that was half shame and half outrage, she whirled on him, sending her platinum hair flying.

"You think this is easy for me?" she demanded, her eyes flashing blue with her magic. "Half of those dullards down at the Bureau think I'm some bubblehead the higher ups are patronizing because my name looks good in the reports. The other half think the director keeps me around to play slap and tickle behind closed doors." Her voice and her anger rose as she spoke. "I've worked damn hard to prove myself, and it doesn't help when your name gets associated with my cases, as if I need my hand held."

Alex knew she was right. She'd agreed to work with the FBI to help them with cases that involved magic, but she'd turned out to be a damn good investigator. The fact that the Bureau was relying on her more and more was a good thing, but he couldn't help resenting it. He worked as hard as anyone, but he still managed to find time for her after all.

"I didn't realize I was such an imposition," he said.

Her look softened.

"You aren't," she said. "And once I get back we'll figure this out. I promise."

Alex sighed. He'd heard that before. More than once.

"All right," he said. He didn't believe she was serious, but his anger at the situation had been sated and he didn't want to argue about it further.

She looked down for a moment, then back up to his eyes, searching for understanding. Alex didn't have any to give, and he just stared back at her.

"All right," she echoed him, then she turned and strode out of the office.

Alex watched her go and continued to stare at the door for a full minute after she shut it behind her. He suddenly identified with the card Sherry had dealt him.

"The Fool, indeed," he said with a nod of acquiescence, then turned and headed back to his office. When he pulled the door to the back hallway open, Sherry and Mike almost fell out into the waiting room.

"You heard?" he said.

Sherry looked embarrassed, but Mike just nodded.

"She's a fiery woman," he said, putting a hand on Alex's shoulder. "Women like that are just like a spirited horse, you need to ease up on the reins, boss. Let her figure out how you fit. If you keep pushing, you'll just drive her away."

Alex scoffed and shrugged his shoulders.

"Thanks, Mike," he said, "but we've got work to do." He looked at Sherry. "My schedule just opened up tonight, so I can take any casework you've got waiting."

"Sure thing, boss," she said, giving him a sad smile, then stepping past him toward her desk.

Alex worked through lunch without noticing, swearing at his mechanical tormentor the entire time. When he finally looked up from the typewriter it was almost three. His stomach growled at him, but he ignored it. He needed something active to do.

"You've been sitting too long," he declared, pushing back in his chair and rising. Honestly, he'd expected Sherry to bring him something to work on already, but he hadn't heard a peep out of her since Sorsha left. Was this her way of giving him room to stew about his love life?

"That's the last thing I need," he said, striding around to the intercom box. Before he could push the call key, however, Sherry's voice came out of the speaker.

"Boss?" she said.

Alex almost laughed. He once asked her if her uncanny ability to appear when he needed her was part of her magic or just good timing. So far she'd refused to take a position on the subject.

"Yeah," Alex said back to the box after pushing the 'talk' key.

"Mr. Barton would like to see you in his office right away," she responded. "He said it's urgent."

Alex hung his head before he replied. He desperately wanted something to do, but meeting with his part-time employer was never high on his list. Barton had a bad habit of either wanting to bounce ideas off Alex or showing up with magical emergencies he needed Alex to fix. Unfortunately both situations usually took far more time than Alex liked.

"All right," Alex replied through the intercom, not bothering to hide the sigh in his voice. "Tell Andrew I'll be up in a minute."

Alex left his office a few minutes later, heading down in the building's public elevator to Empire Station. The only way to reach the upper floors was to take the private elevator behind a security station on the west wall of the station. Alex had been in the building for over six months now, so the guard at the glassed-in booth simply nodded at him as he passed.

Another two minutes and the private elevator deposited Alex in the front room of Barton Electric. From there he moved to Andrew Barton's private elevator and used his key to summon the car. This elevator had only two buttons. The bottom one led to the catwalk that ran around the etherium generators that converted magical energy to electricity. A catwalk led from the landing to the spell room, the nerve center of Barton's operation. In that room dozens of linking runes connected the galaxy-like power spell to the generators, and then connected the generators to the two relay towers providing power to Brooklyn and the Bronx.

The second button in the private elevator deposited Alex directly into Sorcerer Andrew Barton's palatial private office. The room was twice the size of his apartment and two stories tall. Rows of glass windows covered the back wall with an incredible view of the city and Central Park in the distance. A desk the size of a banquet table occupied the center of the room and was made of a single slab of white marble held up by an industrial-looking steel frame. As usual, the desk was littered with papers, folders, rolled blueprints, artistic renderings of buildings and machines, and several scale models of various types of equipment.

Most times, when Barton summoned Alex, he would be waiting, impatiently, for Alex to arrive. This time, however, there was no sign of the sorcerer when the elevator doors slid open.

"Hello?" Alex said after surveying the room.

"Back here," Barton called from somewhere off to Alex's right. Looking in that direction, Alex spotted a door that was set into the wall. He'd seen it before, but it had never been open till now.

Making his way through the open door, Alex found himself in a small hallway that ran down to an elegant foyer. The foyer was currently occupied by two suitcases and a portmanteau trunk all done in burgundy leather with gold accents. Beyond them was an apartment that closely resembled the one Barton had provided for Alex. It was neat to the point of not looking lived in, with a row of bookshelves on one side of the front room, surrounded by a tasteful arrangement of couches for entertaining. A counter ran along the back wall with stools on one side and a cutout that showed a kitchen beyond. Off to Alex's left was a hallway continuing further back into the suite.

"I was about to go and get you," Barton said, emerging from the back room with a valise that he set on top of the trunk. The sorcerer wore a tuxedo that shone glossy black from his shoes to his lapels. His hair was slicked back, and his pencil mustache had been trimmed into two precise lines. "Here," he said, reaching into his jacket and withdrawing a folded paper. "Get whatever you need ready, and meet me downstairs in twenty minutes."

Alex looked at the paper in confusion, then back to the sorcerer.

"What?" he said. Alex was genuinely confused, a condition that wasn't unusual where Barton was concerned. The man seemed to exude chaos and then just sweep people up in his wake.

"It's your ticket, of course," he said as if that explained everything. "Now get a move on, I don't want to be late."

Rather than continue to pursue his futile line of questioning, Alex opened the paper sleeve, revealing a silver square of paper with black printing on it.

"Airship *Merryweather*?" Alex read the name in big letters.

"Yes, yes," Barton said. "I know airplanes are faster, but I dislike being packed in like a sardine. I've got us berths for the night, now get your kit together, we've got to go."

"Where are we going?" Alex asked.

"Washington, of course. The city is run by a board of commissioners and their President wants to talk to me about putting up a relay tower in the city."

"Congratulations," Alex said, holding up the ticket. "And I'm accompanying you for what reason?"

A look of annoyance crossed the sorcerer's face, as if Alex was being deliberately obtuse.

"To make sure the linking runes work over that distance, of

course," he said. "Now pack your bags and put on some decent traveling clothes." He checked his watch. "We've only got fifteen minutes left. Chop, chop!"

Alex shook his head, but decided not to discuss the matter further. The conditions of his employment with Barton Electric were very simple. Barton provided him with office space and an apartment in Empire Tower, and Alex was available to provide runewright services at Barton's discretion. Usually Barton's requests were simple and didn't take too much time, but odd, inconvenient requests were also par for the course.

"All right," he said with a defeated sigh. "I'll meet you in the lobby in fifteen minutes."

Fifteen minutes later, Alex got off the public elevator in the Empire Tower lobby. He'd put on his tux and grabbed one of the spare doctor's bags he kept around in case he had to replace his kit. Since Barton said they'd be traveling overnight, he dropped a pair of pajamas into the bag along with his razor, toothbrush, hair creme, and comb.

"Where are your bags?" Barton said as Alex crossed the gleaming marble floor.

Alex held up the doctor's bag and patted it for emphasis.

"That's it?" Barton asked, incredulous.

Alex just shrugged.

"I'm a runewright," he said. "I'm never more than a chalk outline away from my vault that's got all my clothes and things inside."

Barton pinched the bridge of his nose and then shook his head.

"I'm a sorcerer, Alex," he said, putting his arm around Alex's shoulders. "I could conjure everything I might need out of thin air, but where's the romance in that?"

"Romance?"

"Of course," he went on. "There's something cathartic about traveling in style, just a man, his luggage, and a first-class cabin. You're disconnected from everything, no phone, no newspapers, just the journey. You can't enjoy that if you're popping into your vault every five minutes. I'm surprised you didn't know that."

"Andrew," Alex said as patiently as he could. "I was an orphan by age twelve. That also meant that, until recently, I was church-mouse poor. The longest trip I've ever taken was the time I had to go to Albany to look up some building permits for a proposed hospital in Palmira."

Barton looked confused at that, but it didn't last. His look of delight returned with a vengeance.

"Of course! I should have thought of that," he admitted. "This will be quite the adventure then. Your first time traveling first class. We'll eat dinner in the observation lounge and then sip cognac and smoke cigars as we watch the sunset." He slapped Alex on the chest with a delighted chuckle. "You'll love it."

Alex wasn't so sure, but it was hard not to get swept up in Barton's boundless enthusiasm.

"Okay," he said with a half-hearted grin.

"That's the spirit," Barton said, heading for the street where a gleaming black car waited. "Let's be off. Time and airships wait for no man."

The New York Aerodrome was a complex of buildings and towers built on the southwest end of Manhattan Island. Dozens of airships docked daily, delivering passengers and cargo to one of the busiest cities in the world. Alex followed along in Barton's wake as a never-ending stream of officials, porters, and aerodrome crew escorted him through the terminal to the elevator that would take them up to the *Merryweather* high above.

Alex had seen airships all his life, swimming through the sky like flying whales, but he'd never been this close to one. The aerodrome had a glass roof and Alex looked up at the massive vessel suspended in the air, high above. It was long and cigar-shaped with a large passenger gondola hanging beneath its bulk and heavy gasoline engines protruding out from its body. It was an awe-inspiring sight.

Someone said something, and it took Alex a moment to realize the words were directed at him.

"Your ticket, sir," the uniformed steward said again. He was an older man with white hair and a thick, white mustache.

Alex fumbled for a moment with his pocket, then produced the ticket.

"You have a stateroom," the white-mustached steward said after examining his clipboard. "Number eleven. Enjoy your voyage."

Alex thanked the man as he took his ticket back, then stepped on the elevator beside Barton.

"Exciting, isn't it?" the sorcerer said, nudging Alex with his shoulder.

Alex had to admit that, in truth, it really was.

3

THE JOURNEY

A young steward in a dark green uniform jacket and a pillbox cap took Alex's ticket and his lone bag, then led him down a well-lit stair into the bowels of the massive craft. The *Merryweather* was an American airship, built by the Goodyear Company, and had two passenger decks. The lower deck had staterooms and large viewing areas for first class passengers, while the upper deck had mostly seats and a cafe for regular travelers.

"Right along here, sir," the steward said, leading Alex past a row of wooden doors that gleamed with polish. Each door was narrow, and they were spaced relatively close together, a testament to how compact each stateroom was. A second row of doors occupied the opposite wall, across a wide hallway, which gave plenty of room for the crew to move about with luggage and other necessities.

"How many staterooms are there?" Alex asked as they went.

"Thirty," the young man said. "Fifteen on each side. Here we are, sir." He took out an elaborate key and opened the door to stateroom eleven.

"There's a call button on the wall next to the light switch," he said as he took Alex's bag inside. "Just ring if you need anything."

Alex looked into the little compartment as the steward set his bag on the couch that occupied one wall. It was a tight fit to be sure, but he'd stayed in worse places. There was a series of drawers on the wall opposite the couch, beside a mirror and washbasin, with a tiny bathroom beyond.

"When is dinner?" Alex asked, passing the steward a fiver as the young man exited the stateroom.

"From six to eight in the observation lounge," he replied as the bill vanished into his pocket. "We'll be stopping in Philadelphia to take on cargo around eleven and we'll arrive in Washington at eight the following morning. Would you like a wake-up call?"

"Seven," Alex said as the steward handed him a brass key on a fob with the number eleven stamped on it.

"Very good, sir."

The steward nodded and left, hurrying away along the wide hallway. Alex watched him go for a moment, then realized he hadn't asked the man where the observation lounge was. Since he hadn't passed it on the trip to his cabin from the aft boarding ramp, Alex assumed it was farther toward the nose of the airship. Since he had no real need to unpack, he shut and locked his door and continued forward.

The wide hallway between the rows of staterooms ended in a set of double doors with the words, Observation Lounge, engraved into a brass plate on each door. Beyond was a large, open area filled with sunlight. All of the exterior walls were made of glass and even though the *Merryweather* was still moored to the Aerodrome tower, the view was amazing. Round tables were distributed throughout the room, and already some of the passengers had claimed many of the ones nearest the windows.

"Excuse me," Alex said, stopping a young woman in a white jacket and green skirt. "When are we going to depart?"

The girl looked toward a large clock mounted above the doors Alex had just come through.

"In about ten minutes," she said.

Alex looked around at the seating.

"Where should I sit to get the best view?" he asked.

"Well. that depends," the girl said, her face taking on a conspiratorial aspect. "Do you want to see the city or the ocean?"

"Ocean."

Alex had seen plenty of the city in his lifetime. The girl's expression slid into a grin and she nodded to the windows behind Alex.

"Port side then," she said. "You won't see the sun set, but the reflection on the water is amazing."

Alex thanked her and headed toward an empty table up against the port side glass. Even with the ship moored in place, he could see Empire Tower and even a bit of the Chrysler Building off in the distance. At that sight, his mind drifted to Sorsha. He was still angry that she apparently didn't think enough of him to make him a priority in her life, but that feeling faded quickly. She was a sorceress, after all. A powerful and influential woman whose time, attention, and opinions would always be in demand.

"Maybe she's better off without extra entanglements," he muttered.

"I thought I'd find you here," Barton said, interrupting his thoughts. The Sorcerer slid into the chair on the opposite side of the little table. "I was hoping you'd already got a good table, and this will be quite satisfactory."

Alex shot him a sly look.

"Benefits of not having all that luggage to unpack."

Barton laughed at that, offering Alex a cigarette from a solid gold case.

"I don't bother unpacking for one night," he chuckled. "My trunk is up in the hold. No, I was talking to the captain. They usually expect me to sit at his table during dinner, but since this is your first trip I wanted to have dinner with you and watch the journey. I explained to the captain I couldn't make it."

Alex lit the cigarette he'd selected from Barton's case, then offered the other man a light.

"I hope he's not upset," he said.

"It's not exactly an international incident," Barton joked. "Besides, I smoothed it over with a bottle of Château d'Yquem, '88."

Alex gave the sorcerer a blank look.

"A very expensive bottle of Bordeaux, Lockerby," he said with a grin. "Now that you're becoming a man of wealth and position, I'm going to have to put some effort into refining your palate."

Alex wasn't sure he wanted his palate refined. He really wasn't a man of wealth or position either. The only reason he could afford his fancy office address and the apartment that went with it was his work with Barton. On his own, he'd probably still be in his comfortable mid-ring office on the east side. He'd be doing very well for himself, to be sure, but not get-an-office-in-Empire-Tower well.

"None of that," Barton said, reading the expression on Alex's face. "You work with the greatest sorcerer in the world, you solve murders in the greatest city in the world, your clientele is among New York's elite, and you're dating one of the most beautiful and powerful women on earth."

Alex rolled his eyes at that last one, making Barton eye him intently.

"Trouble in paradise?" he asked. The question had a tone of mirth in it, but no malice.

"It's...involved," Alex said, not wanting to air his dirty laundry in a public place, even one as nice as the *Merryweather*'s lounge.

Barton let out a laugh and leaned over to slap Alex on the shoulder.

"Don't let her throw you, kid," he said. "I know I don't look it, but I'm over one hundred years old. Now, I don't claim any great propensity toward wisdom, but one thing I've learned for certain is that anything worth having is a struggle." He gave Alex a meaningful look. "You of all people should know that. After all, you started off in an orphanage, were taken in by a priest, without anything to your name, and now look at you."

"A man of wealth and position?" Alex said, not really believing it, but knowing it was what Barton wanted to hear.

"Just so," Barton confirmed. "You didn't come all this way by accident. You did it the same way I did it, the same way Edison did it, and even the same way Sorsha did it, by pure stubbornness and hard work."

Alex couldn't argue with that. He'd come a very long way from the Brotherhood of Hope and his little basement office in Harlem. No one had done it for him; he'd had to fight and claw for every inch. He stayed late, came in early, and took whatever cases came his way. He'd once found a dog named Lady Barkley — it wasn't glamorous, but he did it.

The clink of glasses pulled Alex back from his thoughts. A blonde waitress in the white shirt and green skirt uniform had just set down a round bottle of some dark liquid and two glasses.

"What's that?" he asked as Barton removed the crystal stopper and began pouring out.

"The first step in expanding your palate," he said, passing Alex the glass. "This is Louis IV cognac, aged for over 100 years. It is..." he held the stopper under his nose and inhaled, "exquisite."

Iggy was a bit of a connoisseur of cognac, but Alex had never heard of this brand. Once Andrew passed him a glass, he swirled it around for a moment before taking a sip.

He had to admit, the Sorcerer wasn't wrong.

Before he could comment, there was a heavy clank that echoed throughout the airship, and Alex had the sudden sensation that the ground under his chair was moving. Outside the window, the *Merryweather* began to rise up, gaining altitude as it moved to clear the city.

"We're off," Barton said. He tapped out his cigarette and left it in the ashtray. "This calls for ceremony." Reaching into thin air, he produced a humidor about the size of a standard cigar box, opened it, and offered Alex a cigar.

As the airship rose, Alex trimmed the cigar with Barton's pocket cutter. Far above them, the massive engines began to turn, their propellers gaining speed until they became just a circular blur of motion. As the thrum of the engines began to vibrate through the cabin, the *Merryweather* slowly turned south. In the window, the cold, gray waters of the Atlantic came into view along with Lady Liberty, holding her torch aloft in the light of the fading sun.

"Like this," Barton said, pulling Alex's attention from the window. He dipped the end of his cut cigar into the cognac, letting it sit for a moment while the tobacco leaves soaked up the brandy.

Alex moved to copy him as Barton extracted the cigar, tapping the excess moisture from the tip.

"It takes a bit to get it lit when it's wet," he said, holding the cigar in the flame from his lighter.

When Alex finally got his cigar to light, he was surprised at how the taste of the cognac infused the tobacco smoke. He hated to admit it, but he could get used to traveling with Andrew.

"What did I tell you, Alex," the Sorcerer said with a prodigious grin. "Stick with me and I'll make a proper world traveler out of you."

Alex and Andrew sat, smoking their cigars and watching the sunlight on the water far below. When their meal came, the light had shifted from gold to red. By the time the plates had been cleared away, the sea had vanished into the blackness of night, and the *Merryweather* hung in the air like a bat in a dark cave.

The waitress who collected their plates said that once the dinner service had been cleared away, the cabin lights would be lowered so the stars would be visible. Alex decided he wanted to stay a while longer and stare out at the dark ocean below, while Barton excused himself to go read in his stateroom.

The moon had been up before the sun set and when the cabin lights went down, Alex could see its silver light sparkling on the tops of waves far below. It had a hypnotic, soothing rhythm that set Alex's mind to pleasant drifting as he watched.

"Alexander?" a smooth, feminine voice broke through his reverie. "Alexander Lockerby?" The voice was tinged with a hint of southern drawl and had a husky tone that brought an involuntary smile to Alex's lips. He turned to find a woman standing at his elbow. She wore a smart, knee-length dress with a button-up panel in the front that was cut modestly but still low enough to be alluring. As his eyes traveled up, Alex found the speaker to be young, certainly in her early twenties, blonde and pretty. She had a roundish face with a broad smile, a pert nose, and eyes that sparkled blue as she smiled. A tantalizing floral aroma accompanied her, and it triggered something in Alex's memory.

His mind finally catching up with what he was seeing, Alex rose from his chair. He had a good eye for faces, a useful skill as a detective, and he was certain he'd never met this young woman before. She clearly knew him, though.

"Call me Alex," he said. "Miss—?"

"Pritchard," she said, her smile getting wider and more charming as she tilted her head. "Zelda Pritchard."

Alex stepped around her and pulled out the chair Barton had vacated over an hour previously.

"Won't you join me, Miss Pritchard?"

She demurred, then sat in the offered chair.

"I must confess that I don't remember meeting you," Alex said as he resumed his own seat.

Zelda's smile didn't waver.

"I'd be offended by that if we'd actually met," she said with a sly smirk that was more mirth than reproach. Alex waited for her to elaborate but she just kept smiling.

"Can I offer you a drink?" Alex asked, holding his hand in the general direction of the waiter.

"That would be lovely," she said, her gaze sweeping over Alex with an appraising eye. "You look like a bourbon man."

Alex found himself grinning in spite of his general confusion about this amiable encounter.

"I prefer my liquor to be old enough to vote," he said, eliciting a giggle and a raised eyebrow from Zelda as the waiter arrived.

"Whisky it is then," she said to the man in the white coat, favoring him with her enchanting smile.

"Make it two," Alex said. "So how is it that you know me?" he pressed once the waiter departed.

She leaned forward, resting one arm on the table and the smirk she'd given him softened into a radiant smile.

"Your perfume," Alex said, his memory finally putting the pieces together for him. "It's by Enzo Romero."

Her smile somehow got wider, and her eyebrows went up for a moment.

"Very good, Alex," she said. "I love Romero's work, and this one is a blend of ylang-ylang and vanilla. It's one of his most expensive."

Alex had never heard of ylang-ylang, but didn't bother to ask.

"It suits you," he said. "I had occasion to be in Enzo's shop a few months ago; were you there as well?"

Zelda shook her head.

"I was in Milan a few months ago," she said, deliberately teasing him with the mystery of her identity.

"Then how do you know me?"

"How could I not know the man who saved the treasure of the *Almiranta* from a gang of desperate criminals?"

That surprised Alex. There had been several news stories about the incident at the museum, and some of them even included Alex, but none had given him more than a passing mention. There was certainly no reason this young and beautiful woman should know about his involvement with the attempted robbery.

On the other hand, three of the glyph runewrights died during the shootout with the police. Maybe someone she knew...or loved?

Alex shifted his right thumb until it touched the inside of the silver ring on the third finger of his left hand. He wished he had the comforting weight of his 1911 under his jacket, but the bulky weapon would ruin the lines of his tux. If Zelda had ill intent and a partner out in the semi-darkness of the observation lounge, Alex would need to be alert. He resolved that next time he wore his tux, he'd drop his knuckleduster in the pocket, just for good measure.

All of the men involved in the museum robbery were of Mayan descent, which Zelda clearly wasn't.

That doesn't prove anything, he chided himself. *She could have had a lover who was in on the crime.*

"How does such a lovely young woman know about ancient shipwrecks and dusty museums?" he asked, trying not to sound too inquisitive. He made a pretense of looking for the waiter and let his eyes sweep quickly over the nearby tables. Most were empty, but three still had occupants. One well-dressed man and his wife—

Mistress, he corrected. *Her clothes are stylish but clearly not up to his standards.*

The second table held a party of older women who were sipping sherry and enjoying each other's company. They were all far too preoccupied to pay any attention to Alex and his enchanting guest.

A lone man in an expensive suit sat at the last table. He had the long hair favored by men of certain Latin countries and it flopped down over his forehead. Dark glittering eyes peered out, beetle-like, from beneath the hair and when he saw Alex notice him, the eyes slid away toward the table of women.

Zelda laughed a musical little laugh that dragged his attention back to her.

"My father is Beauregard Pritchard," she said, in answer to his question. "He's one of the biggest tobacco producers in the country, and he simply loves to give his money away to museums and art galleries." She paused as the waiter returned with two Glencarin glasses full of dark whisky. "Anyway," she went on, picking up the nearest one, "he decided I needed some culture, so he made me the head of his foundation a few years ago..." She sipped the whisky and closed her eyes, savoring it.

"And what does the head of a foundation do?" Alex asked.

Zelda chuckled.

"I go to museums all over the world, whenever they're having parties or big events, and spend daddy's money. It's all terribly dull, which I'm sure is what daddy had in mind all along."

"So you're going in to Washington for a party?"

She sipped from her glass again, then nodded.

"There's a new exhibit at the Freer Gallery," she said as if Alex might know what that was. He didn't say anything, but she caught his lack of interest just the same. "Let's not talk about boring museum parties full of equally boring people," she said, reaching across the little table to take his hand. "Tell me about the *Almiranta* treasure and how you figured out what those thieves were up to?"

Alex drank his whiskey to give himself time to think. Zelda was pretty and her interest seemed genuine. Since all the relevant details of the robbery had been in the newspaper, he saw no harm in indulging her.

"It all started when a distraught young woman came into my office," he began. "She wanted me to find her missing husband."

Over the course of the next hour, Alex regaled Zelda with the story of the case, ending with the dramatic rescue of Leroy Cunningham, the kidnapped engineer. Whenever he could, Alex stole glances at the lone man in the expensive suit. He didn't catch him watching again, but he could almost feel the man's interest in their conversation.

For her part, Zelda watched Alex closely, listening with rapt attention and asking thoughtful questions.

"You really do like those dusty museums, don't you?" Alex asked Zelda once he finished.

"History fascinates me," she confirmed. "Museum parties bore me, but there's always a few people there who can give you the inside story on a painting or an artifact. You just have to keep an eye out for the right people."

"Like you did tonight?"

She blushed for a moment, then nodded.

"I got to see the *Almiranta* exhibit once they put it back on display, you know," she admitted. "It was beautiful and amazing. I can't imagine it's being lost to thieves, all that gold melted down to make earrings or bracelets."

"Excuse me, Miss Pritchard," a voice intruded.

Alex turned to find a short, red-haired man with wire rim glasses standing beside the table. He wore an expensive suit that had been tailored perfectly and his shoes shone with polished luster.

"I'm afraid it's after ten, Miss," he said in the manner of a schoolmarm calling her class back to their studies. His face was serious with the kind of fussy, intransigent demeanor Alex always associated with government file clerks.

"Alex," Zelda said, her perpetual smile wavering. "This is Hector Cohan. He's my father's watchdog, sent along to make sure I behave as a proper southern lady should."

Hector gave Alex a look that implied a near infinite well of disapproval, then turned back to Zelda. "Katherine has your cabin prepared."

"Thank you, Hector," Zelda said without any trace of sarcasm. "Tell Katherine I won't need her for anything further. I'll be along presently." She held up her glass that still had a bit of whisky in it. "Soon as I'm done, I promise."

Hector gave Alex another look, this one full of suspicion, but he didn't protest, nodding instead to Zelda.

"Very good, Miss."

With that, Hector withdrew. Zelda watched him until he was out of sight before she turned back to Alex.

"Sorry about that," she drawled. "One hundred years ago, I'd have been considered a spinster, but to daddy I'm still his little girl."

"A little girl he trusts to spend his money," Alex pointed out.

Zelda laughed at that.

"Don't let that fool you, Alex," she said. "Remember when I said those boring parties were full of boring people? I think that was part of his plan too. I'm sure he's picked out some young go-getter from one of his companies that he'll introduce me to in a few more years."

"I'm...sorry?" Alex said, not sure what to make of Zelda's predicament.

"Don't be," she said, draining her glass and setting it back on the table. "Hector's not a very attentive guard dog."

She slid her chair back and Alex stood with her.

"Twenty-seven," she said, giving him a sly smirk.

"I would have thought you were younger than that," Alex said.

She leaned close, looking up into his face with a hand on his chest.

"That's not my age," she said in a quiet, conspiratorial voice. "It's the number of my stateroom."

She turned and headed for the doors where Hector had vanished, swaying as she went. Alex was absolutely certain that Zelda was exaggerating that delightful hip swing explicitly for his benefit.

He didn't turn away, reasoning that it would be ungentlemanly not to watch after she'd expended so much effort.

Zelda finally turned and disappeared through the doors that led to the staterooms. The spell that held Alex's attention broke as soon as she was out of sight and he shook his head with a sigh. Before he could even consider the implications of the number twenty-seven, Alex turned to the table where the lone man had been sitting.

He found it empty.

Looking around quickly, he tried to spot the long-haired man, but there was no sign of him.

"Damn," he muttered to no one in particular.

4

LINKS

Washington, D.C. was a federal district rather than a state or a territory. As such, it was overseen by a three-man Board of Commissioners that were appointed by Congress. The head of the Board was one Melvin Hazen, a tall, broad-faced man a bit past his prime. He had a wide nose with dark eyes and his hair was parted in the middle, no doubt in an effort to appear stylish despite the gray creeping into his temples. The office he occupied was large and sumptuously decorated; no doubt he felt it was befitting his position. Alex suspected most of his visitors found it quite impressive, but Alex had seen Barton's office and Melvin's seemed cramped by comparison.

Andrew Barton had informed Alex that Melvin wanted to put up a power relay tower in the nation's capital, so Alex had assumed this meeting was just a formality. He couldn't have been more wrong. As soon as Barton and Alex arrived at the D.C. Administration building, Melvin had leapt into the role of gracious host. He'd shown them around the opulent building and introduced the pair to a legion of various government functionaries that Alex had no prayer of remembering. Eventually the walking tour made its way back to Melvin's office and the board president began his pitch in earnest.

"Look at it," he said, pointing out the bank of windows on the left side of his office. The Capitol building was plainly visible along with several other impressive-looking government structures. "Every state in the union has a contingent here, in addition to their Senators and Congressmen." He pointed off toward the north end of town. "A dozen countries have full time embassies here, and half a hundred more have official delegations. You couldn't pick a better place to showcase your technology, Mr. Barton."

Alex stifled a smirk. Melvin Hazen had clearly done his homework. Andrew had big plans for his wireless power network, and Melvin was spotlighting the opportunity represented by a tower in D.C. Andrew wasn't smiling, but he was nodding along enthusiastically.

"How big is the district?" the sorcerer asked.

"Ten miles square," Melvin replied. He turned back to his elegant desk and withdrew a rolled-up map from beneath it. Andrew stood as Melvin unrolled it and the two men began to discuss the capabilities of a relay tower and where it might best be placed to serve the entire city.

Alex let his mind wander. So far he hadn't said a word beyond his greeting to Melvin Hazen when they'd met. At some point Andrew would want him to see if he could link back to the power room in Empire Tower, but from the snippets of discussion that penetrated his wandering consciousness, it would be some time before he was needed.

Taking a deep breath, Alex let it out slowly as his thoughts drifted back in time.

He'd awoken that morning from the steward's knock on his stateroom door, sharp at seven, just as he'd requested. Despite her unmistakably direct invitation, Alex had not made his way to Zelda Pritchard's stateroom during the night. Here in the cold light of morning, he wasn't sure how he felt about that decision. He owed it to Sorsha to either work things out with her or break it off before taking a lover, even a casual one. Then there was the fact that Zelda was at least ten years his junior. For a man likely to live a very long time, that wasn't much of an obstacle, though.

Something was off last night.

Even as he thought about his encounter with Zelda the previous evening, his stomach felt uneasy. Alex had been so enamored with his first time on an airship that he'd let his guard down. Was Zelda who she said she was? Was the well-dressed man watching them? What about the table of older women? By the time he'd started paying attention it was far too late to notice something out of place.

He cursed his lapse but was grateful that his instincts had been sharp. Something had been wrong, he just didn't know what. Maybe if he had some free time that afternoon, he'd look up Zelda Pritchard in Who's Who and check her bona fides.

That thought made him smile.

Maybe if she is who she says, we could revisit—

"Okay, Alex," Andrew's voice cut through his thoughts. "Time to see if this trip was worthwhile or if we came all this way for nothing."

Melvin Hazen looked distraught at that, but Andrew didn't give him time to speak. He reached out with both hands into the empty air before him and made a grasping motion before pulling back. As he did, a heavy metal box appeared, and Andrew staggered under its sudden weight, then straightened and set the box down on Melvin's desk.

"What is that thing?" the board president asked.

"This is a miniature projector," Andrew said, reaching back into space and pulling out an electric lamp. "Think of it as a portable relay tower." He walked around the desk and placed the lamp on an end table under the bank of windows.

"What's it for?"

Andrew walked back to the box and opened a panel in the side. Alex could see a small sliver plate just beyond and he smiled. He knew this part.

Taking his rune book, he flipped to the back and tugged a folded-up rune paper from the little sewn-in pocket there. He didn't bother to unfold it, just touched it to his tongue and stuck it to the silver plate. Squeezing the side lever of his brass lighter, he held the flame to the delicate flash paper, and it vanished in an eruption of flame. A glittering symbol remained behind for just a moment, shimmering with multiple colors like a faceted gem.

"Is that it?" Melvin asked once the rune vanished.

"Not quite," Andrew said, looking at Alex.

"The rune is active," Alex said. He could feel its connection with its sister rune some two hundred miles to the north.

Melvin let out the breath he'd been holding and smiled in relief. Obviously he hadn't thought that there might be limitations on a sorcerer's power.

"So it works?" he asked, looking from Alex to Andrew.

The sorcerer gave a theatric smile, then stepped up to the box, raising another hidden panel from its top. Beneath the panel, Alex could see a large red button.

"Let's find out," he said, then he pushed the button with his thumb. Immediately the metal box began to hum and a moment later, the lamp on the table turned on, glowing brightly.

Alex closed his eyes and concentrated on the linking rune he'd just cast. He couldn't measure it or test its connection back to New York, but when runes were working properly, they had a certain feel to them. It always reminded him of the way a sun-warmed river rock felt; warm and smooth. Runes that weren't cast properly tended to feel jagged or uneven.

"The link is stable," he reported to Andrew. "Looks like there isn't any magical reason not to put a tower here."

An hour later, Alex got out of a cab in front of the Hay-Adams Hotel. Not knowing how long it would take to get the tower deal ironed out, Andrew had booked them rooms in what was, arguably, the swankiest hotel in the city. When Alex dropped his bag off that morning, he could see the White House from the window of his room.

He'd managed to extricate himself from the tower meeting as Andrew and Melvin argued over where to put the actual tower. Barton wanted to put it up in the center of town, but hadn't reckoned on a law that forbade any building in the city from being taller than the Washington Monument. When Alex excused himself, they were discussing the possibility of two smaller towers on the north and south ends of town.

"Good morning, Mr. Lockerby," a young man in a silk tuxedo greeted him as he entered. Alex remembered the man from when he dropped off his bag. He'd led Alex and Andrew to their rooms, but Alex hadn't spoken to him at the time.

"My name is Julian Rand," he went on. "I'm the concierge here at the Hay-Adams. If there's anything you require during your stay with us, I'm your man."

"Well I've got some papers to look over," Alex lied. "So I'm just going up to my room." With his vault book and a piece of chalk, Alex could open his vault and go back to his New York office where his actual work awaited him.

"So it's true that you're working with the police?" Julian asked. His tone was neutral, nothing more than polite curiosity, but his words stopped Alex in his tracks.

"What now?" he asked.

"Aren't you here to consult with the police?" Julian asked. He quickly read Alex's confusion and apologized. "I was under the impression that you'd come to consult on the murder of Senator Young," he went on. "You being a famous New York detective and all. Forget I mentioned it."

"All right," Alex said with a chuckle. He hadn't heard about any Senator being murdered, but he did like being called a famous detective. Julian knew how to make an apology go down like smooth whiskey.

"Would you like me to have lunch brought up for you, while you review your paperwork?" Julian asked.

"I just ate," Alex lied again. "But thanks for the offer."

The little man gave him a smile and a nod that seemed genuine, and Alex headed for the elevator.

Alex's room was on the top floor of the hotel and right next to Andrew's. His morning meeting had only lasted an hour and a half, but he felt as if it had taken all day. As he pushed his key into the lock of his door, he had a momentary impulse to skip his office and just take a nap. When he opened his door, he realized that wasn't going to be doing either.

"Hello, Mr. Lockerby," said the woman sitting in one of the overstuffed chairs in the room's elegant receiving area. "I've been waiting for you." She looked to be in her early forties, though the beauty of her youth hadn't faded a bit. Her face was lean, with angular cheek bones that gave her character rather than looking severe, and she had a dimple on one side. A long, black cigarette holder was clutched in one hand, trailing smoke as she moved it to her bright red lips. The dress she wore was black and expertly tailored to reveal her figure — busty with a narrow waist and slim hips. Long legs in black stockings were crossed demurely, giving off an almost wanton energy despite that.

Alex looked behind him along the hall, half-expecting the hotel detective or a nefarious accomplice, but he was quite alone.

"You have me at a disadvantage," he said, stepping inside the room and shutting the door behind him. "Miss..."

"Mrs." she corrected. "Young."

Alex felt the hair on the back of his neck bristle.

"As in Senator Young?" he asked.

Rather than seeming distraught, she smiled, giving him a raised eyebrow and a nod.

"The same."

Alex had a momentary impulse to turn around and leave. He had plenty of work to do in New York without opening a branch office here.

"I understand that you aren't in town to work on my husband's case," she continued when Alex didn't respond. "I was hoping I could prevail on you to work for me."

"How did you know I wasn't working with the police?" he asked. Almost before the words left his mouth, he noticed that the chair she occupied was right next to the end table that held the telephone. Add to that her presence in his room in the first place and that meant...

"Julian," he said.

"Don't be angry, Alex," she said. "May I call you Alex?"

"Sure," he said, taking out a cigarette and lighting it.

"Julian is very good at his job, Alex," Mrs. Young went on. "He would never have let me in here if he thought I meant you harm."

"Terrific," Alex said without enthusiasm. He crossed to the little couch that stood opposite Mrs. Young's chair and sat down. "But I'll deal with Julian later. You said you wanted me to work for you, not with the police."

Mrs. Young gave him a smile filled with self-mockery.

"The authorities believe that I killed my husband," she said.

Alex sat back on the couch and crossed his legs, taking a drag on his cigarette.

"Did you?"

She seemed shocked by the directness of the question and her lips tried to form a smile, but instead they dropped into a frown.

"No," she said. "I loved my husband very much. We had no quarrels. I had no reason to want him dead."

"Why do the police think otherwise? I assume you told them of your undying affections."

She smiled at that, her mask of sardonic indifference firmly back in place.

"Because Paul was poisoned," she said, then puffed her cigarette. "In the same hotel room as his secretary."

Alex closed his eyes, resisting the urge to shake his head.

"I thought you said you had nothing against your husband?" he said after a moment. "Did you not know about the affair?"

He expected Mrs. Young to be taken aback by such a frank statement, but she didn't even flinch.

"Of course I knew," she said in a voice that carried neither resentment nor censure. "My husband was a man of..." She paused as if trying to find just the right words. "Appetite," she finished.

"So you approved of your husband's activities?" Alex asked. "Why?"

She blew a smoke ring at him, then sighed.

"A Senator is a man of power," she said. "He wields influence in a way other men can only dream of. A man like that has no shortage of suitors. All of them want favors or consideration. Some pay with favors of their own, and some..."

"Pay a different way," Alex finished. "I see what was in it for him, Mrs. Young, but it still leaves you out in the cold. Why would you put up with that behavior?"

"Because, Alex," she said. "Some of Paul's suitors went to him directly, but some decided to approach him through me."

Alex was sure the woman in the black mourning dress wasn't

implying what she seemed to be implying, but unfortunately he couldn't work out any other meaning to her words.

"Some paid him," he said, "and some paid you."

"I didn't wield the full power of my husband's office," she admitted, "but he made it known that I had his ear. And just like Paul, I was often plied with gifts, money, IOUs and—"

"More intimate favors," Alex finished, feeling a bit queasy at the amount of wanton corruption and depravity Mrs. Young had just confessed to.

"You don't approve," she said, reading his expression expertly. "I don't blame you; politics isn't a game for everyone. That said, power can be a very potent aphrodisiac."

"Look," Alex began, searching for a polite way to extricate himself from this encounter. "Mrs. Young—"

"My name is Tiffany," she said. "And before you come up with some excuse not to take my case, let me tell you one thing. You may not like the way Paul and I lived our lives, but that doesn't matter to me. Paul may have scratched a few backs, but he never stole from his constituents, or sold them out for money. He might not have been an angel, but he didn't deserve to die, and I didn't kill him. I need you to prove that, Alex."

Alex looked longingly at the door to his suite, wishing he'd obeyed his first instinct and not come in.

"All right, Tiffany," he said, turning back to her. "Where was your husband when he was poisoned?"

"At the Fairfax Hotel. It's up by Embassy Row."

"And where were you?"

Tiffany sighed and blew another smoke ring.

"If you're asking whether or not I have an alibi, I don't," she admitted. "I was at our apartment alone the entire night."

"Is there anyone who might have seen you, a maid, cook, the milkman?"

She shook her head.

"I went to bed at ten and slept soundly until the morning."

Alex crushed out his cigarette in an ashtray to give himself time to think.

"Then we need to prove that you knew about the affair and didn't care," he said.

"How can we prove that?" Tiffany asked.

"You said you had your husband's ear, right?"

She nodded.

"So you knew about his other trysts, right?"

"I did," she said, a more genuine smile touching her lips. "And I can give you the names of those women and the dates when these encounters occurred." The smile suddenly faltered. "But how will you convince any of them to come forward to the police? Many of them are married; they'd be ruined."

"There's more than one way to skin a cat," Alex said. "All I need to do is prove that your husband was in a hotel room with a woman that wasn't you on the days you said he was. It proves you knew."

"I still might have killed him," she said. "Maybe I finally got tired of his ways?"

"Yes," Alex said, fixing her with a serious look. "But it will create doubt in the minds of the investigators. If they have doubts, then so will a jury. That will force them to look at other possibilities."

"What if they don't find any?"

Alex shrugged and shook his head.

"In that case, Mrs. Young, I either have to figure out who *did* kill your husband, or you might have to expose your side of your marital arrangement in open court."

Alex expected her to look chagrined, but she didn't even blink.

"I will if it comes to that," she said. "I have no wish to sit in the electric chair. Of course I'd rather you proved my innocence without being exposed."

"All right," Alex said. "Write out a list of your husband's playmates and when he was with them, and I'll track down whoever's in charge of the investigation and see if I can get a look at their case file."

"Thank you, Alex," Tiffany said, then she rose. "I'll check my calendar and have the list delivered here by this afternoon at the latest."

He saw her to the door, then waited for her to board the elevator before stepping back inside.

5

CONFLICT OF INTEREST

It would take Tiffany Young at least a couple of hours to put together a list of her husband's liaisons, so Alex took out the chalk from his pocket and drew a door on the pristine wallpaper of his front room. The suite Andrew had rented for him had two rooms, a front room with a desk for work, a wet bar, and a half-dozen chairs and couches arranged for entertaining. A door in the middle of the left-hand wall led to the bedroom and the bath.

Opening his vault, Alex passed through his work area and into the right-hand hallway that led down to his office door. Taking out his pocketwatch, he released the wards that kept the cover door in place and stepped through. He checked his office, but found his in-box empty, so he headed down the short hall to the waiting area.

"Hey, boss," Sherry said with a grin. She was sitting facing the door with a cigarette in her hand. Clearly she'd been expecting him. "How's Washington? Did you see anything historic?"

"I can see the White House from my hotel room," he said with a chuckle.

Sherry got a pained look and groaned.

"You have to take me next time you go somewhere," she insisted. "I saw Egypt in its heyday, but all I've seen of America is this city."

Alex swept his hand back toward the hallway.

"Do you want to see the White House right now?" he asked.

She groaned again and cast a hateful look at the outer door.

"I'm expecting a couple of Mike's clients," she said. "I can't leave now."

"Don't you know when they're going to be here?" Alex said with a smirk.

She fixed him with a level, unamused gaze.

"That's not how my gift works and you know it. Still," she went on, "maybe tomorrow you could take me to lunch somewhere in D.C."

Alex thought about it and nodded. He'd need to make sure Andrew didn't see her, but he was the only person in Washington who would know that Sherry belonged in Manhattan.

"It's a date," he said. "I've picked up a case, so I don't know when I'll be officially coming back, but I'll be checking in periodically."

"Use the phone in your vault to call," Sherry said. "I've been telling people you're out of town and it wouldn't do for them to think I was lying."

"Will do. Now, do you have anything for me?"

She shook her head with a sad smile.

"Sorry, boss. Everything so far has been pretty basic. Mike is taking care of it all. He'll probably need some more finding runes by the end of the week, but that's it."

Alex sighed. He'd been through dry spells before, but he always hated it. Still, he had Tiffany Young's case to keep him busy; he'd just have to wait for her to give him a place to start.

You could go by the police station, he thought. *See if any of the D.C. detectives would play ball with a P.I.*

"All right," he said. "If anything important comes up, leave it on my desk and I'll take a look later."

Sherry bid him farewell, and Alex turned back toward his vault.

Having never been sightseeing, Alex contemplated the idea as he passed through his vault, heading for his suite in the Hay-Adams

Hotel. Washington was full of monuments and government buildings, after all, so there must be something he'd find interesting.

Maybe a museum.

The thought recalled a young blonde with the dusky hint of a southern accent and ylang-ylang infused perfume. If Zelda Pritchard was who she claimed to be, Alex would probably find her at the Smithsonian. She wasn't likely to be standing in the foyer, so he'd have to ask around. He grinned as he judged his detective skills to be up to the task.

Before he could pursue that line of thought any further, the sound of pounding echoed through his vault, coming from the hotel suite beyond.

That's probably Andrew, he thought as he hurried through his vault. Since he'd locked the door after Tiffany Young, he couldn't just yell for him to come in.

"All right, I'm coming," he called out as he passed into the suite's front room. Andrew just kept knocking as if he hadn't heard. Alex snapped the lock open, then pulled the door handle. "Keep your shirt on, Andr—"

As the door opened it was not a sorcerer he found in the hall, but rather a sorceress.

"Sorsha?" Alex said in surprise. Having no expectation of seeing her until he returned to New York, Alex just stared. That turned out to be a good thing, because as he looked at her, he became very aware of just how angry she looked. Her normally perfect hair was a bit disheveled, and a strand hung down, adorably, over her left eye. She was dressed in a stylish suit coat with a loose skirt over a button-up shirt. It was the kind of dress she favored when working with the FBI.

Alex realized that he'd kept her standing in the hall for several seconds while his mind groped with the incongruity of seeing her in D.C. He quickly stepped back, holding the door open for her.

"Won't you come in?" he said, more to give himself time to think than to breach the silence.

The sorceress stormed in, whirling on him as Alex closed the door.

"Explain yourself," she snapped, her voice full of barely controlled fury.

A sense of basic self-preservation compelled Alex to comply, but that was the problem. He genuinely had no idea what she was talking about.

"I'm sorry?" he ventured.

Her eyes flashed dangerously, and she took a step toward him.

"Don't," she growled. "Don't you dare play dumb. I know we've had some problems of late, but I never thought..." Words seemed to fail her, and she turned her back to him. Alex opened his mouth to try to answer but she whirled back around again. "How could you do this to me?"

"Sorsha?" Alex said, reaching out slowly to take her by the shoulders. "Darling," he pressed his luck. "I'd be happy to tell you anything you want to know, but first I need you to do something."

She sucked in a breath that threatened to return as an explosion, so Alex rushed on.

"I need you to tell me what, exactly, you're talking about."

She pulled away from him, turning her back once more. Alex saw her hands ball into tight fists, and she sucked in a deep breath. Instead of returning as another tirade, however, Sorsha held that breath for a log moment, then slowly let it out.

"Are you *trying* to ruin me?" she asked.

"What? Of course not." Alex wasn't sure he even knew of a way to ruin Sorsha; she was a sorceress with a thriving business that gave her more money than she could spend in several lifetimes.

"Are you trying to get me fired from the Bureau so I'll have more time for you?"

The more Sorsha spoke, the less sense she was making. Alex decided he had to rein in this conversation quickly before Sorsha said or did something they'd both regret.

"I'd love for you to spend more time with me," he admitted. "But working for the FBI is part of who you are. I'd never take that away from you. I wouldn't know how to even try."

She turned back, regarding him with an appraising stare that still carried a good deal of anger with it. Finally she reached into thin air and pulled out a folded newspaper.

"This will get the job done nicely," she said, holding the paper out to him.

Alex took it, unfolding it as he held it up. The name *Capital Dispatch* was printed across the masthead and it appeared to be a tabloid in the flavor of *The Midnight Sun*. Letting his eyes roam down the page, Alex didn't have to look far to find the story that had raised such ire in the sorceress.

"FBI at Dead End with Senator's Murder," he read the headline aloud. "The murder of Senator Paul Young was recently handed off to the Federal Bureau of Investigation, but it seems the crime is too much even for them. Famous New York society detective, Alexander Lockerby was seen arriving in the city this morning, presumably at the request of his girlfriend, Sorceress Sorsha Kincaid. Sorsha is a consultant for the FBI but has been known to rely on Mr. Lockerby for help with some of the Bureau's biggest cases."

As he read, Alex's heart sank. Whoever wrote the story made it sound like Sorsha couldn't solve cases without his help. He understood her anger.

"This is just some yellow journalism," Alex said, tossing the paper onto the little table by the door. "He doesn't know what he's talking about."

"So you didn't come here to work on my case?" Sorsha asked, one eyebrow arching skeptically. "You seem to have a knack for inserting yourself in my business lately."

Alex took her by the shoulders again and leaned down to look her in the eye.

"I'm here because the governing board of D.C. wants Andrew to put a power relay tower in the city," he explained. "I came down with him to make sure my linking rune would work all this way from Empire Tower. Besides, you know that I only got involved in the incident with the German saboteurs because my own case led me there."

"I know that," she said, her anger turning to frustration, "but that's not what the papers say."

Alex shook his head. He read the paper every day, and as far as he knew no one was gossiping about he and Sorsha.

"This is one story," he protested, pointing to the paper. "Nobody will take that seriously."

She gave him a look somewhere between resigned and sad, then reached into the empty air again and produced a fat file folder.

"No," she said, handing it to Alex. "It isn't just one story."

Opening the folder, Alex quickly perused its contents. The stories went all the way back to the first time he'd met Sorsha, when the magical plague had been let loose in the city. Some of them mentioned only Sorsha, implying that the FBI was paying far too much for what they were getting by having her as a consultant. The rest concerned the times he'd been involved with one of her cases. All of them subtly suggested that without Alex, those cases wouldn't have been solved.

A quick check of the writing credits revealed that the stories had been written by different people and for several different newspapers, but the theme of Sorsha's incompetence was all the same. To Alex it felt like a coordinated smear campaign despite the disparate sources and authors.

"So the Bureau knows about all this?" he asked, holding up the folder.

Sorsha hesitated, then nodded.

"I've been told, unofficially, that the higher ups are reviewing my association with them," she said.

"You want me to write up a report?" Alex offered. "Tell them what really happened in all that mess. You and I both know that you were an integral part of those cases."

Her expression softened and for the first time she smiled, albeit a bit sadly.

"They'll say that you're stretching the truth because you're my beau."

"Am I?" Alex said, giving her a sarcastic smile.

Sorsha snorted but her smile didn't waver.

"That's what it says in the papers," she said, "so it must be true." She took the folder full of hostile press clippings and it vanished back into the aether from whence it came. "I'm sorry," she said, moving to embrace him. "I saw that story and I just...I got so angry."

Alex put his arms around her and nuzzled the top of her head.

"You of all people should know better than to believe anything you read in the papers."

Sorsha sighed.

"I'm just glad you're not working on the Senator's murder," she said.

Alex had been feeling pretty good about how he'd handled the sorceress' anger. That feeling evaporated like fog in the sunlight.

"Yeah," he said, stretching the word out. "About that."

Sorsha pushed off him so hard, Alex staggered back a step.

"You said you were here to help Andrew with his business," she said, her eyes wide.

"I am," Alex protested.

"What did you do, Alex?" she growled.

"Tiffany Young came to see me about an hour ago," he admitted. "She said the authorities wanted to pin her husband's murder on her and she wants me to find out who killed him."

Sorsha's hands balled into tight fists and her eyes began to glow with an inner blue light.

"I won't get in your way," he said, holding up a placating hand.

"No," Sorsha said, her voice now deadly quiet. "You aren't going to get in my way because you're not going to be on this case. You call that…that woman, and you tell her that you won't be able to take her case because you're going back to New York."

Alex intended to protest, but Sorsha read the intention on his face and went on.

"In fact, you can tell her that your job is done," she said. "The Bureau no longer suspects her because the secretary left a note in her apartment confessing to poisoning their food."

"Murder-suicide?" Alex asked.

"Not quite, but she tried. She's currently in the hospital but the doctors say she'll recover. As soon as she's well enough, we'll have her confirm her confession and the case will be over."

"Okay," Alex said, resisting the urge to take a step back. "I'll call Tiffany and—"

"Tiffany?" Sorsha growled, her eyes jumping up from glowing to blazing.

"I'll call Mrs. Young," Alex corrected hastily, "and let her know about the secretary and the letter."

Sorsha's eyes dimmed, and a disquieting smile crawled across her face.

"Oh, no you don't," she said. "You call that harlot, and you tell her that you are off the case." She stepped closer and stabbed her finger into Alex's chest. "That's what you tell her."

"All right," Alex said, putting up his hands in a placating gesture.

"I swear, Alex Lockerby," she said, her voice going suddenly calm, "if you mess this up for me," she reached out and smoothed his tie. "If you interfere and I lose my job at the FBI, I will...I will turn you into the weasel you are."

Alex was pretty sure she was bluffing about that, but he didn't want to take stupid chances just in case.

"All right, you win," he said. "I'm off the case. It's already solved, so there is no case anyway."

Sorsha looked up at him for a long moment, then the glow in her eyes faded and she leaned against him once more.

"Thank you, Alex," she mumbled into his chest.

"You should have told me about the newspaper stories," he said, putting a hand on her shoulder. "I could have had Billy Tasker write something flattering about you; he owes me."

Sorsha leaned back far enough to look up at him.

"That's actually a pretty good idea," she said.

"See," he chuckled, "you do need me." That earned him a stern look.

"You're not funny," she said.

"It was a little funny," he said. "Since your case is solved, how about I take you to lunch, or maybe dinner tonight?"

"No," Sorsha said, somewhat emphatically. "Until this case is officially finished we cannot be seen together. That news rag will say I'm consulting with you on the side."

"Well no one can see us here," he suggested. "I'll have Julian send up something and you can hide out here until that secretary wakes up."

Sorsha pushed away from him with narrowed eyes and an amused expression.

"None of that," she said. "I need to stay focused on this case. It might not be as cut and dried as we believe. And you...you need to call Mrs. Young and tell her you're going back to New York."

"You're no fun at all," Alex said, only half kidding.

"I promise when I get back to the city, I'll make you a priority," she said. "Now kiss me before I go."

Alex did as he was told and a far too short time later, he saw Sorsha out. As he relocked the door, he saw the tabloid on the side table. Picking it up, he read the name, Simon Edwards, on the banner over the story about him being called in to work the Senator's murder. Since Alex wasn't going to be working that case after all, maybe he'd make time to look up Mr. Edwards.

"First things first," he said aloud.

Walking to the phone on the desk, Alex set the papers aside.

"I need to speak to Julian," he told the hotel operator. A moment later the concierge's voice came on the line. "I need the number for Tiffany Young," he said.

"I'll have that sent up immediately," Julian said. "Would you like me to connect you now?"

Of course he knows her, that's how she got in here in the first place.

"Yes please," he said.

After a moment, Tiffany answered, and Alex explained about the note left by the secretary.

"So it looks like you're off the hook," he concluded. "I didn't really do anything but make a few inquiries, so you don't owe me anything."

"Maybe not yet," Tiffany said, "but this case isn't over."

"What do you mean? It sounds like as soon as the secretary wakes up, the feds will have their killer."

"You don't understand, Alex," she said. "That story about Helen, it's just not possible."

"According to the note this Helen got jealous; it happens," Alex said, assuming Helen was the secretary.

"As I told you, Alex, the people my husband had business with wanted something he could provide," Tiffany said, clearly unwilling to let this go. "It was a mutual exchange, not a promise of a relationship. Helen wanted to become a legal assistant for one of the city's law firms, one with several young, single, and very marriageable partners. Paul was going to make that happen for her."

Alex felt a sinking feeling in the pit of his stomach.

"So she had no reason to kill your husband, did she?"

"No, Alex. She did not."

"I was afraid of that," he sighed. "All right, I'll keep looking."

"Thank you, Alex."

"You're welcome, Mrs. Young," he replied, wondering just what he was going to tell Sorsha.

6
CLUBS

Alex sat at the little writing desk in his hotel suite, staring at the telephone as if it were the cause of his troubles. He took out his cigarette case and pulled one out, then tossed the case on top of the desk. There was no sense putting it away until he figured out what to do.

Lighting the cigarette, he took a long drag and considered his position. He needed to be done with the case of Paul Young's murder. Sorsha had made that abundantly clear. She wasn't his wife or his boss, and he didn't take orders from her, but he didn't want her to lose her job on his account. She was a good investigator, with good instincts, despite what the tabloids were saying.

It made him sick to his stomach to think that someone was using him against her.

On the other hand, Tiffany was right. Someone had killed her husband and now it looked like they were trying to pin it on a patsy. That fact alone told Alex there was much more to Paul Young's death than met the eye.

Ordinarily a cover up would be reason for further investigation all by itself, but this victim had been a US Senator. Whoever killed Paul might be playing a much larger game, one that could have national or even international implications. Alex simply couldn't let this go.

That realization made him grind his teeth. If he ran around investigating Senator Young's death, someone official was bound to notice and that would inevitably get back to Sorsha. If he tried to work with her, she could keep the locals off his back, but that would raise more questions about her ability to do her job. Questions like that could get her fired.

She'd never speak to me again, he thought. *Or turn me into a weasel for her own amusement.*

What he needed was a way to keep investigating without tipping anyone off. The way Tiffany had described the case made it sound like the local police were handling it, but if Sorsha was here, that meant the FBI was involved as well. Which made sense, with a Senator dead. The story in the paper had said the case was now in the hands of the FBI, but the *Capital Dispatch* wasn't exactly a bastion of good journalism. Alex knew from experience that locals resented it when the Feds showed up and started interfering with their cases. Based on what Sorsha had said, everyone was waiting for the poisoned secretary to recover. Once they had her story, the Feds would either take the case outright if they thought there was something to it, or, if not, they'd back off and let the locals handle it.

So, until Senator Young's secretary recovers enough to give a statement, each agency will be waiting in Limbo.

If it turned out there was something nefarious to the case, each side would want their people on it. Each side would want the credit.

Alex could work with that.

He crushed out his cigarette and stood, a plan finally forming in his mind. With a little finesse on top of a fair dose of luck, he might be able to find a detective in the D.C. office with ambition. Such a man might be willing to partner with an unknown factor, like an out-of-town P.I., and work the case on the sly.

Maybe.

Right now it was the best idea he had; in reality it was the only idea he had. So, pushing his trepidations aside, Alex closed his vault, donned his overcoat, and headed for the elevator. As he rode down, he checked to be sure he had one of his climate runes in his book. The weather had been unseasonably warm, but it was definitely the tail end of a long Indian Summer. If the weather turned cold, he might need more than just his coat. Once Sorsha found out he was still on the Paul Young case, he might really need a climate rune.

Once outside the hotel, Alex looked for a taxi. There weren't as many cabs on the street as there were in Manhattan, so Alex stood on the curb for a few minutes waiting. He'd finally spotted one coming his way when a long, black car rolled to a stop in front of the hotel. The rear window came down, but rather than someone getting out, Alex saw the nose of a pistol pointing squarely at him.

The front passenger door of the car opened and a man got out. He wasn't as tall as Alex, but he had the beefy, muscular frame of a night-club bouncer.

"Get in the car, Mr. Lockerby," he said. His voice was a deep, basso growl, but he enunciated his words as if it were a polite request rather than a threat.

Alex thought about running back into the hotel. He had his shield runes in place, of course, but that would only stop five bullets and he knew from experience that the pistol held up to eight. The odds were probably in his favor, but his curiosity was piqued. Who even knew he was in the city, and what could they possibly want?

His moment of indecision made the choice for him as the big man grabbed his elbow and started him toward the rear door of the car. The pistol pulled back as the man holding it slid over to make room. Alex opened the door and got in, sliding into the middle as the bouncer squeezed in on the other side.

The man with the pistol had a broad flat face with a Roman nose and close-set blue eyes. He was clean shaven but already had a fair five-o'clock shadow coming in. As the car began to move, he kept the pistol pointed at Alex's ribs.

"So, where are we going?" he asked when no one spoke.

"Mr. Casetti would like a word," the man with the pistol said. "Now shut up."

Alex felt a chill go down his back at the name. Anthony Casetti was also known as Lucky Tony and he'd run the Rosono crime family for decades, ever since the actual Rosonos 'mysteriously' disappeared. He'd risen to power and wealth during Prohibition where he'd been the beer king of the West Side. He also had a very highly placed mole in the D.A.'s office — in fact it was the D.A. himself, one Addison "Tiger" Smith. Alex knew this because he and Danny had exposed Tiger, costing him his freedom and costing Lucky Tony his inside man.

It had been ten years since that case, and Alex hadn't heard a whisper from Lucky Tony in all that time. He'd been worried at first, but nothing had happened, so he'd gradually forgotten about it.

Apparently Lucky Tony had not.

Alex felt himself start to sweat. He had his shield runes if it came to that, but Lucky Tony wasn't some thug with a pistol and a vendetta. He was an educated man, one ruthless enough to seize the reins of a major crime family and run it successfully for years. He knew Alex was a runewright and he might have taken precautions. A man of Lucky Tony's power would likely know the limit on how many shield runes any one person could have.

Worse was Alex's lack of an escape rune. He'd used the last one he'd made a few months ago and he hadn't put in the time to write a new one. If he made it back to New York in one piece, he vowed to make that a priority. Right now, that prospect wasn't looking good.

The car had headed north after picking up Alex, and twenty minutes later it felt like they'd left the city. A vast wooded wilderness stretched out on the left side of the road with only a few houses and buildings off to the right. The woods looked like the kind of place a mobster might go to put a bullet into the head of an annoying private detective.

Alex thought about his flash ring, but pinned in the back of the car, it wouldn't do him any good. Even blind, the man with the gun couldn't miss from only a few inches away. Alex would have to bide his time and look for an opening. For the second time in two days, he wished he'd taken the precaution of wearing his 1911, or at least carrying his knuckleduster.

The car slowed and turned off onto a narrow side street. Through the windshield Alex could see that the trees were thinning up ahead, opening into a large open field. As he looked, they passed a large sign that read: *Rock Creek Park Golf Course.*

His first thought was confusion. The middle of a public golf course wasn't the kind of place mob bosses usually chose to have a quiet conversation. Especially not the kind that left a corpse at its conclusion. That said, it was December and there were only five cars in the dirt parking lot at the end of the drive. Alex couldn't see anyone actually out on the course.

The driver pulled up to the first empty spot beside the parked cars. As soon as he shut the engine off, the man who had ushered Alex into the car got out, and the man with the gun gestured for him to follow.

"Strange place for a chat," Alex said as the gunman got out behind him.

"Fewer busybodies," he growled, then he prodded Alex in the back with the gun. "That way."

Alex started walking out onto the golf course. He'd never played golf, but he'd seen plenty of newsreels of politicians and Hollywood actors playing to understand the basics of the game. He passed the eighth hole, designated by the red number eight on the flag sticking out of the cup, and continued down the fairway.

They were heading toward the back side of the course and Alex could clearly see more of the thick woods beyond the course. The trees were winter bare, but there were enough of them to reduce visibility significantly. If his escorts intended to take him in there, they also planned on coming back without him.

Alex wasn't sure how effective his flash ring would be in the bright light of day, and if the second man had a gun, he didn't have anywhere near enough shield runes. If things got desperate, he could try suddenly reversing his stride, slamming into the gunman behind him. He would fire, certainly, but with his gun at waist level, he was most likely to hit Alex's shielded back. The move would work best going uphill, then Alex might have a chance to knock the man off his feet.

Before a suitable grade presented itself, however, they passed around a little copse of trees to reveal the green of the fifteenth hole. A man stood there, dressed in a hideous golf sweater with a pattern of repeating gold and brown diamonds, dark slacks, and a flat cap. He was tall and lean, with a muscular upper body over a slim waist, and he stood with his feet crossed, leaning on a golf club. A white ball sat on the green a few yards from the cup and the man simply stared at it.

As they approached, Alex had no doubt that this was Lucky Tony Casetti himself.

"Go on ahead," the gunman growled at Alex, then he and the other man stopped just beyond the oval of short-cropped grass that defined the green. When the man spoke, Casetti looked up from his contemplation of the golf ball. He had a broad, clean-shaven face and, much to Alex's surprise, had the good looks of a movie actor, with bright blue eyes and straight teeth.

"Ah," he said with a satisfied smile. "Give me just a minute."

Alex wasn't sure what to make of that, so he just stood there while the man who'd owned the west side of Manhattan during the prohibition years made his putt. He moved with the natural grace of an athlete and Alex remembered that he'd been on the cricket team at Columbia. He and former D.A. Addison "Tiger" Smith. Lucky Tony had helped Tiger cover up the murder of his ex-girlfriend and that had made Tiger his man for the better part of thirty years.

Right up until Alex and Danny had tied the dead girl's murder back to Tiger and sent him to prison.

"Alex Lockerby," Lucky Tony said as he fished his golf ball out of the cup and replaced the flag. "I've wanted to meet you for some time."

The words were friendly enough, but a chill ran down Alex's spine. Sure they were out in the open in a public place, but at this end of the course, there wasn't another soul in sight.

"I'm in the book," Alex said, putting on his most pleasant smile.

The mob boss chuckled at that.

"And you've got a fancy office in Empire Tower, too," he said, replacing his club in the long narrow bag that held its brethren. "You must be quite the crackerjack detective to go from that little hole in the wall in Harlem all the way to the Core."

After watching more than a few gangster movies, Alex expected Lucky Tony to speak with a Bronx or maybe a Jersey accent. He'd forgotten that Anthony Casetti was a graduate of Columbia, one of the most prestigious schools in the country, and his accent was one of culture and refinement.

Culture notwithstanding, Alex didn't like the fact that Lucky Tony Casetti knew the details of his entire professional career.

"I do okay," he said, somewhat noncommittally.

"Don't be so modest," Casetti said, hefting his bag over his shoulder. "Anyone who could solve a thirty-year-old murder and oust a sitting D.A. in one fell swoop has got some impressive skills. Walk with me."

He indicated the direction of the next fairway and waited for Alex to accompany him.

"I'm a little surprised you'd find my work that impressive," Alex said, falling into step beside the head of the Rosono crime family. "All things considered."

Lucky Tony scoffed.

"Tiger was getting too full of himself," he admitted. "He started thinking he should be the one calling the shots. I was going to have to do something about him anyway; you just saved me the trouble."

That surprised Alex. He knew he should shut up and take the man at his word, but he couldn't help himself.

"One of yours was killed during that incident."

Lucky Tony glanced at him with a raised eyebrow.

"True," he said, his easy voice acquiring a hard edge. "While he was trying to abduct a policeman, no less. That was Tiger's decision. I never would have approved it. That's the problem with police insiders, they don't understand the delicate balance between the police and independent entrepreneurs like myself."

Alex wanted to laugh at that remark, but decided discretion was the better part of valor.

"You were there when my man was shot," Lucky Tony said, in an offhand manner. "Who was it that shot him?"

Alex suddenly had trouble breathing. That had been over ten years ago, but the memory was clear in his mind. The mobster in question had been blinded by a flash rune but he still had his gun. His vision had cleared just as Alex was right in front of him and when the gunshot sounded, Alex knew he'd been shot. It wasn't him though. Danny's sister Amy had picked up a dropped gun and killed the man with one bullet. The fact that Lucky Tony wanted to know the identity of the shooter terrified him.

"I did," Alex said without hesitation.

Of all the reactions Alex expected, he didn't count on Tony Casetti laughing.

"That's what I like about you, Alex," he said, shaking his head. "You've got chutzpah and you're loyal. I know it was that pretty nurse down in Philadelphia, but you were ready to take the rap anyway."

Alex had to work to keep his breathing even, but his fist clenched in spite of himself. The mob boss noticed and laughed heartily.

"Never fear, Alex," he said. "I have no quarrel with her or her detective brother. That entire incident was Tiger's fault."

Alex spared him a glance, and Tony gave him a knowing look.

"Of course I wouldn't move against either of them even if I did hold a grudge," he said. "They're...protected."

This time Alex wasn't surprised. Danny and Amy's father ran the Japanese Mafia in Manhattan, after all.

"So if you're not upset about the loss of your inside man," Alex ventured, "why did you have your friends back there invite me out for this chat?"

Lucky Tony smiled at him again, and he reached out to put his arm around Alex's shoulder. It made Alex shiver.

"I'm not holding a grudge," he said. "But you do owe me for messing up my organization, so I've come up with a way for you to square your debt to me."

Alex didn't even want to think about what a mob boss might want him to do. That said, settling a marker with Lucky Tony, whether it really existed or not, was definitely a good thing.

"How can I help?" he said.

7

THE LEGITIMATE BUSINESSMAN

"I need you to find someone," Lucky Tony Casetti said as they arrived at a small flat spot that overlooked the next green. "That's your specialty, correct?" The mob boss set down his bag and made a show of selecting one of the clubs with a wide, wooden head.

"That depends," Alex said. "This person you're looking for...why do you want him?"

Tony stopped fiddling with his clubs and turned to give Alex a hard look. For his part, Alex tried not to sweat, the chill weather notwithstanding.

"That's kind of a long story," Lucky Tony said.

"My schedule is clear," Alex replied.

Tony held his gaze for a long moment, then he nodded.

"All right," he said, pulling out one of his clubs. He walked to the edge of the flat space and bent down, sticking a wooden tee into the turf and leaving a golf ball on top of it. "It used to be that a man in my position had the world by the tail," he said with a wistful sigh. "When Prohibition was the law people would beat a path to my door. Everybody wanted a drink, and I was there to supply them. Even if the cops shut down one of my speakeasies, a new one would be up and running the next day." He chuckled, "Sometimes the same night."

"So, you're looking for someone you knew twenty years ago?" Alex asked.

Lucky Tony chuckled. It wasn't a pleasant sound.

"Patience, Alex," he said, stepping up to his golf ball. He held the club against the little white sphere, then hauled back and smacked it down the center of the fairway. "That's a pretty shot," he said, more to himself than to Alex. Turning, he tossed the club to Alex. "Since I'm playing storyteller, you can play caddy," he said. "Grab my bag."

Alex held the club for a moment, but decided not to argue with the crime boss. He dropped the club into the bag and picked it up, slinging the strap over his shoulder.

"Do you know how to make a fortune, Alex?" he asked as they headed out toward where the ball had flown.

Alex shrugged.

"Not really."

"Well, then let me give you the golden key to business," Tony said. "You make a fortune when you provide a good or service that people want badly enough that they come to you to get it."

"Beer during prohibition," Alex said, understanding.

"Exactly. Now that beer is legal again, people aren't beating a path to my door anymore. Sure we've got gambling parlors, bookies, and the odd brothel, but those don't do the kind of volume of the old speakeasies. The only thing that was really raking in the money was the slot machines."

Up until recently, every five and dime and hardware store had a slot machine or two on the counter. Alex had heard that most of them were owned by the various mob families rather than the shop owners themselves.

"And the Governor just banned slot machines," Alex said. "So business is bad."

"Bad is an understatement," Tony said. "The other families don't see it yet, but with business opportunities shrinking, a turf war is inevitable."

Alex didn't want to believe that. It had been over a decade since there was open mob war in the streets of New York, and people still talked about it in hushed tones. Some of the older detectives at the Central Office told stories that gave Alex the shivers.

"So you're looking for a way to get out ahead of all this?" Alex asked, trying not to sound spooked.

"Nope," Tony said, pulling another club out of his bag. He walked up to where his ball lay among the tall grass and squared up to it. "I'm going to do the most cliché thing a mobster can do." He drew the club up over his shoulder, then smacked the ball, sending it hurtling toward the green in the distance.

"What's that?" Alex pressed.

Tony looked at him with a sly grin.

"I'm going to become a legitimate businessman."

"You're getting out?"

It was difficult to believe, but everything in Lucky Tony's story seemed to point to that conclusion as the only viable option available. With the easy cash businesses drying up, the Rosonos would have to fight for the few resources left. Tony might be a mobster, but he was also a graduate of a prestigious business school. If anyone could figure a way to go legit, it was him.

Alex pushed those thoughts aside. Lucky Tony might be smart, and cultured, and a decent golfer, but he was still a mob boss. That was a job you didn't hold on to by being a nice person. It was probably best for Alex to get on with the job.

"What does this have to do with your missing man?" he asked.

Tony slid his club back in the bag at Alex's shoulder, then unzipped his sweater, revealing a button-up shirt. He pulled a small picture from the breast pocket and handed it to Alex.

"That's my nephew, Colton Pierce," Tony said, zipping his sweater closed again.

Alex looked at the picture. It was a close-up of a thin man in his thirties with thick spectacles and dark curly hair that he kept cut short. His face was narrow with a long, pointed nose and a crooked smile. Alex half expected him to be carrying a book, though the picture only showed him from the chest up.

"Colton is a professor at George Washington University," Tony went on. "He's been missing for two days and no one seems to know where he went. The Dean of the Alchemy School said that Colton had been on sabbatical for a semester, so no one at the university knew he was missing. According to his landlady, his rent is paid up through the end of the month. It's like he dropped off the planet."

"Colton teaches Alchemy?" Alex asked, taking out his folding notebook.

Tony nodded, then stopped.

"Hold still," he said, then unzipped a pocket on the outside of the golf bag. From inside, he took two green bottles of beer. Producing a church key from his trouser pocket, he flipped the caps off both of them and held them up to Alex.

"You strike me as the suspicious type," he said. "Pick one."

Alex took the bottle on his right and Lucky Tony took a long swig from the other. Before raising the bottle himself, Alex looked at the printed label on the bottle. There was a picture of a cottage on it, the kind storybooks always used for tales that started with, *Once upon a time*. The word *Homestead* was written in a simple script above the cottage with the words, *Welcome Home*, below it.

Alex had never heard of this brand, but Tony was eyeing him expectantly, so he raised the bottle to his lips and took a drink. As beer went, it was pleasant enough, but nothing compared to a good single malt. He was about to say that when a sudden euphoria washed over him. It seemed to spread out from his middle, tingling as it went. As the sensation reached his head, Alex had a sudden memory fill his mind. It was the smell of potato soup, the way Sister Gwen used to make it. The smell brought with it a thousand thoughts and impressions, memories of growing up at the Brotherhood of Hope, of practicing his runes by candle-light, and of the encouragement and patience that Father Harry had given him.

The feeling lingered for a few moments, then the cacophony of memories faded away, leaving only a warm, comforting feeling behind. It took Alex half a minute to remember he was standing outside, drinking with a mob boss, in the chill December air.

"Quite the kick, isn't it?" Tony said, taking another long pull from his bottle.

"You've added something to it," Alex said, staring at the bottle. "Some kind of alchemical ingredient."

"Euphorian," Tony said. "Colton invented it. A few ounces in a vat of beer and anyone who drinks it will experience the feelings of their best moments."

"What happens if they drink too much?" Alex wondered.

Tony actually laughed at that.

"You can't," he said. "The body can only absorb a small amount of Euphorian at a time. So it's not addictive and you can't overdose. It just does what beer is supposed to do," he raised his bottle in a salute, "it makes you happy."

"Doesn't regular beer do that too?" Alex asked.

"Sure, but you don't have to get drunk this way."

Alex took another swig and felt the emotions of a hundred forgotten memories wash over him.

Lucky Tony is going to make a fortune.

"So you need Colton or this whole deal is moot," Alex said, "but no one knows where Colton is."

Lucky Tony's contented smile disappeared.

"It's worse than that," he said. "I had one of my boys keeping an eye on Colton. Last night they pulled his body out of the Potomac. According to the cops, someone worked him over pretty good before they tossed him."

Alex's mind snapped into focus.

"Could this be some rival?" Alex asked. "Maybe they grabbed him to..."

"To make a point?" Tony said, his voice hard. "Yes, I thought of that. But Colton isn't part of my business, so he's not a legitimate target. Besides, if someone took him to get back at me, they would have killed him and left his body where it would be easy for me to find. You can't make your point if no one finds the body."

The matter-of-fact tone Lucky Tony used when he explained his thinking made Alex shiver. He had no doubt the man knew what he was talking about, likely from experience.

"What about ransom?"

Tony shook his head.

"They would have made their demands by now," he said. "Waiting only works on worried parents."

Alex considered that as he made more notes.

"Who else knows about Euphorian?"

"Nobody," Tony said. "Colton told me and only me."

"You told me," Alex said.

"I did that because of Sal," Tony explained, "that's my man that was found in the river. If he's dead and Colton's missing..."

"Then Colton might be dead too," Alex caught on. "And if Colton's dead, you still need me to find the formula for Euphorian."

Tony nodded and finished his beer, though this time he didn't smile.

"Colton has an apartment in Georgetown," he said. He waved at his goons who had been following along at a respectful distance. "Connie will take you over there. I understand you need something of Colton's to use your finding rune, the more personal the better."

Alex nodded as the flat-faced man from the car stepped up next to him.

"I'll start with the finding rune," Alex said. "Maybe we'll get lucky and it'll locate him quickly."

"What if it doesn't?" Tony asked.

"Then I'll start looking the old-fashioned way," Alex explained. "I'll try to retrace his steps on the day he disappeared. I'll also check his apartment for his recipe book, but that's just as likely to be in a safe deposit box at his bank."

"Colton has an account at Capital Bank," Tony supplied, then he took his bag from Alex and headed toward the green. "Keep me appraised of your progress."

Alex started to turn away, but Tony called him back.

"I'm not a good man, Alex," he said in a mild voice. "I can understand if a man like you doesn't care what happens to me. It might have been a stroke of good fortune that just when I need you, you show up here in D.C., but understand I didn't want you for this job because you're a fellow New Yorker. I've done my homework on you, Alex. You see yourself as a white knight, riding to the rescue of the innocent. So I want to be perfectly clear, Colton is a good man. He's never been a part of my business. He's just someone who's in trouble, and he needs you to find him."

For the briefest of moments, Alex thought Lucky Tony looked small, standing alone in the tall grass with his bag slung over his shoulder. Just like any other person might look when missing a family member. The vision passed quickly as Alex remembered who, exactly, he was looking at, but the impression remained. This was just another case where someone needed his help.

"I understand," Alex said, looking the mob boss in the eyes. "If Colton's alive, I'll find him, and if he's not...I'll find that out, too."

Tony held his gaze for another moment, then nodded and turned away.

The Georgetown townhome of Colton Pierce reminded Alex of Iggy's New York brownstone. It was a tall, narrow building nestled in the middle of a long row of similar homes. The most pronounced difference was the lack of the dark bricks that gave brownstones their name.

As Lucky Tony had ordered, the flat-faced goon, Connie, had driven Alex from the golf course to Georgetown. It was a surprisingly short journey, despite the fact that Connie didn't say a word for the entire trip.

"Do you have a key?" Alex asked as he climbed the stairs to the white front door.

Connie just nodded and produced a small ring of keys from his pocket. He unlocked the door, then reached into his overcoat where Alex knew his holster hung. With his hand on his hidden gun, Connie opened the door and stepped in, turning his head quickly as he swept the room for possible threats.

Alex wasn't particularly worried that someone would be lying in wait at Colton's empty home, but he supposed Connie had been a bodyguard for a long time and old habits died hard.

"It's clear," the broad man said in his deep, growling voice. If Lucky Tony was the exact opposite of a movie gangster, Connie was every stereotype Alex had ever seen rolled into one. He had a slight Jersey accent, but better diction than Alex would have expected; obviously being around Lucky Tony had influenced him. Connie was big and squarish with the kind of face that made you want to avoid him without even trying.

The big mobster stepped to the side and Alex followed him in. The front room of Colton's home was neat with a couch and a coffee table for guests. A round throw rug occupied most of the floor, and there was an end table with a Victor radio on top against the far wall. A mantle of dark wood ran over a small hearth which was covered by a metal screen and looked like it hadn't been used in years. On top of the mantle were pictures and other knick-knacks. Alex recognized Colton in several of the photos that ranged from him as a young man to one of him behind what had to be his desk in the university.

Everything in the front room was neat and orderly, the sign of an organized mind, but a thick layer of dust was also present. Alex took down the central picture on the mantle and wiped away the dust with his handkerchief. Underneath was a picture of a cozy cottage home, probably from somewhere upstate, and an older man and woman standing arm in arm. In their smiling faces, Alex could see the shadow of Colton.

"Must be his parents," Alex said, replacing the photograph. He took out his chalk, then stepped over to the blank wall beside the radio and end table before drawing a door.

"What are you doing?" his watchdog growled. Alex wondered if his voice just lent itself to sounding irritated or if the man was taken aback by the chalk lines on the wall.

"Opening my vault," Alex said, pulling out his rune book. "I need to get my investigation kit. Don't worry...Connie, was it?"

"Constantine Firenze," he said. "But you can call me Connie." He actually smiled, and Alex almost did a double take.

"Well, don't worry, Connie," Alex continued. "I'll clean up after I'm done."

Alex stuck a vault rune paper to the wall, then quickly lit it. Connie took a step back when the heavy steel door melted out of the plaster on the wall. Alex didn't want to give the gangster a good look at his vault, so he unlocked the door with his key and then pulled it open just wide enough to get his bag from the table next to the door.

"There you go," he said as he shut the door and it melted away. "Good as new."

"Mind if I look in your bag?" Connie said in a tone that indicated that he didn't care if Alex minded or not.

Alex did mind, but he pasted on a smile and handed the bag over for a brief inspection.

"That's a hell of a thing," Connie said, nodding at the wall as he handed Alex's bag back.

"It comes in handy," Alex admitted. "Now I want to take a quick look at the rest of the house, then we'll see if we can find Colton."

Alex led the way into the back part of the main floor, where he found a kitchen and a little office. Each were equally neat and dusty like the front room, though the desk in the office looked more used. From there, he went up to the second and then the third floors. Nothing stood out as being out of the ordinary, and the dust was pervasive everywhere but the bedroom. By the time he was finished, Alex was convinced that Colton spent almost no time at his home. Like most alchemists, he had a lab somewhere, probably at the university since he worked there as an alchemist, and it was undoubtedly what occupied the man's waking hours.

"Don't look like the boss' nephew spends much time here," Connie echoed Alex's thoughts.

"I'd say you're right."

"How are you going to find him, then?" Connie asked. "I thought you needed something special to Colton in order to find him. Nothing here looks that special."

"That's where you're wrong, Connie," Alex said, motioning for the broad man to follow as he made his way down the stairs. "What we need is something that means a great deal to Colton."

He moved to the front room and reached behind the picture of Colton's parents and picked up a small vase with a cap over it that sat against the bricks of the hearth.

"What's that?" Connie asked.

Alex held the vase and pointed to a picture of Colton and his father standing by a large wooden sign that read George Washington University.

"Colton's father looks a lot older in that picture than he does in this one." Alex indicated the one in the middle with both parents, then he held up the jar. "So unless I miss my guess, these are his mother's ashes."

Connie got a startled look on his face, then held up a warning hand.

"That's the boss's sister," he said.

"Don't worry," Alex said, cradling the urn in the crook of his arm. "We're not going to do anything to disturb her rest, we just need the ashes to establish a link to Colton. We don't even have to take them out of the urn."

Connie still looked nervous, but he followed Alex to the kitchen without further comment. Alex set the urn down gently in the center of Colton's small kitchen table, then opened his kit. He didn't have a map of D.C., but he did have the old brass compass he'd used since the days of his Harlem office. Without the map and the enhancement circle back in his new office, the finding rune wouldn't have its full power, but there wasn't anything Alex could do about that at the moment.

"How does this work?" Connie asked as Alex set the compass gently on top of the urn.

"I use the rune and if it makes a connection to Colton, the compass will point right at him."

"Then we just go get him?"

Alex added a folded-up finding rune on top of the compass, then pulled his lighter from his pocket.

"It might be just that simple," he said, squeezing the side of the lighter until the cap flipped up and it ignited. "But we have to be careful. If someone has him, they might kill him if we go barging in."

He touched the flame to the delicate flash paper, and it went up in a poof of flame. The orange rune sprang to life over the compass, spinning slowly as it pulsed with life. Alex started to lean in, but the rune faded after only a second and the compass needle below didn't even quiver.

"Damn," he muttered.

"What happened?"

Alex just shook his head.

"Does that mean Colton is dead?" Connie asked with a worried look.

"No. But he might be shielded from scrying, or underground, or even far outside the city. I need to prepare a booster and try again."

He picked up the compass, returning it to his bag, then gently added the urn inside.

"Where are you taking that?"

"Back to my hotel room," Alex said. "It will take time to prepare the booster and I'll need some things."

"So that's it?" Connie said, giving Alex a skeptical look.

"No," Alex said, heading out of the kitchen toward the little office. "I'm going to take Colton's appointment book, his notepad, and these receipts." Alex scooped up the items from the desk and added them to his bag. "If I have some spare time, I'll try to piece together what Colton was doing leading up to his disappearance. That might give me some other way to find him."

Connie's skeptical look turned downright untrusting.

"That's it?" he said. "That's all you can do?"

Alex didn't get upset, he'd heard this complaint many times before from frustrated clients.

"You ever had to stake a guy out?" he asked the mobster.

"Yeah," Connie said with a curt nod.

"You know how most of the time you just sit there in your car and watch the front of a building?"

Again Connie answered in the affirmative.

"Well, that's what this is," Alex said. "There's no sign of foul play here. Look at all the dust." Alex swept his arm around at the room. "If Colton had been grabbed here, even if someone cleaned up after, there'd be big patches where the dust was disturbed. So we know that whatever happened to Colton, it didn't happen here. All I can do now is go through what I've got and look for a clue."

Connie's hard look softened a bit, then he nodded.

"Okay," he said at last. "So where are we supposed to do our waiting?"

"I'm going to go back to my hotel before Andrew Barton starts looking for me," Alex said. "I can work on the booster there and go over all this." Alex patted the side of his bag. "You go back to your boss and report in."

"I'm not supposed to let you out of my sight," Connie said.

Alex chuckled at that.

"By all means, come back to my hotel. I'm sure the Lightning Lord would love to meet you."

Connie's grim expression soured, and Alex could tell he was trying not to show fear. Most people were justifiably afraid of sorcerers, so Alex decided to use that to shake loose from Lucky Tony's watchdog.

"Look," he said when Connie didn't answer. "Give me a number where I can reach you. If I find anything, I'll call."

Connie didn't like that idea, but he seemed to decide that Alex was trustworthy. Either that or he felt that discretion was the better part of valor.

"All right," he said at last.

8

PLANS

"Julian," Alex called out the moment he hit the lobby of the Hay-Adams Hotel. Several of the patrons cast abashed glances in his direction, but he was in a hurry.

"Mr. Lockerby," Julian Rand said, appearing as if from nowhere. "Did you require something?"

If he objected to being summoned so loudly, he gave no sign.

"I need a map of Washington," Alex said, heading for the elevator.

"A street map or a tourist map?" the concierge said, falling into step beside Alex.

"Street map," Alex said. "An accurate one, as big as you can find," Alex added as the elevator door opened. "And I need it as soon as possible."

"Very well," Julian said. "Anything else?"

Alex almost laughed at that as he stepped on the elevator. He'd just dropped a very specific request on Julian and the man had accepted it as if Alex had asked for poached eggs and toast.

"Can you have the kitchen send up a couple of poached eggs on toast?" he asked.

"Of course, Mr. Lockerby," he said as the automatic door slid closed. "Consider it done."

Alex paused outside the door and listened intently for a moment. When he was finally satisfied no one was waiting for him this time, he went in and set his bag gently on the writing desk. Despite Julian's confidence, Alex was relatively sure it would be some time before an acceptable map could be found, so he took out his rune book and opened his vault.

He hadn't been completely honest with Connie. While Alex did need a focusing ring underneath the map to boost the finding rune's power, he already had one he'd painstakingly painted onto a small rug. All he had to do was retrieve it from the vault and roll it out on the floor. It only took a few minutes, but before he had even shut the vault, there was a knock at the door.

"Your food, sir," the short man in the hotel uniform said when Alex answered. He wheeled in a small table with a covered dish on top. "Mr. Rand said to inform you that he'll have your map within the hour."

Alex thanked the bellhop and tipped him heavily before shutting the door. His eggs and toast, simple though they were, appeared to have been done to perfection and the cook had added a side of some kind of white gravy. More impressive, however, were Julian's scrounging skills.

Alex carried his food to the writing desk and sat down to eat. Since he couldn't look for Colton until the map arrived, Alex opened his bag and took out the stack of papers he'd taken from the alchemist's desk. There was an appointment book, a notepad, and a half-dozen receipts from various businesses. Alex stacked the receipts together, and set them aside along with the appointment book. He'd checked that back at Colton's apartment and it had no entries for this week. It still might be useful, but he'd have to go over it in depth to determine that.

Holding the notepad up to the light, Alex saw impressions on the paper, made by whatever had been written on the previous sheet. He considered using a revelation rune to bind graphite shavings into the grooves of the paper, but that tended to make a mess, and he didn't want graphite in his eggs.

Taking a bite of his lunch, Alex turned his attention to the pile of receipts. Two of them were from alchemy shops. No doubt Colton was purchasing ingredients or components used in his profession. One receipt didn't have a shop name or address on it, just the number five hundred written in pencil. Without any identifying data, Alex had no way to interpret the slip of paper, so he set it aside. The last three receipts were for shops around the city. Alex couldn't tell if they were grocers by their names, but he assumed they were. The amounts on the receipts varied but most were small, as if Colton had only purchased one or two things. One receipt was for twenty dollars at a place called Hallman Brothers, but Alex didn't know that name any more than the rest.

"What were you doing?" Alex asked as he went through the grocery receipts. All of them were dated the day he disappeared. "Why buy food from different stores?"

The obvious answer was that Colton was some kind of connoisseur, preferring one store's produce to another's, but the stores in question appeared to be nowhere near each other, based on their addresses. He'd have to check that when the map showed up.

Setting his now empty plate aside, Alex dug into his bag and pulled out a small bottle of black powder with a screw-top lid. He set the receipts aside and picked up the blank notepad. Unscrewing the lid on the bottle, Alex carefully shook out a thin layer of powdered graphite onto the paper. Returning the bottle to his bag, Alex took out his rune book and paged to the back where he kept the useful, but not often needed, runes. Finding a revelation rune, he tore it out and returned the book to his pocket.

The rune on the paper was simple enough, a symbol that resembled a squinting eye inside a circle with a few runic words around the outside. Revelation runes sounded more powerful than they actually were. If you had the right catalyst, they could reveal things like hidden marks or fingerprints, but only over a small area. Alex's lamp could reveal hundreds of fingerprints and many other things over a wide area, so he didn't have much call for revelation runes. When it came to exposing the indentations of writing, however, revelation runes were indispensable tools.

Folding the rune, Alex held it over the graphite-covered paper, took out his lighter, and ignited it. The flash paper burned for a moment with a sooty, gray light, then vanished. Immediately the graphite dust on the notebook jumped up off the paper as if a puff of air had somehow passed up through from the bottom. As Alex watched, the dust drifted back down, collecting in the invisible impressions on its surface. Some of the powder had been thrown up too high and it floated down over the desktop and Alex's now empty plate.

"Shopping," Alex read the word at the top of the paper. "Terrific, I've discovered Colton's grocery list." He continued reading the list that followed.

Quicklime, Hawaiian Ginger, Cashew Apple, Regulus of Antimony, Bourbon Vanilla, Colloidal Silver, Navel Orange.

Alex recognized some of the exotic names as alchemical ingredients. Cashew, Orange, and Apple seemed obvious enough, but he'd never heard of Bourbon Vanilla.

"Must be some kind of fancy liquor," he said. "I'll have to ask Iggy about it."

Alex set the list aside and pinched the bridge of his nose. Based on the list and the receipts, Colton Pierce went shopping for a few things for his lab and some for his icebox. That wasn't likely to reveal whoever grabbed Colton, so he tossed the notepad back into his bag. He could use the receipts to retrace Colton's steps during his strange shopping trip, but if he'd been grabbed when he was out, there wouldn't have been receipts back at his house. Clearly he was taken after he got home from his shopping trip, but after he'd gone out again.

Alex picked up the appointment book, but put it down again almost immediately. Something still bothered him about the receipts.

Reaching into his bag, he pulled the notebook out and tried to compare the receipts with the items on the shopping list. The receipts had the date and the amount of the purchase, but no details on what had been bought.

"Why did he even do this?" Alex fumed out loud. "Doesn't he have an assistant at the university to buy his alchemy ingredients?"

Alex was about to go on, but he stopped.

His question had been correct. As a professor, the university would have provided Colton with all the ingredients he needed to do his job, and they probably fronted his private research as well.

"The only reason for Colton to be buying his own ingredients is if they're for something else," Alex reasoned.

Something like the new business venture with his uncle.

If Lucky Tony and his nephew were the only people who knew about Euphorian, then Colton wouldn't want his secret ingredients showing up on the university's purchase logs. Someone might go looking for what the professor was using and work out the recipe for themselves.

Alex seized the list again and stared at it. He knew that quicklime and colloidal silver were alchemy ingredients. He'd seen them on the shelves in Dr. Kellin's shop often enough. He didn't know what Regulus of Antimony was, but that sounded like something an alchemist would use.

"That's why he shopped all over town," Alex declared, standing up and starting to pace around the room. "He didn't want to risk anyone knowing what goes into Euphorian, so he bought the ingredients from different shops."

It was a fairly paranoid precaution, but Colton was in business with a ruthless mobster, one who presumably had enemies.

"So now what?" Alex asked out loud.

He was pretty sure he understood the strange pile of receipts, but he was no closer to learning what had actually happened to Colton Pierce.

A knock at the door pulled his mind away from the problem and back into the present. When he opened the door, Alex found Julian Rand standing in the hall in his silk tuxedo. He had a pleased smile on his face and a paperboard tube under his arm.

"One map of Washington D.C.," he said, holding out the tube to Alex. "As requested."

Alex took the tube and stepped back, allowing Julian to enter. He pulled off the cap and a rolled sheet of heavy paper emerged. From the look of it, the map was about three feet square. Not as detailed as Alex would have liked, but on short notice, it was nothing short of miraculous.

"Is it to the gentleman's liking?" Julian asked, his crooked smile never wavering.

"Very good," Alex said, taking the map to the low coffee table he'd carried from the sitting area and placed it over his focusing rug.

"What are you doing?" Julian asked.

"Looking for someone," Alex replied. "How well do you know the city?"

"I've been employed here for ten years," he said by way of answer, "and I grew up in Bowie, just east of here in Maryland."

"You'll do," Alex said, carefully removing the urn from his bag. He set it on the map, then added his compass and a folded finding rune. "With any luck I'll need you to tell me what's in a certain part of the city."

Julian was about to ask something, but Alex lit the paper and the rune flared to life. Just like the last time, it spun briefly, then faded out without making the compass needle spin.

"What does that do?" Julian asked.

"Nothing, apparently," Alex growled. He explained the finding rune to the concierge as he moved the urn back to the writing desk, brushing the remnants of the graphite dust away before putting the urn down.

"I'm sorry it didn't work, sir," the young man said. "Perhaps next time."

"Perhaps," Alex said.

"Is there anything else I can do for you?"

Alex was about to dismiss him, but he did have another case he needed to attend to.

"You don't happen to know the concierge at the Fairfax Hotel, do you?"

Julian looked mildly surprised, but he nodded.

"Dustin Mills," he said. "He's not the sharpest tool in the shed, as it were, but he's a decent fellow."

"I need to know who's leading the investigation into the death of Senator Young," Alex said. "Not the FBI, but the local police. Do you think Dustin could, or would, tell me that?"

Julian's perpetual grin turned slightly predatory.

"You? No," he said, shaking his head. "We concierges, however, share information regularly. I'm absolutely certain he would tell me if he knew. He would never betray the confidence of a guest, of course, but the police are tramping around making a mess of his hotel and bothering his guests. I'm certain I can get you a name."

Alex pulled a twenty out of his wallet and passed it to Julian.

"I need that as soon as possible," he said.

The twenty vanished into Julian's pocket and he gave Alex a small bow.

"Right away, Mr Lockerby."

Alex quickly copied Colton's strange shopping list into his flip notebook, then put the alchemist's notepad and the receipts onto the side table inside his vault door for safekeeping. As he picked up the blank receipt with the five hundred written on it, he paused. It had been blank except for the number, he was certain of that. Now, however, there was a circle with a plus sign inside it in the upper left corner.

The lines of the little pictogram were dark and solid. It would have been impossible for him to miss it before, so where had it come from?

"The revelation rune," he muttered as the truth hit him. The symbol must have been on the paper as an impression from a previous paper, or maybe as a faint pencil mark. Whatever the case had been, his rune had affected the receipt as well.

Alex copied the symbol into his notebook along with the number five hundred, then added the receipt to the drawer. He'd only just closed it when there was another knock on his door.

"Alex," Andrew Barton said as soon as the door opened. "What a day! The Board of Commissioners is going to fund not one but two towers to distribute power over the city." He swept into the room and made a mock bow to Alex.

"Congratulations," Alex replied.

"Nonsense," Andrew said. "I owe it all to you and those amazing runes. I can hardly believe we can just link back to Empire Tower and power whatever we want wherever we want. It's fantastic."

Alex almost blushed under the weight of such praise.

"I'm going to stay in town for a few more days," Andrew went on. "Maybe a week. There are details to hammer out, contracts to sign, and plans to oversee. You can head back sooner than that if you want, but I need you to do something for me first." Andrew reached into thin air and pulled the heavy power test box into his arms. "Take this thing," he set it heavily on the floor, "and go around town taking readings. I want to make sure the links will work no matter where we put the towers."

Alex didn't relish lugging the heavy tester around, but then he remembered he could just put it in his vault, and open the door to get it out wherever he wanted to take a reading. He'd have to close the door first, since his vault was connected to Empire Tower itself. If the vault was open the connection would throw off his reading. That said, vault runes were easy to write, so it wouldn't be a problem.

"I'd be happy to," he said to Andrew. "How many readings do you need?"

"Let's call it an even dozen," Andrew said, taking a step toward the door. "I'd love to stay and chat, but I've got a dinner date and I don't want to keep her waiting."

With that, the sorcerer swept out of the room, closing the door behind him.

In the wake of Tiffany Young's visit, his fight with Sorsha, and meeting Lucky Tony Casetti, Alex had quite forgotten about the reason he was in the city in the first place. Since he planned to work on both of his new cases that evening, he was glad Andrew had a date to keep him busy.

Alex donned his overcoat, then opened his vault again and lugged the heavy power tester inside. He was going to the Fairfax Hotel up by Embassy Row, so he'd take a reading there. It would give him a good excuse if Sorsha saw him.

9

PROOF AND POLITICS

The Fairfax Hotel was an eight-story edifice of red brick on the corner of Washington's Embassy Row. As a result it catered to an international clientele, one that wasn't thrilled to have their hotel full of uniformed policeman and suit-clad FBI agents.

"Are you the private detective?" a pudgy, red-haired man asked as Alex stepped out of a cab. The man had a round face with lines that indicated he usually wore a smile, though that was conspicuously absent at present. Like Julian, the red-haired man wore an immaculate silk tuxedo with gold cufflinks and shoes polished to a gleaming shine.

"You're Dustin Mills?" Alex asked.

The man nodded, taking Alex by the elbow and leading him away from the curb.

"Julian said you might be able to help the police with their investigation and get them out of my hotel," Mills said.

"I've been hired to find out what happened to Senator Young," Alex said. "I might be able to point the police in a new direction so they're out of your hair. I just need to know who's in charge. He's the guy I have to convince."

The Fairfax concierge gave Alex a suspicious glance, then sighed with resolution.

"Come with me," he said and turned to the main doors of the hotel. Once inside, Alex saw a knot of police officers in blue uniforms gathered in one corner of the lobby. Several men in suits were there as well, and none of them looked happy.

"That's him," Mills said, pointing to one of the suited men. "Detective James Norton. He's in charge of the police investigation."

"You sure?" Alex said, studying the man. His suit was rumpled, and he looked soft, like he spent more time behind a desk than in the field.

"Oh, yes," the concierge said. "He's very unhappy about the FBI's involvement, as he tells anyone who will listen. Trust me, Mr. Lockerby, that's your man."

"Thank you, Mr. Mills," Alex said, handing the man a fiver. "Do me a favor and tell him he has a call on the hotel phone."

Alex made his way to the front desk as the concierge moved to speak with the detective. Most hotels had a courtesy telephone for guests on or near the front desk and the Fairfax was no exception. A single telephone sat on a shelf in a wall niche just to the left of the main desk. Alex took up a position near it and leaned on the counter to wait. A minute later the detective appeared, rounding the end of the front desk and heading for the phone.

"Hello?" he said, picking up the receiver. A look of consternation crossed his face, and he repeated his greeting.

"There's no phone call, Detective Norton," Alex said, still leaning with his back to the counter. "I arranged a little privacy so we could talk."

Norton looked Alex up and down with an appeasing eye. The police detective was just as rumpled and unkempt up close. His face was soft and jowly under a mop of black hair that ran down in front of his ears to a day's growth of unshaved beard. He had a stain of some kind on his tie, his shoes were scuffed, and the battered fedora he carried in his hand hadn't been blocked in quite some time. The only part of the man's appearance that gave Alex pause were his eyes. They were a lustrous brown and seemed focused and sharp, as if the messy exterior was merely some kind of façade or disguise.

Capital Murder

"Oh, yeah?" he said, his voice somewhere between annoyed and belligerent. "Who the hell are you, and what makes you think I want to hear anything you've got to say?"

Alex was ready for this response and he handed over one of his business cards. Norton read it, then scoffed.

"Well, what do you know," he said, looking up from the card to Alex. "Those muckrakers at the Capital Dispatch finally got something right. I read that the widow Young had hired some hot shot, out-of-state dick to help her beat a murder rap."

"I suppose the tabloids did help, in a way," Alex admitted. "Mrs. Young saw that story, same as you, and sought me out this morning."

"Doesn't make any difference," Norton said, handing Alex's card back. "The powers that be want this case over and done with. They got a note from the Senator's mistress confessing to poisoning their food and they're just itching to declare this case solved. As soon as she wakes up, they'll put the kibosh on any investigation, so you can tell your client she's free and clear. The FBI is satisfied."

"But not you," Alex said. It was a statement rather than a question.

Norton chuckled.

"No," he admitted. "Not me. My money's on your client. I was the one that told her about her husband's affair."

"Let me guess," Alex interrupted. "She wasn't surprised."

"Not one bit. She knew he was stepping out on her, and if she knew," he paused, letting the implication hang in the air for a moment. "If she knew, I'm betting she finally decided she'd had enough. In any case I don't buy that the mistress poisoned the food, letter or no letter."

Alex nodded, following the detective's train of thought.

"If she meant to kill herself, then why is she still alive?" he said.

"Exactly. Did she have second thoughts halfway through the soup? It doesn't add up."

"So you're betting that once she wakes up, she'll deny the whole plot," Alex said. "Say she's never seen the confession letter before."

Norton nodded, then poked Alex in the chest with his index finger.

"And when that happens, everyone's going to look at your client, Mr. Fancy Private Dick."

"What if the mistress claims she wrote the letter?" Alex asked.

Norton sighed.

"Then the FBI gets their wish," he said with a shrug. "Case closed. They'll probably declare it closed no matter what happens. The murder of a U.S. Senator is bad for everyone in this town." He turned and started to leave. "See you round, Lockerby."

"Detective," Alex called after him. "One more thing, if you don't mind."

Norton hesitated for a long moment, then turned back.

"What is it?"

"Let's say for a minute that Senator Young's mistress didn't try to kill herself and her lover."

"Then your client did," Norton said, matter of fact.

"What if she didn't?" Alex suggested. "What if she knew about her husband's proclivities and simply didn't care?"

Norton scoffed but his eyes narrowed at Alex. Clearly he was thinking about what such a scenario would mean.

"If the poisoning and the confession were staged," he said, rubbing the stubble on his chin, "and the wife didn't do it, that would mean someone murdered a U.S. Senator and set the mistress up as their patsy."

Alex gave the man a conspiratorial smile and leaned in as if not to be overheard.

"That's the kind of case that could make a career, don't you think?"

Norton's eyes hardened and he sneered at Alex.

"You're grasping at straws, Lockerby," he growled. "What is it you want?"

"Access to your case files," Alex said, as if that were the most normal request in the world.

Norton laughed at that.

"Figures," he said. "I knew you were buttering me up for something. You can forget about that, or any other help from me. I got enough trouble with the Feds sniffing around, looking to shut me out. I don't need some clever dick muddying the waters any further."

"Think about it, detective," Alex said, putting a restraining hand on Norton's arm as the man started to turn. "If I'm right, my client is innocent, but in order to prove that I've got to find out who actually killed Senator Young. Once I do, I'll need to gift wrap this case and then make sure the word gets out so Mrs. Young will be officially off the hook. Now I can call the papers, and they'd certainly be happy to print the story for the public, but I'd rather have someone on the inside. Someone who could take this case to the feds and get them to back off. Someone official."

"Someone like me?" Detective Norton asked, a sarcastic tone infusing his voice.

"Look, detective," Alex said. "Mrs. Young isn't paying me to get my name in the newspapers, and frankly, that's fine by me. All she wants is to find out who offed her husband. You, on the other hand, could be helped a great deal if your name showed up in the papers."

Alex widened his smile, trying to be as persuasive as possible. He was having to work too hard for this. It felt like Norton was three seconds from telling him to go to hell.

"You know that article in the Capital Dispatch said you work with the New York Police Department," the detective said, his eyes boring into Alex. "You offer them the same deal?"

Alex grinned and nodded.

"Call the Manhattan Central Office of Police and ask for Lieutenant Danny Pak," he said. "After you talk to him, talk to Captain Frank Callahan. They'll tell you."

"Boss," a man's voice interrupted.

Alex turned to find the two other detectives hurrying over. The younger of the two looked worried, but the older man simply looked resigned, as if expected bad news had finally come to pass.

"What is it?" Norton demanded.

The man who had spoken gave Alex a nervous look but only for a second.

"One of the uniforms got a radio call," he said. "Helen Mitchell just died."

Norton's teeth clenched together so hard that Alex could hear them grinding.

"Damn it," he swore.

Alex knew the name, but it took him a minute to put it together.

"Senator Young's secretary?"

Norton nodded and swore again.

"It's the FBI's case now," he fumed. "They'll declare the confession to be genuine and that's that." He waved at the other two detectives. "Go get the car. There's no reason to stick around here."

Norton waited until the men had gone, then he turned back to Alex.

"I was just starting to buy what you were selling," he admitted. "Probably a good thing it's all over now."

"Is it?" Alex asked.

Norton's scowl broke into a grin and he laughed.

"You can't fight the Feds, Lockerby," he said. "Especially on their turf."

Alex shook his head and leaned in close. He would have to talk fast if he had any hope of convincing Norton to help him.

"Assume for a minute that you're right, the mistress didn't poison the food," he said.

"Then the widow did." Norton said. "We've been through this."

"And if it was someone else," Alex postulated. "Then they killed Senator Young for a reason. Now, if you went to all the trouble of arranging a murder, and framed a patsy, and that patsy didn't die, what would you do?"

Norton nodded, catching Alex's train of thought.

"I'd make sure to tie up my loose end," he said.

"According to the papers, Helen Mitchell was supposed to make a full recovery," Alex pointed out.

Norton rubbed his chin again, clearly wavering.

"I'm not just a detective," Alex went on. "I'm also a runewright. I've got magical means to find evidence others can miss. What say you and I go have a look at the room that Helen Mitchell died in? See if there's anything to see."

"Assuming the FBI doesn't throw us out," Norton said.

"Your man said you got a radio call about the death," Alex pointed out. "It's possible the FBI doesn't even know about it yet. There's a good chance we can look at that room before they get there, but only if we hurry."

"What if there's nothing to find?" Norton said. "I'd be taking a hell of a risk bringing you to a crime scene."

"If there's nothing there, then the FBI's version of the case is the final one," Alex said with a shrug. "No one will care what some D.C. cop did after it was over. But if there is something to find…"

Alex stuck out his hand for Detective Norton to shake.

"You sure you can find any hidden evidence?" the detective asked.

Alex nodded and pushed his hand a little closer to Norton.

"Mr. Lockerby," he said, with steel in his eyes. "I may live to regret this, but I'm going to go have a look at the room Miss Mitchell died in, and I'd like you to come along."

He grasped Alex's hand and shook it firmly.

"Detective Norton," Alex said, shaking back. "I'd be delighted."

The police had put Helen Mitchell into a private room because of her involvement with the murder of a Senator. A uniformed officer had been stationed outside the room, but based on the sturdy chair and the stack of dime novels on the floor, the guard hadn't been paying too much attention.

"What happened?" Detective Norton asked the man when he and Alex arrived outside the room.

"Dunno," the officer said with a shrug. "Someone comes by every half hour or so to check on her. The last one found her dead."

"And only doctors or nurses went in?" Alex asked. "No one else?"

The cop gave Alex a quick once over but must have assumed he was FBI because he just shrugged.

"Nobody."

"Find the doctor in charge," Norton told the man. "I want to know her cause of death."

The cop looked like he was about to argue that the poison was what had killed Helen, but he just shrugged again and turned away.

"Okay, scribbler," Norton said once the cop was out of earshot. "I'm sure the FBI is on their way over by now, so let's make this quick."

Alex opened the door and they went in. The room was small, just space enough for a bed with an I.V. stand beside it. A chair stood against the wall with a small table that held a vase of freshly cut flowers, and there was a wardrobe cabinet affixed to the wall by the door. A white porcelain sink stuck out beyond the wardrobe, and Alex could see a mirror attached to the wall over it. The bed was empty, though the sheets had not yet been stripped, and there were two pillows on the floor.

Alex took all this in as he entered, setting his kit bag on the bed.

"Look around for anything suspicious," Alex said as he took out his multi-lamp, setting it on the table by the chair.

"Like what?" Norton said, peering into the wastebasket by the door.

"Empty alchemy vials, used syringes," Alex said. "That kind of thing." He clipped the silverlight burner into the lamp, the retrieved his oculus from the bag. Since discovering the hidden text in the Monograph, Alex had worked on his oculus. The new one, which he called model two, was much smaller and fit directly over his eye. It still had a small tube but unlike his original, it was only about an inch and a half long. Multiple rings ran around the outside for focusing the lens and changing the color, but the new design was all internal. The entire oculus now looked like a weirdly shaped monocle.

Strapping it on, Alex lit the burner, then swept the room. Being that this was a hospital room, the whole place lit up in various shades of silver-white glow. Evidence of bodily fluids was everywhere, even a disturbing spray that ran up the wall to the ceiling that Alex knew to be arterial blood.

Since the walls and floor were too covered with stains both old and new, Alex confined his examination to the blankets and sheets on the bed. These, at least, were washed regularly, so fresh stains should be very evident.

The top of the blanket had a small spot that looked like the remnants of vomit, not surprising for someone who'd been poisoned. The rest of the sheets showed signs of sweat and urine, but nothing that looked suspicious. He checked very carefully up by where Helen's head would have been, looking for drips of alchemical potions, but found nothing.

Frustrated, he turned and picked up the two pillows, setting them on the bed. He shone the light over them, revealing sweat stains, but that was it.

"This place is empty, Lockerby," Detective Norton said, peering under the bed. "You got anything?"

"Not yet," Alex said, turning the pillows over. "Check the cabinets."

"What?" Norton scoffed. "You think someone came in here, killed the girl, and then hid the evidence with her clothes?"

Alex just shrugged.

"You don't know if you don't look," he said.

Norton sighed, but turned toward the cabinet.

"Fine," he said.

Alex felt his skin prickle as the detective opened the wardrobe and there was a brief pressure in his eardrums. He was about to say something, but the silverlight on the second pillow made him stop.

"Detective," he said, beaconing the slovenly man over. "You'd better have a look at this." He slipped his oculus over his head and passed it to Norton. "Hold this over your eye."

The detective didn't bother with the strap, simply holding the little tube up to his eye and closing the other.

"What the hell is that?" he growled once he pointed the oculus at the pillows.

Alex knew what the silverlight was revealing. It had looked like the face of a ghost from a comic book with a title like, "Tales of Terror." There were two holes where the eyes would be, the impressions of cheekbones and a nose, and then a long opening for a mouth.

"It's Helen Mitchell's face," Alex said. "Someone held this pillow down on her hard enough to make that impression from the sweat and oils on her skin."

"You think someone suffocated her?" Norton said. "Gutsy. She might have been unconscious, but there's no way they could be sure. What if she'd struggled?"

"They didn't leave anything to chance," Alex said, blowing out his lamp and swapping the silverlight burner for the ghostlight one. "Have a look over here and tell me what you see."

He lit the lantern, then shone the greenish light on the open doors of the cabinet that held Helen's clothes.

"There's a symbol of some kind on the inside of the right door," Norton said. "It looks like it's moving."

"It's a privacy rune," Alex said. "They usually last about an hour, so whoever killed Helen put it here so he wouldn't be disturbed. It's a good thing we came right over, it'll probably be gone in a few more minutes."

"All right," Norton said, handing Alex the oculus. "How did you know it was there?"

"I felt the air pressure change when you opened the door," Alex said, slipping his oculus back on. He looked at the privacy rune, turning slowly in the light of his lamp. It was similar to the one he had in his own rune book, but this one would only block sound. Alex's rune would also prevent scrying. "Whoever did this knew their stuff," he said, peering at the rune. "That's why they put it on the inside of the door. Privacy runes make it impossible for sound to travel outside of the room they're in, so with the door to this cabinet open, it covers the whole room, but with it closed..."

"It silences the closet," Norton said. "So when our killer left, the cop outside didn't notice anything funny. Smart."

Alex took off his oculus and grinned at the rumpled man.

"Looks like you were right, detective," he said. "Helen Mitchell didn't poison Senator Young. Both of them were murdered."

10

THE BOOKIE

"So where was your client a few hours ago?" Detective Norton said, standing with his hands on his hips.

Alex laughed at that as he packed up his kit.

"You thought she was a suspect," he said. "You and I both know you have someone watching her, and if she was anywhere near this hospital today, you would have led with that."

The , ground his teeth and looked back up at the open closet door. He couldn't see the rune now, but he knew it was there.

"She could have paid to have someone off the girl," he said, sticking to his suspicions.

"Maybe," Alex said with a shrug. "She's got money and a certain amount of power, so she might know someone she could hire for this kind of job."

"But?" Norton said, reading Alex's expression.

Alex pointed to the space where the now invisible rune clung to the inside of the cabinet door.

"This isn't some two-bit thug," he said. "Whoever did this had a plan, and a good one. They wanted to make Helen's death look like suicide, just like it said in that letter you found. Even the most famous mafia hit-men back in the day never bothered with this kind of theatricality. I think you're looking for a pro."

"An assassin?" Norton said, his eyebrows shooting up. "Like in a dime novel?"

"I know it sounds far-fetched," Alex said, closing his bag and standing, "but you and I both know that someone murdered a U.S. Senator and tried to cover it up. That's not a jealous lover or a slighted constituent, this is someone with deep pockets and a motive that would be obvious if Senator Young's death was declared a murder."

Norton thought about that for a minute, stroking his chin.

"You've got a point," he admitted. "Both the FBI and my Captain want this case swept under the rug as quickly as possible. They definitely don't want to hear anything about why Helen Mitchell didn't manage to kill herself when the note said she intended to. So now we need to figure out who had a motive to want the Senator out of the way."

"It has to have something to do with his job," Alex said. "Maybe some law he was proposing or bill he was blocking? Would someone kill over that?"

Now it was Detective Norton's turn to laugh.

"Are you kidding, Lockerby? If the right law gets passed here, it could mean millions to a business back in the Senator's home state."

"So what changes with Senator Young's death?" Alex asked. "Who stands to reap a windfall now that he's out of the way?"

Norton sighed and rubbed his temples.

"That isn't likely to be a short list," he admitted. "And figuring it out is going to be like untangling a big knot. I know a guy over in the Senate clerk's office. I'll call him in the morning and try to find out what was coming up for a vote this week."

It was a sound enough place to start, but the way Detective Norton said it, Alex could tell he didn't have much hope that tactic would bear fruit.

"You might want to ask around about a hit man who has runewright training," Alex added. "That's not going to be a common combination, so maybe you'll get lucky."

Norton sighed and nodded. It was clear he thought it was a long shot as well. The FBI might know more about hitters, but if Norton brought the Bureau in on this, it was likely they'd just take the case from him and leave him out in the cold. Besides, the FBI wanted this case closed. If Norton made waves, someone might decide to make an example of him.

"Call your clerk," Alex said. "I'll see if Mrs. Young can shed any light on possible motives. I've got another case I have to run down tomorrow morning so I'll call you around noon and we can compare notes."

Norton was about to answer when the uniformed officer who'd been stationed in the hall pushed the door open and leaned in.

"The Feds are here," he said.

Alex headed for the door and peered out. A group of men in dark suits were coming up the hall from the direction of the elevator. As they moved, he caught a flash of platinum blonde hair.

"Hold this," he said to the officer as he pushed the door open. The man looked confused but held the door, effectively screening Alex from the approaching group. "Now stay that way till the Feds get here."

"Don't forget," Norton hissed as Alex headed down the hall in the opposite direction. "Noon tomorrow."

Alex gave the man the okay sign as he hustled through the door to the stairwell at the far end of the hall.

Alex paused on his way out of the hospital to make a call. He pulled the card Connie had given him from the back of his rune book and dialed the mobster's number.

"Hello," a gruff voice answered after a single ring.

"I need to speak to Connie."

"He ain't here," the gruff voice came back. "What da'ya want?"

"Get a message to him," Alex said, irritation overflowing in his voice. "This is Alex Lockerby, I have a lead in Mr. Casetti's case and I need him to meet me at my hotel as soon as possible. You got that?"

There was silence on the line for a moment, then Alex heard muffled voices.

"Alex," Tony Casetti's voice came on. "We've been wondering where you got off to."

"Chasing leads," Alex said. "I found a paper with Colton's receipts, it had 'five hundred dollars' written on it and there's a bookie's mark in the corner."

"You think Colton got in bad with a bookie?" Lucky Tony growled.

"I think five hundred is a lot of cash," Alex said.

"Not for me," came the reply. "If Colton was having trouble with some number runner, I'd have taken care of the debt."

"Maybe he didn't want you to know," Alex suggested. "But I figure that rather than guess, Connie and I should go have a word with the bookie."

"You recognized his mark?" Lucky Tony said, sounding impressed.

"No," Alex admitted, "but this is a bill for half a grand, that makes it important to our bookie. That means I can use a finding rune and follow it right to him."

"Connie's already over at your hotel," Tony said. "Do you need him to come get you?"

"No," Alex said, not really wanting to explain to Lucky Tony why he was in a hospital filled with cops and Feds. "I'll grab a cab, and meet him there."

Fifteen minutes later, Alex opened the door to his room in the Hay-Adams Hotel with Lucky Tony's man Connie in tow.

"Nice," the mob man said, looking around at the sumptuous room. "I didn't realize being a private dick paid so well."

"Andrew Barton is paying for the room," Alex said, tossing his hat on the chair next to the door. "He's in town finalizing a business deal and I do runewright work for him."

"So you didn't come to D.C. to figure out who killed that Senator?" Connie asked. There was a note in the man's voice that caught Alex's attention and he turned.

"Why?"

Connie shut the door to the hall, then gave Alex a hard look. It was clearly meant to be intimidating, but Alex knew Lucky Tony still needed him to find his nephew. That meant Connie wasn't about to attack him. Still, he touched his flash ring with the tip of his left thumb just in case.

"I got a call right before I heard from the boss," Connie said. He spoke easily, like any regular conversation, but he was still attempting to stare Alex down. "It was from one of my people at the hospital. We keep a guy there in case one of ours is brought in. Anyway, he said you were there and that you had been talking to some Feds."

"And you figured I was trying to sell out your boss?" Alex asked, letting the ghost of an amused smile play across his lips.

"The thought occurred to me," Connie replied.

"I was at the hospital because the wife of the murdered Senator wants me to figure out who killed him," Alex explained. "The girl he was in the hotel room with just died, even though she was supposed to recover, so I helped one of the local cops figure out she was murdered."

For the first time, Connie's implacable expression split into a sneer.

"And what about the case you're supposed to be working on?" he demanded. "Every minute the boss's nephew is out there the chances get better that he ain't coming home alive."

Alex stared back at Connie for a long moment before answering. He'd heard this complaint before, from many clients. Usually he told them that if they didn't like the way he was handling their case, they could seek out someone else to help. In this instance, he'd have to try something else.

"How long have you been working for Mr. Casetti?" he asked.

Connie's brows furrowed for a moment at the seeming change of subject.

"Twenty-three years," the mobster replied. "Why?"

Alex shrugged and took out a cigarette.

"How long before Tony trusted you with a big job?" he asked, and he squeezed his lighter to life. "Something he let you handle by yourself."

"I don't know," Connie growled. "Four years, maybe five."

"Right," Alex said, blowing out a plume of smoke. "He didn't send you out on your own until you understood the job, until you knew the business." Alex took a step forward and stabbed his finger into Connie's chest. "So don't you dare come in here and tell me how to do my job. Despite what your boss said, he didn't pick me because of some long forgotten, shirt-tail connection. He wanted me because I'm the best. He wanted me because he knows I won't rest until I've found his nephew, preferably alive."

Connie glared at Alex for a long moment, even leaning in toward him a bit.

"You'd better hope you find him alive," he said in a quiet, dangerous voice. "If your running around working on other people's problems costs Colton his life, things are going to end badly for you."

"If there had been anything I could have done to help find Colton earlier, that's what I would have been doing," Alex growled back. "Right now the only clue we've got is a bill from a bookie. It's not the best connection I could hope for, but as long as our man isn't on the move, my rune should be able to find him."

Connie stared into Alex's eyes for another long moment, then he took a step back.

"So you had to wait until the bookie settled into his usual haunt," he said.

Alex nodded and let his angry expression slacken, replacing it with a conspiratorial grin.

"I figure by now he's in a booth in some bar or nightclub where he settles up the day's business," Alex said. He turned and walked over to the coffee table where he'd set up his map of the District. Reaching into his pocket, he dropped the bookie's note onto the map, then added a finding rune from his book.

Connie followed, standing a few feet away from the table as Alex placed the brass compass on top of the note, then added the rune on top. Alex touched the burning end of his cigarette to the flash paper, and this time the glowing rune it left behind began spinning slowly. Beneath where it hovered in the air, the compass needle began to turn as well.

Alex suppressed a sigh of relief. He'd been pretty sure that with the aid of his flash ring he could have taken Connie in a fight, but it would have been a narrow victory. Men like Connie had the air of casual violence about them, and Alex had no illusions that Lucky Tony's watchdog could not handle himself in a fight. With the finding rune doing its job, the odds that Alex and Connie would come to blows were greatly reduced.

As the rune faded and then burst into a shower of orange sparks, Alex took hold of the compass and began sliding it along the map. The needle immediately began turning, indicating a spot in the northeastern part of the city.

"Looks like our bookie is right here," Alex said, circling the corner of a block with the compass, keeping the needle pointing directly to the spot.

"Not bad," Connie said, nodding his approval.

Alex gave him a grin and picked up the compass.

"What say we take a ride over there and find out if he knows anything about the whereabouts of Colton Pierce?"

The Eastern Star was a nightclub located on a corner where two busy streets came together. It wasn't as upscale as a Core nightclub in New York, but it did have a well-dressed man in a suit out front to keep out the riffraff.

"You sure our bookie is in there?" Connie asked as he and Alex crossed the street toward the club.

Alex held out his brass compass, showing that the needle was pointing right to the building.

"It's the kind of place I'd expect for a bookie taking bets for half a grand," Alex said. "You ever been here?"

"No," Connie said. "I'm not much of a dancer."

Alex looked at the mobster, unsure of whether he'd just made a joke. When he looked back up the sidewalk toward the club, however, he stopped short.

"What?" Connie asked, his hand twitching toward the bulge under his coat.

"The doorman," Alex said, nodding to where the man in the expensive suit had stood. "He went inside."

"Probably had to use the can," Connie said with a shrug. "His stand-in will be out in a minute."

Alex couldn't argue with Connie's logic, it made perfect sense, but something about the doorman's disappearance bothered him.

Working with mobsters is making you jumpy.

Alex started forward again but no replacement doorman had appeared when they reached the entrance to *The Eastern Star*. Brassy swing music filtered out through the door and Alex only hesitated for a moment before he pulled it open. The room beyond was typical for a nightclub. A long bar of whitewashed wood ran the length of the left-hand wall where patrons sat on padded stools chatting and drinking. To the right was a raised platform where twenty or thirty tables were arranged for dining and in the center was a packed dance floor.

Since it was just after seven, the club was crowded and raucous with the noise of the band, the dancing, and the incessant buzz of conversations straining to be heard over the music.

"How do we find the bookie in all this?" Connie said, coming up beside Alex.

Alex didn't bother yelling over the din, he just held up the compass, placing it on the flat of his hand. The needle pointed off slightly to the right and Alex nodded that way. He started forward, climbing up the three steps that led up to the dining platform.

Following the compass needle, he threaded his way through the sea of tables and diners with Connie in tow. As he neared the end of the platform, Alex could see that a row of booths lined the back wall of the building. They were beyond the bright lights that hung over the diners, and each booth had a single lamp on its table, no doubt for romantic atmosphere. Several of the booths were occupied, but Alex's eye caught movement at the one at the far end. A man stood there, leaning down over someone who was seated. As Alex watched, the standing man turned and pointed right at him. In the dim light, Alex hadn't recognized the bouncer from the front door, but now he could see him clearly. Below in the booth sat a lean, shrewd-looking man who took one look at Alex, then jumped up and ran.

11

THE FISH

Of all the things Alex had expected to happen when he met Colton Pierce's bookie, having the man take one look at him and run wasn't even on the list. Alex just stood, stunned by the fleeing man. After all, Alex had never been to Washington before, and he didn't recognize the man, so how would the bookie even know him?

"I got him," Connie said, charging past the flat-footed Alex.

The bookie reached the corner where the back of the club met the sidewall and he shouldered his way through a service door into a dark hallway beyond. This finally shook Alex into action. He held up the compass and watched as the needle began to sweep back toward the center of the club. The bookie was still in the building and looking for a way out.

Alex turned and dashed back the way he had come. The front door to The Eastern Star was in the middle of the building, but if Alex could get outside before the bookie, he might be able to prevent the man from jumping in a cab and disappearing. The finding rune would still let Alex track him, but when the quarry knew he was being chased, it made it that much harder to run him down.

Checking the compass as he hit the street, Alex turned right and ran to the corner of the building. Rounding it, he saw a dark alleyway separating the nightclub from the next building down the block. As Alex ran, he could hear the sound of splintering wood and curses. He put on a burst of speed and rounded the corner into the alley just in time to collide with the fleeing bookie. He only came up to Alex's chin, but he'd been looking back over his shoulder when Alex rounded the corner, and despite the differences in their size, the impact knocked Alex back. Losing his balance, Alex fell onto his backside, but he managed to grab the bookie's suit coat, pulling the man down after him.

Alex wrapped his free arm around the bookie, holding him tight, but the little man still had plenty of fight in him. He balled up his fists and started slamming Alex in the kidney over and over. Alex tried to twist away from the blows, taking them on his back, but that loosened the hold he had on his assailant.

"Enough!" Connie growled, and suddenly the bookie was yanked free from Alex's loosening grasp.

Above him, Connie held the bookie by the back of his jacket and without any seeming effort, slammed the man bodily into the back wall of the nightclub. Alex tried to get up, but the pain in his side was making that difficult. The bookie had got several solid hits in, and Alex's side ached.

"Don't you move," Connie said, jamming a snub-nosed .38 up under the little man's jaw. "You all right, Lockerby?"

"My pride's a bit damaged," Alex said, rolling onto his right side, then pushing himself up to one knee. He paused for a moment as the throbbing in his left side quieted down, then heaved himself to his feet. "But I'll live." He turned his eyes on the bookie. The man had the lean, hungry look of a predator with angular cheekbones, thick eyebrows and dark eyes. Alex was about to ask why the man had run, but the answer was plain to see. The bookie wasn't looking at Alex at all, he was staring, wide-eyed, at Connie.

"Friend of yours?" Alex asked, nodding at the bookie.

Connie had been watching Alex, pinning the bookie against the wall with his arm and his gun. He'd lost his hat somewhere in the pursuit and there was an angry welt rising on his forehead that caught the light from the street as the mobster turned to his captive. He looked the bookie up and down for a moment, then his angry expression slid into a wolfish grin and he stepped back.

"Jimmy the Fish," he said with a dark chuckle. "I heard you was dead."

"H-hi-ya, Connie," Jimmy said, pressing his back against the brick wall as if he might somehow melt through it and escape.

"Jimmy the Fish?" Alex asked. He'd heard a lot of underworld nicknames but 'the Fish' was a new one.

"I had the shingles when I first started in the rackets," Jimmy said, taking his eyes off Connie for a brief moment. "The boys said my arms looked like I had fish scales."

That actually made more sense than Alex expected.

"You ain't here about Celia, are you?" Jimmy said, his eyes going a bit wild with fear. "I mean, that was years ago."

"I bet the boss don't think it was that long ago," Connie said, a toothy grin splitting his unshaven face. He looked at Alex, tapping Jimmy with the barrel of his pistol. "You see, Jimmy here had a thing for this girl, Celia," he explained.

"Oh, let me guess," Alex said, catching on. "Celia Casetti?"

"Got it in one," Connie laughed. "When the boss found out, he ordered the Fish here chopped into bait."

"I met her in a nightclub," the Fish pleaded. "She never told me who she was, I swear."

Alex couldn't suppress the grin that was spreading across his face. He only hoped Connie was savvy enough to follow his lead.

"You know what, Jimmy," Alex said, thumping the bookie on the shoulder. "I think today is going to turn out to be your lucky day."

"How do you figure?" the Fish asked.

"My name is Alex Lockerby, and I'm a private detective."

The Fish looked confused, then angry.

"Hey," he protested. "What is this?"

Connie jammed his pistol back into Jimmy's neck.

"Shut up, you," he growled. "Let the man talk."

"Connie and I are looking for someone," Alex continued. "Someone you know."

Jimmy's look of fear and confusion melted into one of calculation.

"And you want me to finger him?" he guessed. "What if I do?"

"Then Constantine and I," Alex nodded at Connie, "might be persuaded to forget we ever saw you."

"Sure, sure," the Fish said, starting to nod, then remembering the revolver just under his chin. "Who is it you're looking for?"

"Colton Pierce."

Alex expected Jimmy to react to the name, but he just looked confused.

"The professor?" he said.

"Colton Pierce," Alex said, letting a tone of anger slip into his voice. "The man who owes you five hundred dollars."

"What?" the Fish protested. "Pierce isn't on my books."

Alex pulled the receipt from his pocket and held it up in front of the bookie's face.

"This is yours," he said. "I know that because I used a finding rune and this paper, and it led me right to you." Alex jabbed the man with his finger. "So don't play dumb with me."

"What happened?" Connie said. "You send some boys over to encourage him to pay his debts? Things get out of hand?"

Jimmy's eyes had gotten wide, and a look of naked fear played across his face.

"I swear, Connie, Pierce doesn't owe me anything," he insisted.

"Then why did he have this bill from you?" Alex yelled, pressing the paper against the Fish's chest. "It says he owes you five hundred, and that's a lot for a college professor."

"Besides," Connie said, his voice dropping to almost a whisper. "He had a bodyguard with him, a friend of mine. Whoever grabbed Pierce beat my friend to death. So I'm going to give you one more chance, Jimmy. One chance to tell us where Colton is." Connie reached up with his thumb and cocked the revolver. "And you'd better hope he's alive."

Alex watched Jimmy while Connie threatened him. The bookie looked like he was on the verge of losing control of his bladder. His face was a mask of terror, not at all the look of someone who still had a hole card to play.

"What's it going to be, Jimmy," he pressed. "You going to play ball, or are we going to find out just how much Lucky Tony loves his little girl?"

"I swear," Jimmy sobbed. "That ain't a bill. Colton has the devil's own luck." He pointed to the paper still clutched in Alex's hand. "That's a receipt. He won that money betting on the ponies at Arlington. I-I paid him a few days ago."

Connie's face twisted into a sneer.

"You expect us to believe that load of horse apples?" He turned to Alex. "Let me shoot him in the knees, that'll loosen—"

Alex held up his hand and Connie's mouth snapped shut so hard his teeth clacked. Taking a breath, Alex turned to the Fish.

"Jimmy," he said, his voice smooth and cajoling. "It isn't widely known, but Colton Pierce is Mr. Casetti's nephew."

Jimmy groaned and started shaking.

"Jesus," he said, though Alex couldn't tell if it was a curse or a prayer. "What is it with that family? I can't get away from them."

Alex put a reassuring hand on the man's shoulder.

"Focus, Jimmy," he said. "You realize that if you have Colton stashed somewhere—"

"I don't," the Fish insisted. "I swear, I don't!"

"If you have him," Alex went on, a bit louder. "All you have to do is give him up, unharmed, and we walk away."

"I don't," Jimmy sobbed. He was weeping openly now. "Look in my shirt pocket."

Alex reached into the pocket and pulled out a pasteboard book similar to his own rune book. Flipping it open, he found flash paper pages inside, each covered with notes. Grinning, Alex turned the pages carefully. The idea of using flash paper for runes had come from bookies, who occasionally had to burn their books to prevent them falling into the hands of law enforcement.

"There's a list of names in the front," Jimmy went on. "Colton Pierce is in there, just look."

Alex found the pages where names were written in a long column with numbers after them. Some of the numbers were underlined, while others had a cross above them.

"The numbers with the crosses are bets and the ones with a line under them are winnings," Jimmy said. "Look next to Colton's name, you'll see. I owed him and I paid him."

Alex ran his finger across the page to where the number five hundred had been written. It had been underlined and crossed out.

"You cross out the entries when the debt is settled?" he asked.

Jimmy nodded, tears streaming down his face.

Alex regarded him for a long moment, then he sighed.

"I believe you, Jimmy," Alex said. "But I'm afraid I'm going to need some insurance." He opened the man's coat, replacing the pasteboard book and then pulling a gold pocketwatch from Jimmy's inside coat pocket. "Where did you get this?"

"It...it was my father's," he blurted out. "My mom gave it to me after he died in the war."

"Very well," Alex said, dropping the watch into his own pocket. "I'm a runewright, which means that all I need to find you is something you have a strong connection to."

Jimmy's eyes went wide, and he looked down at the pocket where his watch had vanished. Alex snapped his fingers and the bookie's eyes darted back up to him.

"If I find out that you lied to me, Jimmy—"

"I haven't," he blubbered. "I don't have Colton. I didn't send anyone after him, I swear."

Alex reached up and grabbed the Fish's ear, pulling his face close.

"If you lied there won't be anywhere on earth you can hide from me. Understand?"

Jimmy's eyes went wide again, and he nodded vigorously.

"Connie," Alex said, stepping back. "You can let our friend go."

"You sure about that?" the mobster asked. There was a note of disapproval in his voice that suggested he thought letting the Fish go was a bad idea.

"Don't worry," Alex assured him, patting the pocket where he'd put Jimmy's father's watch. "We'll be able to find him if we need him."

Connie grunted in a noncommittal way, then pulled his .38 away from the bookie's throat. Jimmy immediately took a step away from his former colleague, moving toward the end of the alley.

"I'll be seein' you, Jimmy," the mobster growled.

That was all it took. Jimmy the Fish turned and fled.

"You shouldn't have let him go," Connie said once the sounds of Jimmy's running footsteps vanished into the noise of the street.

"He didn't know anything," Alex said with an irritated sigh. The bookie angle had seemed like a cinch, Colton gets in deep, and the bookie grabs him for ransom. Now Alex was out of leads.

"How can you be so sure?" Connie said, anger creeping into his voice. "If he does have Colton, he's on his way to kill him right now."

"No," Alex said. "He was terrified you'd take him to your boss. If he had an ace, he'd have played it the moment he knew we were looking for Colton."

"You're playing awful loose with Colton's life," Connie said.

Alex gave the mobster a hard look.

"You telling me how to do my job again?"

Connie growled in a manner that reminded Alex of a junkyard dog. For a moment it looked like the beefy enforcer might take a poke at him.

"Okay, Mr. hotshot detective," Connie said, taking through his teeth. "What now?" He jerked his thumb in the direction Jimmy had gone. "You said that was our only lead."

"Our only good lead," Alex corrected. "We still have the receipts and the coroner's office."

"You think we'll find Colton in the morgue?"

"No, but that's where the bodyguard is. If we can't track Colton, maybe we can figure out where his bodyguard met his end."

"Sal," Connie said.

Alex gave him a questioning look.

"Colton's bodyguard," Connie explained. "His name was Salvador Gerano. He was a good guy, had a family and kids."

"Sorry," Alex said, and meant it. "We'll go over to the morgue in the morning and see if we can get a look at Sal's body."

"They aren't just going to let us waltz into the morgue," Connie said.

Alex knew he was right. Even in his home turf of New York, he was persona non-grata at the city morgue. He suspected he'd be even less welcome as an outsider in town.

Maybe Detective Norton can get me in to look at Helen Mitchell's body. It was a long shot, but not impossible.

"You let me worry about that," Alex said, not letting his uncertainty show in his voice.

"Alex," Connie said, the hard edge in his voice gone. "If you find the sons of bitches that killed Sal...we ain't just letting them go."

Alex sighed and then nodded. He wasn't thrilled with the idea of street justice, but he knew nothing he could do, short of bringing in Andrew or Sorsha, would stop Connie from taking revenge on whoever killed his friend. He was family, after all.

"Don't worry about that," he said. "Once we find out where Colton is, they're all yours." Alex wrinkled his nose as a strong alkaline odor assaulted him. "Let's get out of here. I think Jimmy pissed himself."

Connie laughed at that as the two men stepped to the mouth of the alley.

"You know something, Lockerby," he said. "You're a pain in the ass...but you're all right."

It took Alex almost a full minute to get his key to fit into the lock of his hotel room door. It wasn't particularly late, but he felt as if this had been the longest day of his life. When he finally got the key to turn, he pushed the door open and almost fell into the suite. The lights were off, but the curtains along the row of windows were still open, flooding the room with the glow from the lights outside.

Alex secured the door, then made his way to the adjacent bedroom. When he reached the door, his tired mind snapped into focus. He hadn't been in the suite's bedroom since that morning, and he'd definitely turned the light off. Now, however, a sliver of light was escaping from where the door wasn't quite shut.

Holding perfectly still, Alex listened. If there was someone in his room, they weren't making any noise. He turned and stole to the writing desk that held his kit and the urn containing the ashes of Colton's mother. Opening the middle drawer of the desk, Alex pulled out his 1911. He'd brought it out of his vault right after he'd called Connie to come over.

Better safe than sorry.

Grabbing the slide, Alex cocked it gently, trying not to make any noise. The bolt clacked loudly as it locked into place, but no response came from the bedroom.

Wide awake now, Alex crossed back to the bedroom. Taking a deep breath, he grabbed the handle with his left hand and pushed the door open, following it with his gun at the ready.

Whatever Alex expected to find in the bedroom of the second-best suite in the Hay-Adams Hotel, it wasn't the sight of Sorsha Kincaid asleep on his bed. She was dressed in her professional attire, a woman's jacket cut to look like a man's suit coat, with a button-up shirt and slacks. Her shoes were pumps, mostly to compensate for her stature, but they were on the floor by an overstuffed chair in the corner.

Alex just stood there for a moment, his gun still raised, as he looked at her. Even asleep, her beauty was captivating. He hadn't made any sound, but something woke her.

"Alex," she gasped, sitting up and blushing furiously.

"Sorceress," Alex said, lowering his gun and leaning against the door frame. "If you needed a place to sleep, you should know I'm always willing to share my bed."

He didn't think it was possible, but she blushed even more as she practically leapt to her feet.

"I'm sorry," she said smoothing out her rumpled clothes. "I came for two reasons. First, because...because I wanted to say I'm sorry." She looked up, but had trouble meeting his eyes. "For this morning."

Alex sighed. He was having fun teasing her and then she went and turned the conversation serious.

"I'm sorry too," he admitted. "You and I both know you don't need my help to do your job with the FBI. I never meant for anyone to think that."

"I know," she said. "I was just frustrated, and I took it out on you."

It felt like there was a heaviness in the room, so Alex decided to move the conversation along.

"Well, Goldilocks, if you didn't come over to find out if my mattress is just right, why *are* you here?"

She opened her mouth, but no words came out. After a moment she hung her head.

"I need your help," she whispered.

12

COLLUSION

Alex raised an eyebrow as he watched Sorsha try to meet his gaze. After the tongue lashing she'd given him that morning, her admission must have really cost her. Resisting the urge to tease her further or rub her admission in, Alex gave her a reassuring smile.

"You know I'm always here for you," he said, stepping away from the door frame. "Let's have a drink and you can tell me what you need."

He turned and led the way back out into the suite's front room. A large liquor cabinet with doors of etched glass stood beside the writing desk, and Alex opened it to find a row of glass bottles with liquids of varying colors. Since they weren't labeled, Alex opened the one that looked the most like bourbon, Sorsha's drink of choice. Pouring the burgundy liquid into two glasses, he carried them around to the couches that faced the windows.

"Now," he said, handing Sorsha a glass and directing her onto the couch. "What seems to be the problem?"

Sorsha sat down, setting her drink on the side table with a sigh. She leaned forward, elbows on her knees and her head in her hands. Alex sat in a comfortable chair next to the couch and waited. She stayed slumped forward for a long moment, then looked up at Alex, picked up her glass, and drained it.

"I've been taken off the Young case," she said.

Alex wasn't sure he'd heard her right. Sorsha was the FBI's hotshot, celebrity consultant. Why go through all the trouble of bringing her down from New York just to kick her off the case? Besides, having a sorcerer working with the FBI lent an air of infallibility to any resolution. Even if they didn't need her impressive deductive skills, having her around was a bonus by itself.

"Why?"

"Something stinks about this case, Alex," she said. "Did you know that Senator Young's secretary died this afternoon?"

"I believe I heard something about that," Alex said, not wanting to cop to his continuing involvement in the case just yet.

"Did you know that the doctors initially said she would make a full recovery?"

Alex nodded but then shrugged.

"Doctors aren't always right," he pointed out. "Is there some reason you find her death suspicious?"

"Don't you?" she demanded.

"Yes," he admitted. "I find it highly suspicious, just like you, so what's the problem?"

"The FBI is turning a blind eye to the whole thing," she said, raising her glass before remembering that it was empty.

"No one at the Bureau thinks the secretary's death is suspicious?" Alex asked, handing the sorceress his glass in trade for her empty one.

"Some of the agents do," she said. "But Director Blake of the D.C. field office is having none of it." Sorsha drained her new glass. "He's convinced the note we found is genuine and the Senator's death was a murder-suicide."

Alex rubbed his chin as he watched Sorsha hold up the empty glass, trying to get whatever few drops remained in it. Detective Norton had told him pretty much the same story. Whoever had assassinated the Senator, they had powerful friends, friends who could not only arrange to hide a murder but could call off an FBI investigation when the cover-up didn't stick.

He stood, taking Sorsha's empty glass from her and moving past the couch to the liquor cabinet. Removing the crystal stopper from the decanter, he refilled the glasses.

"I see why you're frustrated," he said, offering her one of the full glasses as he moved back to his chair. "But just what is it I can do to help you? I sincerely hope you're not asking me to get rid of the local FBI director for you."

Sorsha gave Alex a withering look as he sat down.

"Nothing so satisfying," she growled. "That's something I could handle myself."

Alex had no doubt of that whatsoever. If Sorsha wanted to, she could probably make the man disappear without a trace. Unfortunately even an all-powerful sorceress would be brought to account for getting rid of a high-ranking federal agent.

"Alex," she said. "I think someone assassinated the Senator and now they're trying to cover it up."

"Go on," Alex said, not revealing that he already suspected exactly that.

Sorsha sighed and drained her third glass before continuing.

"You were so sure that Tiffany Young didn't kill her husband," she said. "I've learned to trust your instincts, so I did some checking," she said. "I called in a favor from a Senator I helped out a few years ago and he put me in touch with a few of his colleagues." She paused, then glanced at her empty glass and Alex's full one. Alex sighed and handed it over. "Apparently Senator Young was well known as a deal maker," Sorsha continued after sipping from the new glass. "He used his position to trade favors and grease palms all over the city and back at home. According to multiple sources, a lot of the people he did favors for were young, attractive women."

"So his philandering wasn't exactly a secret," Alex concluded.

"No one had any direct evidence," she said "None they were willing to share, anyway, but the inference was clear. I even heard one story of a lobbyist sending his handsome adult son over to the Senator's residence to...persuade Mrs. Young to intervene with her husband regarding some bill or other." Sorsha rubbed her left temple with her free hand. "If even half of what I heard was true, there's no way Tiffany Young didn't know what her husband was up to."

"I know," Alex said. "Tiffany explained to me about their, uh, philanthropic endeavors."

Sorsha glared at him over the rim of her glass.

"You could have told me that," she said, "instead of letting me run all over town finding out for myself."

Alex shrugged.

"You wanted me off the case," he said with an innocent smile. "You were very emphatic about it."

Sorsha hung her head and let out an exasperated grunt.

"Look on the bright side," Alex said. "Now we know that Tiffany's story about her relationship with her husband is true. She also told me that Helen wanted to become a legal secretary for a big firm, one with several young, single partners."

"So she had no motive to kill the Senator," Sorsha confirmed.

"Certainly not one involving him leaving his wife for her."

Sorsha sighed and finished her drink.

"So what do we do?" she said, leaning back into the couch.

Alex stood and refilled the glasses again.

"Here," he said, handing her another one.

"Are you trying to get me drunk?"

"Maybe a little," Alex admitted. "You see, I called Tiffany Young this morning to tell her I was off the case, just like I told you I would."

Sorsha didn't respond, but her expression hardened.

"That's when she told me that bit about Helen wanting to become a legal secretary."

Sorsha groaned.

"What did you do that I specifically told you not to?" she asked.

"I talked with the local police," Alex said. "The detective in charge is a guy named Norton." He went on to explain how the news of Helen's death reached Detective Norton when Alex was there and how they'd gone to the hospital room and discovered the privacy rune.

"So I was right," Sorsha said, sitting up.

"Of course you were," Alex said, sipping his drink. "You're very smart."

Sorsha set down her glass, then reached across the little side table that separated the couch and Alex's chair. Grabbing him by his tie, she pulled him forward and pressed her lips to his. After a kiss that was far too chaste for Alex's liking, she let go.

"That's for not listening to me," she said with a smile.

Alex laughed at that.

"I'll be sure to not listen to you more in the future."

"Don't you dare." She returned his grin but her expression suddenly darkened. "Alex," she said. "If you're right about the rune, that means the assassin used rune magic."

"Very proficiently," he confirmed.

"You don't suppose this is..." she hesitated. "Could this be Moriarty's doing?"

Alex thought about that for a moment, then shook his head.

"Moriarty would never have botched the job this badly," he said. "If he or any of the other immortals were behind this, Helen Mitchell would never have survived to begin with. There wouldn't be any clues for us to find, to say nothing of the police."

Sorsha began chewing her bottom lip, something she did when she was thinking. Alex found it adorable and started to smile...when the sorceress gasped and grabbed his arm.

"Who do we know who uses runes and meddles in politics?" she said, her voice hard and serious. If her tone hadn't sent a shiver down his spine, the realization of who she meant would have.

"The Legion," he answered with a nod. He hadn't thought about that connection, but now that Sorsha said it, it made perfect sense. Their first interaction with the mysterious group of runewrights was when they had tried to rig a New York election. Killing a Senator to move a piece of legislation seemed like it was right up their alley.

"This must have something to do with whatever the Senator was voting on," Sorsha said, finally catching up.

"That's what Detective Norton and I figured," he said. "He's got a contact in the Senate clerk's office and I'm going to talk to Tiffany tomorrow to see if we can't figure out what this is about."

"As I mentioned, I have a contact in the Senate," Sorsha said. "I'll talk to him and see if he can think of anything on the docket that might rise or fall with Senator Young out of the way."

"You want me to tell Detective Norton that you're coming in on this with us?"

Sorsha shook her head, leaning back on the couch with a sigh.

"Just introduce us. If Director Blake finds out you're helping me in any way, that'll be it for my work as an FBI consultant."

"What about Stevens?" Alex said, thinking back to when he met the director of the New York FBI office. "He likes you."

"Director Blake is the Bureau's golden boy," she said. "His opinion carries more weight than that of Director Stevens."

"Well, look on the bright side. If the FBI fires you, you can always come to work with me at the agency."

Sorsha narrowed her eyes and glared at him.

"You are *not* funny," she said, but there was no energy behind her words. She leaned back against the couch and sighed. "I'm tired," she mumbled.

Sorsha's eyes slid shut as the bourbon finally caught up with her.

With a sigh of his own, Alex finished his own drink, then got up and carried Sorsha back into his bedroom. A few minutes later, he returned and opened the door to his vault. Sorsha might have kicked him out of his bed, but with a bedroom in his vault, at least he didn't have to sleep on the couch.

The problem with sleeping in a vault was that there wasn't any outside light to indicate the time of day. As a result, Alex had a large bedside alarm clock in his vault bedroom. The problem with that was that he didn't sleep in the vault very often and that meant every time he did, he had to wind the clock and set it from his pocketwatch. Even when he was sure that he'd done it right, Alex found he slept a bit worse in the vault from worrying he'd wake up late.

When Alex did wake up, however, it wasn't because of the alarm. One minute he was sleeping and the next he was aware of a presence in the room. With an incoherent cry, he grabbed his pistol from under his pillow and leapt out of bed.

"Keep it down," Sorsha said from the doorway. She still wore the clothes she'd had on when he dropped her in his hotel bed but now they were rumpled and untucked. Her eyes were closed, and she had a hand firmly pressed to her forehead. "I've got the mother of all hangovers," she said, her voice barely a whisper. "Where do you keep your medicinal potions?"

Alex lowered the gun he was pointing right at the sorceress' head and tried to slow his thundering heartbeat.

"Why should I waste party blaster on you?" he grumbled, glancing at his clock which read six-twenty. Party blasters were potions that would reduce and sometimes eliminate the effects of a hangover.

"You're the one who got me drunk," she mumbled. "Give, now."

This last was less of a command and more the sorceress' desire to not provoke her throbbing head with an excess of words.

"Fine," Alex said, tossing his 1911 onto the bed. He led the stumbling sorceress across the great room to the hall on the far side. Originally the hall on that side only led to a cover door that connected to his office and one to his apartment. Recently, however, Alex had added a new room. He opened the plain door on the side of the hall and led Sorsha into a white tile room with a doctor's exam table in the center.

This was Alex's infirmary.

It wasn't as large or as well stocked as Iggy's, but then Alex wasn't a doctor. What it did have were all the potions, remedies, and medicinal runes a lay person would need to patch up minor injuries.

On the wall on the left side was a row of glass-front cabinets. Alex passed the doors until he found one with potion bottles inside.

"Here," he said, pulling a small, purple bottle from the top shelf.

Sorsha didn't hesitate, she pulled the cork stopper from the top, then tipped the potion up, swallowing it in one go.

"The sink is behind you," Alex chuckled.

Sorsha pried one of her bloodshot eyes open and regarded him with as much disdain as she could manage with her palm pressed to her forehead.

"I'm not going to throw up," she insisted. "I'm a woman of culture and refine...refinement."

True to her word, she didn't appear sick, but she did turn a lovely shade of green before the potion completed its work.

"Yuck," she said at last, running her fingers through her hair in a vain attempt to smooth it down. "Party blasters are so vile it makes me want to give up drinking."

"Let's not go to extremes," Alex said, trying and failing to stifle a grin. "How did you sleep?"

"In my clothes," Sorsha said with a disapproving frown. "Though under the circumstances. I suppose I'm grateful for that."

"If you want to come back tonight," Alex said, "I'm sure that between the two of us, we can correct that error."

"Don't do that," Sorsha said, putting her hand back on her forehead again. "You're far too charming to make passes at me this early in the morning."

She turned and headed back out in the direction of the hotel suite.

"I can have the hotel bring up some breakfast," Alex offered, following her. "Unless you think eggs are too charming to eat at this hour."

"Eggs would be lovely," she said. "But I suggest you put some pants on before the bellhop brings them up."

Sorsha had slept in her clothes, but Alex had slept in his undershirt and boxer trunks. Trying not to blush, he headed for his room and quickly dressed.

"I ordered breakfast," Sorsha said when Alex finally emerged from his vault.

"How am I supposed to explain your presence in my room at this hour?"

Alex wasn't angry, but if someone decided to bring in the hotel detective, it would cause trouble. Sorsha, however, didn't seem worried about any potential difficulty Alex might have.

"I'm a sorceress, Alex," she said with a bored air. "I can teleport wherever I want, whenever I want."

"Except when you're blind drunk," he retorted.

"Don't be crude," she admonished him as she pulled her long, black cigarette holder from thin air.

A few moments later, the breakfast arrived, and they sat where they'd been the previous night but with the breakfast trolly between them.

"I think we should meet back here tonight," Alex said between bites of bacon and toast.

"I told you not to make passes this early," Sorsha said, though she had a half smile when she said it.

"I mean to coordinate on the case," Alex explained. "You said that if Director Blake catches the faintest hint that you and I are working together, it could be bad for you."

Sorsha's face grew serious, and she nodded.

"I'd forgotten about him," she admitted. "I probably shouldn't have called for breakfast. Blake has informants all over town. He probably already knows you're working for Tiffany Young."

Alex shrugged.

"So? He doesn't know you're here now...or what we talked about. We'll just carry on separately and meet up to compare notes."

Sorsha shook her head.

"We can't see each other," she declared. "You need to go out of your way to avoid me. If you learn anything, leave it with Sherry. I'll call your office every day at five and get whatever you've got from her. If I find anything, I'll pass it on the same way."

Alex sighed. Sorsha was blowing the danger out of proportion, which was usual for her. Of course, it was her consulting job on the line, so Alex couldn't really argue with her precautions.

"You do remember what happened last time you didn't want to be seen with me?" Alex asked.

She gave him a frosty look and he actually felt the temperature in the room drop several degrees.

"Yes," she said in an unamused voice. "You started dating another girl."

"You have to admit, it was the perfect way to throw people off the scent."

"I don't care how well it worked," Sorsha growled. "I expect you to stay away from young, beautiful, single women."

"Don't worry," Alex laughed and shrugged. "There's no chance of that. I don't know anybody in town."

Sorsha held his gaze for a long moment, then went back to her breakfast.

Before Alex could resume his own meal, there was an urgent knock at the door.

"Are you expecting anyone?" Sorsha asked.

"No," Alex said, then he gave her an exaggerated look of concern. "Maybe it's Director Blake."

Sorsha shot him an unamused glare, but she did hide in the bedroom as Alex went to open the door. When he did, he found young, single, beautiful Zelda Pritchard in the hall. Her blonde hair was disheveled, and it was clear she was upset.

"Oh, Alex," she cried, throwing herself into his arms. "You have to help. The most dreadful thing has happened."

"Uh," Alex managed as she clung to him, burying her face in his chest. He couldn't see Sorsha hiding in the bedroom, but he could guess what she was thinking right now. "What's the matter?"

"The museum's been robbed."

13

LOOMING PERIL

"Take it easy, Zelda," Alex said, trying to pry the distraught girl off his chest. "Tell me what happened."

She looked up at him, her eyes brimming with tears.

"There was a robbery last night," a male voice came from the hall.

Alex looked up, expecting to see Zelda's valet, Hector Cohan, but instead he found another man. He was average height and a bit paunchy with dark black hair and a strong chin. As he approached, he stuck out his hand.

"I'm Lyle Gundersen," he said. "I'm the Deputy Curator of the Smithsonian Institute."

"So what happened?" Alex asked, trying to find a polite way to pry Zelda off his chest.

"Someone broke in and ransacked one of our exhibits," Gundersen continued as Zelda wept into Alex's shirt. "They also killed a night guard."

"The police are baffled," Zelda said, looking up at him. "You have to come, you have to help."

"Uh," Alex managed. He could almost feel the temperature in the room dropping as Sorsha fumed, out of sight. He needed to extricate himself from this situation, and quickly.

"I'd love to help," he said, "but this isn't my town. I very much doubt the police will let me just show up and start poking around."

"Please, Alex," Zelda implored him. "The Smithsonian needs you."

Before Alex could reply, Lyle spoke up.

"I can guarantee police cooperation with your investigation," he said. "We have a large amount of pull with the local officials. There are many important citizens on our board of directors."

Alex looked down into Zelda's imploring eyes and sighed.

"All right," he said, finally managing to push Zelda back to arm's length. "Let me get my coat and my crime scene kit, then we'll go over to the museum and have a look, okay?"

"Oh, Alex," Zelda said, her eyes sparkling. "I knew you'd help. You just had to."

Alex stepped back, letting the pair into his room to wait.

"I'll just be a moment," he said, looking down at his mascara-stained shirt.

He left the door to the hall open, then retreated to the bedroom. He was not surprised to find Sorsha glaring at him with her arms crossed. The fact that most of the room was covered in frost was a bit of a shock, however.

"Who is she?" the Sorceress hissed through clenched teeth.

"Her name is Zelda Pritchard," Alex whispered, not wanting to be overheard. "I met her on the airship from New York."

"And you just happened to tell her all about how you're a great detective and impress her enough that she came looking for you?"

Alex's spare shirts were actually in his vault, so he opened his red book and quickly tore out a minor restoration rune.

"She's a museum patron," he explained. "She knew about me from that the *Almiranta* robbery. I guess she's a fan."

Sorsha's expression relaxed, and she actually smiled. Her eyes, however, began to shine with the tell-tale light of her power.

"That wouldn't have been an overnight airship journey," she said, touching the rune paper Alex had stuck to his shirt and setting it alight.

"It was," Alex said as the rune removed the stains of Zelda's mascara. "And before you ask, I slept alone."

Sorsha's smile became predatory.

"I'll just bet Zelda was very disappointed by that."

Alex rolled his eyes, hoping his girl didn't realize how close she was to right.

"Hey," he growled under his breath. "You wanted it to look like we weren't colluding on the Young murder."

"So you're going to date that child out there?"

"No, but I am going to take her case," Alex said, grabbing Sorsha by the arm and giving her a hard look. "We'll walk around the museum, I'll let her hang on my arm, and lots of people will see."

Sorsha pulled her arm away from him, crossing them angrily.

"I suppose that is a good cover," she admitted with a scowl.

Alex turned to go, but Sorsha grabbed his lapel and pulled him back around to face her. Her eyes were glowing again, and she pulled his head down and kissed him.

Kissing Sorsha was always a rush, but this time Alex felt a wave of pure magic go coursing through him. It only lasted a moment, and it left his body tingling in its wake.

"Something to remind you who you're actually dating," she whispered, bringing her mouth close to his ear. "And if you ever kiss that teenager, I'll make you regret it."

Five minutes later, Alex exited the main elevator of the Hay-Adams Hotel with Zelda and Lyle Gundersen in tow. He started across the lobby, but caught movement out of the corner of his eye.

"Would you excuse me for a moment," he said to his companions. "I'll be right back."

Leaving them standing by the front doors, Alex crossed to one of the lobby's large couches where a man in a dark suit had just stood up.

"You're here bright and early," Alex said to Connie Firenze, and the mobster buttoned his coat.

"You have a habit of moving around at odd hours," Connie said. "I was going to come up after eight." He nodded at Zelda and Lyle. "What's all this?"

Alex quickly explained about the museum robbery.

"So you're taking another case?" the mobster growled when Alex finished.

"Easy, Connie," Alex said. "That guy over there is the Deputy Curator of the Smithsonian and he's assured me that he can get the police to cooperate with my investigation."

"So what?"

"So," Alex said, lowering his voice. "They said a security guard was killed during the robbery. I imagine by now his body is over at the city morgue."

Connie's angry scowl slowly vanished, to be replaced after a moment by a conspiratorial grin.

"And you'd have to go look at the body, wouldn't you?"

"I wouldn't be doing my job if I didn't," Alex said. "Now, I'll go to the museum and look around for an hour or so, then I'll ask to have a look the body. Meet me in front of the morgue around nine-thirty and we'll see if we can't figure out how and, more importantly, where Sal Gerano was killed."

"You think they'll let me in?"

"Sure," Alex said. "You'll be my assistant. They won't even look at you twice."

"All right," Connie said, most of the suspicion gone from his voice. "Nine-thirty it is."

Alex started to turn away, but Connie caught his elbow in an iron grip.

"But if you're trying to play me, Alex," he said in a quiet voice. "I'll make sure you get a slab next to Sal. Capiche?"

Alex nodded and Connie released his arm. As he continued on toward the door and his waiting companions, Alex tried to ignore the fact that he'd already been threatened twice this morning and it wasn't even eight o'clock.

The Smithsonian Museum was housed in an enormous brick building known as the Castle. In truth, it looked like a castle, so the name wasn't as creative as Alex had first believed. It had a central rotunda with several wings radiating off it where the various exhibits were housed.

Zelda and Lyle led Alex through the rotunda and down the main hallway to the rear of the building where another set of wings stretched out to the right and left. He'd expected to be taken to a room where the museum's various collections of gold coins and precious gems were kept. Instead, his guides turned down a hallway that was lined with industrial machinery. Alex recognized a few items, including a woodworking lathe and a cotton gin.

In the back corner, there were three policemen in blue uniforms standing around something that looked like the guts of an oversized upright piano. A slender man in a pinstriped suit was there as well, talking earnestly with one of the uniforms, who was jotting notes in a flip book just like Alex's.

"Here we are," Zelda said, tugging on Alex's arm. "Isn't it awful?"

Alex was genuinely at a loss for words. Not only didn't he see anything in the entire hall that he would consider to be worth a thief's time, he couldn't tell what had actually been stolen.

"What?" he said.

"They took the cards," Zelda said, her voice dripping with malice. "They were original pieces. How could someone do that?"

Alex wasn't sure *what* the thief had done yet, so the *how* wasn't high on his priority list. What he did know was that during the time the thief had done whatever he did, someone had been killed.

"Let me explain," Lyle said, sensing Alex's confusion. "This is a Jacquard Loom."

He paused and Alex shook his head.

"Sorry Mr. Gundersen," he said. "You're going to have to do better than that."

"It's the first truly modern weaving machine," Lyle went on. "It automates weaving patterns, even very complex ones, using wooden cards with holes drilled in them."

As he spoke, he pointed to a mechanism with several long needles that were mounted so they could move through holes in the frame around them.

"The cards are all attached together in a long chain and as the machine weaves, they are pulled up here. Each needle is attached to a string and, if the needle is stopped by the wooden card, it lifts its corresponding string."

"That's how it makes the pattern," Zelda finished. "Isn't it fascinating?"

Alex was sure it would be if he had any interest in weaving...or if he were very drunk. What he didn't understand was why someone would kill for a few bits of wood with holes drilled in them.

"Okay," he said, not believing the words that were about to come out of his own mouth. "You're saying that someone stole a bunch of wooden cards from an antique loom? Are they that valuable?"

Lyle nodded.

"The cards are original, part of the acquisition when we purchased this loom," he said. "They're almost one hundred years old, so they'd be quite valuable to a collector."

"Of old looms?"

"You wouldn't believe the strange things people collect," Zelda said.

"Tell me about the murder," Alex said.

Lyle turned to the detective in the pinstriped suit and waved him over.

"This is Lieutenant MacReady," the deputy curator introduced the man. "Lieutenant, this is Alex Lockerby, the man we told you about."

MacReady gave Alex the once-over, sizing him up. It was clear he didn't like private detectives, but Alex's expensive suit seemed to give him pause. Washington was a town run on money and power after all, and they usually came together.

"Pleased to meet you," MacReady said, holding out his hand for Alex to shake. "I'd appreciate any light you could shine on this business."

Alex shook the offered hand. He could tell MacReady still didn't like him, but he was willing to make nice in case Alex had friends in high places.

"What happened to the night watchman?"

The lieutenant flipped through his notes, then pointed up toward the ceiling. A long row of skylights ran the length of the room, bathing the exhibits in the bright light of day.

"Near as we can tell, the thief pried open one of those and came down on a rope," he said.

Alex was impressed. The ceiling had to be fifty feet above the exhibit floor.

"Where'd they exit the building?"

"That's the thing, Mr. Lockerby," MacReady said. "As far as we can tell, our man left the same way he entered. All the exterior doors have bolt locks with keys, and they were all still locked this morning."

"There's no way the thief made that climb," Alex said, still looking at the ceiling high above. "He must have taken the guard's keys."

"That's what I thought," the lieutenant said. "But the guard didn't have a key to the doors."

Alex didn't believe that, and it must have shown on his face.

"That's museum policy," Lyle jumped in. "Night guards are locked in by the person in charge at closing time. That way, no guard could function as an inside man for a robbery."

"So no keys," Alex said, looking back up at the ceiling.

"And no rope," MacReady said. "When Mr. Gundersen got here this morning, there wasn't any rope hanging down from the skylight. We had to send a man up there just to figure out which skylight they opened."

"They?" Alex asked. "You think it was a team?"

For a big heist, like the one aimed at the treasure of the *Almiranta*, you needed a crew, but big crews tended to attract attention. Stealing a couple of cards that would fit in a sack was a one-man job, even if you did have to climb fifty feet of rope.

"We think the thief had a couple of men on the roof to haul him up," MacReady explained.

"That would make it easier to get out," Alex said. "But why split the take with a couple of haulers? Why not just break a ground floor window and escape that way?"

"There are bars on all the ground floor windows," Lyle Gundersen pointed out.

"Also, our thief wasn't alone down here," the lieutenant said, motioning for Alex to follow him. "He'd need help getting out."

MacReady walked around the loom to the aisle where the three uniforms were standing. As Alex followed, he could see they were protecting a patch of the concrete floor that had been smeared with a dark substance. Alex's stomach turned as he realized it was blood.

A lot of blood.

"What happened?" he asked.

"This is where we found Michael Halverson, the unfortunate night guard. The first officer on the scene said it looked like someone hacked him up with a machete."

That explains the blood loss.

"When the coroner arrived," MacReady went on, "he said the man had been mauled."

"Mauled?" Alex scoffed. "By what, a bear?"

"Wolf or large dog," MacReady said.

Zelda made a noise in her throat and turned away.

"Why don't you take Miss Pritchard to your office and get her something to drink," Alex said to Lyle. "I'll look around here and join you as soon as I can."

The Deputy Curator nodded and took Zelda's arm, leading her off toward the front of the building. Alex turned back to the lieutenant, who wore an amused smile.

"Now I see why you didn't object to having me on this case," Alex said. "It makes no sense. If you're right, our thief shimmied down fifty feet of rope with a wolf under his arm, killed a guard, stole something worthless, then climbed back up and hauled the wolf up after him."

"That's just about the way it looks," MacReady said. "The chief is on the Smithsonian board of directors, and he wants this case solved, so any insight you can give would be greatly appreciated."

And if Alex bungled something, MacReady would point to him as the reason the case didn't get solved.

"How much does a full-grown wolf weigh?" Alex asked.

The lieutenant shrugged.

"I don't know, but one big enough to maul a man to death has got to be a hundred pounds if it's an ounce."

Alex whistled. That would be a lot of dead weight for the thief to haul up on a rope, especially after climbing it himself.

"Is there a circus in town?" he asked.

"How would I know?" MacReady said, then he added, "Why?"

"Because," Alex said, "those trapeze guys can climb ropes like monkeys, and circuses work with all kinds of large, dangerous animals."

"What would circus performers want with a bunch of cards from an old loom?"

Now it was Alex's turn to shrug.

"No idea," he said. "But they might just be a hired crew, stealing the cards for someone else."

MacReady flipped his notebook open and began scribbling in it.

"I guess I'll go see if P.T. Barnum is in town."

"All right, lieutenant," Alex said, setting down his bag. "I promised Mr. Gundersen and Miss Pritchard that I'd look around, so I'll do that while you make a few calls."

MacReady nodded, then instructed the three uniforms to stay out of Alex's way before walking off.

Alex took out his oculus and slipped it over his eye, then clipped the silverlight burner into his lamp. In a public space like this, he expected there would be hundreds of biological and chemical markers, everything from saliva and fingerprints, to grease and tobacco. When he lit the lamp, however, he was surprised. Most of the errant marks were confined to the various railings that kept visitors from touching the exhibits.

Turning his attention to the loom, Alex found fingerprints on it, but most of them were old and almost faded completely. There were some fresh prints on the mechanism that read the cards, but they were fuzzy and indistinct. The only time Alex had seen something like that was once when a thief wore gloves but got some grease on them, so they left smeared-out grease prints behind.

Discouraged, Alex turned his attention to the bloodstained floor. The picture painted by his lamp was gruesome. There were bloody footprints where the guard had tried to run away from the assault, and a smear of blood where he'd fallen. All around the area were animal footprints in blood, but they were much larger than Alex expected, almost as big as his hand.

After walking over the area for ten minutes, Alex gave up. There just wasn't any way to tell what had happened during the theft, beyond the obvious, of course. With a sigh, he blew out the silverlight burner and switched it for ghostlight. He didn't expect to find anything magical involved, but he liked to be thorough. Shining the light around at the scene of the attack, he didn't see anything, so he moved on to the loom. Sweeping the beam over the apparatus, he peered at the needles that read the cards and the various strings and gears that made up the machine.

"Nothing," he grumbled. He wasn't excited about solving the theft of a bunch of cards with holes in them, but a man had been killed, a man who was just doing his job. Alex owed the dead guard his best effort.

"Apparently my 'best effort' is confirming the police theory of a rope climbing thief with a wolf in his hip holster," he muttered. It sounded just as ridiculous out loud as it did in his head. "All right," he said to himself. "I've wasted enough time on this. Time to go over to the morgue."

He packed up his gear, then headed back to the front of the building to confer with Lyle and the lieutenant to make sure he had access to the morgue.

14

ACCIDENTS

The office of the Deputy Curator of America's official state museum was far less grand than Alex thought it would be, just a small, well-appointed room off a side hallway. When Alex arrived, Zelda was sipping a glass of some red liquor and seemed to be feeling much better.

"Did you find any clues?" Lyle Gundersen asked as Alex entered.

"Nothing that makes any sense," he said. "For the life of me I can't understand why anyone would steal a bunch of old pattern cards. I mean if I'd been hired for this job, I'd have just faked some in my workshop. They're just strips of wood with holes in them, right?"

"They're much more than that, Alex," Zelda said, turning in her chair to face him. "Those cards are part of history, a part that's gone now. They represent the hard work and ingenuity of the people who made them, and they're a literal pattern of their artistry."

"I don't think Mr. Lockerby was discounting the historical value, Zelda darling," Lyle said, giving Alex an apologetic look. "Just wondering why a thief would pick those particular objects."

Zelda's cheeks flushed a bit in response, but Alex gave her a smile.

"Actually," he said, "you just gave me an idea." He turned to Lyle. "Those cards tell the loom how to weave a pattern, right?"

Lyle looked a bit confused at the question, but nodded.

"Yes."

"And does anyone at the museum know what pattern those cards produced?"

"Uh," Lyle hesitated. "Actually no," he said. "We would never actually use the Jacquard Loom. It's almost one-hundred years old, after all."

"But if you had the cards," Alex pressed, "could someone determine what pattern they would make?"

Lyle thought about that for a long moment, then shrugged.

"I suppose," he said. "But I suspect you'd need someone with an expertise in weaving to figure that out."

"You let me worry about that," Alex said.

"Why does it matter?" Zelda asked.

"You said it yourself," he replied. "The real value of those cards is what they represent." He turned to Lyle. "You said those looms could make intricate patterns using the information encoded on those cards. So what if someone encoded more than just a fancy design?"

Zelda's expression changed from confusion to excitement and her smile lit up her face.

"You mean something like a treasure map?" she wondered.

Alex shrugged.

"Maybe," he said. "Or it could be someone's will, or the co-ordinates to a lost historical artifact, or any number of things. I think it would be very instructive to find out exactly what pattern those cards make."

"I guess that would be a good idea," Lyle said, somewhat hesitantly. "But since they've been stolen, I don't see how I can help you."

Alex put his hand on the Deputy Curator's shoulder and gave him a reassuring smile.

"What I need from you, is for you to call your insurance company."

"Why?" Zelda asked.

"I spoke to him already," Lyle admitted. "The value of the cards is rather minor, so we won't be putting in a claim."

Alex shook his head.

"I'm not interested in that," he said, then winked a Zelda. "In order to insure your loom and its contents, your insurance company would have taken photographs of it, along with all the things that went with it."

"They'll have pictures of the cards," Zelda gasped, her eyes positively glowing. "Alex, that's brilliant."

Alex just grinned.

"You get me those pictures," he said to Lyle, "and I'll show them to a friend of mine in the textile industry. Once we know what the pattern made by those cards is, I bet you we'll have a good idea about who stole them."

"I...I'll call my agent back right away," Lyle said, turning to his desk.

"I want to go over to the city morgue and take a look at the dead watchman," Alex said, taking out his cigarette case and offering one to Zelda. "Will you call your police contact first and make sure they won't give me any trouble?"

Lyle promised that he would, as Alex lit Zelda's cigarette and then his own.

"I expect it will take a few hours at least for them to dig up the photographs," Alex said. "When they get here, call the Hay-Adams hotel and leave word for me."

Lyle nodded and Alex left the office. Before he left the museum, however, he stopped at the public phone booths in the lobby.

"Young residence," a honeyed, feminine voice greeted him when his call connected.

"Tiffany? This is Alex Lockerby. How much do you know about the legislation your husband was involved in?"

"Not very much, I'm afraid," she said. "I usually relied on Duke for that sort of thing."

"Duke?"

"My husband's aide, Michael Harris — he goes by Duke. He oversaw all official communication, kept Paul's calendar, that sort of thing. Do you think my husband was killed over something he was working on?"

"It's a possibility," Alex said. He didn't want to tell her it was the only lead he had.

"I'd say it was a certainty," Tiffany said. "I got a call this morning from the Illinois governor. He's already appointed Paul's replacement, a man named William Unger."

"That's pretty fast," Alex said. "Do you know this Unger guy?"

"Yes, he ran against my husband in the last election."

"Is he a sore loser?"

"I wouldn't think so," Tiffany said. "He's the most typical example of a politician, a greedy coward."

"That sounds like exactly the kind of man who would have a rival killed to get him out of the way."

"In business, maybe," Tiffany said. "But in politics, men like that won't make a dangerous move unless there is a fortune on the line…or if they have no other choice."

Alex wasn't sure her explanation rang true, but she understood politics better than he did. Still, he'd have Sherry look into William Unger and see if there might be a hidden motive for him to kill Paul Young.

"Well, if he's not our man, I'm back to your husband's work," Alex said. "How can I get access to the bills he was involved with?"

"It's public information, but it'll take days for you to cut through the red tape at the National Archives. I'll call Duke and have him give you access to Paul's files."

"He can do that?"

"Not legally," Tiffany said with a chuckle. "You'll have to go over after the Senate office building closes."

"What if Duke objects?"

Tiffany laughed at that, a deep, full-throated sound.

"I have a few very interesting pictures that will guarantee Duke's cooperation," she said. "Remind him of that if he gives you any trouble."

Alex raised an eyebrow at her words. So far the ins-and-outs of politics were leaving him jaded, at best.

"All right," he said, not addressing her admission of blackmail or her intent for him to become complicit in it. "I'll go over after closing and go through everything. If I find anything, I'll call."

"Or," Tiffany purred. "You could come by afterword and brief me on what you found out."

The implication was naked, right out in the open, and Alex shuddered. Tiffany Young was a beautiful woman, there was no denying that, but she had ably demonstrated that she was also dangerous. Alex already had more than enough beautiful, dangerous women in his life.

"I can't," he lied. "I've got another matter to deal with."

"Pity," Tiffany said in a voice that made promises.

Unlike the Manhattan morgue, which was hidden away in the basement of an ordinary-looking office building, the Washington D.C. morgue was its own, unassuming structure in the southeast part of the city. The problem with that was that if you showed up there, you were going to the morgue. When Alex was just starting out as a detective, he'd managed to sneak down to the Manhattan morgue by pretending to be going up to one of the various offices above it. There wouldn't be any way for a young detective to bluff his way inside.

As Alex paid the cabbie, he saw Connie getting out of a car in the morgue parking lot.

"You sure we can get in?" he asked. "A museum guy doesn't sound like he'd have any pull with the cops."

"Welcome to politics," Alex said as the two men headed for the front door.

A bored uniform with a mustache and a paunch gave Alex a hard look when he entered the building's lobby. Putting on a confident smile, Alex walked right up to the man.

"I'm Alex Lockerby," he said. "Someone should have called about me."

The policeman didn't look convinced, but he checked with an equally bored officer behind a tall counter and a few minutes later, Alex and Connie were escorted through a set of double doors and into the morgue proper.

Unlike the morgue he was used to, this one was done up in white tile and looked more like a hospital. Officer Mustache led them back to the office of a gray-haired doctor who looked outraged at the very idea of shepherding a private detective.

"Let the girl deal with them," he said, waving Officer Mustache away.

Rebuffed, the policeman led Alex and Connie back across the building to a tiny office that also seemed to serve as a storage room.

"Miss Baker?" Officer Mustache said, knocking on the doorjamb.

Inside, Alex could see a young woman with mouse-brown hair and thick glasses filling out reports under the harsh glow of a desk lamp. She had a plain face, tired eyes, a messy pony tail, and wore a white coat over her clothes.

"What is it?" she said, without looking up.

"Dr. Reynolds wants you to help these two," Mustache said, jerking his thumb in Alex's direction.

The young woman looked up and took in Alex and Connie with a sweeping glance.

"Who are they?" she asked.

"Private detectives," Mustache said, irritation plain in his voice. "Someone high up wants them to have a look around."

The woman looked back at Alex and he put on his most charming smile. It seemed to work, since she swept a few stray hairs back over her ear self-consciously.

"All right," she said, standing. "I'll take it from here."

The officer thanked her, gave Alex a stern look, then headed back to his post.

"Okay," the woman said, standing up. "Who are you and what do you need?"

Alex introduced himself and then Connie, claiming that the big man was his assistant.

"Lisa Baker," she said, sticking her hand out. "Since Dr. Reynolds doesn't want to deal with you, I'm at your disposal."

"We'll try not to take up too much of your time, Dr. Baker," Alex said, shaking her hand. She had a firm grip and callused hands. Alex suspected that she did a lot of the work around the morgue.

"It's just Miss Baker for now," she said with a self-deprecating smile. "I still have to finish my training, assuming Dr. Reynolds approves my work."

Alex got the impression that Reynolds was holding the girl up; he was certainly in a position to do so, and he could continue to pawn his work off on her as long as he did.

"We're here to see two of your clients," Alex went on, his smile never wavering. "First a Michael Halverson — he would have been brought in early this morning, and then Sal Gerano, brought in sometime last week."

Lisa nodded and headed off down the tiled hall, motioning for them to follow.

"If you're looking for the coroner's report," she said, "there won't be one for the man brought in this morning. We work fast, but not that fast."

"That's all right," Alex said. "I understand that case is pretty cut and dried, but I promised I'd take a look."

When they reached the cooler and Lisa uncovered Halverson's body, Alex wished he hadn't kept his promise. The body was lacerated and torn, the flesh ripped into long strips, and the man's throat had been completely torn out.

"Yuck," Lisa said in the understatement of the century. "What happened here?"

"The initial assessment was animal attack," Alex supplied.

"I concur," Lisa said. She pointed to the ragged edges of the wounds in the man's neck. "You can see the tracks left by the teeth. Some kind of dog, I'd guess."

"Whoever made the initial assessment thought it was a wolf."

Lisa leaned down and examined the wounds more closely, then she shrugged.

"The teeth are a bit large for a dog," she admitted. "But it might have been a big dog."

"Ain't that what a wolf is?" Connie asked. "A big dog?"

Lisa smiled and nodded.

"Pretty much, but it's rare to find a wolf in the city."

Satisfied that he'd done his duty, Alex motioned for Lisa to cover the body again. Once she'd wheeled it back into the cooler, she hunted around for Sal's body, eventually bringing it out. When she pulled the sheet back, Alex found himself looking at what appeared to be a younger version of Connie. The man was large, with big shoulders and a lantern jaw. His body was covered with nicks and scrapes and there was a large depression on the side of his head where he'd clearly been hit with a blunt object.

As Alex began to examine the body, Lisa picked up the clipboard hanging from the end of the gurney and began reading the coroner's report.

"This one was fished out of the Potomac," she said, flipping to the next page. "Multiple broken bones and contusions. Cause of death looks like the blunt force wound to the head. Dr. Reynolds concluded that he'd been beaten by multiple attackers."

"Does he say who did it?" Connie asked.

Lisa chuckled and shook her head, no doubt assuming the mobster's question was a joke.

"I hate to disagree with Dr. Reynolds," Alex said, turning one of Sal's hands over to examine the palm. "But I don't think this man was involved in a fight."

"Oh, really?" Lisa asked, her voice wavering between interest and sarcasm. "And what makes you think that?"

Alex turned Sal's hand back over so the top was visible.

"There aren't any defensive wounds on his hands," he said. "Sal here was a professional bodyguard, so he knew how to fight. Even if he'd been jumped by multiple attackers, he'd have gotten off a few punches before they put him down. But there's nothing here."

Lisa looked from Alex to Sal's hand and back, then she rounded the table and examined the other hand.

"There should be bruising on the knuckles if he'd been in a fight," she said, more to herself than to Alex. Finally she looked up, nodding. "You're right, Mr. Lockerby," she admitted.

Before Alex could respond, she moved back to where she'd left the autopsy report and began paging through it again, mumbling.

"What's she doing?" Connie whispered, moving up beside Alex.

"The same thing we're doing," Alex replied. "Looking for clues."

As Lisa continued to read and mutter, Alex reached under the gurney and removed the cardboard box that sat on its lower shelf. He knew from experience that it would contain the dead man's personal effects.

"Let's see what we can find out while she works," he said, moving to a nearby desk and setting the box down.

"What are we looking for?" Connie asked as Alex began taking out Sal's clothing and patting it down.

"Anything that might give us a clue to where Sal was killed."

Alex squeezed the leg of Sal's trousers, running his hand down each leg. If there had been anything concealed inside he'd have felt it, but there was nothing. Moving on, he repeated the process with the suit coat, the shirt, and even Sal's tie. The only thing he found was a dry cleaner's mark on the inside lining of the jacket.

Next came Sal's shoe — apparently only one had been recovered — as well as a cheap pocketwatch, a gold wedding band, a lighter, and a leather wallet. Opening the wallet, Alex found it empty. With a sigh he checked the box again, looking for anything he might have missed. The only thing left was a property envelope where the coroner would have put any money found on the body.

He was about to start putting everything back, but he'd come this far so he might as well be thorough. With a sigh, he picked up the envelope, turned it over, and tipped it toward his open hand. When nothing came out, he looked inside and found it completely empty.

"Why did they put this here if there's nothing in it," he groused. As he moved to throw the useless paper into the box, he caught the name printed on the outside of the envelope. He'd assumed it said *Capital Police*, but instead, it read, *Capital Bank*.

"What?" Connie said, picking up on Alex's sudden excitement.

"Did Sal have an account at Capital Bank?" he asked.

Connie shrugged.

"Don't know," he said. "But I can tell you who does have an account there, Colton. The boss set it up for him and puts money in there to pay the business expenses."

"As soon as we're done here, I need you to call Sal's wife and find out if he had an account."

"And if he did?"

"We need to know if he took any money out on the day he died."

Connie was about to ask something more, but Lisa's raised voice interrupted.

"I think I've figured it out," she said. "Look here."

Alex and Connie moved over so they could see the clipboard where Lisa was pointing. She had folded the upper pages back, revealing a diagram of a human body that also showed the bones. Several lines had been made through various bones.

"This shows where Mr. Gerano had broken bones," she said. "Look here, at his legs."

Each of the upper leg bones had a slash through it but Alex didn't see why that would be significant.

"These injuries are symmetrical," Lisa said. "They're in almost the exact same position on both femurs."

"So?" Connie said.

"So I think they were caused at the same time by a large, horizontal object."

"You think he was hit by a car," Alex guessed.

Lisa blushed slightly and brushed her hair back.

"Well not a car, exactly," she said. "If this were a bumper, it's too high for a car. I think he was hit by a truck, one moving pretty fast. That would account for his injuries and there wouldn't be any defensive wounds."

Alex exchanged a glance with Connie, then nodded.

"Thank you, Miss Baker," Alex said, offering her his hand. "You've been very helpful."

She smiled again and told Alex he was welcome any time, then she wheeled Sal's body back into the cooler.

"You got that look," Connie said.

"What look?"

"Like you just made your first big score. I'm guessing that means you've figured something out."

"Maybe," Alex admitted as he headed toward the exit. "I'm guessing Sal didn't have an account at Capital Bank. That would mean that the money he took out was from Colton's account."

"Why would Sal take money out of Colton's account?"

Alex pushed the door open but hesitated, waiting for Connie to catch up.

"If you were assigned to guard Colton and he got grabbed, what would you do?"

"Call the boss and start a manhunt," Connie said without hesitation.

"Let's say you can't or won't do that?"

Connie sighed and shrugged.

"I don't know, I guess I'd go out to find Colton myself."

"Exactly," Alex said. "I think Colton got grabbed and Sal tried to just pay the ransom."

"Okay," Connie said, thinking over what Alex said. "But is that good news or bad?"

"If I'm right, it's bad," Alex said. "If Sal was hit on his way to make the ransom drop, it means that whoever grabbed Colton thinks they delivered their ransom demand and they haven't heard back."

Connie swore.

"What if they're the ones who killed Sal?" he asked.

"No," Alex said. "That had to be someone else. If the kidnappers never intended to give Colton back, they'd just wait and take the ransom at the drop. No need to kill Sal."

"So what do we do?"

"You go see your boss," Alex said, waving at a passing cab. "Find out how much money Sal took out and from whose account, then call me at my hotel."

15

THE TIP OF THE ICEBERG

In Manhattan, uniformed policemen had local precinct buildings spread throughout the city, enabling them to respond quickly to any emergency. Detectives, however, were concentrated in the Central Office, allowing them greater access to the resources they needed and allowing them to easily share information. D.C., however, spread its detectives out into three offices around the city. Each office covered a piece of the ten-mile square that made up the district.

When Alex exited a cab in front of Command Office number two, he wasn't impressed. Unlike the towering edifice that was the Manhattan Central Office, this building was a plain, two-story brick structure. If he hadn't known he was in the right place, Alex would have sworn it was an overbuilt warehouse or a small industrial building.

"I'm here to see Detective Norton," Alex told the desk sergeant in the lobby.

"Take a seat," the man grumbled, not looking up from his paper.

"He's expecting me," Alex pressed.

The cop looked over the top of his paper and gave Alex the once-over. His expression said he wanted to make Alex wait just for the crime of interrupting his reading, but Alex was wearing an expensive suit and that might mean trouble. After a long moment, the man sneered and set his paper aside.

"Who wants to see the detective?" he asked as he picked up the phone on his desk.

Alex grinned back at the surly sergeant.

"Tell him Santa Claus is here," he said, "and I've got a present for him."

Ten minutes later, a uniformed officer led Alex to a small office with a desk and several filing cabinets. There might have been a chair for visitors in front of the desk, but it was impossible to tell. Every surface was covered with paper. Not the orderly stacks he'd seen in Danny's office, but what amounted to litter. It looked as if someone had taken the contents of several dozen police reports and simply thrown them up in the air.

In the center of this sea of document chaos sat Detective Norton, wearing a different rumpled suit from yesterday. As Alex entered, his escort stepped back and closed the door.

"All right, Lockerby," Norton growled. "What's with giving my desk sergeant a hard time?"

Alex shrugged.

"He started it," he said. "Besides, I figured you might not want anyone to know we were meeting in case they read that story in the *Capital Dispatch*."

Norton thought about that for a moment, then nodded.

"It's not a bad idea, actually," he admitted. "So, you found something."

"Not yet, but I have good news on that front," Alex said. "How did your investigation go?"

Norton's expression soured and he took out a crumpled cigarette pack.

"My buddy directed me to the National Archives," he said, fishing through the pack for a smoke. "He said all legislation is on file over there. So, I call over and they tell me that the bills I'm looking for are in their legislation storage room." He held up the pack to his eye, then grumbled and crushed it.

Alex pulled out his own case and offered a cigarette to the detective.

"So we can just go over there and look it up?" Alex asked.

"No," Norton said, lighting his borrowed cigarette. "They haven't filed it yet."

"Who cares?" Alex asked, lighting a cigarette of his own. " We'll just go through the newest stack and find it ourselves."

Norton chuckled without any humor in his voice.

"You'd think, but no. According to the helpful clerk I talked to, they just got finished filing the Congressional Record for nineteen-thirty-four."

"So they've got three years of legislation in a big pile in a back room?" he said with a laugh.

"Yeah," Norton said. "And it isn't funny. According to my contact, Congress put a bunch of security rules on their paperwork a few years ago. That means I'd need a warrant just to get a look for some bill for renaming a post office."

"And whatever we're looking for is no post office," Alex said with a nod. He took a drag of his cigarette and smiled at the detective. "Then it's a good thing I've got an in for us."

"Just like that?" Norton said, appraising Alex from under his bushy eyebrows.

"Well, it does come with one caveat."

Norton's face twisted into an expression of disgust.

"Okay, Lockerby, get to the bad news."

Alex put his hand on his chest and gave Norton a look of profound innocence.

"Why detective, you wound me," he said, sarcasm dripping from his words. "Not only have I gotten us in at the Senate offices tonight at six, but I've also recruited some extra help."

"The bad news," Norton demanded.

"Much like your superiors," Alex explained, "the FBI has taken their hotshot sorceress, Sorsha Kincaid off the Senator's murder."

"Isn't she your girlfriend?" Norton asked.

"By a happy coincidence, I believe she is," Alex said. "But what's important is that she believes the Senator was murdered, too."

Norton looked like he was about to object, but he stopped and thought about that for a long moment. When he smiled, Alex knew their little cabal had taken shape.

"Do you think she could get us a look at the FBI's file on the case?" he asked.

Alex bit his lip and shook his head.

"I don't know," he admitted. "The local guy in charge doesn't like her very much. I guess she's interfering with his time in the spotlight. Name's Blake if I remember right."

Norton chuckled at that.

"Sounds like him, the pompous ass. He's the director of the FBI's field office in the city. A man of great ambition and little talent, which means he'll go far in Washington."

Alex wanted to laugh at the detective's words, but it didn't sound like he was joking. That prospect was horrifying.

Reaching into his shirt pocket, Alex took out his flip notebook and tore out a page that contained Sorsha's room number and the number of the Fairfax hotel where she was staying.

"What's this for?" Norton asked as Alex dropped it on top of his paper-strewn desk.

"I'll arrange for Sorsha to meet us at the Senate Offices tonight, but after that you two need to coordinate directly."

Norton picked up the paper, then his eyes narrowed, and he looked up at Alex.

"Why?"

"Because, detective," Alex said, reaching behind him for the doorknob. "Like you, the Sorceress might find herself in trouble if anyone were to know that I was working with her."

Norton thought about that as Alex opened the door, then he nodded.

"That's fair enough," he said. "One less person to share the credit with, I suppose."

Alex grinned at the man, then stepped out into the hall.

"Glad we understand each other," he said. "Six o'clock in front of the Senate Office Building. Don't be late."

With that, Alex headed back toward the stairs and the first floor. For as disorganized as Detective Norton seemed to be, he caught on quickly. Alex could work with that.

He stopped by the pay phone in the lobby and dropped a nickel into the slot.

"Give me room two-eleven," he told the man who answered. A moment later he heard Sorsha's voice come on. "I just talked with Detective Norton," he reported. "He's on board."

"What about looking at the Senate files?" she asked. "My friend in the Senate says it might take a couple of days to track down what Senator Young was working on. He isn't on the same committees."

Alex explained about his conversation with Tiffany Young and how she'd basically blackmailed her husband's aide, Duke Harris, into helping them.

"All right," Sorsha said when he was done. "I'll be there at six sharp, and...and thanks for helping."

Alex bit back a snarky comment.

"Any time, darlin'," he said, then hung up.

He turned to make his way back out to the street, but stopped. It had only been a couple of hours since Alex had left the museum, but it was on the way back to his hotel room, so he decided to check in.

"Alex," Lyle Gundersen's voice greeted him enthusiastically. "I'm glad you called. My insurance man is on his way here with the pictures you wanted."

"That's great work, Mr. Gundersen. I'll be right over."

Twenty minutes later, Alex entered Lyle Gundersen's office at the Smithsonian. To his surprise, Zelda Pritchard was still there, sitting in one of the comfortable chairs in front of Gundersen's desk. She had her legs crossed and the slit in her skirt was open, revealing a generous amount of toned calf.

"Alex," she said as he entered, giving him a smile that reminded him of Leslie Tompkins. "I'm glad you came back," she went on, bouncing her bare leg casually. "You hurried off so quickly before I was beginning to think you wanted to get away from me."

Alex took off his hat and held it over his chest.

"My most humble apologies," he said. "I was obviously too eager to track down the museum's card thief."

"Yes, about that," Lyle said, standing from behind his desk. He indicated a third person in the room, an older, heavyset man with a bowler hat in his hand and a fairly large folio under his arm. "This is Jerry Edwards. He represents our insurance company."

Edwards stuck out his hand, but was still holding his hat. After a moment of confusion, he dropped it on the desk and shook Alex's hand.

"Lyle said these might help you find out who robbed the museum," he said, holding the folio out. "Since the museum isn't going to make a claim, we won't need these right now, and my company is interested in apprehending the thief just the same."

Alex took the folio, but almost dropped it.

"How many pictures did you take?" he said with a grin as he placed the folio on Gundersen's desk.

"There's one of every card that was acquired with the loom," Edwards said.

That didn't sound right, so Alex undid the clasp on the front and opened the top of the folio. Inside there had to be two hundred photographs. Reaching in, Alex pulled out a half-dozen or so and spread them out across the desk. Each was a photograph of a thin wooden card laid out on a white cloth with a ruler plainly visible below it. Comparing them quickly, Alex found they were all different, and each card had a number cut into its bottom right corner, indicating its position in the sequence.

"You say there's only one picture of every card in here?" Alex asked the insurance man.

"That's right," Edwards confirmed, a bit confused by the question.

Alex ignored his probing glance and turned to Lyle Gundersen.

"How many cards do you figure were stolen from the loom exhibit?"

"About fifty," he said. "But I don't know which of those are the stolen cards."

Alex grabbed his forehead with his thumb and index finger, desperately attempting to ward off a frustration headache.

"I've been assuming that whoever stole them did it because they wanted to reproduce the pattern the cards make," he explained, somehow resisting the urge to yell.

"I don't follow," Gundersen said.

"Lyle," Zelda gasped, standing up to better see the pictures on the desk. "Don't you see what Alex is getting at?"

Gundersen looked from Zelda to Alex, then shook his head.

"They can't reproduce the pattern without all the cards," Alex said with exaggerated patience. He picked up one of the pictures from the desk and held it up. "That means they're going to need the rest of these."

"Oh," Lyle said, his cheeks reddening in embarrassment. "I actually...I didn't consider that."

"So where are all of these," Alex said, waving the picture. "There's got to be a couple hundred pictures in here."

"Well, most patterns are very complicated," Lyle said. "It's quite common for these kinds of looms to use several hundred cards in just a simple pattern. As for the cards, whoever set up the exhibit probably took the fifty best cards to be put on display."

"And the rest would be...?" Alex left the sentence hanging.

"Well, in one of our storage warehouses, obviously," Lyle said.

That took Alex aback.

"How many warehouses do you have?"

"About a dozen scattered around the city," Lyle said. "We started with just one, but as the museum grew, we just kept needing more and more."

"But which one has the cards?" Zelda asked; her face was flushed and her breathing was fast and shallow. Clearly she saw where Alex was going with this.

"Well...I don't know," Lyle said, rubbing his chin. "They aren't particularly valuable as they are, so they would have been stored in whichever warehouse had space. I can look it up in the original file on the exhibit, but it might take me a few days to track that file down."

"Whoever stole those cards is going to want the rest of them," Alex said. "The quicker you find that warehouse, the quicker we can use those cards as bait for our thief."

Lyle finally seemed to understand, and he nodded.

"I'll get to work on that right away," he said. "I'm sure I can locate the remaining cards in a few hours if I put my mind to it."

"All right," Alex said, picking up the stray photographs and dropping them back into the folio. "Do you mind if I take this back to my hotel to go through it?" he asked the insurance man.

Edwards shrugged, then nodded.

"Since I doubt the museum would make a claim even if they were all stolen, I don't see the harm," he said. "Just don't lose any, as I'm going to need them back."

"I'll take great care of them," Alex said. "Thank you."

Shaking Edward's hand, Alex nodded to Lyle and Zelda before heading out into the hall. He had only gone a few steps when Zelda's voice rang out behind him.

"Are you running away again, Alex?" she said. "Keep that up and I might develop a complex."

Alex turned with an apologetic look on his face. Zelda was pretty, certainly, and he might have pursued her a few months ago. She certainly made her interest known. But he had a feeling that if he so much as held her hand, Sorsha would make him pay for it. Quite apart from that, he was just beginning to actually melt some of the Ice Queen's frosty façade, and he didn't want to ruin that.

"Well," he lied. "You did want me to solve this case quickly. I can't do that if I'm just standing around talking."

Zelda walked toward him in a way Alex could only describe as 'slinky'. She rolled her hips, emphasizing them with every step until only a foot separated them and the smell of her expensive perfume washed over him.

"Well, I didn't want to tie you up, but I figured you might need a break from the case every now and then."

DAN WILLIS

A tingling sensation raced up the back of Alex's arms and he was suddenly very aware of how close she was.

"I do take the occasional break," he said, magnanimously. "But right now I've got to get these pictures back to my room and go over them. That's going to take a lot of time."

She reached out and slid her finger up the lapel of his suit coat, straightening the knot of his tie when she reached the top.

"I was thinking further out," she said. "There's a gallery opening tomorrow night over at the Freer Gallery. It's just over there," she pointed off to the east. "They've got a new exhibit of American Impressionist paintings and I'd love it if you came with me."

Alex's mind raced, looking for a believable way to bow out of an evening looking at paintings.

"I know these things can be a bit tedious," Zelda went on, reading his expression. "But there's always Champagne, that and good company can pass the evening quite amiably."

She smiled at him in a way that made him really want to agree.

"All right," he said. "I can't promise anything because something might come up with the case, but if I'm free, I'd be happy to escort you."

Zelda's sultry smile grew until it beamed.

"I'll hold you to that, Alex," she purred. "And I do expect you to catch our thief in time for the opening."

She turned and sauntered back to Lyle's office. This time Alex had a perfect view of the little roll she gave her hips as she went, watching until she was out of sight.

Blowing out a pent-up breath, Alex clutched the folio full of pictures. If he was right about the thief's motive, the pictures would help him solve this case. Before he could go through them, however, he was going to need a cold shower.

16

PATTERNS

Alex opted to run a cold towel over his face rather than taking a shower when he got back to his hotel room. Zelda was pretty and very insistent, but her charms faded when compared to Sorsha. The only exception was in just how completely Zelda had shaped her sex appeal into a weapon. He wondered what kind of negotiator she was.

Pushing those thoughts from his mind, Alex set the folio full of card pictures on the little writing desk and opened the door to his vault. He was tempted to look through the pictures, but realistically he simply didn't have the expertise to understand what they meant. Their real importance was what they revealed. So far he knew that the cards that had been stolen from the museum were just a tiny fraction of the ones that had been purchased with the loom. That meant that if the thief really was after the pattern the cards made, he'd be back.

Once Gundersen finds the rest of them, he thought, *we'll make sure people know they exist, then sit on them and see who comes calling.*

In the meantime, he'd give the photographs to someone who would know what they meant. If the thief didn't fall for the bait, maybe Alex could find him by knowing what pattern the cards actually made.

The pattern someone was willing to kill for.

Picking up the folio, he entered his vault and headed to the right-hand hallway, to where the cover door to his Manhattan office stood. Since he was supposed to be out of town, he couldn't just walk into his waiting room where he might be seen, so he entered his private office and sat behind his monstrous desk.

The desk had been supplied to Alex, along with the office, as part of his deal with Andrew Barton. It was far larger than Alex needed, and incredibly ornate, with carved flourishes on the corners and around the panels. The top was covered in green leather that had been stained in a way that made it resemble marble. It was so fancy, he only kept his phone, an in-box, a matching leather blotter, the intercom, and his touch tip lighter on it.

Of course he'd been away for half a week, so Sherry had piled several stacks of case files on his desk, but the top was big enough that Alex didn't even have to move them as he sat down. He pressed the white "talk" key on his intercom twice in quick succession, then retrieved his contact book from the center drawer of the desk. As he opened it, the intercom clicked, and there was a brief burst of static.

Since the door through Alex's vault needed to remain a secret, Alex and Sherry worked out the two-tap signal with the intercom months ago. When Alex returned through the vault, two taps let Sherry know he was back, and she'd answer with a single tap so Alex knew she'd received the message.

Since Alex didn't know if Sherry was busy up front, he proceeded to open his contact book and flipped to the second page where he found the number for Broadline Textiles. He'd done some work for Lewis Clayton, the owner, a few years back and Lewis had promised him a favor if he ever needed it. Looking at the folio stuffed with pictures of wooden cards with holes in them, Alex chuckled. This would be a big ask.

Picking up the receiver on his desk phone, Alex dialed the number for Broadline. A receptionist with a pleasant, Midwestern accent picked up and took his name, then, a few minutes later, Lewis Clayton himself came on the line.

"Lockerby," he said, enthusiasm flowing through his Brooklyn drawl. "Been a long time, what brings you to me?"

"Lew," Alex greeted him. "You ever heard of a Jacquard loom?"

Lew laughed out loud.

"I'm in the textile business," he said, as if that explained everything.

"So?"

"A guy like me not knowing Jacquard is like a painter who never heard of DaVinci. The weaving machines I use are just faster versions of Jacquard's original, that and our cards are made out of paperboard. Why do you wanna know?"

"Someone broke into a museum and stole the cards right off their loom display," Alex explained. "I'm thinking they wanted to get their hands on whatever pattern the cards made."

"That's nuts," Lew said. "It'd be easier and cheaper to just hire someone to make you new cards from the original design."

"What if the design was some kind of secret?"

There was a pause on the line while Lew thought that one over.

"We're talking about pictures made out of cloth," he said finally. "How special could this pattern really be?"

"Well that's what I was hoping you could tell me," Alex said. "The museum had pictures taken of the cards, you know, for insurance purposes. If I showed you the cards, could you figure out what the design they produced looked like?"

"Me?" Lew scoffed. "No. But I've got a girl who makes the cards for all my patterns, and she's amazing. I could have her take a look and let you know, but it might take a week or two."

That wasn't what Alex wanted to hear, but it was better than nothing, so he agreed.

"I'll have my secretary send them over to you by messenger," he added.

"Hey," Lew added before Alex could hang up. "If this pattern is something interesting, do you mind if I use it once you're done?"

Alex thought about that. If the pattern was something important, that would be bad, but it might just as easily have been whatever was fashionable at the beginning of the last century.

"I'd have to check with the Smithsonian," he hedged. "It's their pattern after all. I will ask, though."

"You're a prince, Alex," Lew said, then hung up.

Alex shook his head as he returned the phone receiver to its cradle. Trust Lew to find a way to make a buck off returning a favor.

He copied the address of Broadline Textiles from his contact book onto a notepad and had just torn it free, when the door opened and Sherry came in.

"Hi-ya, boss," she said with an endearing grin. "You ducking out of some boring meetings?"

Alex chuckled at that. So far his trip to the nation's capital had been anything but boring. He was about to explain when he noticed Sherry's attire. She had on a black knee-length dress with white buttons and trim. His secretary didn't usually wear high heels, but the pumps she had on were taller than any Alex had seen before. Not only that, the dress fit her very well and the front was cut lower than usual.

"Who's the guy?" Alex asked, not bothering to hide a grin.

Sherry looked stunned and then her cheeks flushed.

"Can't get anything past you, can I?"

"Not with that neckline."

Sherry blushed further and tugged the front of her dress up a bit.

"Just somebody who came in while you were out," she said. "Now don't change the subject, what brings you back?"

Alex wanted to push, but Sherry's brush-off seemed pretty definite. When she wanted to tell him, she would, so he returned to business and told her about his time in Washington.

"You've got three cases and you've only been in town a few days," she said with an incredulous look. "I'm starting to wonder what you need me for?"

"Don't ever wonder that," Alex said, pushing the folio full of pictures across the desk toward her. "I need you to have these sent over to Lew Clayton at Broadline Textiles right away." He handed her the slip of note paper with the address on it. "Then I need you to call Charles Grier and Linda Kellin." Opening his flip notebook, Alex tore off the top page and handed it over. "Ask them about these things, whether they're used in alchemy and, if so, what they might be used for. I need to know back about that right away."

Sherry scanned the paper and her face screwed up in confusion.

"Regulus of Antimony?" she read, then she shrugged and nodded. "Okay, I'll call them right away. You want me to just put their answers on your desk?"

Alex nodded.

"I'll check back sometime tonight. Last, I need you to run over to the library archives and look up William Unger; he's recently been appointed to the Senate by the Governor of Illinois. He was undoubtedly a local politician before his elevation, so find out how many scandals he's involved in along with any other dirt you can find."

"You need that tonight as well?" she asked, no trace of complaint in her voice. When Alex nodded, she continued. "I'll have to close the office for the afternoon then, Mike's out on a case."

"That's fine," Alex said, rising. "Good luck. Now I've got to get back before I'm missed."

Alex had just shut his vault when there was a knock at his door. This time it was Connie who stood in the hotel hallway.

"What did you find out?" Alex asked, stepping back so the gangster could enter.

"Sal took three hundred dollars out of Colton's account on the day he went missing," Connie said, not moving from the hall. "And the boss wants to see you."

Alex suppressed a sigh and went back to the room's desk and picked up his kit.

The residence of Lucky Tony Casetti was an unassuming house on a rural street. It was surrounded by a wall of red brick with wrought iron decorations running along the top. As Connie maneuvered his car through the open gate and up the short driveway, Alex noted that the decorative iron was pointed on top, turning it into an effective deterrent to any effort to scale the wall.

The house itself was constructed of red brick with white shutters and eaves. It was three stories high with a wraparound porch that kept it from looking too tall and skinny. The little yard inside the wall was neat and orderly with winter-brown grass and evergreen shrubs up against the foundation. Empty flower beds ran along both sides of the walk, no doubt sheltering bulbs that would bloom come spring.

Connie led the way up the walk to the porch, then in through the heavy front door. A sunken parlor opened up immediately to the left as they entered, and Alex found Lucky Tony and several of his men waiting with an expectant air.

"Connie tells me you have a theory," Tony said without preamble. He motioned for Alex to take a seat, then continued. "He says you think someone grabbed Colton and when Sal tried to ransom him on his own, he got hit by a truck before he could. Is that about it?"

"I did think that, yes," Alex admitted.

Tony's brows dropped down over his eyes in an angry scowl.

"And that would mean that they probably killed Colton and dumped him in the drink the same time they disposed of Sal? Well, that's nonsense," Tony went on without waiting for Alex to answer. "Sal knew better than to act without telling me."

"Maybe he thought he could avoid your wrath by getting Colton back on his own," Alex said.

"Wrath?" Tony scoffed. "Guys get grabbed sometimes," he said. "It happens, but the important part is getting them back. The quicker you get on that, the more chance you have of getting your man back in one piece. Sal knew that, so you'd better come up with something else."

Alex could feel the heat of the mob boss's words wash over him. He'd snapped at Connie, when the man had pushed him, but that kind of latitude didn't extend to men like Lucky Tony.

"You're right," he said. "When I first heard that Sal had an empty bank envelope on him, I figured he'd messed up and lost Colton, then tried to make the payoff himself."

Tony glared at Alex then his expression softened a tiny bit.

"What changed your mind?"

"The alleged ransom," Alex said. "We know Colton saw his bookie on the day he disappeared and collected five hundred dollars in winnings. Sal took three hundred out of Capital Bank sometime later. That's a total of eight hundred. What kind of ransom is that?"

"Eight hundred is a lot of cash to most people," Tony said.

"Yeah, but how much do you keep in that account at Capital Bank?"

Tony shrugged.

"Not much," he said. "It's just so Colton can pay incidental expenses. Every month, my accountant tops it up to a couple grand."

"So if there were kidnappers," Alex said, "and they grabbed Colton, they'd find five hundred on him, right?"

Tony nodded.

"So why did they only ask for a measly three hundred more? Why not another five, or a grand?"

Tony raised an eyebrow as he thought over Alex's words. He looked around at his men, ending with Connie.

"I'd ask for more," Connie said. "I wouldn't be satisfied with three hundred, not when the mark had five on him."

Tony hesitated, then nodded agreement.

"So, you don't think my nephew is at the bottom of the Potomac," he said, turning back to Alex. "What now?"

Alex took a deep breath, giving himself a few extra seconds to think. He didn't have a good answer to Lucky Tony's question, not that he was about to tell the gangster that.

"Now Connie and I go back to the receipts we found in Colton's home," he said. "I called all the shops to find out what he might have bought there and all of them matched the list from his desk except one. That was a haberdasher."

"So Colton bought himself a new hat?" Tony said. "How does that help? And if you've already talked to these shops, what are you hoping to find this time?" An edge of irritation was creeping into Tony's voice and Alex could feel himself beginning to sweat. He really wished he'd worked on a new escape rune.

"This time we're going to go to each one in person," Alex explained. "We'll swing by Colton's house and pick up a picture of him, then see if anyone at the stores remembers talking to him."

"What good will that do?" Tony demanded, his voice rising.

"It might tell us where else your nephew might have gone, Mr. Casetti," Alex said. "All we have right now are the receipts, but he might have gone to other places and simply not bought anything."

"That sounds like a hell of a long shot," Tony growled.

"I know it looks bad," Alex said. "But I'm not giving up. Right now the only thing we know for sure is that Sal was hit by a truck. He might have been targeted or it might have been an accident."

"And what, the truck driver just picked up Sal's body and threw it in the river?"

"Or Sal was hit on a bridge and fell in the water," Alex said. "Whatever happened, we just don't have enough information."

Tony held Alex's gaze for a long moment without speaking.

"You wanted me for this," Alex said, "because I'm good at what I do, Mr. Casetti. Your nephew's trail isn't cold, not yet."

Lucky Tony snorted, then waved toward the door.

"Well if that's the case, then get out of here and find my nephew."

Alex stood and headed for the door, taking care not to run, or even hurry.

"And Lockerby," the mob boss called after him. "I'm losing my patience. You need to make some progress this time. Understand?"

Alex nodded. He understood perfectly well the threat underlying the mobster's words and he had no doubt that Tony would be as good as his word on that account.

Alex rubbed his eyes as he stepped out of Carrol Brothers Grocery. He and Connie had been to half the shops on Colton's list so far and none of them had shed any light on the alchemist's activities. Several of the shop-keeps or their clerks had remembered Colton. As Alex had guessed, he wasn't just grocery shopping, he was looking for steady suppliers of the items on his list. Unfortunately no one remembered anything unusual about their conversations or where Colton might have gone next.

"I need a drink," Connie said, coming up to stand next to Alex on the sidewalk. "Is it always like this?"

"More often than I'd like," Alex said.

"Where to next?"

Alex consulted his watch before answering.

"It's after five and we've hit all the grocers. All that's left are the alchemical suppliers and the haberdasher, but they'll be closed by the time we got there." Alex dropped his watch back into his vest pocket and sighed. "I need to take another reading for the Lightning Lord before I go." Since Andrew wanted him to take readings with the power box, Alex had put it in the trunk of Connie's car and checked it at all the places they stopped. "Pick me up at the hotel at nine and we'll hit the rest of them."

"The boss isn't going to like that," Connie said, opening the trunk for Alex. "He's getting pretty worried about Colton."

"Me too," Alex said. He leaned over and hefted the weighty metal box out onto the sidewalk. "I can't see any reason for him to disappear."

"What if you were right about Sal?" Connie said. "What if he was hit while crossing a bridge, and what if Colton was with him?"

"That would mean he's at the bottom of the Potomac," Alex said, pulling out his flip notebook and pencil. "If that's the case, there's nothing we can do, so let's not worry about that yet. We still have four shops to visit, so maybe we'll get some answer there."

Connie didn't look hopeful, and Alex felt how the mobster looked.

"You want me to drop you off at your hotel?" Connie said as Alex wrote down the readings on the power tester.

"No," Alex said. "I'll catch a cab."

"Suit yourself," he said, then climbed in his car and drove away.

After he was gone, Alex stepped around the corner of Carrol Brother's Grocery and chalked a door on the brickwork. He opened his vault just long enough to deposit the heavy power meter inside, then shut it and walked down to a five and dime to use their phone. He still had an hour before he had to meet Sorsha and Detective Norton, but he wanted to check up on Lyle Gundersen to see if he'd found the loom cards in storage.

"Alex!" Gundersen cried when the phone connected. "Where have you been, I've been trying to reach you?"

"I have other things I'm working on, Mr. Gundersen," Alex said, a bit short-tempered after the day he'd had. "Did you find the extra cards?"

"Yes," he said, still agitated. "They were in a warehouse in Silver Spring."

"Great, I can meet you there, just give me the address."

"That's what I'm trying to tell you, Mr. Lockerby," Lyle moaned. "The warehouse was broken into an hour ago."

Alex felt a sudden headache blooming and he grabbed his forehead in a vain effort to suppress it.

"Don't tell me," he said.

"The cards were the only things taken," Lyle continued.

"I told you not to tell me," Alex sighed.

17

PATHS

It turned out that Silver Spring, where the burgled warehouse was located, wasn't even in D.C. It was a rural area north of the city in Maryland. Alex's cab deposited him in front of a run-down building at the far end of a small industrial park. It stood two stories high with a steeply sloped roof and a peeling paint job that had to be a decade old.

Alex stopped at the curb to light a cigarette, letting his eyes wander over the building. The warehouse had two large carriage doors in front along a raised platform where trucks could back in to unload. A standard-sized door for the office stood on the right edge of the building with a long bank of windows running down the right side.

In the time it took Alex to put away his lighter, he'd spotted at least four ways to get into the warehouse without being detected or leaving a trace.

Secure it was not.

Despite the fact that there had been a burglary, Alex saw no sign of a police presence.

"Hello?" Alex called, pushing the office door open. Beyond the door was a table with a telephone and a blotter, three filing cabinets, and a table with a hot plate and a dirty skillet. A door at the back of the room stood ajar and Alex assumed it led from the office into the warehouse proper.

"Alex?" Lyle Gundersen's voice came through the back door. "We're in here."

Opening the door, Alex found the warehouse very much as he expected it to be, one enormous room filled with dusty shelves. Boxes, crates, and paper-wrapped objects littered the place, clogging the shelves and, in many cases, spilling out over the floor. The shelves each had paper cards on their ends with a letter designating each aisle, but beyond that Alex saw no further form of organization.

How do they find anything in this fire hazard?

Walking along the rows, Alex came to the one designated 'E' and found Lyle and a man in work overalls standing about a third of the way along the aisle. A large crate stuck out into the aisle from the shelves, and Gundersen had placed an open, hard-shelled container on top of it.

"Thank goodness you're here, Alex," Lyle gushed. "I just don't understand any of this."

"Is this where you kept the cards?" Alex asked, indicating the hard-shelled case as he walked up.

"Yes," Lyle said. "I had Mr. Grady here," he indicated the man in overalls, "locate them as per your instructions. I had no idea someone would try to take them. This just doesn't make any sense."

On that point, Alex agreed.

"Were you here when the theft occurred?" Alex asked Grady.

"D'know," the man slurred. He was of average height and lean, with a pock-marked face, a bald head, and a lackadaisical expression on his face. Alex got the impression he wasn't the sharpest knife in the drawer. "I found the box of cards like Mr. Gundersen said. I left them right here before I went to lunch and when I came back, they was gone."

Alex resisted the urge to roll his eyes.

"Is there anyone else on duty here?" he asked.

"Mr. Grady is our day clerk," Lyle said, cutting in quickly. "If the museum needs anything from storage, he locates it so it can be moved. He also files anything the museum sends here for storage."

"Is there a night guard?" Alex pressed.

"Nah," Grady said with a dismissive wave. "This is the stuff that ain't worth nuthin'."

"What Mr. Grady means," Lyle explained, "is that this facility is for storing things that, while historically valuable, don't have much..."

"Material value," Alex finished.

So this is the museum's junk drawer, he thought. *Great.*

Alex looked at the open case. It looked like a fancy hat box, but it was square in shape. And it was filthy.

"Did anybody move this after the theft was discovered?" he asked.

Both Lyle and Grady shook their heads, so Alex leaned over the open case and examined it. There were clean stripes in the dust along the top and front of the case and Alex could clearly see where Grady had put his thumbs on the front when he opened the lid.

"You opened this to check the contents," Alex said, looking at Mr. Grady. "Did you leave it open when you went to lunch?"

"I think so."

Alex chewed his lip. With the case open, the thief wouldn't have left any fingerprints on the outside. Still, there were several tracks in the dust that coated the inside of the box, so maybe he'd have better luck there.

"See anything?" Lyle asked.

"Not yet," Alex said, setting down his kit. "But let's take a closer look, shall we?"

He took out his new oculus and went over the case with silverlight. There were several fingerprints on the outside of the case, but those would belong to Grady. Inside there were a few stay marks that could be the oils from the thief's hands, but they were too faint and smeared to be of any use.

"Anybody here," a familiar voice called from up front.

Alex looked at Lyle, who shrugged.

"I also called the police," he explained, then called out to the men in front.

A moment later Lieutenant MacReady made his way down the aisle with two uniformed officers in tow.

"Sorry I took so long, Mr. Gundersen," MacReady said. "This is

Maryland, so I had to get special permission from the State Police to be here." He smiled at Lyle, then turned to Alex.

"Lockerby," he said with a nod. "Find anything?"

Alex was forced to admit that he hadn't.

"I looked into your theory that our wolf-handling thief came from a circus," he said, pulling out a flip notebook and paging through it. "Turns out there is a circus in town, so I went over there and guess what? They have large predators and a dog act."

"Scottish terriers?" Alex guessed, reading the lieutenant's expression.

"Poodles," MacReady said. "They've got some big cats, a few lions and a tiger, but no large canines."

Alex sighed and put his lamp on the floor. Silverlight hadn't revealed anything, but he might try ghostlight just to be thorough.

"At least our thief didn't kill anybody this time," MacReady continued. "Probably left his dog in his other pants."

Alex started to chuckle, but stopped as he reached for his ghostlight burner. Picking up the multi-lamp, he swept it over the floor around the crate.

"No," Alex said. "Our thief brought his wolf with him here too. Mr. Grady was lucky to be out when they visited."

MacReady's face screwed up into a confused expression until Alex passed him the oculus.

"Right here," Alex said, indicating the floor. He couldn't see it without the oculus, but he knew what the lieutenant was seeing. All around the crate were large paw prints.

"I don't get it," MacReady said, passing Alex back the oculus. "How does a man come and go in broad daylight with a wild dog and nobody notices him?"

"Maybe he's the dog," Grady said, scratching his ear.

"What?" Alex and the lieutenant said together.

"You know," Grady explained. "Like that movie where the feller turned into a wolf when he drank liquor."

"You're suggesting our thief is a wolf man," Alex said, not believing he'd heard correctly. "Like in the movies."

"Wouldn't that make him even easier to spot?" MacReady said, his voice dripping with sarcasm. "People are bound to notice a guy walking around with fur and fangs."

Grady just shrugged as if the lieutenant's statement had been a genuine question.

"Dunno," he said. "But it sure would explain why you can't find the wolf."

So would a ghost wolf, Alex thought, *and it's about as likely*. Out loud, he said, "I'm sure we're keeping you from your work, Mr. Grady. Thank you for your assistance."

Grady might have been slow on the uptake, but he knew a dismissal when he heard it.

"I got to go fill out the forms to report this to the museum," he said, then excused himself and headed back in the direction of the office.

"I'm sorry to say it," MacReady said once Mr. Grady was gone, "but so far, the wolf man thief is the best lead we've got."

"Not quite," Alex said. "When I asked Mr. Gundersen to locate these spare cards, I suspected that what our thief was after was the pattern the cards produced. This theft all but confirms that."

"I don't see how that helps us," MacReady said.

Alex explained about the insurance pictures and how he'd turned them over to a friend in the textile industry, though he left out the part about that friend being in Manhattan.

"So we'll know what the pattern is in a couple of weeks," Alex concluded.

"That might help," MacReady admitted, "but the thief has all the cards now, won't he just skip town?"

"We may still have a chance to catch him," Alex said, then he turned to Lyle. "How many people know that I asked you to find the extra cards?"

Lyle looked confused for a moment, then shook his head.

"Just the people in the room when you asked," he said. "You, me, my insurance man, Edwards, and..."

"And Miss Pritchard," Alex finished.

Lyle's eyes went wide, and he stammered in outrage.

"You can't mean to suggest that an upstanding young woman like Zelda Pritchard had anything to do with this unseemly business."

"Think about it," Alex said. "Edwards had the insurance pictures the whole time. If he wanted the pattern, he wouldn't have had to steal anything, he could use the pictures to make reproductions of the cards, then put the pictures back where he got them. Then there's you," Alex went on. "If you wanted the cards, you could have simply removed them from the exhibit for cleaning and kept them as long as you wanted."

"What about you?" Lyle demanded, a bit half-heartedly.

"I have the photos," Alex explained. "If I was after the pattern, I wouldn't have bothered stealing the cards from here. It wouldn't be worth the risk."

"You've convinced me," MacReady spoke up. "Who is this Pritchard woman?"

"For the record, I'm sure she's not involved in any of this," Lyle insisted. "I had to make a dozen phone calls trying to find where the cards were stored. Anyone could know about them in time to arrange this theft."

"I still want to speak to the young lady," MacReady said. "If she has an alibi, I can rule her out."

Lyle hemmed and hawed for a bit longer but eventually broke down and told the lieutenant what he wanted to know about Zelda. While he did that, Alex switched his multi-lamp to ghostlight and swept the scene again. When he was finished, it was half past five and he had to hurry if he didn't want to be late to meet Sorsha. Excusing himself, he packed up his kit and headed to the office to call for a cab.

The Senate Office Building was a twenty-minute cab ride from the burgled warehouse, so Alex had time to stew over his cases. The theft of some worthless cards from the national museum seemed so random and silly. It felt like a badly thought-out prank, and yet a man had been killed over it. Alex was convinced that something big was tied up in the case, but he just couldn't imagine what the card's pattern could be that would be worth the effort of stealing them. And yet someone had.

After a quarter-hour reviewing the Smithsonian theft, Alex's thoughts turned to the disappearance of Colton Pierce. He'd worked missing person cases before, and he knew that the more days went by without a ransom demand or some word from the missing person themselves, the more likely it was that they were dead. When he went over the facts, Alex had a sinking feeling in his gut. If someone had grabbed Colton for ransom, then Lucky Tony would have heard something by now.

But he hadn't.

There were only two possible explanations for that. One, whoever had Colton didn't know he was Tony Casetti's nephew. Lucky Tony said that the relationship was a secret after all. Then again, if they didn't know, why grab a college professor with no relatives to pay a ransom? That didn't make sense.

The other option was equally bleak: Colton had been killed. Maybe Connie was right and the professor had been killed by the truck that hit Sal, or maybe he saw Sal get hit and knocked into the river, and Colton had gone in after him and drowned. Whatever the situation, though, it meant that Colton wasn't coming back.

That wasn't good news. Lucky Tony had been easy and affable on the golf course, but the longer Colton's fate remained unresolved, the angrier he got. Alex had no doubt if that trend continued, the mobster would start making real threats. There were flash runes, shield runes, and even escape runes to help Alex, if it came to that, but Lucky Tony wasn't just some street tough. A man like him could hire an army to go after Alex, or put a bomb in a package and have it delivered to his office, or to the brownstone. Mobsters tended not to care very much about collateral damage, and there were plenty of people in Alex's life that could get hurt if he didn't locate Colton Pierce.

And soon.

His thoughts were interrupted as the cab eased over to the curb in front of a nondescript office building. As he paid the cabbie and got out, he saw Detective Norton having a smoke near the building's main door with a newspaper tucked under his arm.

"I was beginning to think you sent me for a buggy ride," he said as Alex approached.

"Sorry I'm late," Alex said, checking his watch. "I had to go out to Maryland and look at a crime scene."

"The museum case?" Norton asked with a sly grin.

Alex opened his mouth and then shut it again.

"How do you know about that?"

Norton chuckled and handed over his newspaper. It had been turned to the society section as Alex unfolded it and he groaned as he read the headline.

New York Society Detective Steps out on Sorceress Girlfriend.

Accompanying the headline was a picture of Alex in the lobby of the Hay-Adams hotel with Zelda Pritchard on his arm. The article below the picture suggested that Alex had come down from his room with Zelda, which was true, but the story intimated that she'd been in his room the previous night.

"I take it your former girlfriend won't be joining us?" Norton asked with a smile in his voice.

As if on cue there was a soft popping sound and Alex felt a wave of magical energy wash over him. Sorsha appeared at the end of the sidewalk, looking a bit green from the teleport.

"Sorry I'm late," she apologized after taking a cleansing breath. "Did I miss anything?"

Norton chuckled and looked at Alex.

"Do you want to tell her?"

"Tell me what?" Sorsha asked.

Alex sighed and handed over the paper. Sorsha scanned the story then gave Alex an exasperated look.

"You were right," she said, much to Alex's surprise. "With you escorting this child all over town, the FBI is convinced that we aren't working together."

Norton's face fell and he snatched back the paper, looking intently at the picture of the young and beautiful Miss Pritchard.

"You let him go around with her?" he asked Sorsha.

"It wasn't my idea," she said, giving Alex a stern look. "But the FBI seems to think I can't solve cases without Alex to hold my hand, so this actually helps."

Norton rolled his eyes.

"My wife wouldn't let me in the same room with that girl," he said.

Alex thought about commenting on that statement, but decided against it.

"If we're done with the news," he said instead, "I suggest we go find Duke Harris. He'll give us access to the legislation Senator Young was working on."

As it turned out, they didn't have to look far. No sooner had Alex and his companions entered the building lobby than a young man with broad shoulders and a solid build stood up from the waiting area.

"Is one of you Alex Lockerby?" he asked.

When Alex identified himself, Duke led them to the stairwell and up to the second floor.

"Senator Young shares an office with Senator Colins from Wisconsin," Duke said as he unlocked the door. "So don't touch anything. I've got the files you wanted set out on a work table."

The door opened on a rather plain room with two desks, one on either side. Two doors led out of the room, one behind each desk. The desk on the right had a placard that read *Duke Harris*, so Alex assumed Senator Young's office was through the door behind it. In the center of the room, a foldaway table had been set up with three chairs around it. On top of the table were a half-dozen stacks of paperwork, each well over six inches high.

"This is it?" Alex asked incredulously. "All this?"

"No," Duke said. "That's just the stuff for this week and next. Tiff... uh, Mrs. Young said that's what you wanted to see."

"How do Senators keep all that stuff straight?" Detective Norton asked.

Duke just shrugged at that.

"Who says they do? Now I have to get out of here in case someone finds you with this stuff." Duke opened the door and stepped out into the hall. "Remember to lock the door when you're through."

With that, he closed the door, and Alex could hear his footsteps receding rapidly down the hall.

"He seems nervous," Sorsha observed.

"I imagine he could get in trouble for letting us in here," Norton said. "He must have liked his boss a lot."

Alex didn't explain that Tiffany Young had basically blackmailed the young man into helping. Given what he knew of the late Senator's wife, Alex could guess what kind of leverage she had over the young, good-looking clerk.

"Well, gentlemen," Sorsha said, staring at the mountain of paper. "I suggest we each take a stack and get reading."

Alex took one of the chairs and sat down, picking up the nearest stack of bound paper. It was at least an inch thick, and Alex wondered how a simple law could occupy so much paper.

"Report of the budget committee on the request for naval vessel maintenance budget increases," Alex read. He'd barely finished the sentence before a wave of fatigue washed over him.

This was going to be a long night.

18

THE ROAD

For the third time in as many minutes, Alex glanced down at his bag. In the old days, he'd kept a small bottle in amongst his inks that contained cheap Scotch. Now, however, he kept good Scotch in his vault, which was usually just a chalk outline away. But he was sitting in Senator Young's outer office with a D.C. detective he barely knew, so Alex wasn't keen on revealing his vault.

After two hours of reading legislation intended for the Senate, however, he definitely needed a drink.

"Let's break for a minute and compare notes," Sorsha said, picking up on Alex's mood. She lowered her head and rubbed her eyes while Detective Norton tossed a fat pack of paper onto the table.

"I could use a belt," he echoed Alex's thoughts.

"An excellent idea, detective," Sorsha said. She reached out and pulled her hand back, holding a dark bottle of liquor. Setting it down, she added three shot glasses, also pulled from thin air.

Alex picked up the bottle and removed the cork. He'd expected Scotch or brandy, but the aroma was unmistakable.

"Rum?" he asked as he began to pour out.

"Don't judge," she said with an enigmatic grin. "It's not the sort of grog you used to swill in the old days. This has class."

Alex and Norton exchanged an amused glance, then picked up their glasses.

"Sláinte," Norton said, holding his up for the others to toast.

The others repeated the Gaelic salute and drank. Sorsha had been right — the rum was complex and smooth. It wouldn't supplant single-malt at the top of Alex's preferred drink list any time soon, but it definitely made the list.

"Again," Sorsha said, setting her glass down.

Alex poured and they drank again.

"Now," Sorsha said. "What have you found?"

Detective Norton chuckled at that, picking up the stack of paper he'd been going through.

"What do you want?" he asked, exasperation in his voice. "I've got a request by the Army to consolidate their research facilities to some new base in the Nevada desert." He dropped a bound stack of paper on the table. "Here's one from the Navy wanting to build a base on the island of Midway, which is somewhere in the middle of the Pacific. The Army Air Corps wants to build a training facility in Colorado. Here's three requests for budget adjustments, and last, but not least," he tossed a loose folder on top of his pile, "a proposal to take Ben Franklin's face off the hundred-dollar bill because he wasn't a President. What have you two got?"

"Three bills adjusting President Roosevelt's various job agencies," Sorsha said, "a proposal for the TVA to build three new dams, and, if you can believe the nerve of it, a congressional pay raise."

Sorsha finished and both she and Norton turned to Alex.

"Mine's not any better," he said, indicating his stack of legislation. "An adjustment to the Anti-Trust act, this year's budget for a federal highway project, two requests to rename post offices, and a resolution condemning Germany's military build-up."

Alex sighed as he dropped the last bound bundle onto the table. All of the documents he looked at had dozens, if not hundreds of fiddly details, just the kind of things a savvy politician could use to horse trade. That said, none of them seemed to be something worth killing over.

"I'm thinking this is hopeless," Detective Norton said. "I just assumed something would jump out at me as I read through this stuff." He shrugged his shoulders. "You know, something that could be taken obvious advantage of, but this...this is all just so..."

"Arcane," Sorsha added, helpfully.

Norton blew out an exasperated breath and nodded.

"I still think the answer is in here, somewhere," Alex said.

"What we need is a way to narrow it down," Detective Norton said, though his expression said he had no clue how to do that.

Sorsha looked pensive, then she poured out another round of the rum.

"The Illinois Governor already appointed Senator Young's replacement, correct?" she asked, looking at Alex.

"Yeah," Alex said, sipping the rum this time. "A guy named William Unger."

"That seems like an awful hurry," Norton observed.

"Exactly what I was thinking," Sorsha said. "Clearly whoever wanted Senator Young out of the way, no matter what their reason, they wanted this Unger fellow here, voting in his stead, immediately."

Alex nodded along. He'd wondered why the hurry to get Unger in Washington, but if Young had really been murdered over legislation, it made sense. Whoever killed Young needed to have Unger in place before whatever vote they were trying to influence happened.

"So all we need to do," he concluded out loud, "is to find out what's being voted on in the next two to three days."

"And why would you need to know that?" a new voice interrupted.

Alex turned and found the door to the hallway open and a man in an expensive suit standing in the frame. He appeared to be in his forties, with an athletic build that had started to slide toward flab. His face was handsome with a square jaw, thick dark hair, and piercing blue eyes.

"Who are you?" Detective Norton asked.

"Since you're in my office, I'd say that's my question to ask," the man said. "I know you're not supposed to be in here, so who are you?"

When Duke had let them in, he'd explained that there were two Senators who used this office. Since William Unger wouldn't arrive until tomorrow, this could only be Senator Aaron Colins of Wisconsin.

"Apologies, Senator," Alex said, rising. "We're looking into the death of your colleague, Senator Young. We're with the police."

"Like hell you are," Colins snapped. "I was briefed just this afternoon on Paul's death. The police say he was killed by his secretary in a fit of jealousy."

Detective Norton stood up and fished out his badge, holding it up for the Senator to see.

"I'm Detective Norton," he said. "This is Miss Kincaid from New York, she's a consultant for the FBI, and this is Mr. Lockerby who's consulting for the D.C.P.D. I understand that the official story is being told as if the case is closed, but a few of us are still investigating other possibilities."

Colins looked around at the three of them. His eyes went wide when he got to Alex, but they quickly darted back to the woman in the middle.

"Kincaid?" he said, as if just registering the name. "As in Sorsha Kincaid, the sorceress?"

Sorsha gave the man a radiant smile and nodded.

"Yes," she said. "I apologize for being in your office at this hour, but my colleagues and I are attempting to determine if anyone had a motive to replace Senator Young with the incoming Senator Unger." She went on to explain about the timing of Unger's appointment and his eminent arrival.

Senator Colins listened but his expression didn't soften noticeably.

"I'm sure if you call the main office number in the morning they can tell you the schedule," he said. "Off the top of my head, there's hearings tomorrow, then Friday we have sub-committee meetings in the morning followed by votes on the TVA bill, the Highway bill, the pay increase, and the Anti-Trust adjustment. Now if you don't mind, kindly get out of my office."

Sorsha's eyes narrowed, and it was clear she wanted to argue, but Alex stood up quickly and put on his hat.

"Of course, Senator," he said, pasting a smile on his face. "Thank you for your help."

Sorsha drained her tumbler of rum, then the glasses and the bottle vanished back where they had come from. Detective Norton put on his hat as Alex offered Sorsha his arm and the three of them left the office.

"I could have bullied him a bit more, you know," Sorsha said under her breath as they walked down the stairs to the street.

"If he makes a case of it, we could all get in trouble," Alex whispered back.

"He's right," Norton confirmed. "Capitol Hill has their own cops, and my badge wouldn't have helped us."

"At least the Senator gave us some useful information before he threw us out," Alex observed.

Sorsha sighed and squeezed Alex's arm affectionately.

"He did narrow our search a bit," she admitted. "All we have to do is dig into the three bills he gave us."

"Four," Norton corrected.

"I doubt the pay increase has anything to do with this," Sorsha said. "I'll take the TVA dam projects."

"I'll do the highway bill," Alex said.

"That just leaves me with the anti-trust changes," Norton said. "I'll get on this first thing in the morning. We should have lunch at noon and coordinate."

Everyone agreed and Norton headed off to where his car was parked. It was still early, so Alex and Sorsha walked a block to where they could get a cab.

"You seemed eager to take that highway bill," Sorsha said as they went.

"And you find that suspicious?" Alex grinned at her.

"Coming from you," she said, giving him a penetrating look. "Excessively."

Alex laughed and patted her hand where she held his arm.

"Did you notice where the highway is being built?"

"You know I didn't see that bill," she said, irritation in her voice. "It was in your stack."

"Part of that highway, where the government is going to pour millions of federal dollars, goes through southern Illinois," Alex said. "Whoever controls that bill holds sway over a lot of money."

Sorsha's face split into a wide grin.

"That sounds like motive," she said. "No doubt some construction company would like all that lovely government money to come to them."

"And Young didn't agree," Alex said.

Sorsha pulled him close, pressing her head against his shoulder.

"I like working with you," she purred. "You're very handsome when you're figuring things out."

Alex looked down, only to find her pale blue eyes shining up at him and a devious grin on the sorceress' lips.

"You're not so bad yourself."

"What say you take me back to my hotel and we have dinner in?"

Alex couldn't help but grin at her. After months of putting off being together, she was upping the ante. He wasn't sure if it was the rum or Sorsha's risqué suggestion, but Alex was starting to feel a little tipsy.

"Your hotel is crawling with Feds," he pointed out. "Feds that can't see us together."

She stepped in front of him, pressing up against his chest.

"Your hotel, then."

Alex felt an actual pain in his side as he looked down into the sorceress' smoldering eyes.

"I'll have to take a rain check," he said, hating the words as he said them.

Sorsha pushed back from him with an incredulous look.

"I need to do a few things on this highway bill tonight," he said, the excuse sounding both hollow and insulting as the words left his mouth. "It's more important to get Director Blake and the FBI off your back," he added. "Show them you're worth keeping."

A war of emotions played across Sorsha's face as she looked up at him. Finally she smiled shyly and stepped back in close.

"Thank you, Alex," she said, quietly.

A few moments later, Alex managed to grab a cab and Alex gave the driver the name of the Fairfax Hotel so he could drop Sorsha off. To his surprise and delight, the sorceress pulled him down and kissed him for the entirety of the trip.

Half an hour later Alex opened the door to his suite in the Hay-Adams hotel. He stopped in the washroom to check that he'd managed to get all of Sorsha's lipstick off his face, then opened the door to his vault. He had a feeling that the key to solving Paul Young's murder was in the details of the highway bill, but he'd need help to find it.

Picking up the phone next to his writing desk, he dialed Sherry's number.

"Boss?" her tired voice came across the line a few moments later.

"How'd you know it was me?" Alex chuckled.

"You're pretty much the only person who has my number," she admitted. "What do you need?"

"Do you have a suitcase?" he asked, remembering the conversation he'd had with Andrew Barton on the airship.

"Yeah," she said, somewhat hesitantly. "Why?"

"Get packed for a couple days, then get over to the office," Alex said. "I'll have train tickets for a pullman car delivered by the time you get there and a car to take you to Grand Central Terminal."

"And where am I going?" she asked, not bothering to argue.

"Springfield, Illinois. I need you to do a record search when you get there, probably pull some business licenses, too. I'll have all of that for you in the morning."

"What do I do when the train gets in?"

"Just get a hotel room somewhere near the city offices," Alex said. "I'll have some cash for your expenses and I'm giving you a key to the back door."

He waited for her to ask questions, but all he could hear over the line was the sound of scribbling as Sherry wrote his instructions down.

"Okay," she said. "I should be over to the office in about half an hour. I'll see you then."

Sherry hung up and Alex pressed down the receiver hook, then let it up again. He waited for the operator, then had her connect him to Grand Central so he could purchase Sherry's train ticket.

A few minutes later, he set down the phone and returned to the hotel room. This time he picked up the phone on the little desk and dialed the number for Tiffany Young.

"Didn't Duke get you into my husband's office?" she asked once Alex identified himself.

"Yes, but Senator Colins came along and threw us out," he explained. "He didn't seem too happy that we were there. Was there any bad blood between him and your husband?"

"No," Tiffany said without hesitation. "They weren't on any of the same committees, so they rarely worked together. As far as I know, he and Paul barely spoke."

Alex brushed the thought aside. Senator Colins' reaction to finding people in his office seemed a bit strange, but the man might just appreciate his privacy.

"Since we got kicked out, we didn't get a chance to finish our investigation," Alex said. "Do you think you could get me a copy of the federal highway bill that's going up for a vote on Friday?"

"Of course," she said, as if it would be the easiest thing in the world.

"Tonight if possible."

Tiffany chuckled softly over the line.

"I could bring it over personally, if you'd like."

"Just the bill will be fine," Alex said, feeling himself actually blush. He was starting to understand why Tiffany and her husband made such a good team; the woman was practically a force of nature.

"All right," she purred at him, being sure to add just a slight note of disappointment to her voice. "I'll make a few calls and have a copy of the bill over to you within the hour."

Alex thanked her and hung up. He still needed to get cash out of his hidden safe for Sherry, along with a sealed envelope and a special cigarette case he'd prepared for just such an occasion. Whistling as he set about his tasks, Alex felt confident that once he knew why Senator Young had been killed, the 'who' would become painfully obvious. Once he knew that, all he had to do was pass the information to Sorsha, let her catch the bad guy, and restore her reputation.

Easy.

19

TRAVEL

The Pullman conductor knocked on Sherry's door sometime after six in the morning. Groggily, she pulled her eyes open and tried to focus on the bedside clock she'd brought with her, but it was still too early.

"Coming in to Springfield," he called. "Ten minutes to Springfield."

"Thank you," Sherry called, forcing herself to throw aside the blanket and expose herself to the frigid air of the train compartment. Shivering as she stood, she moved to the washbasin and ran water to splash on her face.

It was amazing to her how she could go to sleep in New York and wake up several states away. When she was born, the fastest way to travel was on a horse. To make the journey that had happened while she slept would have taken weeks. It was a strange and wonderful world she had awakened into.

She spent a few minutes fixing her face at the mirror as the train swayed gently from side to side. When she finished, she reapplied her lipstick and packed her makeup bag away in her suitcase. Just as she finished, she felt the train lurch slightly as the brakes engaged and it began to slow.

Five minutes later, Sherry stepped down from the train onto the

DAN WILLIS

platform in the capital of Illinois. She just stood for a moment, holding her suitcase, and took it in. Since she'd awakened in New York, she'd never even been off the Island of Manhattan, and now she stood on new ground and she could hardly suppress the grin that spread across her face.

It took Sherry almost an hour to locate a hotel near the state records office. It would have gone faster if she hadn't asked the cabbie to take her all over town so she could see the city. When the bellhop of the Lincoln Hotel finally set her bag on the bed in her room and withdrew it was almost eight o'clock.

"Better get going," she said to the empty room. "The boss is waiting."

She locked the door and set the bolt to make sure she wouldn't be disturbed. The room she'd rented was simple, just a bed, dresser, chair and an end table in a single room with a washroom attached. A large window occupied the outer wall with the curtains open to let in the pale morning light. Since the room faced a wide street, Sherry didn't feel the need to close them for what came next.

When she picked up her tickets at the office the previous evening, Alex had given her cash for the job, and a cigarette case without any cigarettes in it. When she opened the case, it contained several items; an old-fashioned key, a folded piece of fragile flash paper, a book of matches, and a small stick of chalk. As she removed them, she laid each one out in a neat line on the hotel bed.

This was Alex's latest experiment. He called it the back door and he'd given Sherry very specific instructions on how to use it. First she selected the stick of chalk, then moved to a bare patch of wall and carefully drew the outline of a door. She'd seen Alex do this before, and he never seemed to pay too much attention to it, but it was her first time, so she spent a minute or two going over the drawing to make sure there weren't any gaps.

Satisfied, she returned to the bed and selected the next item, the folded rune paper. Alex told her she just needed to stick it to the wall inside the chalk outline, but Sherry couldn't resist opening the paper. The rune inside was much more complex than most of the runes she worked with as Alex's secretary. A little chill of fear swept through her as she remembered the last time she'd seen such complex and elegant designs.

In her former life.

The constructs the Rune Lord had made had this kind of complexity. Unlike the one she held, which was limited to a small sheet of paper, his runes covered walls and even entire buildings.

She shivered again at the comparison. When she'd awakened in this age, her magic had told her that there was a potential Rune Lord close to her. That knowledge had sent her into a fit of apoplexy that had lasted almost a day. Every Rune Lord she'd ever known or heard about had been tyrannical monsters, buoyed by near god-like power. They took what they wanted and crushed all who opposed them. The only thing that gave Sherry hope was the fact that Alex hadn't ascended to his power yet. That gave her the courage to insinuate herself into Alex's life, to become his secretary.

And, if necessary, to kill him before he became a threat.

Fortunately, against any odds she would have given, Alex turned out to be a good man.

Good men go bad, the voice in her head whispered.

"Shut up," she told the voice. She believed in Alex. She had to. The alternative was too horrible to even contemplate.

You know I'm right.

Sherry squeezed her eyes shut tight and clutched the rune paper to her chest. Summoning her magic, she focused on the paper and its connection to the hand that had written it. Her gift wasn't like Alex's or Andrew Barton's, it wasn't hers to command, it came and went as it would. Sometimes she could compel it to reveal things, but it almost never worked.

This time she felt a tingling in her hand, and she saw a strange place. It looked different than New York or Springfield; the roads were narrow, and the buildings seemed older in their design. The image seemed perfectly ordinary, but then it flickered and changed. The streets were broken up and the buildings were shattered with slumping walls and exposed innards. Bodies lay strewn throughout the scene, some burned and black, while others were covered in blood.

As she watched, the scene jumped forward to envelop her and she found herself standing on the broken road. An acrid stench of fire and decay assaulted Sherry and it was all she could do not to gag. She turned, taking in the destruction and the death until she saw what was behind her. A man stood on the road, not ten feet from her.

It was Alex.

"No," she gasped, tears filling her eyes.

Her boss and friend stood wearing a business suit, though it was dirty as if he'd crawled on the ground. A smear of blood covered his right arm, but he didn't seem to notice, or maybe he didn't care.

Sherry avoided Alex's eyes, dreading what she would see in their brown depths. Satisfaction for magic effectively used? Fear from losing control?

She took a breath and looked.

Anger.

White hot, burning anger.

Sherry sobbed and her legs gave out, driving her to her knees. Alex hadn't done this. The scene filled him with rage for whoever had caused it. He hated them in the way only a good man could, with righteous anger in the face of evil.

"Thank you," she gasped as the vision faded.

When Sherry came to herself, she was kneeling on the floor of her hotel room with tears ruining her makeup. She unclenched her hand and smoothed out the wrinkled rune paper.

"See," she said to the voice. "He won't fall."

You thought that about another once. Have you forgotten what he did to you? The things he made you do? The blood that's still on your hands?

"Rage all you want," she sneered, getting to her feet. "I'm not that person anymore, and Alex isn't him."

The voice remained sullenly quiet, and Sherry snorted derisively at its silence. She set the crumpled rune on the bed and went to the bathroom to repair her makeup. It had been a while since she'd heard the voice. Alex's rising skills as a runewright had dredged it up. The voice wasn't part of her, or at least she hoped it wasn't. It always seemed to be an outsider, looking in and observing her life but not able to see inside her heart. Somehow it was related to her gift, but how exactly remained a mystery.

Satisfied that all traces of her tears were gone, Sherry returned to the room and picked up the rune. Without ceremony, she touched the paper to her tongue as she'd seen Alex do a hundred times, and stuck it to the wall. That done, she picked up the book of matches, tore one out, and lit the rune. The paper vanished in a puff of heat and flame, leaving the rune behind, glowing with silver, purple, and orange lines.

Alex had warned her that the rune might not work. It was something Alex had thought up but hadn't yet tested. Sherry held her breath as she watched the glowing rune pulse with light. After what seemed like half a minute, the rune vanished and a heavy steel door melted out of the wall.

With a wide grin, Sherry picked up the old-fashioned key and inserted it into the keyhole in the center of the door. Everyone knew that only a runewright could open the door to his vault, but Alex had managed to open multiple doors, so hopefully the key would work for Sherry. Alex assured her it would, but since it hadn't been tested, the only way to know for sure was to try.

She took a deep breath and held it, then turned the key. A moment later there was a click, and the door began to open.

Alex sat, dozing in his reading chair in the library area of his vault's great room. He'd been up late going through the copy of the federal highway bill that Tiffany Young had sent him, but he wanted to be up in time to meet Sherry.

Assuming the back door works, he reminded himself.

The rune was much more expensive to make than he'd counted on, requiring three different infused inks that used costly ingredients that were difficult to make. Even then, he only had enough of the ink to make two of the back door runes. That being the case, Alex wanted to wait for the right opportunity to try them out.

He was brought back from the edge of sleep by a deep thrumming sound that seemed to fill his entire vault. A moment later the wall just down from his regular door began to ripple, resolving into the inside of a steel vault door.

Alex swore and jumped to his feet.

"It worked!"

He hurried to the door, looking to see if there was any way to open the door from the inside. In all the times he'd opened a door into his vault, he'd never been on the inside. Unfortunately the back of the door was entirely smooth except for the handle that would allow the door to be closed from the inside.

I'll have to work on that, he thought.

He wanted to grab the door and push, but until Sherry used the key on the other side of the door, nothing he could do would budge it.

"Assuming the key works," he said out loud. He'd gotten the idea from the limelight-induced rune he'd created to get into the vault of the Brothers Boom after their deaths. There wasn't much of that rune he could understand once the limelight had worn off, but he'd figured out enough to make the back door key — a key that, hopefully, could be used by anyone.

Alex didn't realize that he'd been holding his breath, but the moment the door clicked and began to open, he gasped.

"Hi'ya, boss," Sherry said once Alex pushed the door all the way open. She stood in a plain hotel room that was hundreds of miles from the one where Alex had slept. When he had a chance to think about it, Alex was sure it would boggle his mind.

Before he could respond to Sherry, she stepped over the vault threshold and threw her arms around him in a tight hug.

"I saw you ten hours ago," he said with a chuckle. "What's this for?"

"Just for being you," she said. "You're the best."

"It's true," Alex said with an air of magnanimity.

Sherry looked up at him with a look of exasperation and elbowed him in the ribs.

"So it all worked," Alex said as she let him go and stepped back. "Did you have any trouble?"

A shadow of emotion passed quickly over Sherry's face, but she smiled and shook her head.

"It went just like you said."

Alex sighed and felt tension release across his shoulders. Apparently he was more worried about the back door than he'd admitted to himself.

"Do you have the research notes for me?" Sherry prodded when he didn't answer.

"Right," he said, turning back toward his reading chair. He'd left the notepad with the details of the highway bill on it sitting on the little table with the lamp.

Crossing the stone floor, he picked it up and returned.

"Here you go," he said, handing it over. "There are two main things I need you to check. In the bill there are four construction companies suggested to get the work of building the new road."

"Got 'em," Sherry said, running her finger along Alex's notes.

"Then there's two proposed routes that are being debated," he went on. "I need you to find out who owns the land for both of them."

"Okay," Sherry said. "As long as the land office is organized it should only take a few hours, then a few more at the hall of records to get a look at the construction companies' business licenses. I'll check at the local paper to see if there are any scandals involving anyone involved."

"Good," Alex said.

"Did you read my notes on the Unger guy?" Sherry asked.

Alex had to focus on not blushing. He'd asked her to look into the man replacing Senator Young and he'd forgotten all about it.

"You left it on my desk, didn't you?" he said, a bit sheepishly.

Sherry snickered but managed not to laugh out loud.

"Sorry."

"Don't worry about it," she said. "There wasn't that much on him, since up till recently he wasn't involved in politics. He was a state senator for the last two years and a lawyer before that."

"Anything else?"

Sherry shook her head.

"I couldn't find anything on him before his election. Do you want me to go digging in the local papers now that I'm here?"

"Only if you have time," Alex said. "I need the other stuff by tomorrow morning at the latest."

"I should be done by this afternoon," she said. "Can I just come home through the vault?"

Alex nodded.

"Once you shut the door, just leave the key in it," he said. "Since you opened the door the first time, it won't turn or come out for anyone else. When you're done, just open the door again, take the key out, bring your bag inside and just shut the door behind you."

"How do I get out of this vault?" she asked.

Alex hadn't thought about that. His cover doors were magically locked from both sides, after all.

"See that hallway?" he said, pointing to the hall on the right side of the great room. "Down at the end there is the cover door to my apartment in Empire Tower. I'll leave that door open for you, so just close it behind you when you leave."

"Okay, boss," she said, stepping back through the door. "Wish me luck."

Alex did, then reminded her not to take the vault key out of the door as she pushed it shut. Since the door didn't disappear immediately, he knew Sherry had followed his instructions.

With nothing else to do in the vault, Alex used his pocketwatch to open the cover door to his apartment and left it open about an inch. He hated the breach of security, but figured that since his apartment was on a secure floor, it was the least likely to be broken into. He could have sent Sherry to the brownstone, of course, but he hadn't talked with Iggy all week and if his mentor was out for any reason, Sherry would just be trapped there.

Satisfied that his secretary would be able to get home on her own, Alex headed back to his suite in D.C. . It was almost ten in Washington, and Connie would be by any minute so they could continue checking shops.

20

THE ALCHEMIST'S CASE

The temperature in D.C. had dropped precipitously in the last few days. Unlike when Lucky Tony had been playing golf, now it was definitely overcoat weather. Since Washington had been built on a swamp in the crook of a river, the damp, humid wind cut right through Alex's overcoat, forcing him to turn up the collar and button it to the chin.

Normally he would have used one of his climate runes, but with Connie chaperoning him around, he didn't dare. So far only his close friends knew he'd developed a new rune. While that wasn't terribly unusual, he definitely didn't want the word getting out. There were already enough people that suspected he had the Archimedean Monograph, and he didn't want to add fuel to that particular fire.

"What say we find some place to eat after this?" Connie said as they got out of the car in front of Hallman Brother's Haberdashery. It was an upscale shop on the ground floor of a professional building, and the window was full of the usual wares: hats, coats, ties, belts, and so forth.

As they approached, braving the frigid wind, Alex felt that stopping here was a waste of time. All of Colton's other stops had been about his upcoming brewery.

"He probably came here to get a heavier coat to keep out the damn wind," he growled under his steaming breath.

It's not like all the other shops were relevant either, he reminded himself.

So far his investigation had turned up nothing more than an alchemist looking for suppliers of fresh ingredients. No one remembered Colton seeming nervous or out of sorts. No one saw anyone following him. No one had noticed anything suspicious or out of place. He still had three more shops to visit after this one, but he suspected their stories would be the same.

"Yeah," Alex answered Connie's question. "Lunch would be great. Maybe we can find somewhere with a nice hearty soup on."

The mobster nodded with a chuckle as he held the door to the haberdashers open.

"Can I help you gentlemen?" an older man in an immaculate suit said, approaching them even before Connie had the door shut.

Alex pulled out the picture of Colton he'd taken from the missing man's house and handed it over.

"This man came in here last Saturday," he said. "Do you remember him?"

The man in the suit had a long thin face with a pointed nose and a salt and pepper mustache. His eyes roamed over the picture without his lowering his head, then he looked back at Alex.

"Is he in some kind of trouble?" the man said, somewhat defensively.

"That's what we'd like to know," Alex said with his most reassuring smile. "He disappeared shortly after he was here, and his family is very worried."

The man sighed and looked at the picture again.

"I recall him," he admitted. "But I don't remember why he came in."

Alex pulled the shop receipt from his pocket and held it out.

"Maybe this will help."

"Oh, yes," the man said once he'd looked at the slip of paper. "I remember the gentleman, he was here to buy a travel case. Very keen to get one if I remember right."

"A...what?" Connie said.

"A suitcase," the man clarified. "One of our best."

He turned and walked to the back wall, pulling down a large, sturdy-looking suitcase with brass guards on the corners and an ivory inlaid handle.

Well, that explains the thirty-five dollars Colton spent.

"He bought one of these?" Connie asked.

"Yes," the salesman said. "As I said, he was very eager."

"Did he look at other suitcases?" Alex asked.

"Not that I recall. I showed him this one and he bought it right then."

Alex nodded as several facts lined up in his mind.

"Well, thank you very much," Alex said. "You've been a great help."

The salesman said something, but Alex was already on his way back to the car.

"Okay," Connie said once they were both inside. "That didn't seem like anything to me, but it meant something to you."

Alex nodded.

"I think we're going to miss lunch," he said. "It's time to go see your boss."

Twenty minutes later, Connie pulled the car into the driveway of the neat house where Tony Casetti resided. Alex felt a tingling in his hands and squeezed them into fists to force himself to relax.

"Get the boss," Connie said to the goon who opened the door. He led Alex down into the sunken parlor to wait. A moment later the man himself arrived.

"You have something for me?" Lucky Tony asked. He stood in front of the chair where he'd been the last time Alex was here, but he stayed standing.

He was eager to hear news.

That'll change, Alex thought, checking to make sure he had his flash ring on.

"I think I know what happened to Colton," Alex said, standing as well.

"Is he dead?" Tony asked.

"No," Alex said. Tony's face turned into a mask of relief and he took a deep breath.

"Where is he, then?"

Alex hesitated only for a moment, then he pushed forward.

"He's on the run."

Alex expected anger, or an explosion of disbelief, but Tony simply raised his eyebrows.

"Explain," he said.

Taking a breath, Alex launched into the tale of the haberdasher and the suitcase.

"As I've been recently reminded, if you're going to travel, you need a suitcase, and according to the salesman, Colton bought the first one put in front of him. That sounds like a man in a hurry. Add to that the cash he had from his bookie and the three hundred he took out of the bank, and he's got everything he needs to get out of town."

Tony's face was a solid mask as he listened to Alex, giving no sign what he thought of the story.

"So why is Colton running?" he said after a long pause.

Alex was ready for that question.

"Did he bring the Euphorian formula to you, or did you approach him looking for help?"

Tony chuckled, shaking his head.

"This guy's too much," he said to Connie and the other gangster in the room. "He thinks Colton is running from me."

Connie and the man who had answered the door both laughed as Tony turned back to Alex.

"I'm not sure if you're a fool or not," he said, "asking me a question like that. Colton came to me with the idea. He figured I could use my connections to help him sell his discovery. And, before you ask, he was thrilled when I suggested we go into business together. Does that answer your question?"

Alex nodded.

"Then who, exactly, is my nephew running from?" Tony demanded.

"I don't know," Alex said. "Everything I've got is circumstantial. Based on what I know, it looks like Colton left town in a hurry. He also didn't call you to tell you he was leaving, which could mean whatever trouble he's in could be political."

"It might surprise you, Lockerby, but I have plenty of political connections," Tony countered.

"It was just a guess," Alex said. "The point is, if I'm right, Colton will call you sooner or later to tell you what's going on."

"And if you're not right?"

Alex steeled himself.

"Then I suspect Colton is dead."

Tony looked at him, anger ghosting across his face.

"That's it?" he demanded.

"You haven't received a ransom," Alex pointed out. "Neither has the university. You said no one outside this room knows about Euphorian, so that can't explain Colton's disappearance. You checked the hospitals and the morgues before you brought me on. If there's another option, I don't know what it is."

Tony stepped close to Alex for a long moment, then he sighed and turned away.

"Sit down, Alex," he said, crossing to an oak and glass liquor cabinet. "I can't argue with your logic, but I'm not ready to give up on Colton." He poured some red liquid into square tumbles. "I'm not letting you off the hook either," he continued, returning and offering a glass to Alex. "This isn't about a business, this is about family." Tony sat down in the chair opposite. "You understand family, right?"

"I do." Alex nodded.

"Good. I wanted you to understand what this job means to me. You've done what I asked, but Connie tells me you've got other things you're working on. I can't help wondering if you're not spending enough time looking for my nephew."

That last bit was delivered with ease, but the menace beneath it was plainly evident.

"Don't worry about that," Alex said. "It looks like the murder of Senator Young was to get a better vote on one of the bills before the Senate. The D.C. police and the FBI are looking into it, so I won't need to be involved further."

Alex expected Tony to like that, but he scowled.

"Are you telling me that you think someone paid to have a Senator killed, and set someone up to take the fall, just to fix a vote?"

"Looks that way," Alex said.

Tony actually laughed.

"Let me tell you a story, Lockerby," he said as Alex sipped his drink. "A couple of years ago, Congress passed a law that alchemical additives to foodstuffs had to go through an approval process."

Alex wasn't surprised; that would have been right after the attack on New York with the alchemical plague.

"That's the primary reason I'm here in Washington instead of New York," Lucky Tony continued. "I came to help Colton get set up, of course, but the other is to make sure Euphorian gets approved. Just so you understand, I had to bribe three Congressmen and a Senator to get quick approval. That cost a lot less than hiring the kind of hit man who would kill a Senator and frame a patsy."

Alex felt a chill run up his spine. If Tony was right, and there was no reason to believe he wasn't, that meant killing Senator Young wasn't about changing a vote.

"Anyone willing to drop that kind of scratch would just bribe someone else if your Senator wouldn't play ball," Tony finished. "It's cheaper and far less messy."

"Right," Alex said, resisting the urge to sigh. "I'll call the , on the case and tell him he's looking in the wrong place."

"Probably a good idea. And once you're done with that, I want you back looking for my nephew." The mob boss' tone told Alex in no uncertain terms that was not a request. "So what's your next step?"

Alex finished his drink, giving himself time to think. There weren't many clues left in this case, but some things still bothered him.

"The only thing I don't have a good explanation for is Sal's death," Alex said. "Colton was in such a hurry that he had Sal take money out of the account at Capital Bank...and then Sal ends up dead."

"How are you going to figure that out?"

"I'll go back over to the morgue," Alex said. "I don't think the autopsy they did on Sal was very thorough, so maybe I can talk one of the assistants into taking another look. I'll also ask some alchemists I know about the things on Colton's shopping list. Maybe they'll see something I don't."

Tony raised an eyebrow at that.

"I don't want anyone knowing about Euphorian," he said.

"Don't worry," Alex placated him. "I'll split up the list so none of my guys has the whole thing."

Tony didn't answer, just gave Alex a hard look. Unfazed, Alex simply shrugged.

"It's all I've got left to try," he said.

"Fine," the mob boss growled.

Alex finished his drink and stood.

"In that case, I'd better get over to the morgue."

The last time Alex visited the D.C. morgue, he had official sanction to do so. This time no one would vouch for him, so he'd have to play it smart.

"Alex Lockerby here to see Lisa Baker," he told the uniform at the front desk. "She has some autopsy results for me."

The cop snorted, then moved to the other side of the long counter and picked up the phone.

"We should have gone to lunch first," Connie said, leaning close so he wouldn't be overheard. "This is going to ruin my appetite."

"Better ruined than you lose your lunch here," Alex pointed out.

The desk sergeant turned and looked at the two visitors, then went back to talking on the phone.

"What if he doesn't go for this?" Connie asked.

Alex was wondering the same thing, but Lisa seemed interested when he was here before. With any luck, she'd take the excuse to see him again.

"If she doesn't vouch for us," Alex whispered as the cop hung up, "then we get lunch and go looking for someone who will."

"Through there," the cop said, pointing to the double doors that separated the lobby from the morgue proper.

Alex thanked the man and crossed the floor without appearing to hurry.

"Mr. Lockerby," Lisa said as soon as he passed the doors. She was wearing her white coat over a light green dress with her hair done up in a messy bun. "I don't remember doing an autopsy for you, so if you're expecting results, I don't have any."

"Results?" Alex said, looking confused, then he put on a smile and shook his head. "No, no. The Sergeant must have gotten mixed up. I need you to do an autopsy."

"Oh," she said, her face brightening. "That's fine. I just need your JA-207 form and I can get right on it."

"Well, that's the problem," Alex said. "We're here in a…well, let's just call it an unofficial capacity."

Lisa grabbed Alex by the arm and pulled him close.

"I can't just do an autopsy for you," she hissed. "If there isn't official paperwork, I could get fired. I need this job."

"To finish your training and become a doctor," Alex said. "I remember."

"Then you know why I can't help you," she said. "Now get out of here before you get me in trouble."

Alex leaned down to look her in the eyes.

"When I was here the other day, you implied that the coroner here, Dr. Reynolds, was holding you up. Making it impossible for you to finish your training."

"That's my problem," Lisa said, somewhat sullenly.

"Well what if it was a problem I could help you with?"

She looked up at him, her eyelids mere slits, then cocked her head to the side.

"How?"

"First of all, I have connections with the New York Police Department. I could get you a job in a morgue up there."

She considered that for a long moment.

"Sounds like I'd just have the same problem in a different city. A lot of doctors don't like the idea of women joining their ranks."

Alex gave her his most charming smile.

"That's the best part," he said. "My mentor is a retired British doctor. He helps the police from time to time and is well liked. He would review your work and make sure you got your license, presuming your work is 'up to scratch,' as he would say."

Lisa was skeptical, Alex could see it written plainly on her face. At the same time there was a glimmer of hope in her eyes. All he needed to do was fan the flames of that hope.

"I'll tell you what," he said, pulling out his notepad and jotting down the number of the brownstone. "This is the number for Dr. Ignatius Bell; he's the doctor I mentioned. Why don't you go give him a call, tell him what I told you, and see what he says?"

Lisa took the paper, then hesitated.

"I can't do an off-the-books autopsy while Dr. Reynolds is here," she said. "It would have to be this evening, right after five. That's when he leaves. If I can get set up before the night shift comes in, they'll think I'm just staying late to finish up. Who is it that you want autopsied?"

"Sal Gerano."

Linda made a face.

"You already had me look at him," she hissed. "And Dr. Reynolds already autopsied him."

Alex moved next to Lisa and put his arm around her shoulders.

"Yes, but you found a mistake on that autopsy after looking at the cart for five minutes," he said. "Imagine what you could find if you took a better look."

She hesitated, then gave a quick nod.

"Okay, come back at five-ten and I'll have everything ready. Don't talk to the desk sergeant, I'll come out and get you."

"We'll be here," Alex confirmed, then let go of her shoulder and stepped back toward the doors.

"And I'm calling this Dr. Bell," Lisa said after him. "If you're giving me a line, don't come back."

With that, she turned and walked away.

"You're pretty smooth when you want people to see things your way," Connie said with an approving grin.

"That's an important skill for a detective," Alex said.

"You'd make a good con man."

Alex gave Connie a sly grin.

"Who says I'm not one already?"

"Nah," Connie scoffed, "you're too honest. So where to now?"

"Where you wanted to go in the first place," Alex said. "Lunch."

21

THE FORUM

Alex dropped a nickel into the diner's pay phone and waited as it clacked and rolled down through the mechanics of the machine. A moment later an operator's voice came over the wire.

"What number, please?"

"Embassy Hotel four, two-eleven."

There was a click as the operator connected the call, then the buzzing noise that indicated a ringing phone.

"Hello," Sorsha's voice answered after a few rings.

"It's Alex," he said with a sigh.

"I take it your investigations aren't going well," she said.

"I had a meeting with someone this morning," he began. "Someone who's currently trying to get something through government regulations. He told me that it would be far cheaper to buy a Senator or two than to hire the kind of hit man that could make murder look like an accident."

There was a pause on the phone while the sorceress processed that information.

"How would this person know about that?"

"Trust me," Alex said. "He knows. I think we may be looking for the wrong things."

"If your contact is right, he might have significantly narrowed our search. The only reason to spend the money to murder Senator Young would be if the murderers needed him, and only him, out of the way."

"It would have to be about something only he had control over," Alex said.

"There are ninety-six Senators, Alex. What could Senator Young possibly have exclusive control over?"

"I'll call Mrs. Young; maybe she'll know. In the meantime, we need to keep searching. Can you call Detective Norton and pass this on?"

"He's going to want to know where you got your information," Sorsha said. "I want to know too."

Alex chuckled and shook his head even though Sorsha couldn't see him. There was no chance he would tell his FBI consultant girlfriend that he was working for the likes of Lucky Tony Casetti.

"Sorry, doll," he said. "That's confidential."

"Don't call me doll."

She said it with a growl in her voice, but Alex could tell she was smiling.

He hung up and called Tiffany Young, but got no answer. Scooping his nickel out of the coin return, he dropped it back into the phone and gave the operator the number for Lieutenant MacReady.

"How did it go with Zelda Pritchard?" Alex asked when the police lieutenant came on the line.

"The only way she's our thief is if she's got a twin sister," MacReady said.

"Her alibi's tight?"

"Waterproof."

Alex stifled a curse.

"There's some good news though," MacReady went on. "I looked into little miss debutante, and did you know there have been four robberies of museums and art galleries in cities where she's been staying?"

"That's mighty coincidental," Alex said. "I hate coincidence."

"Me too," MacReady agreed. "I just don't know what to make of it."

Since Alex didn't have anything helpful to add, he bid the lieutenant good afternoon and hung up. He hadn't exactly figured Zelda for the thief, but she might be the spotter for a gang, picking out the targets and casing the buildings ahead of time. Determined to find out, he fished another nickel out of his trouser pocket and dropped it in the coin slot.

"Hello, Alex," Lyle Gundersen greeted him once Alex identified himself. "Have you had any luck with our case?"

Alex explained his fruitless conversation with MacReady.

"I could have told you that Miss Pritchard wasn't involved," Lyle said when Alex finished. "In fact, if I remember correctly, I did tell you. And I wouldn't put too much stock in that bit about museum robberies occurring in cities where Zelda's been. Criminals attempt to rob museums and galleries almost as often as they do banks."

Alex hadn't thought of that, but Lyle was the Smithsonian's Deputy Curator, so he would know about such things. Despite that, Alex wasn't ready to give up yet.

"I think we might still have a chance to catch your thief before he blows town," Alex said.

"You think he hasn't already left?" Lyle wondered. "I mean, he's already got all the cards."

"You know that," Alex said conspiratorially, "and I know that, but our thief doesn't know it. I want you to start calling around to your warehouses just like you did before, and ask them if they have more of the loom cards."

"No one would believe that, Mr. Lockerby. We never split up pieces of an exhibit."

Alex ground his teeth and thought fast.

"What if some of the cards had been damaged?" he asked. "Would you have sent them out to be repaired?"

"That's done sometimes," Lyle admitted after a pause. "But in this case, with so many cards and us only needing a few for the display, that wouldn't have been done."

"Again," Alex said with exaggerated patience, "we are the only ones who know that."

"I see," Lyle said, catching on at last. "You want me to pretend that cards were sent out to be repaired and then not returned to the box with the others."

"You call around, ask people to look for them..."

"And the thief has to stay close until they're found," Lyle finished. "Assuming he finds out."

"He found out last time," Alex pointed out.

"I see your point, but I don't understand how this is going to help you catch the thief?"

Alex had a date with Zelda Pritchard tonight, to an opening at an art gallery. If she was the inside man for a gang of thieves, she'd press Alex for details of these new lost cards.

"For now, it just gives us time," Alex said, not wanting to tip his hand.

There was a long pause on the line while Lyle thought Alex's plan over.

"All right, Mr. Lockerby," he said at last. "I'll do as you ask."

Alex thanked him and hung up. He decided he'd be very glad when his trip to the nation's capital was over. It was early afternoon and he still had to check on Sherry, meet Lisa Baker for Sal's second autopsy, and get back to his hotel in time to take a shower and go to the gallery opening with Zelda. Before he could do any of that, however, he'd need to ditch his mafioso babysitter. It used to be that his life would get in the way of his cases. Now it was his cases getting in the way of his other cases.

"I really need to get Mike trained up so he can start doing more of this," he said to himself, then pushed the glass door to the phone booth open and headed out.

Benjamin Robertson exited the Senate office building and headed along the paved walk to the street. Ben was a young man, in his twenties, with a lean, athletic build, handsome features and dirty blonde hair. For the last three years, he'd served Senator Dixon of Maine as an aide. Dixon was a corrupt, pompous ass, which suited Ben just fine, since it made being the Senator's aide an easy job.

As Ben reached the street, he had the outward appearance of a man without a care in the world, even stopping to light a cigarette before flagging down a taxi. In reality, it was all he could do to keep his hands from shaking as he took a drag.

"You know the Forum?" he asked the cabbie once the Taxi pulled up.

"Sure," the man said in an easy drawl. "The fancy club over in Georgetown."

"That's the one," Ben said as he slid into the back seat.

Fifteen minutes later, the cabbie let Ben off in front of a simple brick building in the middle of a long row of businesses. The only thing that set it apart was a brass plaque at the top of the stoop with an engraving that read, *The Forum*.

Known as one of the most luxurious and exclusive private clubs in the city, The Forum had been around almost as long as the capital itself. Only the most elite of Washington's power brokers were granted membership.

Well, them and Ben.

Digging into his pocket, Ben produced a heavy medallion made of brass. It had a book on one side with an eagle on the reverse and he handed it to the man at the door. A few moments later, the man handed the token back and pulled the door open.

"Enjoy your time with us," he intoned.

Usually Ben loved to hear those words. Words that powerful men all over the city lusted to hear, but most never would. Today though, his mind was preoccupied with the news he bore.

The lobby of the Forum was sumptuous and elegant, done in dark woods and brass with Persian carpets on the floor. A stair ran up on the right side, leading to the upper floors, with a coat check to the left. Ben handed over his overcoat and headed through the central doors to the lounge.

Normally, this was where business took place. The Lounge at the Forum had been the scene of many a brokered deal or political maneuver. There were leather couches and overstuffed chairs scattered about, with bookshelves along the walls and a great hearth at the back. It still being early, only a few of the club's members were present, reading the paper or engaging each other in a game of chess.

Ben passed through without giving the room or its occupants any notice. At the end of a small hallway on the left side of the chamber, there was a small room with writing desks, stationery, and a few telephones. A full-length mirror hung on the wall, surrounded by a carved wooden frame, inviting members to check their appearance before reentering the lounge. It was the mirror that Ben sought so earnestly.

When he reached it, he took a small book from his jacket pocket and tore out a page with a simple rune on it. After taking a moment to fold it, Ben tucked it between the mirror and the carved frame, then touched it with his cigarette. The pass rune blazed to life in a burst of gold and green, then the mirror wavered, like rippling water, and disappeared.

In the space the mirror used to occupy was an opening that led to a stone hallway. Ben knew it was a vault, an extra-dimensional space created by a powerful runewright. One more powerful than he was, at any rate.

Stepping through the carved frame, Ben moved down the hall to the library. It was the main room of the vault, and spiraled up for several stories. Rows and rows of books on art, history, science, and most importantly, magic occupied the ever-present shelves. Several men were scattered throughout the space, each reading quietly. Again, Ben ignored them. He climbed the grand staircase up to the second floor and moved to a heavy oak door that had been polished until it shone. Being careful not to touch any part of the gleaming door, Ben lifted the knocker in its center and let it fall.

"Come," a voice said after a moment.

Ben took a moment to make sure his tie was straight and his suit coat was buttoned, then he took hold of the door knob and pushed. Beyond was a cozy reading room, with a hearth at the back and comfortable chairs arranged around a low table in the center. Three men sat in the circle, each with a book in their laps.

"I bring you greetings, masters," Ben said formally.

"Who are you?" the eldest asked. He was a man in his late sixties at least, with gray hair and a gray beard that hung down several inches from his chin. Ben knew him, of course; his name was Rupert Simons, a Master in the Legion.

"Journeyman Robertson," Ben said.

"You work at the Senate office building," Master Torrence said. He was a heavyset man in his forties with bushy black eyebrows and a bald pate.

"That's correct, Master," Ben said.

"Since it is not yet the end of the workday," said Master Morrow, the youngest of the men, "I assume your reason for coming is somewhat urgent. Please have a seat, Journeyman Robertson, and tell us what urgency concerns the Legion."

"Thank you, Master," Ben said, taking the first convenient seat. "I learned today that the D.C. Police are still investigating the death of Senator Young."

Master Torrence scoffed, squeezing his book shut with a bang.

"The Police have no authority," he said. "The case has been handed off to the FBI, and I've been informed by our man inside that they've already closed the books on the Senator."

"I understand that, Master," Ben said, being careful not to sound disrespectful, "but three people went through Senator Young's papers last night after the Senate offices closed. One of them was a D.C. Policeman and, he was overheard saying that he had evidence that Senator Young was murdered."

The three masters exchanged looks, and the room was still for a long moment.

"You said there were three people at the offices last night," Master Morrow said. "Was he the only policeman? Who were the others?"

"I got this information from a source outside the Legion," Ben said. "He said only one was a policeman. As for the others, there was a blonde woman, dressed fancy, and a man in an expensive suit who was some kind of detective."

Master Morrow swore.

"A blonde woman with expensive clothes," he said to the others,

DAN WILLIS

then shook his head. "That has to be the New York sorceress, Sorsha Kincaid."

At that revelation, Master Simons leaned forward in his chair.

"The other man," he asked Ben, "you heard he was a detective."

When Ben nodded, the old man pressed on.

"A private detective?"

"I doubt it, Master," Ben said. "No private detective could afford an expensive suit."

Simons scoffed.

"This one can," he growled.

"Something wrong, Rupert?" Master Morrow asked.

"Yes," Simons said, setting his book aside. "You remember that operation in New York last year, with the election?"

Morrow nodded.

"That's where Master Jones failed to deliver on his promises."

"I knew Malcom longer than you," Simons said, wagging his finger in Marrow's face. "He didn't botch that job, a private detective named Alexander Lockerby figured it out and threw a monkey wrench into the whole business."

"How could a lowly PI figure out about the mind runes?" Master Torrence asked, disbelief plain in his voice.

"Lockerby is a runewright," Simons said. "Claims to have a powerful finding rune."

"That would make sense," Morrow said. "It's the perfect rune for a detective."

"He must have more than just one powerful rune," Simons said. "He didn't just figure out what Malcom was up to, he figured out a way to stop it."

Morrow and Torrence exchanged questioning glances while Ben observed quietly. He didn't know who Alexander Lockerby was, but the fact that three Legion Masters seemed to regard him as a danger gave him the shivers.

"We should relieve this Lockerby character of his lore book," Morrow observed.

Simons shook his head.

"We considered it," he said, "but shortly after Malcom's death,

Lockerby started working directly with Andrew Barton, even has an apartment in Barton's fancy lighting rod."

"Empire Tower has heavy security," Torrence said with a nod.

"On top of all that," Simons continued, "Lockerby is known to have a vault. If his lore book is in there, we'll never get it."

The three of them sat for a moment, each seemingly lost in their own thoughts.

"Malcom Jones died in police custody if I remember correctly," Master Torrence said, folding his arms over his prodigious gut.

"Lockerby works with the police," Simons said with a shrug. "No doubt he tipped them off."

"How did he get the police to believe that Malcom was using mind runes?" Morrow pressed. "It's not like he could show them any evidence."

"The sorceress," Simons said. "Lockerby convinced her, and she got the cops on board. And it might interest you to know that at the time Malcom died, he was being questioned by Sorsha Kincaid herself."

"You think she killed him?" Torrence asked with a raised eyebrow.

"It doesn't matter," Simons answered. "Sorcerers are a dangerous lot, and the fact that she's here is trouble."

"It isn't very likely that she'll be able to figure out our plans," Morrow said.

"They were reading Senator Young's bills," Torrence said. "That fact alone says that they're on the right track."

"True," Morrow admitted. "But have you ever read legislation? Most of it is written in legalese, and it's practically unintelligible. The odds of her or the detective discovering anything they could trace back to us are remote."

"Remote or not," Simons barked, "I have no intention of ending up like Malcom. I say we make sure Mr. Lockerby doesn't figure anything out."

The statement hung in the air for a moment, then the other masters nodded.

"What about the sorceress?" Master Torrence asked.

"According to the papers, Lockerby is the brains of their partnership," Simons said. "If we remove him, she'll be no threat."

"What if the papers are wrong?" Torrence added.

"Sorcerers are powerful," Morrow said, "but there are ways to deal with that."

"I don't want to tip our hand," Simons said. "Leave the sorceress alone unless it becomes absolutely necessary. For now, focus on the detective."

"All right," Morrow said, setting his book aside and picking up a pad of paper from the low table. "I'll see that the P.I. is taken care of before he can interfere further."

"I'm worried that too many people believe Senator Young's death wasn't an accident," Torrence said as Master Morrow scribbled. "I think we should move up our timetable."

"That would require overt action on our part," Simons said. "Right now we're just a fairy story, a fantasy made up by people who see conspiracies in every shadow. If we move openly, we confirm our existence. The government will start looking for us."

"Yes," Torrence conceded, "but this is worth the risk and we both know it."

"Fine," Simons said. "Make the arrangements."

Master Morrow finished writing on his pad, then reached into his jacket and pulled out a rune book. Paging through it, he tore a page out, then dropped it on top of his pad. A moment later he lit it with a gold cigarette lighter and the rune paper vanished, leaving an embossed pattern behind on the paper. Ben knew from experience that it was his personal mark, put on the paper to guarantee its authenticity. After a moment, the lines of the rune faded and disappeared. They were still there, just invisible to the naked eye.

"Here, Ben," Master Morrow said, handing the paper over. "Take this down to the coat check and give it to Henry. He'll know what to do with it."

Ben accepted the paper, then stood to leave.

"And Journeymen Robertson," Morrow continued, more formally. "Good work bringing this to our attention."

"Thank you, Masters," Ben said, inclining his head to the three men, then he turned and strode from the room.

22

THE FREEWAY AND THE DEAD

Alex returned to his suite at the Hay-Adams Hotel shortly after four o'clock. He'd spent the bulk of the afternoon visiting the last few shops for which Colton Pierce had receipts, and taking power readings for Andrew. Each was an alchemist or alchemy supply shop full of bottled potions, jars of powdered ingredients, brewing and lab equipment, and pamphlets and periodicals on everything from home remedies to advanced alchemy. What they didn't have, however, was any new information on Colton. All of them remembered him, but none could shed any light on his mysterious disappearance.

At least the power tester showed a strong connection to Empire Tower back in Manhattan, he thought. *Andrew will be happy*.

Shutting the door behind him, Alex tossed his hat on the writing desk. He wanted nothing more than to sit on the excessively comfortable couch by the window and just stare at the scenery. Unfortunately, he had to be at the morgue to meet Lisa Baker in less than an hour. Hopefully her review of the coroner's autopsy would shed some light on the bodyguard's death and, by extension, the disappearance of Colton Pierce.

With a sigh, Alex took out his rune book and removed a vault rune, sticking it inside the chalk outline he'd simply left on the hotel suite wall. He paused to light a cigarette, then used it to ignite the flash paper and reveal his vault. Fishing the key out of his pocket, he slotted it into the hole in the center of the steel door and turned it smartly. There was a twenty-year-old single malt Scotch in his liquor cabinet and a comfortable reading chair in his library where he could sit and wait for Sherry.

He almost sighed with anticipation as he pulled the heavy door open, and the urge made him chuckle. There had been many years when the best Alex could do was dime-store bourbon and the hard chair behind his old desk.

"I must be getting soft," he said.

When he got the door open, however, he found that both his chair and his Scotch were occupied.

"Sherry?" he said as he entered.

His secretary looked up from his reading chair. She had the lamp on the side table on and there was a book in her lap.

"Hi'ya, boss," she said, setting down the tumbler of Scotch from which she'd been drinking. "I didn't intend to make myself at home, but I accidentally closed that door you left open." She looked a bit sheepish and went on. "I went in to make sure I was in the right place, then when I came back for my bag, I shut it behind me without thinking."

Alex chuckled.

"Not to worry," he said. "Tell me what you found and then I'll open the one back to my office. I assume you finished up in Springfield."

Sherry picked up the tumbler then drained it and stood, handing Alex the glass and the book.

"*A Christmas Carol*," Alex read off the spine. "Very seasonal."

"It's one of my favorites," she admitted as she made her way to the drafting table where Alex wrote his runes. She scooped up a folder that had been left on top, and returned while Alex put the book back in its place on the shelf.

"Here you go," she said, handing it over.

Alex took the folder and flipped through it. Inside were several pages of Sherry's neat, tightly packed handwriting.

"Care to summarize?" he said, motioning for her to sit in his chair.

She smiled and sat, crossing her legs while Alex pulled up the padded ottoman he kept by the chair.

"There are two possible routes for the new freeway," she said, taking the folder back from Alex. Pulling out two different papers, she passed then over. "This is the northern route, and this is the southern."

Alex looked down the pages. Each of them contained a list of counties where the route would travel, a long list of numbers with names next to them, and some references to newspaper stories with notes.

"So, what am I looking at?" he asked.

"Nothing special," Sherry admitted. "As you can imagine, the local papers were full of stories about each route."

"Is there a favorite?" Alex asked. "Maybe something Senator Young disagreed with?"

Sherry shook her head.

"You'd think so, but no. The stories in the papers were pretty evenly split in their preference."

"Was anyone objecting to the project as a whole?"

"A few, but mostly everyone is excited to have the road."

Alex sighed.

"I guess a major scandal of some kind would make this too easy," he said. "What about the people who own the land?"

Sherry grinned and leaned forward to indicate a name on the paper with the northern route.

"It took a while, but I finally found Harriet Wilson."

Alex waited, but Sherry just sat there with a wide grin on her face, waiting for him to ask.

"And who is Harriet Wilson?"

"She owns a large part of a long valley where the proposed road will be built," Sherry explained. "There's pretty much no way to build the road around her land."

"So if the road goes through the northern route, she's guaranteed to have her land bought out by the government."

"Uh-huh," she said with a nod. "What's better is that right now, most of this land is worthless. It's too steep to make residential buildings cost effective and it's too far off the beaten track for commercial development."

"So Harriet stands to reap a major windfall when the government pays her fair market value for her land."

Sherry nodded and tapped her nose.

"Is she connected to Senator Young somehow?" Alex asked. "Maybe through his wife's side of the family?"

Sherry shook her head, but her smile didn't falter.

"Harriet Wilson is the sister-in-law of a woman named Leslie Marcello."

She paused again, grin never slipping.

"And?" Alex finally answered, giving her an unamused glare.

"Leslie Marcello is the maternal grandmother of one Michael Harris," Sherry finished with an ear-to-ear grin.

Alex cast his mind back over the case but came up short. Was there a Michael Harris associated with the Senator? What about Tiffany? He was sure she'd mentioned someone named Harris.

"Duke," he exclaimed when his mind finally made the connection. "Michael 'Duke' Harris, Senator Young's aide."

"Got it in one, boss," Sherry said. "As far as I can tell, Duke Harris is Harriet Wilson's only living relative. If Senator Young picks the northern route, he stands to inherit about a quarter of a million dollars when Harriet dies. She'll be eighty next April, in case you were wondering."

Alex whistled.

"It sounds like a quarter-million reasons to want the northern route," he said. As the possibilities of Duke's involvement in his boss's death started to play through Alex's mind, he suddenly realized what Sherry had said.

"What did you mean if Senator Young picks the northern route? Isn't that picked by some committee or other?"

Sherry looked at him, confused for a moment.

"I read in one of the papers that the route would be chosen by the state Senators," she explained. "Apparently the other Senator has a brother in the construction business, so he recused himself to avoid charges of nepotism."

"So Senator Young had total control over what route will be chosen," Alex said. "That's the connection."

"I couldn't find any connection to the new guy, though," Sherry said, consulting her notes. "Senator Unger."

"There wouldn't have to be," Alex said. "Duke will just hand him papers that he claims are Senator Young's notes, and Unger will go along. He won't want to make waves on his first day. Great job, Sherry."

She grinned and picked up the empty tumbler from the side table.

"I'll take some more of this as a thank you," she said.

Ten minutes later, Alex made his way back to his hotel suite, having let Sherry out into his office. She'd broken the murder of Senator Young wide open, so he'd sent her home with the rest of his twenty-year-old Scotch. A small price to pay for such excellent legwork.

Checking his watch, he still had a few minutes before he needed to meet Connie and head over to the morgue. He felt better than he had when he'd arrived, despite not getting any real rest, so he decided he'd have a drink and then head down to the lobby. When he exited his vault, however, he realized he was, in fact, late.

"There you are," Connie said. The mobster was sitting on the overstuffed chair next to the desk. "I thought I'd wait here, seeing as you had company."

Alex felt his jaw tighten. His vault was his sanctum, the repository of his secrets. The idea that anything about it might become public knowledge, or worse, come to the attention of Lucky Toni Casetti made him furious.

"How did you get in here?" he asked, mastering his anger.

"Nice to see you, too," Connie chuckled, then he nodded at the open vault door. "Wasn't that your secretary? The one from New York? That's some doorway you've got there."

Damn it.

"Not that it's any of your business," Alex growled. "Let's just say there are perks to working with a sorcerer."

"Barton did that?" Connie said, his eyebrows raising.

"Yes," Alex bluffed. "And he doesn't want people talking about it."

Connie gave Alex a speculative look, but even the right-hand man of a mob boss knew better than to muck about in the affairs of a sorcerer. It wasn't a sure thing that Connie would keep his mouth shut about what he'd seen, but it was all Alex could do.

"You ready to go?" he asked, standing.

Alex turned and shut his vault, then got his hat from the desk.

"Yes."

Alex and Connie waited in the car until the day staff were gone and the desk sergeant had locked the front entrance. They gave it another five minutes, then went around to the back where Alex tapped on the rear door.

"Hurry," Lisa said as she pushed the door open. "Someone will be along to check this door any minute."

She shut the door behind them and led the way along the hall to an operating theater at the end of a short hallway. A body, presumably Sal's, lay on a wheeled gurney in the center of the room under a white sheet.

"I took a look at Mr. Gerano before you got here," she said. "Dr. Reynolds' report documents the injuries pretty conclusively. What is it you want me to look for?"

"Anything that isn't in the report," Alex said.

Lisa gave him a sideways look, then sighed.

"You should settle in," she said, rolling up her sleeves. "This could take some time."

Alex stood where he could watch while Connie sat on a bare metal chair next to an instrument cabinet. Lisa took the sheet away, revealing the dead man. It wasn't a new sight for Alex by any means, but even so, he wasn't really experienced enough to be used to it. He'd seen broken and bloody corpses, but they were somehow better than the naked man on the gurney. Alex could look at the victims at crimes scenes as objects, things that were broken and twisted, devoid of life. With the exception of the long Y-shaped incision across Sal's chest, however, the man could just be sleeping.

It gave him the creeps. One minute you were alive, the next you were dead, but you looked the same.

Lisa pulled a wheeled tray of instruments over next to the gurney, then selected a small knife and turned to the body. With a deftness born of practice, she cut through the catgut Dr. Reynolds had used to sew up the incision.

Alex held on to his stomach as Lisa peeled back the folds of skin, exposing the man's guts. Without any hesitation, she reached in and pulled out the center of the rib cage.

"Breathe, Alex," Lisa said, giving him an amused look. "He's dead; it doesn't hurt."

"Right."

Now that he considered it, Alex could see that the ribs had been cut cleanly by a bone saw. Reynolds would have had to cut them to perform the first autopsy.

"There's a lot of damage in here," Lisa said, as she leaned close to the open cavity. "But it doesn't look like Dr. Reynolds took out the organs."

"Is that unusual?" Alex asked.

Lisa considered her response, then shrugged.

"No. With this much damage, it's safe to assume that the trauma is what killed him."

"What do you think?"

"It doesn't matter what I think," she said with a grin. "You want me to be thorough, so I'll take a closer look."

From there, Alex watched as Lisa removed Sal's major organs, laying each one carefully on a nearby counter. When she was done, she moved her tray to the counter and began examining each of them in turn. More than once Alex had to look away and take a few deep breaths before he could continue. He found the whole thing macabre and fascinating at the same time.

"Well, I know what killed Mr. Gerano," Lisa said at last. "He drowned."

"I thought you said he was hit by a truck," Connie said from his chair.

"And I stand by that," Lisa said. "But that's not what killed him."

"So you were right," Connie said to Alex. "He was hit and fell off a bridge."

"That makes sense," Lisa said. "With these injuries, there's no way Mr. Gerano could swim."

For his part, Alex just nodded, while he stared at the hollowed-out shell of Sal.

"What?" Connie asked, suspicion crawling across his face.

"Lisa," Alex said, turning to her. "Thank you for your help. Give me a few days to arrange things with Dr. Bell and then give him a call."

"We already talked," she admitted. "He's pretty sure he can get me on with one of the hospitals in Manhattan as a resident."

Alex congratulated her, then looked at Connie and nodded toward the door.

"We'll show ourselves out," he said.

Together Alex and Connie headed out into the hall.

"You know something," the mobster said as they walked. It wasn't a question but a statement of fact.

Alex was reminded just how observant Connie was. He worried again what Lucky Tony's man had really seen in his vault.

"Did Colton own a car?"

"What's that got to do with anything?" Connie demanded.

"Did he?"

"Yeah. Why is that important?"

"Because I came down from New York in an airship," Alex said. "The D.C. Aerodrome is just over the river on the Virginia side."

"So?"

"So if Colton took an airship, he probably parked his car at the Aerodrome."

"That doesn't explain why Sal would be walking over the bridge," Connie pointed out.

"Unless Colton ditched Sal," Alex said.

Connie gave Alex a sideways look, and his eyebrows dropped down over his eyes.

"I'm pretty sure I don't like where you're going with this," he growled.

"You're going to like it a lot less," Alex cautioned. "What if Colton was on the run from his uncle?"

"That's ridiculous, and you know that. He came to Tony about his discovery. He wanted to go into business, not the other way around."

"Maybe he got cold feet," Alex said. "Maybe he learned something he didn't know, something that spooked him."

"So you're saying that Colton gave Sal the slip and took an airship out of town?"

"It explains the suitcase and the cash," Alex said.

"And then Sal tracked him to the Aerodrome but got hit crossing the bridge?"

"No," Alex said. "Well, not exactly. Put yourself in Colton's shoes. You want to get away from your rich and powerful uncle. The only way you're going to have a chance is to get a big head start, so what do you do?"

Connie stopped and grabbed Alex's shoulder, spinning him to face to face.

"You think Colton ran Sal down with his car."

"That's exactly what I think," Alex said. "Colton had to get away clean and he couldn't do that if Sal knew when and how he left town. Your boss is a very smart man, so it would be child's play for him to figure it out."

Connie held his gaze for a long moment, looking for any holes in that argument.

"I still don't buy it," he said at last.

"It's just a theory," Alex said. "It fits the facts, but that doesn't make it true. Tomorrow we'll go over to the ticket office and find out what airships departed on the day Colton disappeared. With any luck, we'll be able to learn something new."

"You'd better hope so," Connie growled. "Because I'm not going to be the one to tell the boss your theory."

23

THE OPENING

Alex rode the elevator up to the top floor of the Willard hotel. He was dressed in his black tuxedo and his shoes were polished. As the operator slowed the car, Alex patted his pockets one last time: rune book, cigarettes, lighter, chalk, wallet.

Check.

When he'd first gotten his P.I. license, Iggy had accompanied him on his cases. Back then, Alex would show up at a client's home or to a crime scene having forgotten his rune book or his crime scene kit. Iggy spent weeks drilling him, every time Alex left the brownstone, to check that he was properly equipped. And the routine of patting down his pockets was born. It didn't help with the crime scene kit, but that was why Iggy taught Alex the old safe rune in the first place.

"Top floor, sir," the elevator operator said, pulling the grate back to allow access to the hall. "Room five-oh-two is to the left."

Alex thanked the man as he stepped out. The hallway was sumptuous, with elegant carpeting, crystal light fixtures, and polished wood tables holding paper tissues and touch-tip lighters. Despite the atmosphere of genteel elegance, Alex's eyes darted back and forth quickly, and he even checked behind him. His plan of getting Zelda to out herself during their date now seemed ill thought out. If Zelda were really the front man for the burglars, all they would have to do was grab Alex when he picked her up.

He patted his pockets again, regretting his decision not to bring his knuckle duster. At least he had his flash ring if he needed to make a hasty exit.

His glance darted to the end of the hall where the door to the stairs stood on the left wall. Zelda's door was a good fifty feet away so if he had to use his flash ring, he needed to run. A man running down a hallway would be a sitting duck for anyone not affected by the flash.

Of course if it were me, I'd have someone in the stairwell in case my target ran.

Alex shook his head to clear it, then took a deep breath and rapped on Zelda's door. A moment later it was opened by Zelda herself.

Alex had been ready for a confrontation with her watchdog, Hector, and he had to quickly readjust his thinking. Clad in a low-cut dress made of some shimmering gold fabric, Zelda was a vision. She'd done her makeup conservatively, accenting her youthful features rather than trying to hide them, and her unique perfume was subtle but present. Her butter-blonde hair was in an updo, on top of her head with a small beaded strand hanging down behind her right ear. A pair of intricate gold and emerald earrings dangled from her ears, with a matching pendant that had an emerald the size of Alex's thumb. The design was art deco, all straight lines and angles, and it reminded Alex of the Aztec treasure from the *Almiranta*.

"What do you think?" she said, turning around so he could see.

The dress had long trailing pieces from the sleeves, and they whirled around her like the rings of Saturn. They were the only loose piece of the dress, though. As Zelda spun, every facet of her excellent figure was on full display.

Alex might have accepted this date as a way to publicly separate himself from Sorsha, but Zelda didn't know that, and the girl was playing for keeps.

"You look beautiful," he said, not having to lie even a bit.

"You're not so bad yourself," she said, donning a white fur coat before taking his arm. "I hope you're wearing comfortable shoes," she said as she steered him down the hall toward the elevator. "The new exhibit is quite extensive."

Alex wasn't really a gallery kind of guy, but the company promised to be pleasant and if Zelda was involved with the museum thefts, he'd have plenty of time to ferret it out.

He escorted Zelda down to the lobby, then secured a taxi for their relatively short trip to the Freer Gallery, which was right next door to the Smithsonian's main building.

A man in a silk tuxedo met Zelda at the Gallery door and began showing her and Alex around the exhibit. Most of what was on display were American impressionists, which Zelda found fascinating. Alex thought most of the paintings looked like the artists had washed out of art school and had to find work.

After an hour and a half, Alex and Zelda ended up in a large exhibit room filled with the rumble of conversation. A dozen or so well-dressed men and women were milling about, drinking Champagne that was being passed around by waitresses in surprisingly short skirts. Zelda quickly excused herself and headed over to speak with a group that she seemed to know well. Left to his own devices, Alex grabbed a flute of Champagne from a passing waitress, then headed for a chair that stood along one wall.

As soon as he sat down, however, Alex wondered if he'd made a mistake. The chair was hard and cold, like stone. A quick check revealed it to be made of concrete. He started to rise, but the man in the silk tux who had been his tour guide waved him back down.

"Don't worry," he said with a chuckle. "It's not a piece of art, it's just a chair."

Clearly others had reacted to the strange chair before Alex.

"Who makes a chair out of concrete?" Alex asked, sitting back down.

"Edison," the man replied. "He's convinced that concrete is a viable furniture material. He sent us a dozen of those, so we have them scattered around."

As unconventional as the chair was, it was surprisingly comfortable, so Alex leaned against the back and enjoyed not being on his feet. So far, all Zelda had talked about was the exhibit and which painters she liked, and which she considered frauds. He'd thought she wouldn't be able to resist talking about the museum theft, whether she was actually involved or not.

She'll ask, he told himself, sipping his drink. As he sat, his eyes roamed over the artwork on the walls, wondering what the various artists had been thinking when they created the work.

"Don't tell me you're tired already?" Zelda's voice jarred him back to reality.

His mind was clearly drifting, since he hadn't noticed her approach.

"No," he said, standing quickly. "Just staying out of the way until you need me."

She flashed him a wide smile and took his arm.

"Sorry," she said. "I do have to conduct a bit of business at these affairs. That said, there are some perks to my job."

She led him out of the room and along a short hallway to another space. Unlike the tour, which had only taken them to rooms with paintings, this room held sculpture and what appeared to be Chinese vases.

"This is my favorite piece," Zelda said, stopping in front of a tall, slender vase. The figure of a Chinese dragon circled around the vase, with its head up near the top and its tail at the bottom. The undulating, snake-like body had been painted in a vibrant blue, and the detail was exquisite.

"What do you know?" he said, pointing at the vase. "It actually looks like a dragon."

Zelda laughed and bumped him with her shoulder.

"Not a fan of impressionism, I take it?"

"Not really."

"Well then, what shall we talk about?" she pondered. "How's the case coming?"

Alex felt a rush of excitement as Zelda pulled the conversation around. He sighed and shrugged, keeping his expression neutral.

"Not much to go on, I'm afraid," he said.

She looked a bit disappointed, then she snickered.

• • •

"I had a visit from your friend, Lieutenant MacReady today," she said. She gave Alex a sideways glance, as if she was gauging his reaction.

"What did he want?"

"He seems to think I had something to do with the museum theft," she said, tugging on his arm. "I have to admit, I've never been suspected of a crime before; it was an exhilarating experience."

"He probably just wanted to rule you out," Alex replied. "I doubt he thinks you went crawling over the roof of the Smithsonian."

"I should hope not," she said. "So what have you been doing while the lieutenant is ruling out suspects?"

"I went over the cards with Mr. Gundersen. Unfortunately, he called just about everyone in the museum looking for them, so the thief could have learned about them from anybody."

Zelda tugged on his arm and looked up earnestly at him.

"Does that mean you're giving up?"

She sounded genuinely disappointed.

"I don't know what else I can really do," Alex said. "Unless the thief has already figured out that he's missing a dozen or so cards, he's probably long gone."

"What do you mean, missing cards?" Zelda asked, her eyes sparkling with interest.

It took considerable restraint for Alex not to grin. He'd played along and she'd done exactly what he expected.

Now to bait the hook.

"Gundersen discovered that some of the cards were damaged when the Smithsonian acquired the loom," he said. "They were sent out to be repaired, but they must have been returned to the wrong storage facility. Gundersen is looking for them, but last I heard, he hasn't found them."

A look of confusion crossed Zelda's exquisite features.

"But if the thief doesn't know about them, how does that help?"

"As soon as Gundersen finds them, he'll lock them in the safe in his office," Alex explained. "Then Lieutenant MacReady will have a story appear in the paper saying that the exhibit is reopening with the remaining original cards."

"So you're setting a trap for the thief," Zelda said, her voice breathy with excitement. "He'll see the story and come for the cards, but you'll be waiting for him."

Alex gave her a smile, and nodded.

"That's the plan. The thief might also find out from whoever tipped him off before, but once the cards are located, they'll be well guarded. His only chance will be when they're back on the museum floor."

Zelda leaned close to him, pressing herself against his chest.

"That's brilliant," she said, giving him a smoldering look. "I knew you wouldn't let the me down — or the museum," she added as an afterthought.

She wanted Alex to kiss her. It was written all over her face. He'd expected her to be persuasive, but clearly she had more than one motive in bringing him to this remote gallery. Her body pressed against him, and her more than willing smile made it hard for his brain to come up with an excuse to refuse.

At that moment, the lights went out.

Alex's first thought was that Zelda had arranged it, but her gasp of surprise and sudden death grip on his arm told him otherwise.

"What's going on?" she said, an edge of fear creeping into her voice.

"Just the power," Alex said, fishing his lighter out of his pocket. Thanks to the windowless room, it was pitch black. "I'm sure they'll have it restored in a few minutes."

He squeezed the lighter to life and led the way to the door by the faint glow of the little flame. The hallway beyond was a hole of midnight with a tiny patch of brightness at the far end where it emptied out into a room with windows and the faint glow of moonlight.

"Just take it slow so you don't stumble," he told Zelda and she smiled up at him in relief.

Before they'd gone more than a couple of steps, however, there was the sound of breaking glass from the main gallery, followed by a woman's scream. Gunshots rang out next and the scream was suddenly cut short.

"What was that?" Zelda gasped, clutching Alex's arm in a death grip.

Alex extinguished his lighter and shushed Zelda. It sounded like two people were fighting somewhere in the darkness ahead. Next another shot boomed out of the darkness, followed by a shriek of pain, then silence.

"Alex," Zelda whispered. "What's going on?"

He was about to answer, when he heard the sound of running feet in the hallway. The feet sounded heavy, but there was a clicking noise along with them, as if the runner had studs on his shoes.

Or he's barefoot with long nails.

Alex remembered the attack dog from the museum robbery and his blood went cold.

"Cover your eyes," he hissed, then threw out his left hand and activated his flash ring.

Agonizing light bloomed in the narrow hallway as if someone had just turned on the sun. Even with his head turned, the light hurt Alex's eyes. From the other side of the light, Alex heard a yelp, though it was pitched wrong for a dog.

Too low.

As the light began to die, Alex shook off Zelda's death grip and turned. Every beat cop eventually had to deal with an aggressive dog, and Alex had heard their stories. The best tactic was to shoot, but failing that, a punch to the nose would usually send them running.

Before he could deliver the blow, however, a clawed hand lashed out blindly and Alex felt sharp nails gouge out tracks across his chest. Forcing his eyes open in the fading light of the flash ring, Alex came face to face with a nightmare. The creature was no dog, it was a man — or at least most of man. His face was twisted out of shape with a long snout filled with yellow teeth and his naked upper body was covered with coarse reddish hair.

With only the briefest moment of hesitation, Alex slammed his fist into the man's jaw and his attacker stumbled back, lashing out blindly. One of the clawed hands caught his jacket, tearing a large gash out of the fabric, but missing flesh. The sudden loss of resistance caused the attacker to lose his balance and fall backward onto the tile floor.

Alex grabbed Zelda and pulled her along the hall, back toward the gallery room, igniting his lighter as he went. He didn't know if the attacker was wearing some kind of prosthetic, or if he was some freak of nature, but he needed to put enough distance between them to get inside his vault.

"What happened?" Zelda hissed as her vision started to return. "What was that light?"

"Quiet," Alex hissed, holding his lighter up again. "Get behind that," he said, pointing to one of Edison's concrete chairs in the corner. If worst came to worst, the chair would at least offer some protection.

"Stay here," he whispered as Zelda knelt. He dipped his hand into his pocket for his chalk...but there was nothing there. No chalk and no pocket. The man-dog had torn the pocket right off his tux.

Alex started to swear, but the door to the room was suddenly thrown open with a bang. The attacker's vision wouldn't have returned completely yet, but Alex extinguished his lighter just in case.

Zelda found his arm again and held it in a death grip, pulling Alex down to kneel beside her. He could feel her body convulsing in terror, but she made no sound.

From the door came a snuffling noise, like someone sniffing the air.

"I can smell you," a guttural voice broke through the dark. It was halting and inarticulate, as if the speaker's tongue didn't work quite right. "Tell me where the cards are, and I'll kill you quick."

Alex pulled his hand free from Zelda's grip and took out his rune book. In the dark he couldn't see the pages, but he opened it to the back, then held it flat on the floor with his right hand. Wishing for a slug of whiskey, or better yet his shotgun, Alex took a breath and flicked his lighter to life.

In the faint glow he quickly turned pages until he found the rune he wanted.

"There you are," the halting voice said.

Alex reached up over the top of the cement chair and triggered his flash ring again. The other man growled in pain as the light flared, but Alex paid him no mind. He guessed he had about ten seconds as he tore the rune out of his book with one hand. Licking it, he stuck it to the underside of the cement chair, then held his still burning lighter to the paper.

"Your light won't work this time," the man said. "I'm gonna bite off the woman's fingers until you tell me what I want to know."

The rune on the paper flared to life, a gold and red construct that shimmered and moved as it activated.

"Down," Alex hissed, wrapping his arm over Zelda's head and pressing her to the ground.

"Got you," the voice said from only a few feet away.

Then the world vanished in a flash of light and an ear-shattering wave of sound.

24

ARLO HARPER'S LEGACY

Chunks of the concrete chair rained down on Alex as he tried to shield Zelda with his body. He could feel her convulsing as she screamed in terror, but the only thing that existed in Alex's world was a sound in his ears, like the tone radios made when their stations went off the air.

Opening his eyes, Alex couldn't see anything, but he still had his lighter, so he squeezed the mechanism and it bloomed to life. All that remained of the cement chair were two of the legs, lying a few feet away from where it had been. Alex held the lighter up as he pushed himself to his knees, waving it in an arc, but there was no sign of their attacker.

Getting to his feet, he took a couple of cautious steps toward the door. The only trace of the man-dog was a bit of fur and a smear of blood on the ground. The shrapnel from the chair seemed to have done its job, but Alex was reluctant to take chances. Leaning down, he picked up a piece of the broken concrete about the size of a marble, then he made his way back to the corner where Zelda sat looking around in astonishment.

Her lips moved, and he knew she was speaking, but nothing came through the ringing in his ears. Ignoring her, Alex pressed the bit of crumbling cement to the wall and proceeded to draw a doorway with it. It wasn't as straight or as complete as he could have done with his chalk, but it would do.

Reaching for his rune book, Alex had a moment of panic as he found his pocket empty. Since he was sure Zelda's hearing was just as bad as his, he didn't bother to stifle a curse as he turned back to the remains of the chair. He'd left his book lying on the floor, and now it was under a thick layer of dust and debris. Still, it was only paper and pasteboard, so he picked it up and shook it off.

No harm done.

A moment later, he inserted his antique key into the door and pulled it open, revealing his vault. After Connie had seen it and worse yet, guessed what it was capable of, Alex didn't want anyone else inside ever again, but he grabbed Zelda by the arm and physically hauled her to her feet. The man-thing was gone, but that didn't mean he'd stay gone.

Pulling Zelda after him, Alex entered his vault. He immediately turned and grabbed the heavy cage door that he'd installed on the inside. In the old days it was there to keep people out while making it impossible for anyone to close the vault door and trap him inside. Now that his vault was connected to multiple locations, the second part wasn't really necessary, but Alex hadn't removed the security door. It had too many potential uses.

Shutting the door, Alex slid the heavy steel bolt closed and locked it in place, securing the vault from the outside world. The cage was just an old jail cell door he'd bought at a police auction when one of the local precinct buildings had been renovated. It was made of heavy bands of steel that had been riveted together and Alex knew it would keep out any number of rabid freaks. Notwithstanding that fact, he moved to the other side of the door and opened the cabinet that served as his weapons locker.

Inside was his arsenal: his Colt 1911 pistol with three loaded magazines, a police issue .38 revolver, a Thompson submachine gun with three loaded stick magazines and two loaded drums, and his semi-automatic Browning A5 shotgun. With a sigh of relief, Alex took down the shotgun and pulled back the lever to load a shell into the chamber. Toggling the safety off with his thumb, he stepped back around the door and peered out through the cage. Light from his vault was spilling out, illuminating the room beyond, but there was no sign of life.

"I think it's gone," he yelled over his shoulder. When he got no response, he turned to find Zelda standing behind him, trying to see over his shoulder. She gave him a worried look and he shook his head.

"Gone!" he yelled louder.

She seemed to hear him this time and nodded, then pointed at him and yelled. Alex had heard himself yelling, but Zelda's words were nothing more than faint, incoherent sounds.

"—eeding," she tried again, pointing to his chest.

Alex looked down to see that his shirt was in tatters and two long gashes ran across the front of his chest. The lower half of his shirt was soaked with blood that was beginning to seep down onto his pants.

He'd forgotten the wound the creature had given him, but now that the adrenaline was beginning to wear off, the pain started to break through.

"Ow," he growled as Zelda tried to peel the shirt away to get a better look at his injury.

"This way," he yelled, and headed off to his new infirmary with Zelda in tow.

"This place is amazing," Zelda yelled.

She should see Iggy's vault. Well, actually no, she shouldn't.

Alex stripped off his torn coat and tattered shirt, dropping them in a hamper he'd put in the corner for just that purpose. Normally the kind of damage his tux had been through would be enough to call it ruined, but Alex had access to restoration runes and even major restoration runes if it came to that.

He also had access to wound salve.

Raising his arm to open the potion cabinet sent pain lancing across his chest, so he just pointed.

"Get the jar on the right with the yellow stuff inside," he yelled and immediately winced at how loud it seemed. He could still hear the off-the-air radio tone, but it wasn't as loud as it had been.

Zelda found the jar, a short, round one with a wide opening covered by a screw-on lid, and opened it.

"What is this stuff?" she asked, recoiling at the harsh odor.

Wound salve was an alchemical suspension of several healing liquids. It wasn't as powerful as the potions Iggy had access to, but drinking the wrong one of those could kill you, so Alex went with something a bit more foolproof.

"There's a box in the cabinet with folded papers in it," he said, taking the jar. "Bring me one."

Zelda complied and, moving carefully, Alex reached in his pants pocket for his lighter. Sticking the folded corner of the flash paper into the yellow gel, Alex quickly lit it. The activating rune glowed yellow for a moment, then the glow faded from the rune and transferred itself to the gel.

"What did you do?" Zelda asked.

"Wound salve has to be magically energized before you use it," he explained, slowly dipping two fingers into the glowing liquid. "The upside is you can store what you don't use pretty much forever once the charge wears off."

Alex tried to smear the glowing goo into his wound, but moving his arms was getting more and more painful.

"Give me that," Zelda said, taking the jar from him. Without hesitation, she dipped her hand into it and began smearing the contents on the gashes across his chest.

The salve burned as it covered his ragged flesh, and Alex bit his lip to keep from cursing. Zelda noticed and gave him a patronizing smile.

"Be a good boy and I'll get you an ice cream on the way home," she said.

"You're taking almost being killed rather well," he said.

Her smile slipped at that, and he saw the fear hiding behind her eyes.

"I'm sure I'll be a wreck later," she admitted, "but right now you need my help. And it keeps my mind occupied."

She finished applying the paste, then returned the jar to the medicine cabinet. Alex had her get a roll of gauze next and wrap it around his torso until the wound was covered.

"Is that thing gone?" she asked as Alex led the way back out into the main room, shotgun in hand. As he went across to his library area, Zelda cast a nervous glance at the metal cage door. The lights were back on, but because Alex had opened the door right next to the corner of the room, not much was visible.

"Even if it isn't, it's not getting in here," he said, standing his gun against the little reading table. He went to his liquor cabinet and took out a bottle of brandy; unfortunately he'd given his best bottle of Scotch to Sherry, so this would have to do.

"Have a seat," he said, as he filled up a tumbler. Since there was only one chair in the area, Zelda sat down, wrapping her arms around herself as if she wanted to keep from shaking. "Drink this while I go change clothes," he said, handing her the glass.

Alex moved to the hallway on the left side of his vault and went down to the first door on the right, opposite the opening to his little kitchen. Since he'd changed at the hotel, the suit he'd worn earlier was still laid across his bed, so he stripped out of the bloody tuxedo pants, removed his undershorts, and used a towel to wipe off any remaining blood. Once he was satisfied he was as clean as he could get without a shower, he dressed in one of his remaining suits and headed back out to the main part of the vault.

Zelda still sat in his reading chair, but she'd emptied the brandy in her glass. Alex took it and refilled it before squatting down beside the chair.

"It's going to be okay," he said in a soothing voice.

Zelda took the glass from him and sipped it.

"I know," she said. "I heard someone moving around in the museum, but it just sounded like they were walking around."

"You stay and finish your drink," Alex said, giving her a reassuring pat on the knee. "I'll go see who's at the door."

Zelda took a deep breath, then nodded.

Alex stood, but he wasn't quite as confident as he let on. He walked around to the far side of his reading table and picked up the Browning A5 before heading toward the vault opening and its closed cell door. Before he could reach it, a uniformed policeman stepped up to the bars and peered through. He looked to be in his mid-twenties with broad shoulders, a beak-like nose, and thick, dark hair. When he saw Alex approaching with a shotgun, he let out a curse and jumped away from the door.

"Put down that gun and come out with your hands up," he called. Alex could just see the side of the man's nose as he hid beside the vault opening. It wasn't a particularly good place to seek shelter. In a normal building, Alex could have simply shot him though the wall if he'd wished the man ill. This being his vault, the inside and the outside weren't even connected, so it wouldn't work here, but there was no way for the policeman to know that.

"Identify yourself," Alex called. He was pretty sure the man was legitimately a cop, but after the night he'd had, he wasn't taking chances.

"I'm Officer Henderson of the D.C. Police Department. Now put down that gun and come out."

"You have a lieutenant in your precinct named MacReady?" Alex asked.

"We do," Henderson said. "He's taking statements right now."

"Go get him, and tell him Alex Lockerby is back here with Miss Zelda Pritchard. Got it?"

Henderson didn't answer right away, no doubt weighing his options. Finally he agreed, and Alex could hear him moving away across the gravel-strewn floor. Alex waited until he was sure the man was gone, then headed back to Zelda.

"The police are here," he said. "I asked them to go get Lieutenant MacReady. Do you think you're up to making a statement?"

"I'm all right, Alex," she said, smiling up at him. "I'm shaken, but I'll get over it."

Alex had to admit, she was tougher than he had given her credit for.

"All right," he said, taking the empty glass from her and setting it on the side table. He offered her his arm, and she took it before standing. Alex flicked the safety switch on his shotgun and left it standing against the chair.

"Lockerby," MacReady's voice came through the bars a moment

before the man himself appeared. "Where are..." The lieutenant peered through the bars and whistled. "What's all this?"

"My vault," Alex explained, as he released the heavy bar holding the cell door in place.

"It must be nice to be the Duke of Ellington," MacReady said. "Officer Henderson said you had a shotgun."

Alex pulled the heavy cell door open and locked it in place against the inside wall, then he pointed to where his gun stood by the chair. MacReady leaned in, still looking around, then nodded.

"You want to step out and explain what, exactly, happened here?" he said, moving back from the door. "I've got another dead museum guard out by the front door, looks like a dog attack like before, only this time there's two swells with him."

"Some of the patrons are dead?" Zelda gasped. "Who?"

"I don't know yet," the lieutenant admitted. "People were just starting to give statements when Henderson showed up and called me away."

Alex let Zelda go out before him, then he followed. He wanted to close his vault before anyone got too nosy about it, but as he reached for the door, Zelda gasped, and a soft cry of dismay escaped her lips.

"What it is?" both he and MacReady said at the same time.

She rushed to the pedestal where the antique vase had stood. The explosion that destroyed the cement chair had shattered it. All that remained was the round base still sitting atop its perch.

Zelda leaned down and picked up several pieces, setting them gingerly next to the forlorn base. Alex saw a tear run down her cheek, and it felt like a knife twisting in his guts. He'd thought Zelda might have been involved with the robberies, but the woman before him had far too much respect for museums to ever rob one. The way she handled the fragments of porcelain reminded Alex of the way Father Harry handled the communion wafers. To her, they were sacred.

"What happened in here, Lockerby?" MacReady said, taking in the destruction. "Do you have dynamite in your vault?"

He shook his head, still watching Zelda pick up the pieces of the vase.

"Back in March a couple of brothers started knocking over banks in Manhattan by blowing holes in their walls," he explained.

MacReady nodded.

"The Brothers Boom," he said. "I heard about that case."

"Well one of the brothers, Arlo Harper, was a runewright, and he figured out how to make a blasting rune. The police called on me to consult, and I may have happened upon one of Arlo's unexploded runes."

The lieutenant gave him an alarmed look.

"And you've just been carrying it around? Isn't that dangerous?"

"No," Alex said with a shake of his head. "Runes aren't like sweaty dynamite, they only work when I tell them to."

To illustrate his point, Alex pulled out his rune book and paged to the back, just past where he'd recreated Arlo Harper's blasting rune. Finding what he sought, he tore out a page with an intricate rune on it, done in five separate inks. He quickly folded it and stepped over to where Zelda was crouched, looking for more fragments of the ruined vase.

"Let me show you something," he said, offering her his hand. She took it and stood, leaning against him for support. Alex set the folded paper on top of the pile of broken porcelain, then lit it. The paper vanished in a puff of fire, leaving behind a rune that always reminded Alex of a stained glass window. It pulsed with colors, and Alex could feel the magic rolling off it in waves.

Putting his arm around Zelda, he leaned close and whispered.

"Watch."

The rune pulsed, faster and faster, until finally it gave off a burst of light and broke apart into glittering crimson sparks that settled down among the fragments. Zelda gasped as first one, then another of the fragments jumped up and attached itself to the base. One by one more of them appeared, some leaping up from the floor to snap back into place. The entire process only took half a minute, but by the end, the vase stood fully restored, just as it had been when Alex first saw it. Major restoration runes were costly to make, but they certainly were impressive to watch.

He looked down where Zelda was still leaning against him. The pressure of her cheek on his chest made his wound ache, but he'd endured worse than that. He thought she'd smile or clap, but instead an unbroken stream of tears rolled down her face.

"That was beautiful," she managed after a moment. "Thank you, Alex."

She sagged against him, the emotion of her ordeal finally overtaking her.

"Take Miss Pritchard out front and find her somewhere comfortable to sit," MacReady said to Officer Henderson.

"This way, Ma'am," Henderson said, taking her hand.

"Go with him," Alex said when she hesitated. "I'll be along in a minute."

Lieutenant MacReady waited until Zelda and the officer were gone before turning to Alex.

"Okay," he said. "I know what the people up front said about what happened. Now I want to hear your version."

"Did they say that a wolf man jumped through a window and attacked a bunch of people until an explosion drove it off?"

"You can't be serious," MacReady said with an unamused expression.

"Look," Alex said. "You know and I know there's no such thing as a wolf man, but whoever this freak was, he had claws, fangs, and a muzzle."

"If I hadn't just seen you turn a pile of junk into a priceless vase, I'd haul you in for impeding an official investigation," MacReady said. "You think a sorcerer did something to him? Twisted him up like that?"

Alex could only shrug.

"It's possible," he admitted, "but why? I mean, if a sorcerer wanted the cards from the display all he'd have to do is ask. I'm sure the museum would bend over backwards to help."

"So is this another runewright who's figured something out?" the lieutenant pressed. "Like that Andrew Potter?"

"Arlo Harper," Alex corrected, "and no, I've never heard of any rune magic with enough power to change a man into a half-wolf."

That wasn't strictly true, of course. Alex thought that Moriarty or one of his Immortals might be able to do something like that, but they were powerful enough to steal the cards themselves and leave no trace. There was no way they'd need help.

"So where does that leave us?" MacReady asked, irritation creeping into his voice.

"I've got one more card to play," Alex said. "And with luck, this time when our wolf-boy shows up, we'll be ready for him."

25

BEARER FACTS

After waiting for Zelda to give her statement to Lieutenant MacReady, Alex took her to the hospital where their top doctor checked her over. Alex had managed to keep her out of the path of the man-wolf, but she still had a dozen or so small abrasions from sharp bits of concrete from the exploded chair. By the time he returned her to her apartment, it was well after ten o'clock.

Her valet, Hector, was livid.

He yelled at Alex for putting Zelda in danger for a solid ten minutes while her maid whisked Zelda away to her room. By the time Alex extracted himself from the situation, the little man's red face matched his hair. Alex was surprised that he got away without Hector taking a poke at him. Whatever Zelda's father was paying the man to keep an eye on his daughter, he was getting his money's worth.

All of this ran through Alex's mind as he trudged, wearily, off the elevator at the Hay-Adams hotel and made his way along the opulent hall to his room. The adrenaline from the fight and the subsequent pain-killing effect of the wound salve had worn off, and his chest throbbed with every step. His knuckles were bruised from where he'd punched his attacker, and his ears were still ringing a bit from the explosion.

"Just another day at the office," he mumbled as he fished the hotel key out of his trouser pocket.

When he pushed the door open, he found the light in the suite's main room on, and his nose was assaulted by the smell of expensive tobacco.

"Sorceress?" he said, looking around.

"Well here you are," Sorsha said, standing up from the couch that looked out the long bank of windows. She wore dark, loose-fitting pants with a light blue shirt and a mock suit vest cut that accentuated her slim figure. It was the kind of thing she wore for her work with the FBI, professional but still feminine, much like the woman herself.

"You waited up for me," Alex teased. "I'm touched."

Sorsha gave him a hard look as her brows dropped low over her eyes.

"You're home awfully late for an event that ended almost two hours ago," she said. Before he could respond, she seemed to notice something, and she rolled her eyes. "Is that what you wore?" she demanded. "To a gallery opening in the Nation's Capital?"

"Of course not," Alex protested without thinking. "I wore my tuxedo."

Sorsha's lowered brows twisted into a scowl before Alex even realized what he'd said, and the temperature in the room dropped by ten degrees.

"Easy," he said, holding up his hands. "What's left of it is in my vault covered in blood."

Sorsha had taken a deep breath, presumably to yell at him, but she stopped with her expression wavering between concern and disbelief.

"Show me," she growled at last.

Alex took out his rune book and proceeded to open his vault. Without any ceremony, he led Sorsha to his infirmary where his shredded shirt and tuxedo jacket were still in the hamper. Alex wasn't surprised when the sorceress simply reached in and pulled out the bloody garments, laying them on his examination table. After tracing her finger along the gashes, she looked up at him, and her expression softened somewhat.

"You go to the most interesting parties," she said with the hint of a smile caressing the corner of her mouth. The smile was instantly replaced by the scowl as she added, "Without me."

He gave her a sheepish grin and an apologetic shrug.

"Take off your shirt," she said, the scowl never wavering.

Alex did as he was told, giving Sorsha the abbreviated version of his evening encounter. For her part, the sorceress carefully unwound Zelda's work and checked his wounds. Healing ability was rare among sorcerers, but Sorsha had famously helped out recovering soldiers at Manhattan hospitals during the big war, so she knew her way around injuries.

"You need to go to the hospital," she said. Two of the man-wolf's claws had managed to penetrate his coat and shirt and tear open his flesh. Sorsha examined the upper gash, probing the edge of the wound with her finger.

"I'll be fine," he said dismissively.

She gave him a stern look.

"First of all," she said in her take-charge voice, "these wounds are too deep for wound paste, they need to be sutured. And secondly, if it was some kind of animal that did this, there's no telling what kind of disease it might be carrying."

"Normally you'd be right," Alex said, handing her some fresh gauze to wrap up the wound again. "In this case, however, that's Iggy's special wound paste. Guaranteed to kill off Bubonic Plague, and as long as it's not bleeding faster than the paste can seal it, I'll be fine."

She gave him a penetrating look, then sighed.

"All right," she conceded. "Whatever attacked you wasn't any movie monster, so what was it?"

"A wolf-man," he said, with no trace of a smile.

"You're not funny," she said, just shy of exasperation.

"Oh, come on," he said, buttoning his shirt back up. "I'm a little funny."

That actually got a smile out of the sorceress, and she shook her head.

"A very little. Now what are you thinking?"

"Alchemy," he said. "I've seen people completely transformed with the right elixir."

"You mean Dr. Kellin," Sorsha said. "And...and Jessica. But weren't they fundamentally the same person?"

"Yes," he admitted, "but Jessica was physically taller than Andrea, and Lilith was shorter than both of them. If someone has figured out a formula like Andrea's, they're smart enough to figure out how to blend a man with a wolf."

Sorsha shivered at his words.

"Well, that's not terrifying," she said, sarcasm plain in her voice. "You think someone got ahold of Dr. Kellin's formula?"

Alex shook his head.

"I have the only copy of that formula, here in my vault," he said. "Linda knows it exists, but she doesn't know how her mother made it. She might be able to figure it out in a couple of decades, but she's not up to it yet."

Moving carefully, he slipped his coat back on. The wound paste was doing its job, but it wasn't like an expensive healing potion, so it would take a week or two to work.

"No," he said, leading Sorsha back out into the vault's great room. "I think this is someone else."

"I thought you said the..." she made a face, "the wolf-man demanded you turn over the remaining cards? The ones from the museum robbery."

Alex nodded as he headed for the open door back to the hotel suite.

"Grab some of your good Scotch," Sorsha said. "I think this is going to be a conversation where it's required."

Alex stifled a groan, but turned toward the liquor cabinet in his library area. He picked up the bottle of brandy he'd left out on his reading table.

"To answer your question," he said, "I don't know how this alchemist is connected to the museum robbery, but he clearly is."

"You sound like you have someone in mind," Sorsha said, as Alex pulled a fresh glass out of the cabinet and filled it.

Noticing that he didn't need a new glass for himself, Sorsha picked up the one remaining on the sideboard and examined the lipstick on the rim.

"Miss Pritchard's color." It wasn't a question, just a statement of fact.

"We hid in here until the police arrived," Alex said, passing her a glass of brandy.

The sorceress looked like she wanted to discuss that statement, but her curiosity about the attack won the fight for her attention.

"So who is this alchemist that you think is involved?" she wondered, sipping her drink as she led the way back toward the open door and Alex's hotel suite.

Alex drank half his brandy, then made his way to the comfy chair he'd used the last time he'd had Sorsha over for drinks. As soon as she was settled, he launched into the story of Lucky Tony Casetti and his missing alchemist nephew.

When he finished, Sorsha was stone-faced.

"Is this mobster going to be a problem?" she asked in a voice that clearly indicated that she would handle Lucky Tony herself if the answer was yes.

"I can take care of him," Alex said. "But I'm starting to think there's more going on with his nephew than he knows."

"People like him don't like being told they're wrong, Alex. Have you replaced your escape rune?"

"No," he admitted. "It takes weeks to make one, and I just haven't had the time."

"So you think this Colton can make some kind of transformation potion," Sorsha said. "If he can do that, why does he want pattern cards from an antique loom?"

Alex had no answer for that, so he just shrugged.

"I admit that part doesn't fit," he said. "But it's awful convenient, him being a highly skilled alchemist and missing right when someone starts making alchemical monsters. I'll have to ask him when I find him."

"What if he is being forced to do this, just like Charles Grier?"

Alex actually hadn't thought of that. If someone grabbed Colton Pierce because of his alchemical prowess, that would explain a lot. Of course they would still need the recipe for a transformation potion;

there was no way Colton had cooked one up out of thin air in just a few days.

Still, it was the best lead he had on where the wolf man potion had come from.

Sorsha reached out and took his now-empty glass, setting it aside on the little end table in the corner between couch and chair. When she was done, she grabbed his hand and held it.

"Be careful," she said, squeezing gently.

"Don't worry," Alex said, putting on a confident grin. "Once I figure out where Colton Pierce is, I'll be done with Lucky Tony for good."

She didn't respond, and the silence stretched out between them.

"I heard back from Sherry," he said at last.

Sorsha sat up straighter, releasing his hand.

"Did she find out anything about that highway bill, something we can use, I mean," she amended.

Alex chuckled, then revealed what Sherry had learned about Senator Young's assistant, Duke, and the quarter of a million dollars he stood to make on the deal.

"So he has motive," Sorsha said, a predatory smile spreading across her perfect face.

"Two hundred and fifty thousand of them," Alex concurred.

"You need to thank Sherry for me when she gets back from Illinois."

"She's already back," Alex said, refilling his brandy. "I used the vault to get her home."

When Sorsha didn't respond, Alex stopped pouring and looked up. She sat, regarding him with a quizzical expression.

"You were here all day yesterday," she said. "How did your secretary, who isn't a runewright, open a door into your vault from Illinois?"

"Oops," Alex said, trying and failing to avoid blushing.

"Are you keeping secrets from me again?" she demanded, though her voice was playful.

"Of course not," Alex said with exaggerated sincerity. "I figured this out a few weeks ago, but I didn't know it would work until Sherry tested it by managing to open the back door. Even Iggy doesn't know it worked; you're the first person I've told."

She gave him a dubious look, and rolled her eyes as he sat back down.

"By accident," she said.

"I promise I'm not trying to hide anything from you," he said, taking her hand this time. "But I'm not going to tell you about every wild idea I have, 'cause that'd take all day. I'll just bring you in the loop once I know they work."

She held his gaze for a moment, then smiled.

"You'd better," she said. She withdrew her hand and drained the last bit of brandy from her cup. "Now that we've got that worked out," she said, setting the glass aside, "where does young Duke Harris live?"

Having only met the Senator's aide in professional settings, Alex didn't know.

"I'm sure Tiffany Young knows," Alex said. "We can call her in the morning. Of course, by then Duke will be at work, so we might as well confront him there."

Sorsha's expression soured.

"I want to roust him out of bed and hit him with this tonight," she said, fervor creeping into her voice. She held that thought for a moment, then sighed and slumped back into the couch. "But I guess we'll have to wait."

"Well, I'm going to bed," Alex said, setting his glass aside and standing. He gave Sorsha a sly grin and she raised an eyebrow in return. "You're welcome to join me, of course," he said. "Purely professionally, of course. I won't make any advances."

Sorsha tried to suppress a snicker and failed. She stood slowly, sensually, like a snake uncoiling, moving toward him until she stood only a few inches away. A half smile played across her lips, then she rose up on her tiptoes and kissed Alex lightly on the lips.

"Thank you for the offer," she said, her smile blossoming into a wide grin. "But if you're not going to make any indecent advances, it doesn't sound like it'd be much fun."

Alex opened his mouth to reply, but Sorsha just winked at him and disappeared.

He stood there for a long minute, looking at the space the

sorceress had occupied before she teleported away, then he chuckled and shrugged.

"Me and my big mouth."

Early the following morning, Alex collected Sorsha at her hotel. She answered her door in a dark blue pencil skirt, a white shirt, and suspenders. Being nicknamed the Ice Queen for her business enchanting refrigeration disks, she played into the moniker by not wearing a coat despite the winter chill in the air. Her makeup was more subtle than it had been the night before, attempting to de-emphasize her femininity.

As if she could do that.

Alex pointedly ignored Sorsha's inquiry about how he slept, and they headed to D.C. P.D. Command Office number two to pick up Detective Norton. The , was in a meeting when they arrived, so it was after ten when they finally managed to explain what Sherry had uncovered. A few minutes after that, they piled into Norton's car and headed to the Senate office building.

"Nice to see you all again," Duke Harris said when they walked into Senator Young's office. "Have you made any progress on the case?"

"In fact, we have," Norton said, giving the Senatorial aide a smile that was all teeth. "We discovered that the Senate has a highway bill before it this week."

"The Hayden-Cartwright Federal Highway Act," Alex supplied.

Norton hesitated at the interruption, but rallied quickly.

"It turns out that Senator Young had sole discretion over which of the two proposed routes is actually going to be used when the highway goes through Illinois."

"That's right," Duke confirmed. "Senator Mills had to recuse himself because his brother owns a construction company bidding on the work."

"What is a Senator supposed to do when his aide stands to inherit a fortune based on his vote?" Sorsha asked.

Duke looked shocked, but only for a moment. The mask of helpful friendliness returned quickly, and he just sighed.

"I take it you know about my Great Aunt Harriet," he said.

"So you admit you stand to make a substantial amount of money, depending on the way your Senator votes," Norton said, flipping open his notebook and jotting the comment down.

"That land has been in Aunt Harriet's family for generations," Duke said. "There's nothing untoward about her owning it or about my being her only living relative."

"Unless Senator Young decides to pick the other route," Alex pointed out. "If that happened it might push a clever man to…remove Young as an obstacle."

Duke chuckled at that.

"I can tell by the questions you asked a few days ago that Mrs. Young told you about the real reason he was in that hotel room with his secretary," he said.

"Yes," Norton confirmed. "We know all about the Senator's predilections."

Duke looked at them each in turn as if the detective's admission answered their accusations.

"If you know what kind of man Paul Young was," Duke said, speaking slowly as if he were talking to children, "then you know he had no intention of picking the alternate route."

"You cut him in," Alex guessed. "If Senator Young didn't vote the way you wanted, he wouldn't get paid."

Duke didn't answer, he just tapped the tip of his nose with his finger.

"You couldn't do that," Norton said. "He'd never take your word for it; you'd have to have a contract drawn up. That would leave a paper trail a mile wide, especially when Young tried to collect. Even with a contract, you could stiff him and bet that he wouldn't ruin his good name by suing you in open court."

"You make it sound like such a difficult problem," Duke said with a sly smile. He turned and walked around his desk, withdrawing a large manilla envelope from his center desk drawer. "Here," he said, handing the envelope to Norton.

The , turned it over and pulled out a thin pack of official looking certificates.

"What's the Jeff Wilson Memorial Land Trust?" he asked, reading the name off the top of the first certificate.

"All of my Aunt Harriet's land is held in trust by that corporation," Duke said. "What you're holding in your hand is fifty shares out of a total of two hundred and fifty."

"I don't see how that helps," Alex said. "I get how it keeps your hands clean but Young still has to sell the shares to get his money. Stock sales have to be recorded."

Duke actually laughed out loud.

"That's the beauty of it," he said, still chuckling. "These are bearer shares; you don't have to sell them at all."

Alex had never heard of 'bearer shares,' and from the look on his face, neither had Norton.

"So?" the , said.

"So these shares belong to whoever holds them," Sorsha supplied. "All Duke had to do to keep the Senator in line was hand him that envelope before the vote. If he votes the right way, that paper becomes worth fifty thousand dollars; if he doesn't, it's worthless. Then all Young has to do is trade the shares to someone else for fifty thousand in cash or goods, less a transaction fee of course, and no one would ever be the wiser. The new owner of the shares then cashes them in, but since they aren't connected to Senator Young, no one cares."

"I see why the FBI keeps you around, Ms. Kincaid," Duke said with a nod that was both acknowledgement and admiration.

"None of that lets you off the hook," Norton said. "You still could have killed your boss to save yourself fifty Gs."

"No," Alex contradicted. "Duke couldn't have known who the Governor of Illinois would appoint to fill Senator Young's seat. If the new Senator had some other interest in the deal, he might vote the other way in spite of the bribe. The risk would be too great."

"That doesn't prove he didn't do it," Norton said.

"No," Sorsha admitted with a sigh. "But anyone smart enough to put this together," she indicated the bearer shares, "is smart enough to play it safe."

Duke didn't respond, he just smiled.

"I'm still going to run you in for criminal conspiracy," Norton said, dipping into the pocket of his suit coat for his handcuffs.

"What conspiracy?" Duke shrugged. "All you have is an envelope full of bearer shares for a company I happen to be a part owner of. None of that is illegal."

"Bribing a Senator is," the , growled.

"What bribe?" Alex asked. "Senator Young never received anything from Duke. Nothing you can prove anyway, since the shares are currently in your hands, and therefore owned by you."

"And I'll make sure my lawyer asks you if you ever owned any shares in the trust," Duke said. "I"m sure that'll play well with the jury."

"He can still stop you from bribing Senator Unger when he gets here," Alex said. "All Detective Norton has to do is hang on to those shares as evidence."

This time Duke's laugh was loud and went on for half a minute.

"That's the joke," he said through tears. "That idiot Unger got here this morning. Since he didn't know the bill, he asked me what Senator Young was going to do."

"And you told him," Sorsha said.

"Of course," Duke practically shouted. "The old fool didn't even question it. He walked right onto the Senate floor and recommended the northern route."

"When are they voting on this?" Alex demanded.

"They had the vote twenty minutes ago."

26

ALCHEMY AND BULLETS

After the morning he'd had, Alex needed a drink when he got back to his hotel room. He'd left Detective Norton and Sorsha arguing with Duke Harris. As much as Alex wanted Duke to be the killer, it just didn't make sense. Duke's scheme to get rich came off successfully, but the death of Paul Young could have easily messed it up. There just wasn't any upside for Duke in killing his boss.

Sorsha and Norton still wanted to arrest him for something, but the only evidence that he'd actually done anything wrong was his own admission and he'd simply deny that in court. Alex hated the idea that Duke would get away with his insider dealing, but that wasn't really his problem. Washington seemed to be full of those kinds of back room deals, enough to spend his whole life tracking them down, so he resolved to stay focused on the case for which he was being paid.

"Mr. Lockerby," a voice called as he was shutting the door to his suite.

Alex peeked out quickly, in case of trouble, then opened the door wide as Julian Rand came trotting down the hall from the elevator.

"I saw you in the lobby, but I was with a guest," he explained, then handed Alex a sealed envelope. "This was left for you at the front desk."

Alex took the envelope and turned it over. His name was printed on the front in a legible hand, male if he had to guess.

"Thanks," he said, pulling a fiver from his wallet. He hesitated, then pulled out another one. "Can you get me a good bottle of Scotch?"

"How good?" Julian asked, taking the cash.

"Single malt, old enough to vote. Smoky, a bit of peat; easy on the iodine."

"I have several excellent Scotches fitting that description in my office," he said with a conspiratorial grin. "For just such emergencies. I'll have one sent up right away."

Alex thanked him and went inside to wait. There was still some brandy left in the bottle from last night, but he was a dedicated Scotch man, and he needed a serious drink. While he waited, he sat down on the couch facing the window and opened the envelope. Inside was a single line of text followed by a name.

Call me when you get this.
 Connie

Alex dropped the paper on the couch next to him and sighed. After his experience with Zelda, and the subsequent discussion with Sorsha, he wasn't looking forward to explaining his thoughts to Connie.

"Or his boss," he mused out loud.

At that moment, a knock sounded at the door, no doubt the busboy with his Scotch.

"Thank God," he said, standing up. He had a feeling he was going to need a drink.

"Where have you been?"

Alex was greeted by Connie's irritated face when he opened the door. It took his mind a moment to adjust from what he expected to what he saw, then he stepped back, holding the door open.

"I was just about to call you," he said. "Come in."

"I thought we were going over to the aerodrome this morning," Connie said, striding through the door.

"Change of plans," Alex said. He was about to close the door when a man in a hotel uniform approached with a bottle. Alex accepted the liquor, tipped the man, then shut the door.

"Drink?" he asked Connie, holding the bottle up.

"Tony is getting impatient," the mobster said by way of an answer.

"Did you tell him our theory?"

Alex removed the paper seal from the bottle, then the stopper.

"Your theory," Connie growled. "And no, I like breathing."

Alex poured two fingers in a clean glass and handed it over.

"I have new information," he said. "You're going to need this."

Connie accepted the glass, somewhat apprehensively, then Alex sat down on the couch and spun the tale of the robbery at the museum and his subsequent evening with Zelda Pritchard.

"Alchemy can't do that," Connie scoffed in response. "There's no such thing as a potion that can turn a man into a wolf."

"And there wasn't a potion that could make one sip of beer feel like going home again, either," Alex pointed out. "But Colton invented it. It isn't crazy to think he might have invented the other one as well. And it is possible...I've seen something like it with my own eyes."

"I don't care if your mother turned into a wolf," Connie said. "This doesn't make sense. Why would Colton want some old cards from a...a..."

"Loom," Alex supplied.

"Yeah. What possible use could he have for something like that? I don't know whether your wolf man is an alchemist or not, but it's not Colton."

"It is quite the coincidence, though," Alex said.

"I suppose that's just what it is," Connie replied. "A coincidence."

"I hate coincidences," Alex admitted. "My mentor told me that there are no coincidences in murder."

"Colton didn't make a potion that turns men into murdering monsters," Connie insisted, though he sounded much less sure than he had a moment ago.

"There's one way to know for sure," Alex said, standing. "If Colton was involved with the heist, there's bound to be something at his house that will link him to the museum."

"You already looked there," the mobster pointed out.

Alex shook his head and drained the remainder of his glass. The liquor singed his throat and fired his synapses.

"The last time we were at Colton's house, we were looking for evidence of where he'd gone on the day he disappeared," Alex said. "This time he's a suspect. I'm going to look in every nook and cranny of that house, and if there's any secret compartments, hidden caches, or hollowed out books, I'm going to find them."

Connie fixed Alex with a challenging look.

"And if you don't find anything?"

"Then we go to the aerodrome," Alex said. "We keep following the trail until either it disappears, or we find Colton."

Alex stepped out of Connie's car in front of Colton Pierce's townhouse, being careful to hold the urn carrying the ashes of Colton's mother firmly. He should have just put it in his vault and opened it inside, but Connie had already seen far too much of Alex's vault already.

"You have the key?" Alex asked as they headed for the concrete stairs that led up to the building's stoop.

"Relax," Connie said, holding up a ring of keys as he came around the front of the car.

Alex started to turn back to the building, but Connie's eyes suddenly went wide, focusing past Alex on something behind him. Not hesitating, Alex took a big step sideways and turned to face whatever it was that Connie saw.

Gunfire erupted and the urn in Alex's arms exploded, giving Alex a face-full of ashes. Three more shots rang out, but nothing hit Alex as he struggled to clear his vision and spit out the remains of Colton Pierce's mother.

Another shot split the air and Alex felt a slug hit him square in the chest. His shield runes were in place, and they stopped the bullet from killing him, but it still hurt like crazy, and he slumped forward at the impact. A bullet hit him in the shoulder and another in the thigh of the leg carrying most of his weight. The muscle spasmed, and it stopped supporting him, dumping Alex in an unceremonious heap on the sidewalk.

Belatedly Alex thought of his flash ring. The attack had come out of nowhere, so he wasn't prepared. Despite the ache in his shoulder and chest, he pushed himself up. He could hear footsteps approaching, but his shoulder wasn't responding properly.

"He's got a shield rune on his coat," someone said. "Shoot him in the head,"

Before Alex could turn or bring his flash ring to bear, the gun boomed again, sending a bullet slamming into the back of his head, and the world went dark.

Someone was shaking him.

Blissful unconsciousness faded into painful awareness and Alex groaned as he tried to lift his head off the concrete sidewalk.

"Don't move, mister," an unfamiliar voice said as a restraining hand grabbed his shoulder. "You've been shot."

"I'm fine," Alex slurred, pushing the hand away. His shoulder ached where he was lying on it, but the spasm that resulted from the bullet impact had passed and he was able to lift himself up. An older man in a woolen overcoat and dungarees was kneeling beside him with a shocked look. He had a haggard face with a short gray beard and spectacles.

"Where am I?" Alex asked, trying and failing to remember what he'd been doing, or why he was face down on the ground. As he sat up the pain in his head almost forced him back down and a wave of nausea swept over him.

"You're in Georgetown," the man said. "Someone shot at you and your friend. I thought you were a goner for sure."

"Friend?" Alex said, reaching up to feel a large, painful bump on the back of his head.

The bearded man looked past Alex and nodded.

Moving gingerly, Alex turned to see a man in a dark green suit lying on the sidewalk a few feet away. There was blood on his chest, dripping down into a pool on the sidewalk.

"Connie," Alex gasped as everything came rushing back to him. Ignoring the aches in his body and the pain in his head, Alex lurched to his feet and staggered over to the mobster. He lay on his back, and Alex could see that he'd been shot multiple times in the chest and at least once in his left hand. The middle finger on that hand was missing, but that was minor compared to the amount of blood soaking through Connie's shirt. As he watched, Connie's chest rose and fell, so at least he was alive.

For the moment.

Alex swore.

"Stay with him," he said to the bearded man. Without waiting for a response, Alex hurried up the stairs to Colton Pierce's stoop, which consisted of a large, concrete porch. Yanking out his chalk, he drew a door next to Colton's actual front door, then pulled a vault rune from his book.

"Come on," he urged as the rune burned and vanished. After what seemed like an inordinately long time, the steel door melted out of the brick of the town house front and Alex jammed the key inside.

Pulling the door open, he limped through his great room to the hallway on the left side. Down past his little kitchen on the left and his bedroom on the right was the door to the brownstone in Manhattan. Or at least it used to be.

Alex pulled up short in front of the blank wall where the opening to his bedroom in the brownstone should have been. That vault door was always open, blocked off by a magically protected cover door on the other side. Now it and the door were gone. They'd vanished like they'd never been, leaving a blank, gray wall at the end of the hallway.

Without the door, Alex had no chance to bring Iggy, and at the rate Connie was bleeding, he'd have to do something quick, or the big mobster was a goner.

Wincing as he turned, Alex hurried to his infirmary as fast as his numb leg would carry him. Most of the supplies in his medicine cabinet had been given to him by Iggy, and the old doctor had spent several hours going over the treatment for wounds of all kinds. As Alex pulled open the cabinet door hard enough to crack the glass, he tried to remember that lecture.

Pushing labeled bottles and jars out of the way, Alex finally found what he was looking for. In the back corner was a wooden box just large enough for a cigarette lighter. It was painted black with a red X on it, and Alex grabbed it and popped the lid off. Inside was a glass vial about two inches long with a rubber stopper in the top that had been sealed with lead. A sickly yellow fluid sloshed heavily inside as Alex grabbed the little glass tube and lurched back toward the open door of his vault.

He paused to close his vault door as he emerged, then hobbled back down the steps to the street. Connie was still lying on the sidewalk in a pool of his own blood, but the bearded man was now kneeling beside him, holding the mobster's hand.

"Connie," he called as he knelt painfully next to the bleeding man.

"Alex?" he gasped. His eyes were open, but he didn't seem to see anything. "Tell Tony this wasn't your fault. I shoulda seen them tailing us."

"Here," Alex said, breaking the lead seal with his thumbnail and carefully pulling out the stopper of the vial. "Drink this."

Without any other warning, Alex shoved the open top of the glass container between the mobster's lip and tipped it up. Connie gagged for a second, then swallowed.

"What was..." he gasped. "What was thaaaa..."

Connie's words drifted off to nothing and his body lay still.

"Is he dead?" the bearded man asked, shock and fear in his voice.

"I hope not," Alex said, lurching back to his feet. "Help me get him in the car."

Between the two of them, they managed to get Connie into the back seat of his car. Once he was secure, Alex headed around the car until he remembered something important.

"Do you know where the nearest hospital is?" he demanded of the old man.

"Sure," he said. "Just go down this street—"

"You drive," Alex said, pointing to the car.

The bearded fellow looked like he might withdraw, but Alex grabbed him by his lapels.

"Do you know how to drive a car?" he demanded.

"Yes," the man admitted, "but—"

"I don't know how to drive," Alex said. "If you don't take us to the hospital, he's a dead man."

"All right," the fellow said after a moment's hesitation. He climbed into the driver's seat and pressed the starter as Alex went around to the passenger side.

"You're going to need to hurry," he said, climbing in. "Can you do that?"

The old man gave him an astonished look, then did something Alex found very disturbing — he smiled.

"Hang on to your hat, youngster," he said, then slammed the car in gear and pulled out so fast the tires squealed.

Alex had once been in Danny's '27 Ford when Danny's sister Amy drove it. The experience was still a recurring nightmare that left Alex awake in a cold sweat. What happened over the roughly ten minutes it took to get from Colton Pierce's town house to the nearest hospital drove every memory of Amy's driving from his mind. It wasn't that the bearded man was a bad driver; quite the opposite. He handled Connie's car with the skill and precision Alex expected from a professional, he just did it at speeds humans were only meant to achieve in airplanes. Once, Alex was afraid the car was going to roll over as it lurched around a tight corner at what had to have been thirty miles an hour.

While Alex clung to his seat for dear life, the old man in the driver's seat didn't even look nervous. In fact he even took time to yell at a slow-moving delivery truck to get out of his way. By the time he skidded to a stop in front of the hospital, Alex resolved to learn to drive, so he'd never have to ask anyone again.

"What's all this?" a uniformed policeman demanded, stepping up to the car as Alex got out. "You can't park here, and I ought to run you in for driving like that."

"I've got a wounded man here," Alex said, brushing past the cop and opening the car's rear door. "He's been shot, get a doctor."

The cop hurried away, and Alex and the old man pulled Connie out, supporting him between them. They'd made it halfway to the building when three men in white coats came hustling out carrying a stretcher.

"Put him down," the one in the lead said as the other two laid the stretcher down on the walkway.

Alex and his driver did as they were told, and the lead man knelt over Connie.

"He's not breathing," the man said.

"I gave him hibernation oil," Alex said. "It slowed his body down to give us time to get him here."

The man in the white coat looked up at him in surprise, then nodded.

"I know what it is," he said, turning back to Connie. "He's been shot multiple times in the chest." He stood up and motioned to the orderlies. "Get him inside right away." As the men picked up the stretcher, the leader turned to Alex. "What's his name?"

"Connie...uh...Constantine Firenze."

Before Alex could ask anything, the man turned and hustled away after the orderlies and the stretcher. Alex wanted to follow, but Connie was out of his hands. Instead, he turned to the bearded man. "I'm sorry about your coat."

The man looked down, and his face soured when he saw the blood covering the lower quarter of the woolen fabric. Alex pulled out his wallet and handed over a ten.

"Here's cab fare to get you home and enough to have that coat cleaned," he said.

The man took the money, and then chuckled.

"I hope your friend pulls through," he said. "And don't worry about me, that was the most fun I've had in years, young fella."

"Alex Lockerby," he said, sticking out his hand.

"Eli Oldfield," the man said. "I'll park your car up the street for you, then catch a cab."

Alex thanked him, then headed inside. He'd done all he could for Connie, but he needed to call Lucky Tony and fill him in, then he needed to go back to New York.

27

EXTRACTION

"Tell me you have something from Grier or Kellin," Alex said, storming into his office waiting room. Sherry almost jumped out of her chair, and her nearly-empty coffee cup spilled across the desk.

"Boss," she gasped, trying to blot up the coffee with a piece of paper.

"Sorry," Alex sighed, pulling out his handkerchief and helping. "It's been a rough day."

"You got shot," Sherry gasped.

Alex stood up straight, his wet handkerchief dripping on his shoes.

"How?" Alex asked, then stopped. Sherry must have received a vision of it before he came in, he decided.

"There's a bullet hole in your shirt," she said, pointing to his chest.

He looked down, and sure enough there was a bullet-sized hole with singed edges just under his breast pocket.

"Looks like your linked shield runes worked," his secretary went on.

"Yeah," Alex replied, wadding up his handkerchief and heading for the washroom to wring it out. Once he'd discovered that he could use linking runes to connect himself to other runes, trying it out with shield runes was an obvious first step. Rather than writing the runes on his suit coat or vest, he wrote them on paper that he kept in his vault. From there, a linking rune would connect him to the runes no matter where he went, protecting him even if he was shot in the head.

Fortunately.

He touched the lump on the back of his head as he turned on the water in the washroom sink. If he hadn't done it, he would have been dead right now.

Alex rinsed the coffee out of his handkerchief, then wrung it out and shut off the water.

"You want to talk about it?" Sherry asked, as he emerged back into the waiting room.

"No," he growled. "I've got an hour, two at most, before I have to explain to an angry mob boss how the bodyguard he lent me got shot and whether or not his nephew had anything to do with it."

"Okay," Sherry said with a worried look. "I heard from Charles Grier." She picked up one of her many notebooks, shook a few drops of coffee off it, then began flipping pages. "Here it is. According to him, most of the things on your shopping list are commonly used in alchemy. The only one that was kind of rare was Bourbon Vanilla. He said your alchemist might have trouble finding that fresh, since it comes from Madagascar. The extract is much easier to find, but might not work for every recipe."

Alex chewed on his lip as he absorbed that information.

"You want me to get Linda on the phone?"

Alex shook his head.

"I'll call her," he said, heading for his office.

"What are you going to tell the mob boss?" Sherry's voice trailed after him.

That was the million-dollar question and so far, Alex didn't have an answer.

Sitting down behind his enormous desk, Alex pulled out his directory book and flipped to the letter K. He dialed Linda's number and waited until the familiar voice came on the line. A momentary pang went through Alex that had nothing to do with the bruises the bullets had left on his body.

She sounds so much like Jessica.

"I was just about to call you," Linda said, after Alex identified himself. "I went over that list you gave me, even checked the ingredients against Mom's recipe book. Nothing really stood out, since lots of recipes use those ingredients."

Alex sighed.

"All right," he said, managing to keep the frustration out of his voice.

"There was one thing, though," she went on.

Alex's fading hopes perked up.

"Go on."

"When Sherry gave me this list, she had cashews and apples listed, but those aren't typically alchemy ingredients."

That might be what made Colton's Euphorian special, but neither of those ingredients were hard to find. Cashew nuts were expensive, but it wasn't anything that would faze Lucky Tony.

"I'm thinking she might have given me the wrong ingredients," Linda went on.

Alex pinned the phone receiver between his ear and shoulder, then pulled his flip notebook from his pocket. Finding the page where he'd transcribed Colton's list, he ran his finger across it.

"No," he said. "Both cashew and apple are on here."

"Are you sure that's what he meant?" Linda asked.

Even as she said it, Alex noticed what wasn't on the list. He'd copied the text exactly as Colton had written it. There was a comma after every item but there wasn't one between 'cashew' and 'apple.'

"Hm. Is there such a thing as a cashew apple?"

"Yes," Linda said. "Cashew nuts are actually seeds, and they're part of a fruit known as a cashew apple."

You've been looking for the wrong stuff, he chided himself.

"Are you sure about that?" he asked, not wanting to be sent off on a wild goose chase.

"That's what's funny," she said. "There was an article in this month's AAC Journal. It was about a South American alchemist named Rafael Bolsonaro. Apparently he just developed a process to make cashew apple extract."

Alex wrote that down in his notebook, but it didn't make any sense. "Why is that important?"

"Because," Linda said, with a smile Alex could hear. "Cashew apples are used in lots of Brazilian alchemy. There's demand for them all over the world."

"How come I've never heard of them?"

"The fruit spoils very quickly," Linda said. "And until Rafael Bolsonaro came along, it was impossible to ship very far."

"But with the extract, it will become a viable ingredient for alchemists anywhere," Alex said, nodding even though Linda couldn't see him. "Thanks, doll. You've been a big help."

He hung up and headed back to the waiting area.

"Any luck?" Sherry asked.

"Maybe," he said, jotting a note in his flip book, then tearing the paper out and handing it to Sherry. "I need you to send a telegram."

Alex shut his vault behind him as he re-entered his hotel suite. He went immediately to the little writing desk and poured himself two fingers of scotch in a tumbler before picking up the telephone.

"MacReady," the lieutenant's gruff voice greeted him after half a minute.

"It's Alex Lockerby," he said. "I don't have a lot of time, so I need you to just listen. Call Lyle Gundersen over at the Smithsonian. Tell him to go out immediately and visit three of those storage warehouses the museum maintains. Any three will do, but make it at least three. He should talk to whoever is there and spend ten or fifteen minutes alone in the storage area."

"Slow down, Lockerby," the lieutenant said, and Alex could hear the sound of scribbling.

"When you're on the phone with him," Alex went on, speaking a bit slower, "arrange to meet him somewhere before he goes out to the first warehouse and give him a manila folder with a bunch of blank paper inside. Then, once Gundersen gets back to the museum, tell him to go straight to his office and lock the folder in his safe."

"You think the thief is going to fall for that?" MacReady asked, catching Alex's train of thought.

"Whoever is behind this is desperate," he replied. "If they weren't, they never would have sent their wolf-lackey after me."

There was a long pause accompanied by scribbling, then MacReady came back on the line.

"All right, Lockerby," he said. "It's worth a shot."

"Tell Gundersen to get lunch and go to the bathroom while he's out," Alex added. "He needs to stay in his office for the rest of the day once he gets back."

MacReady promised that he would, and Alex hung up. He was tempted to call the hospital where he'd left Connie and check on the man's condition. If the big mobster was dead, it might be better for Alex to just leave town. Instead, he downed his Scotch, picked up his hat, and headed for the elevator.

Lucky Tony Casetti's face turned an angry shade of red when Alex looked into the recovery room where Connie was resting. He sat in a chair next to Connie's bed with two of his men sitting on the far side. Connie lay asleep in the bed, looking pale. His left hand was wrapped in a bandage, revealing that his middle finger was missing. Alex felt a pang of guilt about that. If he could have reached Iggy, the finger might have been saved, but the doctors at the hospital had to prioritize saving the man's life. Alex didn't blame them.

"There you are," he growled as Alex came in.

Alex had expected this kind of a response and he made sure to keep his face calm. Behind Tony, his goons stood as well, easing to each side so they had a clear line of sight on Alex.

"How's he doing?"

"The doctor says he has a fifty-fifty chance," Tony said. "Which is more than I can say for you, unless you've got a damn good excuse for why you left Connie here and just took off."

"Connie needed surgery," Alex said as if that explained everything.

"I called you, so he'd have someone here, but that's all I could do for him."

"So you just decided to go out for lunch?" Tony said, balling his hands into fists.

Alex shook his head.

"No," he said. "I went out to find out who shot him."

Tony stepped up so close Alex could smell his last cigarette.

"Connie was awake a little while ago," he said. "He told me you think Colton was involved in a theft at the museum, that he's developed some kind of monster potion."

"That's the way I had it figured," he admitted.

"That's nonsense," Lucky Tony fumed. "Colton's not a thief, and even if he were, there's no potion that can turn a man into a monster. You'd better start talking fast."

The 'or else' was implied, and even though Tony was two inches shorter than Alex, his presence filled the room. Alex took a calming breath and let it out.

"First off, there is such a potion," Alex explained. "I've seen it work with my own eyes."

Tony sucked in an angry breath, but before he could interject, Alex continued.

"But Colton didn't make it," he said. "In fact Colton didn't have anything to do with the museum thefts or with the attack on me that got Connie shot."

Tony closed his mouth for a moment, his face shifting from angry to shrewd.

"Connie got shot because of you?" he asked, his voice quiet and dangerous.

"Unfortunately," Alex said. "I suspect the people who were behind Senator Young's murder didn't like me asking questions."

Alex knew that Colton hadn't been behind the attack when the gunman shot him in the back of his head. His companion had known about shield runes and directed the shot to a location he didn't believe they could cover. An alchemist like Colton wouldn't know that, but someone working for the Legion would.

"If you had stuck to the case I gave you, then Connie wouldn't be laying here clinging to life," he fumed. "You'd better hope he lives, scribbler. If he doesn't, I'm going to make sure you join him."

Alex tried to look nonplussed. He was relatively sure that if Tony came after him, Sorsha would turn him into a ferret, but that didn't mean Tony couldn't have Alex killed in an apparent accident. The mob boss was not an enemy to be taken lightly.

"I did what I could for him," Alex said, nodding at Connie's sleeping form.

"The doctor told me," Tony said, still inches away. "That's the only reason we're talking here, and not down by the river while we wait for your cement shoes to harden. So tell me why we should keep talking here, and be quick about it."

Alex reached into his coat pocket and the goons on either side of Tony reached into their coats.

"Easy," Alex said, slowly pulling out a yellow envelope.

"What's this?" Tony asked as Alex handed it to him.

"Telegram from the Hotel Americana in Rio de Janeiro. It's from Colton. He went down there to secure the rights to the newly invented Extract of Cashew Apple; it's one of the ingredients he needs to make Euphorian on a large scale."

Tony tore open the telegram and read it, his face relaxing as he did so. When he finished, he sighed and crossed himself.

"Thank God," he said. A moment later, his skeptical face came back. "But what about Sal? How did he end up dead?"

"That one's easy," Alex said. "The Aerodrome is on the other side of the river. Colton drove his car over there to catch an airship for Brazil. According to the timetable, one left at four thirty-five that afternoon. Sal, being a good bodyguard, went with him, then walked back across the river to the city."

"And some random person just hit him while he was on the bridge?" Tony said.

Alex shrugged and nodded.

"Looks that way."

"Why didn't he just get a cab at the Aerodrome?"

"I suspect Colton needed more cash than he realized," Alex said. "Sal probably gave him whatever cash he had on him, figuring it was only a couple of miles to your house once he'd crossed the bridge."

"So Colton leaves town," Tony summarized. "He expects Sal to tell me where he went, but Sal gets hit before he can. Why didn't the driver of the truck report the accident?"

"No idea," Alex said. "He may have had contraband in the truck, or maybe he was wanted. There are plenty of reasons the driver would just keep driving."

Tony didn't like that answer, but he couldn't fault it, either.

"All right," he said at last. "You're off the hook — for now. But I'm going to confirm this telegram and it had better be on the level."

"I told him to wire you as well," Alex said. "I suspect you've got a telegram waiting for you at your house."

Tony turned to the tall, thin goon on his right and nodded toward the door. The man grunted an acknowledgement and headed out past Alex, presumably to call the house and confirm the telegram. Alex was relieved that Tony was easy to predict; he was a businessman and behaved like anyone whose life was made up of transactions. He'd wanted to balance the scales for Connie's injuries, and Alex had brought him something of value. He wasn't sure he was out of the woods with the gangster yet, but it was a good start.

"One more thing," Alex said, nodding at Connie's unconscious form. "Once he's back on his feet, I know a runewright who can do a regrowth rune. It's a variant of a major restoration rune, and it can restore Connie's missing finger."

"I know what it is," Tony said, giving Alex a wary look. "Those are expensive."

He wasn't wrong. Major restoration runes could cost up to a grand to produce normally. Fortunately Iggy and the Monograph had a few shortcuts that reduced the cost by half.

"Consider it an apology for putting Connie in harm's way."

Tony chuckled, then he smiled and nodded at Alex.

"You're all right, kid," he said. "You understand how to take responsibility for your actions, and how to make amends. These are things men do," he said, and put emphasis on the word 'men.' "Unfortunately there aren't enough people who understand that anymore."

"It's the least I can do."

"There is one more thing I want you to do," Tony said, resuming his seat by Connie. "I want you to find out who did this," he jerked his head at the bed. "You find them, and you come and tell me."

His voice hadn't changed. It was still the cultured businessman, but the implications were loud and clear. Alex had no wish to get on Tony's bad side, having just managed to get off it, but he had no intention of bringing Connie's shooters to the mob. If he was right, they were members of the Legion, and he and Sorsha had first claim on them.

Out loud he said, "I'll see what I can do."

28

NOT IN THE CARDS

Alex got out of a cab in front of D.C.P.D.'s Command Office one with just 30 minutes to spare. He needed to be over at the Smithsonian before the doors closed at seven, and he was cutting it close. It had been several hours since he left Connie in his hospital room, but his experiences in D.C. had prompted him to make some much-needed changes to his vault before he met Lieutenant MacReady.

"You're late," the lieutenant said as Alex entered the building. MacReady and six large uniformed policemen waited for him in the lobby. MacReady carried a shotgun over his arm and the uniforms were armed with billy clubs, pistols, and a large, heavy net.

"We've got time," Alex said.

"You still haven't told me how we're going to sneak all these boys into Gundersen's office," MacReady said, jerking his thumb at the men behind him.

Alex held up a bit of chalk and smiled.

"With this," he said, heading for the stairwell to get some privacy.

Once the lieutenant and his men had crammed into the space, Alex opened his vault against the side wall of the landing. The space beyond was radically different than it had been, and it surprised Alex for a moment. The door used to lead directly into his great room, but now it opened into a rectangular room with a large conference table in the center and chairs all around. At the back of the room was a plain wooden door that Alex knew none of the police would be able to open. It was one of three spare cover doors he had on hand in case he ever needed to leave his vault door open for some reason.

The table and chairs had come from the unused conference room in Alex's office in Empire Tower. He and Mike had muscled them in once Alex pushed the wall of his great room back and created the space he was now thinking of as his vault's vestibule. Unlike the fancy, stained-glass-enclosed one at the brownstone, this one could be used for meetings, to hold gear he might need at a moment's notice, or as in tonight's case, a place to man a stakeout.

"What is that?" one of the uniforms asked.

"This is my vault," Alex said. "It's a magical space I can use for any number of reasons, In this case, I'm going to use it to transport all of you to the museum without being noticed."

"You want me to get in there?" MacReady said, his skeptical look bordering on hostile.

"It's perfectly safe," Alex said. "I've done this before."

"What if something happens to you while I'm in there?" MacReady asked.

"My secretary has a key," he said. It wasn't exactly a lie, but Sherry had no real way to get the lieutenant and his men out of Alex's vault if something were to happen. Of course, Iggy could still get in from the brownstone.

You mean from your office or apartment, he reminded himself. He still didn't know why his door to the brownstone had closed, but he'd worry about that later.

What if the brownstone door closed when Sherry opened the back door?

That thought brought him up short. What if he could only have a certain number of doors open at once?

Shaking his head to banish that train of thought, Alex stepped inside the vestibule.

"Everyone come in and grab a seat," he said. "Once you're in, I'm going to close the door and it will disappear. Don't be alarmed, because it will open up again as soon as I get to the museum."

MacReady gave Alex a long, penetrating look, no doubt searching for signs of deception, then he stepped inside. One by one, his men followed.

"Okay," Alex said, stepping out again. "Sit tight and I'll see you in a few minutes."

"You'd better," MacReady said. "It's my wife's birthday tomorrow."

Alex gave him a reassuring look, then he shut the big steel door and waited as it vanished back into the gray wall of the precinct stairwell.

Alex caught a cab to the Smithsonian, and managed to make it inside just as the guards were ushering people out.

"Mr. Gundersen is expecting me," he said as he hurried along the first side hallway to the Deputy Curator's office.

"Oh!" Gundersen said, almost leaping out his chair when Alex came in. "There you are, Mr. Lockerby. I was beginning to worry."

"Did you do as I instructed?"

"Yes," the balding man said, nodding. "I felt as if I would be attacked by monsters at any moment, but I followed your instructions to the letter."

"Good," Alex said, moving to the back wall of the office and taking out his chalk.

"Do you really think the thieves were watching me?" he said, his voice quavering at the thought.

"Maybe not watching," Alex said, sticking a vault rune to the chalk door he'd drawn. "But somehow they found out about those cards in storage and managed to get to them before you. Then there's the attack at the gallery. The thing that did it wanted to know where the cards were. Asked me specifically, so we know they believe there are more, and they want them."

Alex ignited his vault rune, then pulled the heavy door open.

Lieutenant MacReady practically ran out of the vestibule into Gundersen's office.

"I don't ever want to do that again," he gasped, shivering at the thought.

"It's just like being in this office," Alex protested.

"If this office didn't have any windows or way out," MacReady grumbled.

Gundersen's eyes got big as the policemen kept emerging from the new door in his wall. He looked around at his well-appointed office as if he had just realized what might happen in it during the night.

"Don't worry," Alex said, clapping the balding man on the shoulder. "We'll be as careful as we can. Now that we're here, however, it's time for you to go home."

"Home?" Gundersen said. "But what about tonight? Aren't you expecting the thief to try to break into my safe?"

"Yes," Alex said with exaggerated patience. "But I don't expect them to do it while you are still here."

"Right." Gundersen nodded, picking up his briefcase. "Good luck, gentlemen." With that, he let himself out of the office and locked the door behind him.

"Get the light," MacReady said to one of the officers and a moment later the office was plunged into darkness. "How do you want to play this, Lockerby?" the lieutenant went on as everyone waited for their eyes to adjust to the moonlight filtering through the windows. "There isn't a lot of space in here."

"Two of us will wait in here, up against the back wall," Alex said. "The rest will wait in my vault and we'll rotate every hour."

MacReady made an unconvinced noise in the dark.

"I'll leave the door open, of course," Alex explained.

"Uh-huh," the lieutenant said, not sounding like that made the idea any better.

"How much longer is this going to take?" one of the uniformed policemen hissed in the dark of Alex's vault.

He was seated somewhere off to Alex's left along the conference table, but with the lights off, he was just a disembodied voice.

"Relax, Hannigan," Lieutenant MacReady's voice came from Alex's left. "It takes as long as it takes."

Alex pulled out his pocketwatch and flipped open the cover. The runes inside glowed faintly, but it was enough for him to see the time.

"It's just after midnight," he whispered. "I expect our thief will be along soon."

"What makes you think that?" Officer Hannigan asked.

"According to the almanac, the moon set almost ten minutes ago, so the sky is as dark as it's going to get," Alex replied. "I suspect our thief usually tries to be subtle, to sneak in and out without being seen, like he did at the warehouse. This is his best opportunity to do that."

As if on cue, the room was suddenly filled with the sound of breaking glass. Not the sound of someone delicately fracturing a window-pane to allow entry, but rather the sound of an entire piece of sheet glass being shattered into a million pieces.

"What?" one of the officers outside in the vault said.

"Look out," the other yelled, then the vault filled with ruddy light as an explosion rocked the office.

Alex was thrown to the floor by the blast, and flames rolled into the vault, singeing his suit coat.

"What the hell?" MacReady swore. "Get out there, boys."

Alex pushed himself up as the cops ran past him and poured out into the office. As he got to his feet, an unearthly roar tore the air, followed by screaming men and gunshots. MacReady rushed by, gripping his shotgun, and Alex lurched after him with his ears still ringing.

The scene beyond his vault door was something out of a nightmare. The explosion had blown out the windows in the office, and glass shards covered the floor. The two officers who had been in Gundersen's office were crumpled on the floor, their flesh blackened and charred from the blast. Another uniform was down, lying in a pool of his own blood, while the remaining officers shot at the creature in the middle of the office. It was just as Alex remembered, the twisted form of a man, covered in fur and with a long, protruding snout.

As Alex entered, the wolf man picked up one of the cops and bodily threw him out the opening where the windows had been. Bullets slammed into the wolf man's hide and Alex could see blood leaking from wounds, but they all seemed minor, barely more than scratches.

One of the cops attempted to tackle the beast, but the creature seized the man with its jaws and tore his throat out.

"Keep away from that thing," MacReady roared as he unloaded a blast of buckshot right into the monster's chest.

The wolf man reared back under the impact, dropping the dead cop to the floor. Blood was pouring from its chest, but as Alex watched, the flow began to dwindle. A memory of Dr. Kellin leaped to his mind, of a bullet being expelled from a hole in her side as the wound closed itself.

Alex hadn't expected to be needed for anything other than his vault. Six cops and a lieutenant with a shotgun should have been more than enough to take down a thief, even one magically mixed with a dog. As a result, his 1911 and his heavier weapons were still in his vault. He could run back and try to get them, but by the time he got back, the monster would have time to kill the remaining cops and flee.

Reaching into his jacket pocket, Alex's fingers slipped through the finger holes in his knuckle duster. He'd put it in his pocket after Connie got shot, purely as a precaution. It wasn't much, but it wasn't nothing.

The wolf man backhanded Lieutenant MacReady, knocking him across the room. Alex took advantage of the creature's distraction to step in and deliver an uppercut to the monster's kidney. Normal knuckle dusters amplified their user's striking power, but like most things Alex used, this one had been enhanced with rune magic. The engraved impact runes along the side made it hit like a sledgehammer, and on each end were Iggy's 'stinger' runes. These added pain to any blow akin to an electric shock, and left the area numb and unresponsive.

The wolf man howled in a strange mix of man and beast as the blow landed and he jumped away, cradling his side. It turned its burning eyes on Alex and a low, rumbling growl issued from its snout as it pulled back, ready to spring.

At that moment one of the cops lashed out with his nightstick. Alex didn't know if he was out of bullets, or just emboldened by the creature's reaction to being punched. The club cracked the monster in the shoulder, and it shied away for a moment. Without the aid of the impact and stinger runes, the club didn't hurt the wolf man as much, but it wasn't nothing.

"Going to kill all of you," the thing growled, taking a swipe at the cop, who had wisely retreated out of range.

It turned back to Alex just as Lieutenant MacReady shot it full in the face. The monster howled and clawed at its face as blood ran from a ruined eye socket. Alex seized the opportunity and lunged in, bringing the metal front of his knuckle duster down on the wolf man's thigh. The stinger did its job and the creature stumbled and fell heavily to the floor.

Alex didn't relent, stepping over the alchemical creature and punching it repeatedly in the back. Each time he hit, the monster shuddered in pain. It tried to fight back, but the stinger had numbed its muscles, making them sluggish and slow to respond.

The creature looked up with hate in its eyes as Alex raised his hand for a final blow to the face. Before Alex could strike, however, someone jumped on him, grabbing his arm. He staggered, trying to find the person grappling with him, but nothing was there.

"What are you doing, Lockerby?" MacReady yelled as he struggled to reload his shotgun. "Finish him off."

"Something's got me."

As Alex struggled, he became aware of a distortion where his attacker should be. It was more pronounced as he moved, so he twisted his upper body quickly back and forth.

Pain lanced through his shoulder as something bit him, hard.

Alex charged the office wall, slamming the invisible attacker against it. The distortion wavered, then resolved itself into the form of a man, though it was still indistinct.

"I see him," MacReady snarled. Stepping up to Alex, he slammed the butt of his shotgun into the largest part of the blurry mass.

There was a high-pitched squeal and Alex was suddenly free. His attacker dropped to the floor and in a blink it was suddenly visible. It was another alchemical monster, but this time the features were bulbous and reptilian. Its eyes were round, and protruded like a lizard's; it also had a wide mouth filled with needle-like teeth. The body was small, with feminine curves, and though the creature wore no clothing, it was covered in tiny, multicolored scales.

Alex was frozen in fascination at the thing, and didn't react when its scales began to shift, adapting to the background and causing it to vanish. MacReady didn't hesitate; he fired his reloaded shotgun right where the thing had been, and it screamed. This time when it reappeared, there were bloody tears in the creature's torso, and it wasn't moving.

"No!" the wolf man roared.

Too late, Alex turned back to his most dangerous opponent. The wolf man rose up from the floor, catching Alex in the chest with its shoulder and hurling him right through the office door and into the hall beyond.

Alex lay stunned for a moment as his ribs screamed at him to take it easy. He heard another two shotgun blasts and the wolf man howled again.

"Stop him," MacReady yelled as Alex struggled to his feet, ignoring the pain in his bleeding shoulder and chest.

Several more shots rang out, but by the time Alex managed to limp back to the gaping hole in the wall the wolf man was gone.

"He won't get far," MacReady said, surveying the room. "Hannigan," he barked at the cop who had hit the wolf man with his nightstick. "Take charge. Find out who's still alive and keep 'em that way."

With that, the lieutenant went to the phone that had fallen off Gundersen's desk in the explosion. Picking it up, he pressed the switch until he got an operator, then called for more cops and at least one ambulance.

While the lieutenant was on the phone, Alex knelt down by the dead woman. Whatever alchemical potion had caused her to change had lost its effectiveness and her features reverted to normal. She was small and pale, with a prettyish face, a pert nose, and fiery red hair. Other than the brutal gashes torn in her torso by the shotgun, she had no marks or tattoos, not that Alex expected any of the latter.

Moving to take off his suit jacket and cover the naked dead woman, Alex winced. She'd bit his shoulder in her chameleon form, and lifting his arm was a new exercise in pain. Biting back a curse, he managed to get his coat off and leaned down to lay it over the body.

MacReady hung up the phone and barked at Hannigan for a report.

"Wills and Peterson are in bad shape, but they're alive," he said, his voice a growl. "The rest are dead."

MacReady cursed, then turned to Alex.

"We need to end that thing, Lockerby," he said. "I've got some boys coming over with bigger guns, but we need to be able to find it before we can kill it. You got any ideas how to do that?"

Alex looked down at the dead girl, then sighed and nodded.

"I know where he's going," he said. "We'll need to hurry."

He turned, but instead of heading out through what remained of the office door he headed into his vault.

"Where are you going?" MacReady demanded.

"To get a bigger gun."

29

HAIR OF THE DOG

Someone screamed as Alex and Lieutenant MacReady stormed through the front door of the Willard Hotel. Each man's clothing was smeared with drying blood, and they both carried repeating shotguns.

"Easy, folks," MacReady said, holding up his badge. "Police business. There's going to be a whole lot more cops behind us," he continued to a slim man in a hotel uniform. "Send them up to the top floor."

The man stuttered a reply, but Alex just pushed past him with MacReady in tow. He hauled the collapsible cage to the open elevator and stepped in. The operator was an older man in an impeccable tuxedo, and his eyes widened at the sight of his new passengers.

'Wh-what floor?" he squeaked.

"Twelve," Alex replied, as MacReady pulled the folding door closed again.

The elevator operator pulled the handle that made the car ascend, and it lurched upward.

"Now you want to tell me why we're here?" MacReady asked Alex.

"The monster is going to Zelda Pritchard's room," Alex said.

"You still on her?" the lieutenant asked, his voice incredulous. "I told you she had an ironclad alibi for the first two robberies, and she was with you when the gallery was hit."

"I don't think Zelda is involved," Alex explained. "Not directly anyway."

"Then I repeat, why are we here?"

"Ylang-ylang and vanilla."

"What?"

"Zelda wears very exclusive perfume," Alex said. "It's made by a friend of mine in New York by the name of Enzo Romero and it uses very exotic ingredients."

"Yang-yang and vanilla extract?"

Alex didn't bother to correct MacReady, he just nodded.

"Zelda travels with a valet and a ladies' maid," he explained. "They're brother and sister. I met the valet on the trip down from New York. He had the reddest hair I've ever seen."

"Just like the dead girl at the museum," MacReady said, rubbing his chin thoughtfully. "Might be a coincidence."

"When I covered the girl with my coat, I noticed that she smelled faintly of ylang-ylang and vanilla, but only faintly."

"Like she was around someone who wore that scent on a regular basis."

Alex nodded as the car slowed to a stop.

"Top floor, gentlemen," the elevator operator said, his voice still trembling.

"Get back down to the main floor and stay there," MacReady said as Alex pulled the cage open.

Alex led the way toward Zelda's suite. As he went, he grabbed the charge handle on his Browning A5 shotgun and pulled it back, loading a shell into the firing chamber.

"How do you want to play this?" MacReady asked, chambering his shotgun as well.

"Let me knock and see if she answers," he said. "The wolf man was wounded pretty good, we might have beat him here."

A high-pitched scream erupted from the end of the hall followed by an animal snarl.

"We didn't," MacReady yelled as both men broke into a run.

Transferring his shotgun to his left hand, Alex jammed his right into his trouser pocket. Looping his fingers through his knuckle duster, he pressed his thumb down on the rune carved on the top end.

"Stand away," MacReady said as they reached the door, no doubt intending to blow the lock off with his shotgun.

But Alex didn't hesitate; he lashed out at the metal plate covering the lock mechanism, releasing his thumb as the steel knuckle duster made contact. All the remaining impact runes went off at once in a blow that shattered the lock and blew the door wide open.

In the room beyond, Zelda Pritchard stood behind a decorative couch, dressed in a pair of silk pajamas. She had what looked like a hatbox clutched to her chest and she didn't turn to see what had happened to her front door. Her eyes were fixed on the ragged and bloody wolf man limping toward her from a side room.

The creature's yellow eyes darted to the ruined door, then it snarled and lunged forward. Alex opened his hand, letting the knuckle duster fall to the floor as Lieutenant MacReady raised his weapon and fired. The blast caught the wolf man in the chest, and he flinched. Clearly the shot hurt him, but not enough to stop him. The creature crouched, ready to spring over the couch at Zelda.

Alex raised his own weapon. It was the same model Browning that Lieutenant MacReady carried, but it had something the police issue shotgun couldn't match. All along the side of the stock, Alex had painstakingly carved runes. Three were for accuracy if long shots were required. Three would force the pellets apart as they exited the barrel, providing for a more devastating spread, and the final three increased the mass of the pellets, giving them far greater penetrating power.

As the wolf creature leaped, spreading its clawed hands to rend Zelda apart, Alex leveled his weapon, touched a mass rune with the tip of his finger, and fired. The pellets slammed into the creature's side and it howled in agony, missing Zelda as she darted away, and landing heavily on an expensive Persian carpet.

"Alex," Zelda shrieked, noticing him for the first time. She charged at him and threw her arms around him, burying her face in his shoulder as she sobbed hysterically. "It came back!"

"Get behind me," he ordered, shoving her back as he tried to keep his weapon trained on the wolf man. It was down and not moving, but Alex could see its chest rising and falling, so it wasn't dead.

Stepping carefully, he and MacReady approached the prone figure. As they moved, it struggled to raise its head.

"Keep your hands where I can see them," MacReady growled, pointing his weapon directly into the wolf man's face.

"S-should have killed you before," it growled at the lieutenant, eyes glittering with hate. "When you k-k-killed her." The sentence devolved into a growl of pain, and the man-animal's teeth clenched together.

"Her?" Zelda said, peeking out from behind Alex. "What's he talking about?"

"Katherine Cohan," Alex said to the wolf man.

"Katie?" Zelda gasped. "What do you mean she's dead, what's going on?"

"She came with this one to plunder Mr. Gundersen's safe tonight," Alex explained. "They were smarter than I gave them credit for, recognizing the trap I'd laid. They used some kind of bomb on the room before coming in."

The wolf man huffed a laugh, then winced in pain.

"Almost got you, too," he said.

Alex just shook his head sadly.

"Instead it was Katherine."

"Katie wouldn't go anywhere with this...this...thing," Zelda insisted.

"She would," Alex said with a sigh. "She was his sister, after all."

Zelda's hand on Alex's arm suddenly clenched.

"Hector?" she said.

"Yes," the beast said. "Take a good look, you bitch. This is what you did to us."

Zelda just stood, looking down at the dying wolf man with her mouth open.

"Miss Pritchard didn't give you whatever potion you took that made you a monster," Alex said.

"No," Hector sneered as best he could around his dog muzzle. "She just opened the door for the monster and let him in."

"Hector," she gasped. "What are you saying?"

"When Katie was sick," he groaned. "That doctor in Copenhagen. He's the one that...that gave her the p-potion. Got her hooked." His snout turned up in a growl of pain and he shuddered.

"What are you talking about?" Zelda demanded. "I got Katie a doctor, but he didn't give her anything strange."

"That you know about," Lieutenant MacReady said.

"Sh-she needed more," Hector moaned through clenched teeth. "Had to do what he wanted to get it. He gave us the transformation potions. T-told us what to take."

"This doctor," Alex said. "What's his name?"

"D-doesn't matter. He works for the Alchemist."

"His name was Dr. Fisker, and he came highly recommended," Zelda said, her voice wavering between shock and offense.

"M-made us his stooges," Hector said, his voice becoming clearer. "Your fault."

Alex could see his wolf snout shrinking and the ruddy fur on his body beginning to thin.

"He doesn't have much time," Alex said.

"Hector," Zelda implored as her valet began to resemble his old self. "I didn't know. Why didn't you tell me? My father could have done—"

"Nothing," Hector growled. "Take a good look, princess. You d-did this to us." He laughed and blood oozed from his mouth. "I'll see you in H-Hell," he groaned, his breaths coming quick and shallow.

"Hector," Zelda implored him, but he was beyond caring.

He was beyond anything.

Alex knelt down and closed the man's eyes. He had returned to the short, red-haired man Alex remembered from the airship.

Zelda buried her head in Alex's shoulder and sobbed.

"I didn't know," she kept insisting.

Right then the sound of running erupted in the hall and a moment later a dozen heavily-armed cops burst into the room.

Alex put an arm around Zelda and led her to a chair where she couldn't see the naked, ruined body of Hector Cohan. The box she had been clutching in her nerveless fingers turned out to have the Smithsonian's missing cards in it. Zelda had been laying out her clothes for the following day and wanted a particular hat. Since it was her maid's night off, she went looking herself, and found them in a hatbox.

They sat on the couch for almost an hour as the police went over every inch of Hector's room and Zelda's suite. Eventually a female officer came to take Zelda's statement, and Alex was able to slip away.

"How's she holding up?" the lieutenant asked as Alex approached.

Alex looked back to the couch where Zelda sat talking with the officer. She had her arms wrapped around her body as if she were cold, and even across the room, Alex could see that she was trembling.

"About how you'd be if you found out two of your top cops were thieves and killers," he said. "I suspect she'll be okay eventually, but not for a while. You need to have someone call her father."

MacReady nodded and scribbled in his notebook, then he flipped to an earlier page with a confused look on his face.

"Didn't you say that when Hector attacked you and Miss Pritchard at the art gallery, that he wanted to know where the remaining cards were?"

Alex nodded.

"But you said that Miss Pritchard didn't know about the cards until you told her at the gallery," MacReady went on. "How did Hector know about them?"

"Katherine," Alex said. "I'm guessing she used her invisibility trick to keep an eye on Gundersen."

"Then why didn't she just follow him when he went out?" the lieutenant countered. "She would have known the card story was a fake."

"She couldn't get too far away from the hotel where her mistress was staying," he said. "How could she explain her absence if Zelda came back unexpectedly?"

MacReady nodded and scribbled more notes in his book.

"So they believed there were still missing cards, but not what happened to them. Why go after Miss Pritchard when Gundersen knew where the cards were?"

"They weren't after her," Alex said. "They were after me and, thanks to my date to look at impressionists, they knew right were to find me. I suspect they had no idea where Gundersen lived."

"I guess that does make sense," MacReady said.

"Did you find anything in either of their rooms?" Alex said, changing the subject.

MacReady glanced at Zelda, then jerked his head to the side, indicating for Alex to follow. They went out into the hall, then down to the next room. Unlike Zelda's suite, this room was small and not as richly furnished.

"These are for rich folk's servants," MacReady explained.

The single chest of drawers had been opened and emptied, along with the wardrobe on the wall. Clothing and personal effects were strewn around, but the only thing on the bed was a wooden case with brass fittings and a heavy latch in the front.

"This was in his bottom drawer," MacReady said, opening the lid.

Inside were three rows of glass vials, each resting in its own padded pocket. The two upper rows held small vials, barely more than an inch long, but the ones in the bottom row were twice that length and thicker. Each of the bigger vials had a colored stopper that was either blue or red in equal numbers.

"This mean anything to you?" the lieutenant asked.

"These are the doses," Alex said, pointing to the rows of small vials. "Whatever this Dr. Fisker hooked them on is in there. The ones on the bottom are the transformation serums."

"Okay," MacReady said, "but what do I do with them?"

"Pour them down the sink," Alex said. "They're too dangerous to leave lying around."

"They're evidence, Lockerby," he said with a roll of his eyes.

"My point stands," Alex replied. "But I think I know how to make them someone else's problem."

"You do that, I'll buy you a beer," MacReady said, looking at the case full of alchemy. He shook his head, then turned to Alex. "Who would do something like this?"

"Someone who wanted to rob museums and needed people who could travel in those circles to do the job."

"I get that, but this," the lieutenant indicated the vials. "This is sick."

Alex nodded agreement, but didn't respond. He could think of several people who would happily engineer and carry out such a scheme. It was a bit ham-fisted for the Legion, but not outside the realm of possibilities. The glyph rune practitioners weren't above such tactics either. Then there was his brother in magic, Paschal Randolph, assuming he was still alive.

Shuddering at the thought, Alex changed the subject.

"Let me make a call and I'll take care of this," he indicated the box.

"I'll be in the main room," MacReady said, then he withdrew.

Alex picked up the receiver of the phone mounted on the wall near the door and dialed the number of the Fairfax Hotel.

"Room two-eleven," he said when the hotel operator picked up.

A moment later, he heard Sorsha's voice on the line. Since it was after midnight, he'd been worried about waking her, but from the level of pent-up frustration in her voice, he knew she'd been awake.

"Bad day?" he asked.

"Yes," she growled back. "There's simply no motive for Duke Harris to have killed Senator Young. In fact, the Senator's death could have ruined his plans altogether."

"I know," Alex said. "And now you've got no suspect." He could relate to that frustration. Even though he'd found the Smithsonian's missing property, he now had another mystery on his hands. One with no hard suspects, just two names, Dr. Fisker and 'The Alchemist.'

"At least you can get Duke on fraud," Alex pointed out.

Sorsha gave out an exasperated grunt.

"You'd think that, but you'd be wrong," she said, her voice artificially sweet. "Apparently confessing to planning a crime isn't actually the same as committing one," she added.

"What about conspiracy?" Alex offered. "That's literally planning to commit a crime."

"It only counts if the crime was actually committed," she explained. "Detective Norton and I tried to push it, but no one wants to hear about any corruption here. Not the Capital Police, not the D.C. Police, not Sherman Blake, the wonder boy of the FBI field office."

Alex sighed and nodded to himself.

"Too many skeletons in their own closets."

"What a depressing thought," she conceded. "So what's on your mind at this hour, Alex? More good news?"

"Not exactly," he said. Taking a breath, he launched into an explanation of how Hector and Kate Cohan had been blackmailed into committing robberies for some shadowy person known only as 'The Alchemist.'

"Do you know why they were instructed to steal the things they took?" Sorsha asked when he finished.

"No," he said. "I'll have to track all the robberies they committed, then find out what was actually taken, before I could even begin to guess at the reason."

"If you can figure out what your Alchemist wants, you might be able to figure out who he is," she said. "But since I wouldn't know in any case, I'm assuming you didn't call to hear me speculate about the identity of this criminal mastermind."

"No," Alex said. "I think I've got a way you can score some points with the FBI. I've got a case full of glass vials here and, unless I'm very much mistaken, it's the stuff this Alchemist fellow used to control the Cohens and to change them into monsters. The D.C. Police don't want it and it isn't the kind of stuff to leave lying around."

"How does this get me back in the Bureau's good graces?"

"Won't they want to examine it?"

Sorsha sighed.

"I doubt it," she said. "The government does have research facilities for magical things, but that's not the FBI's jurisdiction."

Alex knew about the government labs, because he'd first met Sorsha when someone stole copies of Archimedean Monograph runes from the lab dedicated to rune research.

"Like as not, the Bureau won't want the stuff either," Sorsha went on.

Alex ground his teeth. No wonder magic was getting out of control; no one wanted to know about it.

"Okay, but I need you to come get it, anyway," Alex pressed. "Just tell them you'll turn it over to the FBI."

"Why?"

"Because if this stuff sits in an evidence room for long enough, someone is going to learn about it. The way I see it, the fewer people who know about this, the better."

"I see your point," Sorsha said wearily. "I'll come over and take charge of the case with the vials, but you understand you owe me a nice dinner for going out of my way."

"Of course," he replied with a smile.

30

ARMORED

Someone was knocking on Alex's door in an annoyingly chipper manner.

"Come on, Lockerby," a familiar voice called, much too loud and too close to be at his front door. "It's after ten."

Alex pried an eyelid open wide enough to glare at the bedroom door, barely visible with the blackout curtains closed. After far too short a time, the door opened and brilliant daylight spilled inside, burning his open eye and forcing him to roll away from the assault.

"Why are you still in bed?" Andrew Barton wondered, entering the room.

Alex groaned in response as the sorcerer waved his hand in the direction of the curtains. As he did, they slid open, filling the entire room with light.

"Go away," Alex mumbled, covering his face with the pillow.

Barton laughed at that.

"That must have been some party you went to last night," he said. "I'm a little bit insulted that you didn't invite me."

"You didn't want to go to this party," Alex grumbled as he forced himself to sit up. "Three cops dead, two bad guys dead, and a young woman traumatized."

A surprised Andrew hesitated.

"How do you manage to find murder and mayhem when you're out of town?" he asked.

"It's a gift," Alex said. He stood up wearing only his boxers and undershirt and searched for his pants. "Can I ask why you're here?"

"I wrapped up my business yesterday," the sorcerer said, obviously pleased with himself. "I'm planning on taking an airship home this evening, and when I went to check out and settle up downstairs, Julian told me you were still here."

"What did I ever do to him?"

"Oh, don't be like that," Andrew said. "I've got to go sign some papers in a few minutes, but then we can have lunch, and I'm supposed to meet the President after that. I thought you'd like to tag along."

Alex groaned. He'd just about had his fill of politics, but how could he say no to meeting the President?

"I need to talk to Sorsha," he managed, buttoning up his shirt.

"Is that blood?"

Alex looked down to see the dark stain across the bottom of his white shirt. To his credit, he resisted the urge to swear as he searched for his suit jacket. It took him almost a full minute to remember that he'd left it draped over Katherine Cohan's body.

This time he did swear.

"What's the matter?" Andrew asked.

Alex explained about his jacket as he found his rune book on the nightstand under his shotgun.

"You don't have a piece of chalk on you by chance?" he asked the sorcerer.

"No," Andrew said with a laugh, then he snapped his fingers, and a glowing line ran up the wall. It reached about the height of a door, then turned ninety degrees, ran across and then back down, forming a door of light.

Alex gave the sorcerer a sour look and tore a vault rune out of his book. He licked one edge, stuck it to the wall inside the door tracing, and ignited it.

"Show off," he grumbled as his vault door melted out of the wall. He pulled the door open and stopped short.

"What happened to your vault?" Barton said, looking past Alex.

Alex had forgotten that he'd put up a vestibule to keep people from seeing inside. He moved through the conference room, explaining about it to Andrew, who followed him in.

"Not a bad idea," the sorcerer admitted as Alex used his pocketwatch to open the cover door that separated the vestibule from the rest of his vault. "You really have an amazing space here. I'm actually jealous."

"You can teleport to your massive building in Manhattan in less time than it would take me to open the front door to this 'amazing space'," Alex said, heading toward the left hall where his vault bedroom was located.

"True," Andrew admitted, heading over to Alex's bookshelf in the reading area. "But there's something so elegant about having a portable home you can access from wherever you happen to be."

Alex rolled his eyes and left the sorcerer in the great room. It was true that his vault was an impressive bit of magic, probably the most impressive in his repertoire, but it was nothing to a sorcerer.

Comparing his magic to that of Andrew or Sorsha was a losing proposition, so Alex pushed the thought from his mind and concentrated on retrieving one of his spare suits. Three minutes later he emerged, properly dressed, with his hair slicked back.

"Now you look awake," Barton said with a chuckle. "Go ahead and call Sorsha, you can invite her to come with us, and we'll go sightseeing in the afternoon."

"I thought you had papers to sign," Alex pointed out.

Barton waved his hand dismissively.

"That will only take a few minutes," he admitted. "Talk to your girlfriend and tell her we'll meet her in the hotel restaurant in an hour."

"Speaking of papers," Alex said, taking out his notebook and tearing out a page. "Here are the power readings you asked for." He handed the paper to the sorcerer. "The readings were pretty constant across the city, but we expected that."

"Excellent,' Andrew beamed. "It's nice to have that confirmed, well done."

"Your power tester is over there," Alex said, pointing at the box on one of his workbenches.

Andrew moved to retrieve his tester as Alex headed toward the vestibule to call Sorsha.

"What about that phone?" Andrew asked, pointing at the candlestick phone on the rollaway cabinet next to Alex's drafting table.

"I hook that up to my office when I'm in here working," he lied. "That way Sherry can call me without having to leave the waiting room."

Andrew considered that for a moment, then nodded.

"Clever," he said. "You always impress me, Alex. I'm very glad you're not a sorcerer."

"Why's that?" Alex asked, leading the way back into his hotel bedroom.

"You're too clever," Andrew said. "If you were a sorcerer, I'd be in danger of you outshining me." He gave Alex a smirk and a wink as they left the vault. "As it is, however, I reign supreme."

Alex rolled his eyes, but he laughed in spite of it. Barton had an ego as big as the outdoors, but he also had the power to match it.

"I'll leave you to bask in your glory," Alex said, picking up the telephone. He dialed the Fairfax and asked for Sorsha's room.

"Alex?" Sorsha's groggy voice greeted him. "Why are you awake?"

"Andrew is here," he said, knowing that would explain everything. "He wants to have lunch and then go sightseeing."

"Does he want a balloon and a ride on the carousel in front of the Smithsonian as well?" she grumped.

Alex snorted in laughter at the mental image of the Lightning Lord on a carousel horse.

"I suspect it's a possibility," he said. "In any case, I need to talk to Tiffany Young before I do anything else."

"What are you going to tell her?"

"That the case is at a dead end," Alex admitted. "There are just too many potential motives. I don't have any idea where to even begin weeding out the possibilities for a proper suspect."

Alex didn't like the truth of it and, based on the sound of Sorsha grinding her teeth, neither did she.

"Well, we'd better tell her in person," she said. "This isn't the kind of news a woman wants to get over the phone."

"We?" Alex asked, noting her phraseology.

"Someone needs to apologize for how badly the FBI bungled this case," she said. "Since no one else even thinks there is a case, I suppose it falls to me."

"How soon can you get here?"

"Soon," she said, then the line went dead.

Did she hang up?

He had his answer a moment later when Sorsha popped into existence right beside him.

Not expecting that, Alex jumped, causing Sorsha to lose her balance, and she grabbed for him.

"Don't move," she gasped, her face a bit green.

Alex knew teleporting nauseated her, so he grabbed her arm and held her steady as she got her stomach back under control.

"Didn't I just wake you up?" he asked as Sorsha straightened up. She was wearing an open-collar white blouse with a high-waisted black skirt and heels. It was simple, but like all things Sorsha wore, she made the outfit, not the other way around.

She smiled up at him and patted his cheek. As she did so, he noticed that her makeup was subtle and flawless.

"You're sweet," she said, a bit of a patronizing tone in her voice. "You don't bat an eye when I teleport into your hotel room, but you wonder how I got dressed so quickly."

Alex felt a bit sheepish for not thinking of that. No matter how amazing Andrew found his vault, sorcerers were way out of his league when it came to raw power.

"Sorsha," Andrew said, coming over from where he'd been drinking Alex's Scotch. "Nice of you to join us. I didn't think you were interested in sightseeing."

"I enjoy many things," she said with a coy smile and a sideways glance at Alex. "But unfortunately, Alex and I need to wrap up a case before we can join you. Perhaps this afternoon?"

A momentary shadow of irritation flickered over the sorcerer's face and Alex almost laughed. For a century-old, nearly all-powerful sorcerer, he looked like a kid who'd been told the candy shop was out of his favorite sweet.

"If you must," he sighed, rallying. "But I have to meet Roosevelt at two, so it will have to be after that. Unless you want to come see the White House?"

Sorsha looked at Alex, then smiled sweetly.

"We should be done by then," she said, then turned to Alex. "But we do need to get going."

Alex offered her his arm, and they headed for the door.

Tiffany Young lived in a modest town home in Georgetown not very far from where Tony Casetti had taken up residence. When Alex and Sorsha arrived by cab, there was a truck in the driveway and several men in coveralls were removing trunks and pieces of furniture from the house.

"Alex," Tiffany said when he entered the foyer through the open door with Sorsha. She stood at the top of a long staircase watching the workmen as they went about their tasks. "Who's your fashionable friend?"

"This is Sorsha Kincaid," Alex explained as Tiffany descended the stairs. She wore a short cream-colored dress that hugged her curves expertly. "She's a consultant for the FBI and she's been looking into your husband's case."

"The sorceress?" Tiffany said with a raised eyebrow and an expression of delight. "It's a pleasure."

"Are you leaving town, Mrs. Young?" Sorsha asked.

Tiffany's smile slipped, just for an instant, then her look of pleasant affability returned.

"Sadly, this home is owned by the Illinois delegation, so I have to yield to Mrs. Unger. She's following her husband out next week."

"Isn't that kind of sudden?" Alex asked. "Your husband just died."

Tiffany gave him a sad little smile and nodded.

"That's politics for you," she said. "My husband was on several important committees and Bill Unger had to be here to cover his duties, at least until they reorganize everything."

"What happens then?" Sorsha asked.

"Oh, committee assignments are highly coveted," Tiffany said. "My husband had a great deal of seniority and influence, so his committee assignments will go to someone else with similar pull."

"So once the Senate reorganizes the assignments, Senator Unger will be on different committees?" Alex asked. It made sense, in a mercenary way, but it just seemed unseemly.

"That's right," Tiffany said. "But you didn't come here to talk about the inner workings of the Senate. Have you learned anything new about my husband's death?"

Alex took a deep breath and told the Widow Young what they knew and what they suspected. He knew it wasn't what she wanted to hear, but she was due the truth.

"So my husband's killer won't be brought to justice?" she confirmed when Alex finished.

"I won't say it's impossible," Alex prevaricated, "but right now the only thing we know for sure is that he was murdered."

"Given your husband's position," Sorsha interjected, "there are simply too many potential motives to narrow down a suspect."

Tiffany sighed, folding her arms, then she nodded.

"I understand," she said in a small voice. She rallied almost instantly, though the sadness remained in her eyes. "I owe you for your work," she said. "My handbag is upstairs."

She turned and headed back up, leaving Alex and Sorsha in an awkward silence.

"Mrs. Young?" a new voice called.

Alex turned to find a young man in a cheap suit standing just outside the open door. He had dark hair and eyes, with a pale complexion, and a look of earnestness on his face.

"Mrs. Young, I'm here for your husband's files," he called again.

"I'll be with you in a moment," Tiffany said from the top of the stairs.

"I'm sorry, Mrs. Young," the young man continued, "but this really can't wait. Senator Unger is already in the committee meeting, and he'll need those papers once they vote."

Tiffany blew out an exasperated breath and returned down the stairs. When she reached the foyer, she turned and opened an ornate door, revealing a well-appointed office beyond. She went to the desk inside and retrieved a folio that had been tied closed with a heavy string. As she returned to the foyer, Alex noticed that there was also a paper seal securing the folio's lid.

"Here," she said, thrusting the folio at the young man.

"This was everything your husband had in his safe?" the young man asked as he checked to see that the paper seal was intact.

"Of course it is," Tiffany said, indignance in her voice. "I'm not a fool. Now you've got what you came for, be on your way."

The young man tucked the folio under his arm and nodded to Tiffany before withdrawing.

"Idiot," Tiffany fumed once he was gone.

"What was that about?" Sorsha asked.

"My husband was on the Armed Services committee," Tiffany said, turning back to them. "The Army is very peculiar about their secrets. Whenever anything classified is discussed in committee, they're only given the relevant details. The rest is held by the committee chair, in this case my husband, until whatever they're voting on is approved."

"They vote without knowing everything?" Alex asked, flabbergasted by the idea.

Tiffany smirked, then favored him with a smile.

"Of course," she said. "You can vote on whether or not to move a military base without knowing how many planes are stationed there, for example. The number of planes or trucks or whatever is only disclosed if the committee votes to approve the move."

"I suppose that makes sense," Sorsha said, though she wore a look of disapproval on her otherwise perfect face.

"I'll get you a check for your fee," Tiffany said to Alex, heading for the stairs again.

"Would you mind if I used your phone while you're gone?" Alex asked.

"Not at all," she said, pointing at an open door on the opposite side of the foyer from the office. "There's one in the kitchen, just through there."

"I know that look," Sorsha said as she followed Alex into the kitchen. "What are you thinking?"

Alex didn't answer, instead picking up the phone and dialing the number for the D.C. Police.

"Detective Norton, please," he asked once the police operator came on. While she worked to connect him, Alex looked at Sorsha. "Remember when we were going through Senator Young's pending legislation?"

"Of course."

"Norton took the ones dealing with the Army," he explained, "and—"

"Norton," the detective's voice interrupted him.

"Detective," he said into the receiver. "Alex Lockerby. The other night in Senator Young's office, you went through all the military stuff. Do you remember anything that was secret, or classified?"

"No," Norton said. "Some of it was pretty light on specifics, but there wasn't anything with redacted information or anything like that."

Alex chewed his lip for a second, trying to remember while Sorsha crowded close, pushing her ear against the side of his head in an attempt to hear the conversation.

"Didn't you say you there was a proposal for the Army to take over some government research project?"

Norton hesitated for a long moment.

"It was called the Armored Initiative," he said at last. "The Army wanted to consolidate a bunch of government research labs into one location. Somewhere in the middle of the Nevada desert."

That sounded like some kind of new tank or maybe a way to reinforce transport ships. Alex sighed.

"I remember because Armored was an acronym," Norton said. "You know, ARMRD." He laughed at that. "The government really loves their alphabet soup."

"What did it stand for?" Sorsha interjected, breaking Alex's train of thought.

Norton hesitated again.

"Something about an army research division," he said.

"Well if it was called Armor, the AR could be for Army," Alex said.

"And on the end RD would stand for Research Division," Sorsha added.

"I don't remember," Norton apologized. "Why is this important?"

"Magic," Alex said. The second the word was out of his mouth he knew he was right. "ARMRD, the Army Magic Research Division."

Sorsha looked at him with confusion on her face.

"Think about it," he said to her, excitement creeping into his voice. "Tiffany said that the Army is careful about its secrets, so much so that they had her husband keep the relevant details locked in his office."

"So?"

"So if they're that careful about secrets, why did they send some kid to retrieve them, by himself?"

"What are you talking about, Lockerby?" Norton asked through the headset.

Alex ignored him as he looked at Sorsha.

"No," Sorsha said at last. "Government secrets would have been picked up by a courier with an escort, either from the Capitol Police or the military."

She looked in the direction of the front door, and the expression on her face told Alex she'd arrived at the conclusion he'd already reached.

"That courier is long gone," she said. "So what's in that pack of secrets he wants so badly?"

"Remember how we met?" Alex prompted.

Sorsha though a moment, then gasped.

"The government's rune research lab."

"Where is it?"

"I don't think they ever told me," Sorsha said. "I only know it was in Tennessee somewhere because that's where the thief, Quinton Sanders, lived."

"I think you'd better find out," Alex said, hanging up on Detective Norton. "Unless I'm very much mistaken, the Legion now has the address of that facility."

Sorsha grabbed Alex's arm with a sudden fierceness.

"They have hundreds of rune books there," she said. "Maybe thousands."

"And the Legion is gaining power by pooling rune lore," Alex said.

"From what I was told, the government got those books by purchasing them from the families of deceased runewrights," Sorsha said. "Most of them probably aren't important—"

"But some of them might hold powerful secrets," Alex finished.

"They have to know we've linked them to Senator Young's death," Sorsha said. "That's why they tried to kill you."

Alex nodded.

"We've upset their plans," he said. "They know they don't have much time."

"They're going to move as soon as they can," Sorsha said.

Alex flipped open the lid of his pocketwatch, then headed back out into the foyer.

"Talk to your FBI contacts," he said over his shoulder. "Find out where that rune lab is located and get as many agents as you can ready to move."

"What are you going to do?"

Alex put on his hat as he headed for the curb.

"Call out the army," he said.

31

OAK RIDGE

"Thank you, lieutenant," Alex said, not bothering to hide the frustrated sarcasm in his voice. "You've been a big help." Without waiting for the man to say anything more, Alex slammed the receiver of the phone down hard enough that the bell inside its body rung. "Stupid son-of-a-whore," he growled at the phone.

Alex felt the tingle of magic run up his spine, and Sorsha suddenly appeared in the room. Her face bore the greenish tinge he'd come to associate with teleportation, but there were lines of anger around her eyes.

"I take it you've been having as good a time as I have," he said.

"Bastards," she swore in a gasping breath. "They...they wouldn't listen to me. I came this close to turning that smug jackanapes Sherman Blake into the weasel he so obviously is."

Alex offered her a cigarette once she'd calmed her stomach.

"I'm getting the same run-around from the Army," Alex said, squeezing his lighter to life for her. "If Walter was still alive, he'd have offered a few squads of Marines just on my say so."

Admiral Walter Tennon had run the Manhattan Naval Shipyards and had used Alex to help unravel several cases relating to the Navy. He'd also been Alex's friend. Alex had called on him to help stop a

German saboteur just a few months ago and Walter had jumped at the chance. It was a decision that had cost him his life. Strictly speaking, it wasn't Alex's fault. In his head, he understood that, but the rest of him — wasn't so sure.

"What about Commander Vaughn?" Sorsha asked.

Alex shook his head.

"Vaughn's been promoted to Captain, and is out in the Atlantic somewhere with his new ship. What about that General over at Fort Hamilton, what was his name? Blake?"

Sorsha nodded, then sighed.

"General Blake and I aren't on speaking terms at the moment," she said. "He wanted to give all the credit for saving the flying bomb experiment to his security force. Naturally the FBI disagreed, since the Army really didn't do much. He took it rather personally."

Alex ground his teeth. A group of powerful and dangerous runewrights were going to be raiding a top secret government facility any minute...and no one cared.

"What we need is access to someone in charge," he said, beginning to pace.

"Ooo. Like the President?" Sorsha said, a half-smile ghosting across her face.

"Andrew," Alex said, slapping his forehead. How could he have forgotten the sorcerer's two o'clock meeting? Consulting his pocket watch, his excitement evaporated. It was well after three. "We're too late," he said.

"Even if their meeting is over, I'm sure Andrew can get Roosevelt on the phone," Sorsha said. "He's very persuasive. We just need to find him."

Alex grinned and motioned for Sorsha to follow.

"He's checking out today, so if his meeting is over, he's probably packing his trunk."

They left Alex's suite and headed down to the end of the hall to the corner suite. The door stood open, and all Alex could do was gape. His own suite was enormous, but this one was twice its size. There were at least three rooms off the main room, which itself included a full bar and formal dining area.

Two packed suitcases stood in the little foyer area by the door, next to a large portmanteau trunk that stood open. Before Alex could say anything, a man's shirt came flying out of one of the room doors, swung itself around a hanger that leapt up out of the case, and then dropped down onto a rail with the other articles of clothing. A pair of socks followed, twisting together into a rolled-up bundle as they flew.

"Andrew?" Alex called, assured the sorcerer was present.

He stepped inside the room and had to dodge a flying suit coat and a pair of trousers that joined the white shirt and the socks in the trunk.

"Is that you, Alex?" the sorcerer's voice preceded him into the main room. "Well, here you two are," he said in the manner of a schoolmaster admonishing wayward students. "Do you realize what pains I had to endure without you? I had to meet with the President without anyone there to act as a buffer. It was frightfully dull."

Alex turned to Sorsha with a sly grin on his face.

"Apparently our friend is in need of some excitement," he said. "Should I tell him?"

"No, no," Sorsha said, picking up on Alex's game. "Let me tell him."

"Oh, I couldn't do that," Alex protested. "Make you do all the work? That would be ungentlemanly."

Both of them understood that the longer they kept Andrew on the hook, the more eager he would be to help.

"But I insist," Sorsha said, pulling Alex close and leaning against him.

"Absolutely nauseating," Barton said. "If you two are quite through being cute, perhaps you could tell me about this adventure you keep hinting at."

"A dangerous group of runewrights is about to raid the government's rune research facility in order to steal the lore books that are housed there," Alex said. "They just learned of its location today, so the attack could come at any time."

Andrew started to laugh, but when neither Alex nor Sorsha smiled, he did a double-take.

"You can't be serious," he scoffed. "How much threat could a gang of angry runewrights..." His sentence trailed off as he looked at Alex. "You are serious," he said at last.

"You wanted adventure, Andrew," Sorsha said with an arched eyebrow. "Here's the kicker. No one will listen to us."

"These people call themselves the Legion," Alex explained. "They've been collecting all the rune lore they can get their hands on, and they're sharing it among their members. They aren't to be taken lightly."

Barton put his hand to his chin, then stroked his pencil mustache as he considered what they'd said.

"We want you to contact the President and have him mobilize some soldiers to stop it," Sorsha said.

"No," Andrew said with a note of finality. "If you're right about these Legion people being dangerous, then we need to move fast."

"Isn't the President in charge of the Army?" Alex asked.

"Yes," Andrew said, waving his hand in a dismissive gesture, "but he'd have to issue orders to some general or other, then they'd issue orders to a colonel who would issue orders to a lieutenant who would call up a sergeant...and by the time it was all said and done, they'd be ready next week. Maybe. What we need is someone who can just order up some men on their say-so."

"Do you know anyone like that?" Alex asked.

Andrew let a slow grin play across his face and he waggled his eyebrows.

"As a matter of fact, I do," he said. "Where, exactly, is this top-secret rune library?"

"Oak Ridge, Tennessee," Sorsha said.

"Is there a military base nearby?" Andrew pressed.

She shrugged in response.

"I have no idea. I had to threaten my government contact with frostbite in his nether regions to get that much."

Alex managed not to chuckle at this serious moment. He would have given a lot to be a fly on the wall for that conversation.

"That's going to be a problem, then," Andrew said. "I know a guy who will issue the order, but there needs to be soldiers nearby. I could teleport three or four, but after that, I'd be exhausted. I assume we need more troops than that."

He looked at Alex and Sorsha, who could only nod.

"In that case," Andrew went on, "we need to find out where the nearest military base is to Oak Ridge. I know a few people I can call, but if it's too far away, I don't know what we're going to do."

"We don't have time for that," Sorsha said, turning to look up at Alex. "You'll have to handle getting the soldiers from wherever they are to Oak Ridge."

"How will Alex do that?"

"I'll have to go with you to get them," Alex said to Barton. "We'll put the men in my vault, then once I'm in Oak Ridge, I'll open the vault to let them out."

"I've never been to Oak Ridge, Alex," Andrew said. "I won't be able to teleport there."

"It will be Sorsha's job to get me there," he explained. "All we have to do is call the local sheriff and she can use his voice to teleport to him."

The sorcerer's face lit up like a kid on Christmas.

"You can do that?" he said, turning to Sorsha.

"I do more than make cold disks, you know."

He clapped his hands and rubbed them together.

"That's fantastic," he said. "I'll call George and get the ball rolling."

He turned to the phone, and Sorsha leaned close to Alex.

"I've been thinking. I believe I can get the FBI's help after all," she whispered.

"How?"

"By using the branch of the Bureau that likes me," she said.

Alex nodded, catching on. Sorsha had a team of FBI agents at her beck and call back in New York, not to mention that Director Stevens of the Manhattan field office liked her. She could probably round up a force of several dozen heavily armed agents without too much trouble.

"One problem," she went on, "or rather the same problem Andrew has."

"Have everyone meet at my office," Alex said. "I'll make sure the door to my vault is open, then I'll just take your agents along with the soldiers."

"How are you going to explain that to Andrew?"

Alex sighed and shrugged.

"I'll have to show him how my vault really works," he said. Alex didn't particularly like that idea, because Andrew had a way of trying to utilize any of Alex's abilities in his business. Still, he couldn't just let the Legion make off with hundreds of unknown lore books. There was no telling what might be lost in the government's collection.

As if sensing his inner conflict, Sorsha stood on her tip-toes and kissed his cheek.

"I'll get going," she said.

"Wait," Alex said. "Save your strength. I'll open my vault and you can just walk through and make your calls from my office."

"All right," Andrew said, hanging up the phone. "My friend George is at Fort Riley in Kansas. You ready to go?"

"You've been to Fort Riley?" Alex asked.

Barton's face turned a bit smug.

"During the big war, the army had me visit quite a few of their bases to look for possible points of magical attack," he said, reaching for Alex's sleeve.

"Just a second," Alex said, pulling his arm away. "Before we go, I need to get Sorsha situated, and you might as well come along.

"I'm shocked," Andrew Barton said. He stood with his hands on his hips in Alex's office on the twelfth floor of Empire Tower. "You've been holding out on me. What other miracles can you perform that I don't know about?"

"That isn't any of your business, Andrew," Sorsha admonished him in a hard voice.

"It most certainly is," he protested. "Do you know how many times a week I have to teleport back and forth to the relay towers just to check on things? Alex here could put a door in each tower and one in my office. I could just walk there in seconds without expending any power."

"I don't know how many doors I can open at once," Alex said. "One of my doors disappeared about the time I opened a fifth one. I don't know if it's related, but it might be."

Andrew waved his hand dismissively.

"Nothing we can't figure out, I'm sure," he said. "Just imagine what this magic is capable of. You could have doors to warehouses all over the world and move goods almost instantaneously. Think how much travelers would be willing to pay to go to Hawaii, or Europe, or Australia by just walking down a short hallway. The possibilities fire the imagination."

"I'm more worried about some government using it to send troops to attack other countries from inside their borders," Alex said.

Andrew's smile evaporated, then he sighed.

"They would use it like that, wouldn't they," he said with a sour expression. "Why must politicians and despots always ruin everything?"

Alex was raised by a man of amazing faith, yet he still didn't have an answer for that particular question.

"The more people who know about my vault, the more chance there is for trouble," Alex said. "We need to keep this quiet."

"I suppose," Andrew sighed. "But I still want doors to my towers, if you can manage it."

"I'll see what I can do," Alex said, glancing at Sorsha, who was deep in conversation with someone on her team. "Right now, though, we need to go to Kansas."

"Right," Andrew said, clapping Alex on the shoulder.

The next instant they were gone.

There was an old joke Alex once heard about Kansas, something about it being so flat you could stand on a fruit crate and see the back of your own head. Alex had never understood that until he and Barton appeared in front of the administration building on Fort Riley.

To be fair, the surrounding land was made up of low, gently rolling hills, but they seemed to go on forever like an undulating, featureless sea of winter brown grass. Beyond the few decorative trees planted on the Army base, Alex couldn't see anything sticking up in any direction.

"This way," Andrew said, heading right through the front doors of the Administration Building. A startled soldier inside leaped to his feet and ordered them to halt as Alex came in behind the sorcerer.

"At ease, son," Andrew said, not slowing at all. "I'm here from Washington and I need a word with the duty officer."

The man behind the front desk hesitated, but he'd clearly seen Andrew and Alex appear out of thin air. After a moment he sat back down, clearly deciding that whatever was happening was above his pay grade.

"George, you old horse soldier," Andrew said as he opened the first door down the corridor. When Alex caught up, he found the sorcerer shaking hands with a hard-looking man in the uniform of a Lt. Colonel. "This is my friend, Alex," he said, pointing to Alex.

"I understand you've got a problem on your hands," the Lt. Colonel said, limping out from behind his desk. "And you want a few dozen men to take care of it."

Alex noted that the Lt. Colonel kept his left leg straight, as if he couldn't bend it, and there was a well-worn wooden cane in the corner.

"That's it, George," Andrew said. "If Alex here is right, a group of runewrights is going to attack the government's rune research facility."

"Runewrights?" the Lt. Colonel scoffed.

"I know what you're thinking," Andrew said. "But you can take my word for it, these people are dangerous. Whatever they want at that research facility, it isn't good."

The Army man gave the sorcerer a hard, calculating look and for a moment Alex thought he was going to turn them down.

"If you're wrong, there'll be hell to pay," he said.

"I'll take the blame," Andrew said. "You can tell whoever is above you that you owed me from that time I saved your life during that business with Pancho Villa."

"As if they'd believe that," George said. "I'm not worried about the blame," he went on. "I can always play it off as a necessary precaution to preserve the Republic."

Andrew's face grew shrewd as he looked at his friend.

"Then what are you worried about?"

George leaned heavily against his desk and slapped his bum leg.

"This," he said. "Damn horse kicked me six months back. If I'm not ready to return to full duty soon, they'll...well they'll retire me. Drum me out of the Army."

"And you'd rather not be a civilian again," Alex guessed.

"That's exactly it," the Army man said. "The Army won't spring for a doctor with alchemy training. This leg will take a major restoration potion to fix."

"And you can't afford that on an Army salary," Alex said.

"Your wife's family has plenty of money," Barton said.

"They want me out of the Army, too," George said. "And things have been a little strained in that area lately."

"All right," Andrew said. "You get us the men and I'll bring you the best doctor in New York to fix your leg, deal?"

He stuck out his hand and the Lt. Colonel took it.

"How long will it take you to get ready?" Barton asked.

"I got the men ready to go out back," George said. He opened the drawer to his desk and pulled out a gun belt with a Colt Army revolver in a leather holster.

"Where do you think you're going?" Andrew said, a look of amusement on his face.

George limped right up to the sorcerer and stood nose-to-nose with him.

"Those are my men," he growled. "I'm responsible for them, and I won't send them into harm's way while I cower in my office like a schoolmarm."

By the look on his face, Andrew wanted to argue, but he just as clearly saw no point.

"All right," he said. "Let's go."

An hour and a half later, Sorsha took hold of Alex's arm and sent them spinning through the clothes wringer that was magical teleportation. Feeling like his entire body had been compressed flat and then shaken violently, Alex staggered against a papered wall as he re-emerged into the world.

He felt like his long-ago breakfast would return, but a few deep breaths calmed his quavering stomach. Beside him, Sorsha clung to his arm and panted like a dog on a hot day.

"Well, that was pretty quick," a portly man in a tan police uniform said, hanging up the phone receiver he had in his hand. He sat behind a plain desk in a little office with a door off to Alex's left. It looked remarkably like the office Danny Pak occupied back in Manhattan, except the only glass was a frosted panel in the single door.

"Thank you, Sheriff Tibbs," Sorsha said, finding her voice.

"Always happy to help the FBI, ma'am," he said with a folksy smile. He had a round, grizzled face with a bushy mustache that grew out to the sides, like a furry handlebar. The hair on his head was black, but the mustache had begun to go gray at the roots, as had the Sheriff's eyebrows.

"Now," he said, standing up from his desk. "Do you want to tell me what this is all about?"

"Sheriff!" a woman's voice interrupted from outside the little office. The door burst open and a short, busty brunette entered the office. "We just got a call from old man Whittaker," she gasped, out of breath. "He says someone's shooting guns over on the far side of his property, a lot of guns."

"That wouldn't be anywhere near the government building outside of town, would it?" Sorsha asked.

"Uh, yeah," Sheriff Tibbs said. "What's going on here?"

"Get your car, Sheriff," Sorsha said. "I'll explain on the way."

32

THE BLOWUP

By the time Sheriff Tibbs' patrol car rounded the last bend in the long gravel drive there was no gunfire to be heard. Six large trucks were parked in front of three small, unassuming buildings and men in work clothes were busily hauling armloads of books and crates of files into the vehicles. When they saw the sheriff's car, most of them dropped their burdens and pulled pistols from their belts.

Shots rang out, and the windshield of the car shattered. Alex ducked down in the back seat as glass flew everywhere and Sheriff Tibbs swerved off the road. Bullets pinged off the sides and roof, until Sorsha raised her hand and a glowing shield leaped up just outside the car.

"Get to cover," Alex said as he reached up past the sorceress to open the car's passenger door.

"My shield will hold," Sorsha replied as Alex leapt out.

"Too late for that," Sheriff Tibbs groaned, pressing his hand to his side where blood seeped through his uniform shirt.

"Lay down," Sorsha ordered.

"No," Alex said. "They've stopped shooting."

"They realize they're up against a sorceress," she said, trying to lay the Sheriff on the front seat.

"They're casting spellbreaker runes on their guns," Alex hissed, grabbing Sorsha and pulling her from the car. Before she could protest, a shot rang out and her glowing shield cracked.

The Sorceress gasped and pressed her hand to her stomach as if she'd been punched. Spellbreaker runes caused feedback that manifested as physical pain for sorcerers.

"See," Alex said, reaching past her to grab Tibbs by the shoulders and haul him out on the far side of the car from the gunmen.

"You're very smug when you're right," Sorsha growled at him as three more spellbreaker shots slammed into her shield, causing it to shatter. Immediately the constant fire continued, and bullets tore into the side of the police car.

"We need to even the odds," Sorsha said. She lifted her hand as if she were directing a church choir to rise and a blue mist came up from the ground between them and the now bullet-ridden car. In a moment, it solidified into a thick wall of ice. "Let's see them dispel that," she growled.

"Clever," Alex said with a grin. Spellbreakers could affect magic but once Sorsha's ice was summoned, it was just ice. He took out his rune book and paged through until he found his flash runes. Tearing three of them out, he crumpled each page up into a ball. "Can you set fire to these if they're inside a snowball?"

Sorsha looked at the crumpled pages, then grinned, catching his train of thought.

"Of course," she said, snapping her fingers. The crumpled paper on Alex's outstretched palm was instantly enveloped in a ball of fluffy white snow.

"Here," he said, passing the remaining papers to Sorsha. "Light this as soon as I throw it, then wait ten seconds and throw the next one, then the next. I'm going to try to get around to the side of that nearest building and open my vault."

Sorsha took the paper, then grabbed his wrist. She pulled him close and kissed him.

"Don't do anything stupid," she admonished once they separated.

Alex chuckled and shook his head.

"Do I ever?"

"Remind me to give you a list," Sorsha said, as he cocked his arm back and threw the snowball.

Alex covered his eyes, then heard Sorsha snap her fingers again. Blinding light erupted over the drive between the trucks and the Sheriff's car, and Alex could hear shouts of alarm and cursing from the far end.

He waited a second for the light to dissipate, then ran forward in a crouch, around the side of the bullet-ridden car. He didn't dare look at the gunmen, but he knew some of them were probably behind cover when the flash went off. That meant they would be looking out any moment. He still had his linking rune connecting him to the shield runes in his vault. He'd written two groups of five and put them on opposite sides of his vault to keep them from interfering with each other. The attack earlier had burned through six, leaving only four. As he ran along the trees toward the first building, he hoped it would be enough.

Just as he expected, shots began to ring out and bullets tore into the trees around him. Alex stopped crouching and ran flat out, just as another snowball flash went off. This time there was more cursing, but the bullets shredding the trees kept up. One slammed into Alex's knee, making him stumble, but the shield rune kept it from crippling him.

After another few seconds of frantic running, Alex outdistanced the shots. The men firing were blind or mostly blind, and they couldn't see where he'd gone. Huffing and puffing from running, Alex reached the building he'd been aiming for. There were windows in the front, and he could clearly see men inside, scrambling to drop armloads of books into wooden crates for transport. One of the men, a heavyset man with a thick, single eyebrow, looked up just as Alex passed. He raised his hand, pointing at Alex, and screamed a warning to his companions.

Alex kept running, past the windows, to where the wall of the building was plain brick. Fumbling his chalk from his pocket, he traced a line up from the ground as the third flash snowball went off. He'd forgotten about it and was dazzled for a moment before he continued drawing the door.

Reaching into the outside pocket of his suit coat, Alex pulled out the vault rune he'd prepared. As he licked it and stuck it to the brick wall, he could hear the shouts of men coming closer. Squeezing his lighter to life, he raised it to the paper just as a bullet slammed into his hand. The lighter spun away, and Alex cursed as he jerked his hand back. A second shot whizzed by him, impacting the brick to his right.

Dropping to his knee, Alex searched for the lighter as more shots whizzed by him. The little brass rectangle lay just a few feet away in the grass and he lunged for it as another shot hit him square in the back.

Lighting it as he surged to his feet, Alex touched the flame to the paper and the rune flared to life. Beyond the glowing rune, Alex could see three men standing by the corner of the building. They had been blinded by the flash rune, but they could clearly see enough to shoot.

As the heavy steel door of his vault melted out of the brick wall, the gunmen regained their vision. They poured lead toward Alex and bullets exploded against the brick all around him. A slug clipped him in the hip, and another grazed his side. With his shield runes gone, the second hit felt like someone seared his ribs with a branding iron, and he grunted in pain.

Hands trembling, Alex shoved his key into the vault lock and turned it. As he pulled for all he was worth, another bullet sank into the meaty portion of his thigh, and he fell.

"We got him now," one of the men yelled as they closed in.

Alex lost his grip on the vault door, but it didn't matter; as soon as the door had begun to open, someone inside pushed it the rest of the way.

"Look out," one of the gunmen yelled.

He started to say something else, but was cut off by the roar of a shotgun blast. More gunfire erupted from beyond the open door that was now shielding Alex from the conflict.

"You dead, son?" the Lt. Colonel said, limping around the door.

"Nope," Alex said, trying to get his good leg under him. "They hit me in the leg."

"Well, up and at 'em," the Army man said, limping past. "My boys and I are going around the back to catch them unaware, and you don't want to be late for the party."

As Alex struggled to his feet, the Lt. Colonel limped past him with a line of soldiers carrying rifles behind.

No wonder Andrew likes that guy, he's nuts.

"You all right?" Barton himself asked as Alex limped around the door and into the vault. He was standing just inside the vestibule holding Alex's Thompson submachine gun.

"Got me in the leg," he reported. "Stings like the dickens, but it isn't bleeding too much."

Andrew handed him the Thompson and gave him a roguish grin.

"Well let's get out there, then," he said. "I don't want to miss all the fun."

Alex pulled the charge lever on the Thompson, then gripped it in both hands before nodding back to Andrew.

"I've had about all I can take of these Legion jackasses," he growled, then limped back out into the evening light.

The three men who had been shooting at Alex were down, and two of them were obviously dead. Alex could hear gunfire coming from around the corner, and he could see one man up by the trucks who stood with his gun raised, but he was encased in a block of ice.

Clearly Sorsha had entered the fray.

Hurrying as best he could, Alex made his way to the corner of the building. A dozen FBI agents were engaged with about twenty gunmen. Agent Redhorn stood at the front, firing his shotgun with little concern for his own safety.

As Alex watched, one of the Legion men darted out from around the cover of one of the trucks and shot Redhorn in the chest. The man tried to fire again but his revolver clicked empty. Redhorn raised his shotgun, but it was empty as well. Snarling in defiance, the Legion man pulled a wicked-looking knife and rushed the FBI agent. Two more men appeared from around the truck and followed their companion.

Redhorn didn't even blink. As the man with the knife came in, he lashed out with the butt of the shotgun, slamming it into the attacker's face. Before the assailant could crumple to the ground, Redhorn dropped the shotgun, grabbed the knife out of the man's hand, then stepped forward to slash the throat of the second man. The third assailant didn't have time to halt his forward momentum, and Redhorn raised the bloody blade just in time for the man to impale himself on it.

As a fourth man stepped out from behind the truck and raised a rifle in the FBI man's direction, Alex shouldered the Thompson and cut the gunman down with a short burst of fire. Startled by the sudden barrage, Redhorn turned, and Alex could see blood leaking from a wound in the right side of his chest. Ignoring the bleeding, Redhorn saluted Alex with his bloody knife, then dropped it and picked up the discarded shotgun.

Beside Alex, Barton raised his hand, and a bolt of raw, sorcerous lightning slammed into an armed group that had just emerged from one of the buildings.

"Can't let you have all the fun," he said.

Off to Alex's left, Agent Mendes leaned around the cover of a truck and fired two shots from her service weapon. As she ducked back, she caught sight of a Legion man who rushed her with his rifle raised like a club. Mendes watched him come, then sidestepped the blow at the last second. As the man passed, she jammed her 1911 pistol up under his arm and pulled the trigger. He went down like a puppet whose strings had been cut and lay, kicking the dirt for a few seconds until he stopped moving.

Turning his attention back to the fight, Alex found the FBI men giving ground. Close to thirty Legion gunmen were pouring fire into their cover and already several of them were down. Alex leaned against the corner of the building, using it to steady his aim, and unloaded with the Thompson. Chattering and jumping, it cut down a half-dozen men before the drum ran empty.

Fire began coming at Alex, and he had to duck behind the corner. Andrew just stood in the open, bullets deflecting around him as tiny bolts of electricity leapt from his body, intercepting them. He raised his hand and blasted the line of gunmen. Many went down, but they kept coming.

"Fall back," Redhorn yelled, scrambling to take cover.

The Legion men heard the call as a sign of victory, and they charged forward. The thunder of long guns dwarfed the sound of the handguns and a chunk of the Legion men went down. Thunder roared again and more fell.

Several dropped their weapons and attempted to flee down the road, only to be frozen to the ground by Sorsha. Others continued charging the FBI men, who cut them down with withering fire. The rest turned to face the new threat: George and his soldiers had taken up positions behind them, and were cutting them down in the crossfire.

Alex sighed as his leg throbbed. They had managed to neutralize the Legion's manpower advantage, but it had been a narrow thing, and there were losses on both sides. A shot broke the glass window on the back side of the building and Alex realized the people inside were shooting out at him. He ducked back, but caught sight of several men going through the crate full of books. One of them gathered up as much as he could carry, then stood up, touched his hand to his heart... and vanished.

Alex swore.

The Legion members were using escape runes to get out with whatever they could carry.

Dropping the Thompson, Alex pulled out his rune book. In the back, where he kept the more expensive, less-used runes, was one he hadn't written. This one was one of Iggy's creations. Complicated beyond what Alex could currently manage, it was made of multiple layers of overlapping lines, and carefully created symbols. To Alex it resembled a bouquet of flowers.

No matter what it looked like, the rune had one basic function: it blocked linking runes from working. Since Alex worked with linking runes all the time, it was the most dangerous rune he carried.

Sticking it to the brick wall beside him, Alex touched the paper with his lighter, and the rune flared to life. Unlike standard runes that would burn in place and then fade, this rune jumped off the wall, then began to swirl. The text appeared to unravel, sending out a ring of crimson light that grew bigger and bigger until it encompassed an area about fifty yards around.

Through the window, Alex watched as the next man to stand

touched his heart, then glanced around as nothing happened.

"Throw down your weapons," Alex yelled. "We've got you surrounded, and your escape runes have been neutralized."

It was very handy that escape runes were just a fancy kind of linking rune.

A few of the men inside started shooting, but Alex just retreated behind the brick. A moment later the Army long rifles boomed and several of the men inside crumpled to the floor. After that, everyone else raised their hands in surrender.

The battle for the rune lab was over.

Alex stood outside the little room where Sorsha was interrogating the ringleaders of the Legion raid. Medical personnel had arrived outside, but Alex's leg wound was superficial comparatively speaking, so he waited inside.

"What are you here looking for?" Sorsha asked the man handcuffed to the metal chair. He was an older man, perhaps in his late fifties, with gray hair and a goatee. Alex had pointed him out as one of the men telling the others what books to take.

As Sorsha glared at him, the man stubbornly refused to answer.

Alex felt a ripple of power as the Sorceress summoned her power.

"What were you looking for?" she asked again, although this time her voice was unnaturally deep and echoed as if she were in a vast cave.

"Th..." the gray-haired man stuttered. "The rune book of F-Felix Markel." He gasped and slumped forward as if that answer had cost him his strength.

"Why?" Sorsha pressed, throwing the weight of her truth spell into the question.

"Gordian rune," he gasped, then his body trembled, and he sat up straight as if he felt no strain at all.

"I think that's enough of that, Miss Kincaid," a new voice said, emerging from the man's lips.

The voice and the posture were easy, but Alex could see the gray-haired man's eyes, open wide and filled with terror.

"Mind rune," he whispered to no one in particular. It couldn't have functioned while the link blocker was active. but that rune only lasted five minutes. Once it was gone, the links would reconnect, just as this one had.

"Who are you?" Sorsha asked, her voice was back to normal.

The new presence must have distracted her enough to lose the spell.

"Where is the Archimedean Monograph, Miss Kincaid?" the voice asked.

Sorsha's eyes went wide, and she gasped.

"Don't know," she said, her voice stilted.

"Get her out of there," Alex hissed to Andrew's Army friend.

"Why?" George asked.

Alex didn't know how to explain that in the aftermath of a truth spell, sorcerers were susceptible to the same truth compulsion for a few moments. It was clear, however, that whoever the voice belonged to knew it.

"Who has it, Sorsha?" the voice pressed.

This time Sorsha just smiled, and Alex heaved a sigh of relief. The after-effects of the truth spell had passed for her.

"If I knew," she said, "I certainly wouldn't tell you."

The gray-haired man's expression changed to a sneer. Paradoxically, he also began to sweat. Alex could see that his eyes were still wide with terror.

"I guess in that case, we really don't have anything more to discuss," the voice said.

"Who are you?" Sorsha asked.

"I am Legion," he said. "For we are many. Was there anything else you wanted to know before I go?"

"Why is he asking for questions he's not going to answer?" George asked. "It's just a waste of time."

Alex felt a cold chill go down his spine.

"He's stalling," he said, looking hard at the sweating man. His body had begun to tremble.

"Sorsha!" Alex yelled. "Get out of there!"

Just as she looked up at Alex, the gray-haired man exploded.

33

MEDICAL ATTENTION

Alex's eyes slid open amid a haze of pain. Everything hurt, including his eyelids. As his vision swam in circles, he became aware of someone standing over him with a weapon of some kind.

He gave out a war cry and forced himself up, only to have his hands intercepted.

"Whoa there, champ," a familiar voice said.

Alex jerked his hands, trying to get them free, but his assailant had too firm a grip.

"Easy, Alex," the feminine voice said. "It's okay."

"Agent Mendes?"

"Welcome back, killer," the Latin woman said with her lopsided grin. A bloodstained bandage was wrapped around her head, but she seemed none the worse for wear. She released her hold on his wrists, and Alex noticed a timid looking nurse standing over him with a clipboard in hand.

"Where—" he began but then he remembered. "Sorsha!"

He tried to lurch up again, but the pain in his body hampered him so much that all Aissa Mendes had to do was lay her hand on his chest to force Alex back down.

"She's alive," Mendes said. "There are doctors with her right now."

"Iggy," Alex gasped. "Got to get Dr. Bell."

"Lay down, Mr. Lockerby," the nurse said. "You have a concussion."

"They found you buried under what was left of that building," Mendes said. "You're lucky to be alive."

Alex ignored both of them, and pushed himself up to a sitting position.

"What happened?" he growled through teeth clenched in pain. Everything seemed to hurt, even breathing.

"You yelled something," Mendes explained, "and then a bomb went off in the room the Ice Queen was using to interrogate the bad guys. It blew a hole in the side of the building."

Alex struggled to pat his pockets, and found both his rune book and his chalk.

"Where are we?" he insisted, bracing himself for the push to a standing position. "And how long have we been here?"

"This is the hospital in Oak Ridge," the nurse said, "and you were brought in about half an hour ago."

"Is Andrew Barton okay?"

Mendes nodded, and grabbed Alex's arm to study him as he forced himself to stand.

"Where is he?"

Mendes sighed and looped Alex's arm inside hers as if he were a girl on a date.

"Come on," she said, giving the nurse a knowing look. "I'll take care of him."

The nurse just shrugged and turned to the next bed. As Alex allowed himself to be led unsteadily to the aisle, he became aware of the room around him. This was obviously an emergency ward and at least two dozen men were laid out in beds. Some of them wore green Army uniforms while others had white shirts, most likely the FBI men. Others wearing workmen's clothes were scattered about as well, the Legion's men. All of those patients had handcuffs on one of their wrists, locking them to the metal frame of the hospital bed.

As Alex moved down the aisle, he noticed that many of the occupied beds had sheets pulled all the way up, obscuring the occupant.

"Is your partner all right?" he asked Mendes.

She grinned at him and nodded.

"He took a slug in the chest, just above his lung, according to the doctors," she said. "But he's too stubborn for that to slow him down. Since it's not life threatening, he's in the waiting room reading a magazine until there's a doctor free to dig the bullet out."

Alex remembered seeing Agent Redhorn get shot and taking out three of the Legion's men in the immediate aftermath.

"Sounds about right," he said.

Aissa led him through a set of double doors at the end of the hall and into a smaller room with a nurse at a desk. Standing next to her was Barton, along with his Army friend. The Lt. Colonel was on the phone and looked to be speaking very quickly.

"The situation required decisive action, sir," he said. "You know I'd have run it up the flagpole if I thought there was time, but the situation was exigent. As it was, we arrived just in time to prevent the wholesale theft of top-secret government research."

"Alex," Andrew said, catching sight of them. "They said you likely have a concussion. You need to lie down."

"I'm fine," Alex growled. "How's Sorsha?"

"Well, no, sir," George's voice broke in. "We got here thanks to Andrew Barton, the Sorcerer."

Andrew held up a finger to ward off further comments from Alex.

"Yes, sir," George went on. "I'll have a complete report for you in the morning."

Andrew turned back to Alex as George wrapped up his call with his superior.

"Sorsha will be fine," Andrew said. "She managed to shield herself from much of the blast and the doctors took a few chunks of table out of her, but they say she'll make a full recovery."

"Where is she?" Alex persisted.

"The doctors have her in an observation room," Andrew said, keeping his tone even. "Her body has started healing itself, but it's going slower than expected."

Alex ground his teeth as a wave of anger flowed through him, hiding the guilt he felt for not catching on to the Legion's booby-trap sooner.

"I need you to do something for me, Andrew," he said.

"Of course."

"Go to Dr. Bell's brownstone and tell him what happened, then get him back here as quickly as possible."

Andrew thought about that for a moment, then nodded.

"I think I've got enough energy left for that," he said with an encouraging smile. "Sit tight." He drew himself up to his full height of nearly six feet, then took a deep breath and vanished with a soft popping noise.

"That was good work you did, Alex," George said once Andrew was gone. "I'm glad we could help."

"That book they were after," Alex said. "The rune book of Felix Markel. Did anyone manage to find it?"

"They're looking now," the lieutenant colonel said. "I don't imagine they'll have much luck until the explosion is cleaned up, but you never know."

Alex didn't like that answer, but it wasn't the lieutenant colonel's fault, so he excused himself and headed through the doors on the far side of the nurse's desk with Agent Mendes in tow.

"Where are we going?" she asked with a smirk.

"Sign above the door said treatment," Alex muttered, not really in the mood to make conversation. "That means the observation rooms are this way."

"Let me get you back to bed and you can visit when the doctors are sure you're not bleeding into your brain," Mendes said. "They're not going to let you see her anyway."

Alex still ached everywhere, but Aissa's comment brought a fierce grin to his face.

"I'd like to see them try to stop me," he said.

"Alex, honey," Mendes said in a patronizing voice. "Right now a stiff breeze could stop you."

Alex's grin grew wider, and he took a deep breath.

"Sorsha!" he called, his voice echoing down the hallway. "Where are you?"

Mendes opened her mouth to shush him, but suddenly the air in the hallway dropped a few degrees.

"I said, out of my way," Sorsha's voice came from farther down the hall. A moment later a door burst open and a large, muscular orderly was thrown out into the hall. Following shortly, Sorsha appeared. She was dressed in a hospital robe and her hands and arms were bandaged. A sizable chunk of her lovely platinum hair was missing, and Alex could see a bandage on the bare part of her head.

Almost immediately, she sagged against the door frame, but she smiled when she saw Alex limping down the hall toward her. He'd forgotten the bullet wound in his leg, but now that the rest of his body was starting to hurt less, he could feel it again.

"You're all right," Sorsha gasped, throwing herself into his arms as he reached her.

"Me?" Alex said, incredulously. "You're the one who got the explosion in the kisser."

"I'm all right," she said, pressing her cheek to his chest. "I'm not back to one hundred percent yet, but that's only a matter of time. I'd be a lot worse if you hadn't warned me," she went on. "I managed to get a rudimentary shield up just in time. It deflected the worst of the blast."

Alex didn't respond; he just held her while she held him back. He'd been worried about her from the moment he woke up, but he'd never allowed himself to consider that Sorsha Kincaid, the all-powerful Ice Queen, might have actually died. A sickening dread accompanied the thought, and he had to will himself not to tremble as it washed over him.

"Sorsha..." he began, not really knowing what to say.

"Idiots!" a familiar voice hollered from down the hall. "Both of you, get back into the room and sit down."

Alex turned to find Iggy marching down the hall toward them with his doctor's bag in hand. Andrew Barton was coming behind him, but the sorcerer looked spent and was moving fairly slowly. Clearly he had been more tired than he let on before he went to get Iggy.

Something else you owe the Lightning Lord, Alex thought, though he didn't really mind this one.

"Iggy," Alex said, relief finally flooding his system. It had only been a few minutes since Andrew had left, and he expected it would be at least half an hour before he returned. "What brings you all the way out here?"

"Don't give me that," he growled. "Now do as I say, or I'll have the nurses give you an eight-hour enema."

"Yes, Dad," Alex grumbled under his breath, then he helped Sorsha stand on her own again before helping her back to her room. He led her to her bed and made sure she didn't fall as she sat down, then he shuffled to a chair by the door and fell heavily onto it.

He growled as he was forcibly reminded of the bullet in his leg. The pain felt like the only thing keeping him conscious.

"Is that your blood?" Iggy asked, standing over him and pointing to his leg.

"Take care of Sorsha," Alex mumbled.

"According to the doctors, she's stable and healing," Iggy said, "so she can wait. You take off your pants."

Alex fumbled with his belt while the orderly from the hall tugged on his trouser legs.

"Just as I thought," Iggy growled when he saw the wound. A moment later a vial of some nasty fluid was shoved into Alex's mouth. "Drink," Iggy commanded.

Alex didn't remember much of the following hours. At some point, he'd been moved to Sorsha's bed so Iggy could dig the bullet out of his leg and examine him properly. After that, he'd dozed in the wooden chair while Iggy worked on Sorsha. Finally, after what seemed like a very long time, Alex's mind began to focus again.

When the world around him stopped being a fuzzy blur, Alex found himself seated by Sorsha's bed as the Sorceress slept. He'd only just tried to stand when the room door opened, and Iggy came in.

"How is she?" Alex croaked, his voice not fully working yet.

"You're fine," Iggy said, his voice cross. "The bullet missed the bone and your femoral artery. Of course, if it hadn't, you'd have been dead long before I could have helped."

"Sorry," Alex slurred. "My vault door to the brownstone disappeared."

"Oh," Iggy said, looking somewhat abashed. "After that Randolph fellow tried to explode his way into the place I figured I'd better increase the potency of our wards. It must have cut the link to your vault. Sorry, lad."

"No problem," Alex said. "I'll open a new one once we get back. Now, how is Sorsha?"

Iggy sighed and jerked his head toward the door. A wave of fear washed over Alex and he was suddenly and painfully awake. Rising as best he could on his still throbbing leg, he limped after his mentor.

"The doctors said her sorcerer's healing isn't working right," Alex began once the door was closed.

"They're correct," Iggy said. He reached into his suit coat pocket and pulled out the pair of green spectacles Moriarty had given him a few months previously. "Go have a look at Miss Kincaid."

Alex stepped back into the observation room and slipped the spectacles on. The great thing about these glasses was that they could see magical residue without the necessity of ghostlight. As of yet, Alex hadn't been able to figure out how they worked, but that was only a matter of time.

He hoped.

As he looked through the green lenses, a massive magical ring appeared over Sorsha's chest. It looked like a rune, but no rune Alex had ever seen before. It was rounded, like a doughnut, and magic symbols seemed to swirl and move inside the shape. There was runic text that spiraled around the outside of the doughnut shape, while power symbols swirled inside. The whole thing was both alien and familiar.

As Alex watched, blue lines of force rose up from Sorsha's chest, like steam. When the lines touched the strange construct, they glowed brightly and vanished. Alex had no idea what was happening, but it certainly didn't look good.

Stepping back outside, Alex handed the spectacles back to Iggy.

"What is that thing?" he asked.

"It's a rune," Iggy said. "That much is certain, though it's not like any rune I've ever seen before."

"What is it doing to her?"

Iggy sighed and stroked his mustache.

"As near as I can tell, it's siphoning off her magic," he said. "That's why she's not healing normally, some of her power is being drained by the rune."

Alex's fists clenched involuntarily.

"Well, then let's get her inside my vault and we'll shut all the doors," he said. "That'll break whatever connection it has to whoever cast it."

"Maybe," Iggy said.

"Definitely," Alex replied. "You know links can't survive being separated from this plane of existence."

"You're assuming it's a purposeful rune," Iggy said. "From what Andrew told me, someone high up in the Legion was speaking through the man who exploded. That means he had a mind rune on him in addition to the blasting rune."

"He might have had any number of runes tattooed on him or maybe linked if they know how to do that," Alex said.

"Which is my point," Iggy said. "What if that isn't an intentional rune, but rather an accidental one?"

Alex processed what Iggy said for a moment, not sure he understood.

"You mean it's some kind of magical residue?" he guessed. "Something made up of random runes that were mashed together by the explosion?"

Iggy nodded.

"It's a possibility," he said. "It would explain why it looks the way it does."

"So what do we do?" Alex asked. "Just wait for it to dissipate? What if it kills her?"

Iggy put a restraining hand on Alex's arm.

"So far, her magic is stronger than that thing's ability to drain her power," Iggy said. "It will take her longer to heal, but eventually, she'll be fine."

"What if that Frankenstein's Monster of a rune absorbs so much power it explodes?" Alex demanded.

"I'm not suggesting we give up," Iggy said. "Just that we don't run off half-cocked. So far, it doesn't seem to be absorbing power so much as diffusing it. We'll need to keep a close eye on Sorsha in case that changes, but for now, let's proceed with caution."

"So what do we do?" Alex asked, trying not to scream in frustration.

"For now, we let her heal," Iggy said, putting his hand on Alex's shoulder. "When she's feeling better, we'll try and get a better look at that mess of a rune and figure out how to untangle the gordian knot."

"Didn't that have to be cut?" Alex asked.

"I'm hoping that between the two of us, we can do better," Iggy said. He picked up his doctor's bag and turned toward the nurse's station. "Now if you don't mind, my boy, I'm told they're a bit short-handed here, so I thought I'd pitch in and help."

"I've got to get back to Washington tonight," Alex said, his mind working overtime. "Will you check in on Sorsha for me?"

Iggy promised that he would, and headed off to find out where he could best be utilized. Alex waited until he was gone before following. Instead of heading into the emergency ward, however, he turned and headed out into the waiting area. There he found Andrew chatting with George.

"I need to get back to Washington," Alex said as he joined them.

"We need to get George and his men back to Fort Riley first," Andrew protested.

"No need," George said. "My CO wants me to stay here until everyone's healthy enough to return, then we'll catch a train."

Alex looked expectancy at Andrew, who groaned.

"I don't know if I've got another teleport in me today," he said. "I've been all over the place. Tell you what, if I can sleep in my own bed tonight, I'll take you to Washington first thing in the morning. Deal?"

"Fine." In all honesty he was exhausted and a night in his comfortable apartment bed sounded good. "Come on."

Alex led the way back to the treatment wing and into an empty room. A few minutes later, he pulled his vault door closed behind him and left Oak Ridge, Tennessee behind.

34

THE BLACK CHAMBER

True to his word, Andrew knocked on the door to Alex's Empire Tower apartment bright and early the next morning, and whisked them off to D.C. . Alex left him to finish his packing in the hotel and went to see Tiffany Young.

"You're lucky you caught me," she said, once she'd answered the door. "I just got back from church, and I catch a train in an hour. I assume you have something more to report after you and the pretty Sorceress ran out of here so suddenly yesterday."

Alex sighed, then launched into the explanation of the Legion and what they were really after.

"I suspect their original plan was to be the winning bid to move everything from the facility in Oak Ridge," he finished. "Then they'd just load up their trucks and drive away, never to be seen again. The only thing I don't understand is why they resorted to murder. I'm sure your husband would have been amenable to a...a different arrangement."

"You mean a bribe," Tiffany said with no trace of self-consciousness. She sighed and shook her head, dabbing a tear from the corner of her eye. "Paul has a cousin with a fleet of trucks," she said. "He was going to give him the job of moving the files from the research facilities. Believe it or not, that would have made more for us than any bribe."

That was the last piece of the puzzle, and Alex felt a wave of relief wash over him as he understood. The Legion had probably tried to bribe Senator Young, but he wouldn't budge on the moving contract. When that happened, the Legion simply had him killed.

"These Legion people," Tiffany said. "You disrupted their plans?"

Alex nodded.

"They did manage to get away with some rune books," he said, "but a force from the Army and the FBI stopped them."

"Were any Legion people killed?" she asked, intensity creeping into her voice.

"Yes, quite a few."

"Good," Tiffany said with bleak, vengeful satisfaction. She took in a deep breath and let it out again. "Thank you, Alex," she said. "At least I know what really happened."

She gave Alex a check for his work just as a cab arrived to take her to the train station. Once she was gone, Alex returned to the cab he'd left idling at the curb, and headed into the city proper.

Three-quarters of an hour and one stop later, Alex paid the cabbie and headed inside the front doors of Providence Hospital. He rode the elevator up to the third floor, then down to room three fifty-eight. Pulling the door open, he found Connie sitting up having a conversation with Lucky Tony, who sat in a chair beside the bed. Tony's two bodyguards stood over by the window, and they had both moved toward the door the moment it opened.

"Alex," Connie exclaimed as the bodyguard hesitated. "I was wondering if you'd come to see me. The boss," he nodded toward Tony, "tells me you found Colton."

"Yeah," Alex said, stepping inside the room.

"See," Connie said, his voice going back to its gruff timbre. "Told you he didn't run out on the boss."

Alex chuckled and nodded.

"You were right," he said. "I wanted to say thanks for helping me, and I'm sorry you got caught up in something that wasn't your problem."

"Did you find the man who shot Connie?" Tony asked in a manner far too casual.

"No," Alex said with a sigh. "I expect that it was a professional, so he's long gone."

That was only a guess, but it was the answer most likely to get Lucky Tony off the idea of looking for a little payback. Before anyone could ask more, Alex placed a rectangular package wrapped in brown paper on the table next to Connie's bed.

"What's this?" the gangster asked.

"I figured after all your hard work, you could use some nice single-malt Scotch," Alex said.

Connie picked up the box and felt its weight.

"Good stuff?" he asked.

"Thirty years old," Alex said. "Best I could find. Save it for special occasions."

"You're all right," Connie said with a grin.

Alex hesitated, then turned to Tony.

"Can I have a word?" he asked, nodding toward the hallway. His bodyguards bristled, but Tony waved their concerns away.

"Sure," he said. "Why don't you break out that Scotch?" he said to Connie. "We'll toast your recovery when I get back."

Connie grinned and tore the paper off the box as Alex and Tony moved to the hall.

"What's on your mind, Alex?" Tony asked once the door was closed.

Alex steadied himself. He knew what he was about to do was dangerous, but it was necessary, and there really wasn't any other option.

"I need to get my hands on a book in the government's rune research facility in Oak Ridge, Tennessee," he said.

Tony failed to hide the ghost of a smile.

"And you think I can get it for you?"

"You said the way to get things done was to buy a Senator," Alex said. "I figure a Senator would be able to request the book and then conveniently lose it."

Tony chuckled and shook his head.

"You're thinking too big," he said, putting his hand on Alex's shoulder. "Just find someone who works there and bribe them to slip you the book. But use a go between," he added. "That way, if your inside man gets caught, he can't finger you."

Alex ground his teeth. Tony's explanation sounded reasonable, but it was well beyond Alex's experience.

"What's so important about this book, Alex?"

"Yesterday a bunch of rogue runewrights raided the place," Alex said. "Sorsha Kincaid and I managed to get there in time to stop them, but they set off some kind of magic bomb. It went off in Sorsha's face."

"Is she alive?" Tony asked, his expression neutral.

Alex nodded.

"But something about the spell is weakening her, and the rune is unlike anything I've ever seen. It twists around itself like a complex knot."

"And this book you want will help you figure it out?"

"Sorsha used a truth spell on one of the Legion men," Alex explained.

"Those are illegal," Tony said with a grin.

"He said they were looking, specifically, for the rune book of a man named Felix Markel, a book that describes something called a Gordian Rune."

"Gordian? As in the Gordian Knot?"

"I don't know," Alex admitted. "But the Legion knew about it, and one of their runes looks like a knot, and it could kill Sorsha."

Tony nodded, then shrugged.

"Why don't you tell this to your friend, Andrew Barton? I heard he met with the President; surely he can get this book for you."

Alex had asked himself the same question, but if he managed to unravel the rune, that would raise suspicions. People would wonder how he knew so much about rune magic. Questions would be asked about how much he really knew about the mythical Archimedean Monograph...and how much his mentor knew.

Questions like that could destroy his life, and Iggy's to boot. If he was going to save Sorsha, no one could know how he'd done it.

"Let's just say that's complicated," he answered Tony. "I need that book and I don't have time to wait for six months of meetings and government red tape."

Tony laughed at that, but there was no malice in his tone.

"You've learned a lot since you came here," he said.

"You have no idea," Alex said. "I want you to get that book for me and in return, I can help you with your brewery problems."

Tony raised an eyebrow at Alex.

"What problems?" he asked. "Colton is safe and well in Rio, and soon he'll have the last ingredient he needs to go into full production."

Alex reached into his outer coat pocket and pulled out a folded magazine.

"Colton found out about Dr. Bolsonaro's cashew apple extract from an article in the American Alchemical Journal," he said, handing over the copy he'd purchased that morning. "I knew Colton had gone to South America, because one of the alchemists I know saw the article on Dr. Bolsonaro's extract and realized that Colton was looking for a source of cashew apples. The reason you can't get cashew apples here in the states is that they go bad very quickly after being picked."

"Okay," Tony said.

"My friend called me yesterday because she re-read the article and pointed out that Dr. Bolsonaro's extract will last longer than the fruit, but it still spoils. You'd have to fly the extract up here if you want to use it in time, because a boat trip will take too long."

Lucky Tony's face hardened as he calculated the increased costs of such expensive transportation. Alex knew he was reaching the same conclusion he had when he cooked up this scheme last night.

"And you can fix that problem?" he asked after a moment.

"I can," he said, reaching into his shirt pocket. "Preservation rune," he said, handing over the folded paper.

Tony accepted the paper, but looked at it as if it were a piece of trash.

"These'll keep milk from going bad in your icebox for a week," he said, holding it out to Alex. "They won't work on a shipment of delicate fruit."

"Don't be so sure," Alex said with a predatory grin. "That rune is much more powerful than your standard preservation rune. It can protect a greater volume for far longer. Call it a...major preservation rune."

Tony opened the paper and looked at the incredibly complex rune inside. It was one of Iggy's inventions that he'd made Alex draw several years ago as part of his training. Alex had never needed it before, but he was glad to have it now. It would take him several days to write another one, but that wouldn't be a problem.

"This will keep the cashew apples fresh for their boat ride from Brazil?"

Alex nodded.

"Sure, but why do that?" he said. "Tell Colton to buy Dr. Bolsonaro's process, then set up a shop down there. You make the extract, then load it in a shipping crate, hit it with the preservation rune, and ship it up here to your brewery."

Tony's face was one of naked calculation, then he smiled.

"I get you your book and you'll provide me with as many of these as I need?" he said.

"One a month," Alex said. "That should cover more than enough extract to run your brewery."

"For how long?"

"Let's say a year," Alex answered.

"Let's say five," Tony countered.

"Three."

"Okay," Tony said, "but what about after that? Where am I going to get this very special rune once our deal is over?"

"I'll sell them to you," Alex said.

Tony chuckled.

"I like you, Alex," he said, shaking his head. "You've got just enough of the killer instinct to be dangerous. But what happens to my business if you have a change of heart?"

"I told you I'd sell you major preservation runes, and I will."

"And I believe that you believe that, here and now."

"But?" Alex asked.

"But what happens when dear Sorsha is all better? What if you decide to change your mind? What if you need some other favor from me? You could use these runes as leverage and put me over a barrel."

Alex wanted to protest that he would never do that, but a world-weary businessman like Lucky Tony Casetti would have heard that song and dance many times before.

He sighed.

"What do you want, then?"

"I want you as my partner, Alex," Tony said, putting a friendly arm around Alex's shoulders.

"Partner?"

"I'll get you your book, and you join me in my business venture at… let's say five percent."

Alex followed the chain of causality fairly easily.

"That way I'm making money off your beer sales," he said, "and I'm incentivized to make sure the extract shipments go on uninterrupted."

"I said you were smart," Tony said. "You get what you want. I get what I want, and you can't hold me up over it without hurting yourself. That's a pretty good deal."

Alex thought about the offer. Tony was right. It was a good deal, one that could make Alex a great deal of money if Homestead Beer sold as well as he suspected it would. The only real downside was that he would be in business with someone who wouldn't hesitate to put a bullet in him if things went south.

He shook his head to clear it.

It didn't matter what Lucky Tony the gangster had in mind. All that mattered was getting Felix Markle's Gordian Rune book before whatever the Legion did to Sorsha killed her.

Alex held out his hand to Tony.

"Deal," he said, hoping that if he regretted it in the future, he'd actually live to regret it.

Tony took his hand and shook it firmly.

"Deal," he said. "Now, since we're partners, that makes you…well, it makes you a member of the family."

Alex suppressed a shiver when the mob boss said 'family.'

"Why don't you come back inside and have a drink with Connie and me to celebrate."

Alex trudged down the hall of the Hay-Adams hotel for what he hoped would be the last time. Retrieving his hotel key, he let himself into his room. It was as he had remembered it, with his oversized map of D.C. sitting on the coffee table he'd dragged over by the desk, and his kit sitting on the floor nearby. He hadn't really unpacked anything other than the tools of his trade, leaving his clothes in his vault bedroom, so there wasn't really very much to pack up.

As Alex shut the door behind him, his senses snapped into sharp focus. There was the faint aroma of cigar smoke in the room. His eyes sought out the chairs and couches by the windows, but no one was there.

He turned toward the bedroom just as the door opened and a man emerged. He had a broad, rectangular face with a large nose and thinning white hair. His suit was stylish and well-tailored, and his hands were manicured. If this man was here to cause trouble, he certainly wasn't dressed for it.

"I thought I heard someone come in," he said, giving Alex a genuine smile.

"What are you doing in my room?" Alex asked. His voice was somewhat testy after the day he'd had.

"Nothing too objectionable," the man said, his grin never slipping. "I always like to see the washroom. You can tell a lot about a man from his washroom."

He chuckled as if he'd made a joke, but Alex didn't respond.

"Sorry," he went on. "Old habit."

"Who are you?" Alex asked, his temper under better control now.

"Name's Donovan, Bill Donovan, and you are Alex Lockerby." He held up his hand in a theatrical sweep. "Runewright extraordinaire, detective to the stars, solver of cold cases."

"You've been reading my press."

"Yes, and I like what I've seen," Donovan continued, his smile never wavering. "That bit with the rune research facility down south was quite the feather in your cap, at least in my circles."

Alex got gooseflesh on his arms. The operation in Oak Ridge was supposed to have been a secret, yet Donovan knew about it.

"Yes, I know about that," he said, reading the expression on Alex's face.

"What can I do for you, Mr. Donovan?" Alex asked, hoping to get to the point of the strange man's visit.

"Have you ever heard of the Black Chamber, Mr. Lockerby?" he asked.

"No," Alex admitted.

"It was an organization of code breakers during the big war," the man explained. "It was their job to intercept and decrypt coded messages. The members of the Black Chamber were very good at their jobs and, at the time, they were the only intelligence gathering organization in the entire US government."

"Intelligence," Alex repeated. "You mean spies."

"I mean that exactly, Alex," Donovan said. "Would it surprise you to learn that the government disbanded the Black Chamber almost a decade ago?"

"Why would they do that?"

"Because some snooty congressman didn't think keeping an eye on our neighbors was honorable."

As a detective, Alex understood the power of, and need for, surveillance.

"That's all very interesting, Mr. Donovan," Alex said, "but I doubt you're here to recruit me to be a codebreaker for an organization that closed down. So why are you here?"

"As I said, the US government doesn't have a *formal* organization to gather intelligence," Donovan said, emphasizing the word 'formal.'

"So you're the informal one," Alex guessed.

Donovan chuckled.

"Something like that."

"And you want to offer me a job as an official government snoop?" Alex scoffed.

"Not right now," Donovan said. "You and your partner in crime,

Miss Kincaid, have exactly the kinds of skills we could use, but now isn't the time."

"Well if you're not going to offer me a job that you seem to already know I'd turn down, what are you doing in my room?"

Donovan reached into his pocket and pulled out a business card, handing it to Alex. There were only two things on the card, the name 'Bill Donovan,' and a phone number.

"You and Miss Kincaid wasted almost an entire day putting your strike team together," he said. "Next time you run across something that needs decisive action, don't bother hunting up Captain Vaughn or Lieutenant Colonel Patton."

Alex was more than a little disturbed by how well-informed Donovan was.

"Next time, you call me," Donovan continued. "If you tell me there's a group of power-mad runewrights about to storm a top secret government facility, then I'll believe you."

"I thought you weren't an official part of the government," Alex said, tucking the card into his shirt pocket.

"I'm not," Donovan said. "But I know things, like who among the official government types can be trusted, and who to call in an emergency."

Alex smiled in spite of his annoyance. If Donovan was telling the truth, he was a very useful friend to have.

"There is one other thing, Alex," Donovan said, reaching down to pick up a gray fedora from the couch facing the windows. "I've had my eye on you for a while, but your recent activities have attracted other attention as well."

Alex didn't like the sound of that.

"What attention?"

"The museum robberies," Donovan went on. "An alchemical potion that turns regular people into monsters is pretty sophisticated, don't you think? Does it remind you of anything you might have seen before?"

That shiver that had gone down Alex's back before returned, and it brought friends.

"No," he lied. As far as he knew, only Danny and Sorsha knew about Dr. Kellin's Jekyll and Hyde formula, and neither of them would betray the secret. Either Donovan was fishing, or he had a different connection in mind.

"Do the names Helge Rothenbaur, Greta Albrecht, and Dietrich Strand mean anything to you?" Donovan asked.

Alex nodded.

"They were responsible for that magical plague a few years back," he said, keeping his response vague. Donovan seemed very well informed, but Alex didn't know how much information the spy really had, so he resolved not to let anything slip.

"You read Dietrich Strand's confession, so you know they were trying to stop the plague from being used," Donovan went on. "Do you remember why they developed it in the first place?"

Alex searched his memory. He'd been told a great deal of technical details about the plague, by Iggy and by the incomprehensible Dr. Halverson, but most of it was over his head and thus quickly forgotten.

"Something about its being used to help cure diseases?"

"Very good," Donovan nodded. "The three unfortunate alchemists were lied to by their boss, the man who now runs Hitler's alchemical weapons lab."

"Joe something?" Alex said, straining his memory for the name.

"Josef," Donovan corrected. "Josef Mengele. He's an alchemist and a medical doctor."

"And he's coming after me now?" Alex asked, an amused expression on his face. "That was five years ago. This Mengele fellow sure holds onto a grudge."

Donovan gave Alex a penetrating look, and Alex connected the dots.

"He's 'The Alchemist,'" Alex guessed. "He made the drug that hooked Zelda Pritchard's domestics, and he supplied them with the transformation serum."

Donovan nodded.

"The Germans call him Führer der Alchemisten," Donovan said. "It just means 'leader of the alchemists,' but everything sounds more impressive in German. This is the second time you've interfered with his plans, and my reports tell me he's not a very forgiving sort of man."

Alex suddenly felt the need to work on more shield runes and maybe even a new escape rune. It would take more time than he could spare, but it didn't sound like he had much of a choice.

"I'll keep my eyes open," he said.

"Do that," Donovan said, heading for the door. When he arrived, he reached for the handle, but stopped short and turned back. "One more thing, Alex," he said. "I expect that the next time we meet, it'll be about that job offer."

"I'll save you a trip," Alex said. "Not interested."

"You're not interested now," Donovan said. "But things are changing fast. You might feel differently, and sooner than you think."

"You mean when war breaks out in Europe."

It was a statement rather than a question, and it got a knowing smile out of Donovan. He regarded Alex for a long moment, then took hold of the door handle and pulled it open.

"Most people aren't willing to admit to themselves that war is coming," he said, stepping out into the hall.

"So people keep telling me."

"Sounds like you know some smart people," Donovan said. "You should listen to them." He started to shut the door but hesitated. "Don't lose that card, Alex," he said. "And give Miss. Kincaid my regards for a speedy recovery."

Without another word, he shut the door and was gone.

Alex pulled the card from his pocket and examined it. Having someone who could mobilize the Army whenever Alex found something worthy of their attention was a good thing, but he wondered exactly what strings came attached to that deal. For its part, the card was just a card, and it gave him no answers.

35

LOOSE THREADS

For the second time in as many weeks, Ben Robertson passed through the door of the Forum club. Last time he'd been excited to report to the Legion, but this time he dreaded every step. When he reached the private reading room inside the vault, his hand was trembling so violently he had to take a moment to center himself before he raised the knocker and let it fall.

"Come," a gruff voice called.

The last time Ben had been in this room, he'd found the three local Masters reading. This time Masters Torrence and Simons had moved their chairs near the low table and were engaged in a game of chess while Master Morrow looked on.

"Journeyman Robertson," Master Morrow said, recognizing him. "What news from our venture?"

Ben took a breath, giving himself a brief moment before he had to begin.

"It is as we feared, Master," he said. "The only books we were able to secure were the ones our brothers brought back when they used their escape runes."

"No one else managed to escape?" Master Torrence asked. "How disappointing."

"What about Felix Markel's rune book?" Master Morrow asked.

"It wasn't among the books we recovered," Ben reported. "I managed to learn that the FBI is looking for it in the ruins of the destroyed building. They thought they had found it, but it was a false report. So far it's still missing, and they've recovered most of the surviving books."

Master Simons snorted angrily and Torrence swore.

"When I think of the time and money we spent on this operation," Torrence said with a sneer. "All of it wasted."

"Maybe not," Master Simons said, moving his knight to queen's bishop five. "What about the Sorceress?"

Ben felt his mouth go dry. The description of what happened once Sorsha Kincaid had started interrogating his fellow Journeymen would give him nightmares for the foreseeable future.

"A-after you spoke to her through Journeyman Phillips," he said, forcing his voice to work, "his failsafe rune activated. I found someone in the local hospital who confirmed she was seriously wounded."

"Not dead?" Master Torrence growled, shifting a pawn. "I'd have thought she would have been taken by surprise."

"I wondered that too, Master," Ben interjected, earning him a sour look from the bald man. "I impersonated an FBI investigator and interviewed several of the survivors."

"And?" Simons snapped.

"All the ones who were present told the same story," Ben went on. "Someone warned her just before the blast."

"That would be your private detective, Rupert," Master Morrow said to the elder Master. "Your queen's in danger."

Simons scoffed as he surveyed the board, and Morrow turned to Ben.

"Is it enough to hope that he was killed in the blast?" he asked.

"No, Master. He had a concussion, but apparently he recovered quickly."

"Too bad," Simons said, teasing Torrence by pulling back his rook.

"There is some good news," Ben said as the Masters focused on their chess game. Clearly they hadn't expected him to tell them anything they didn't already know. He decided to press on. "Some of

DAN WILLIS

the doctors were talking, and they said the Sorceress wasn't recovering as they expected." That got a reaction out of the three men at the chessboard, and they all turned to look at him. "Well, I assumed that means the spike rune took hold."

Morrow and Simons exchanged a knowing look, and the elder man tugged thoughtfully on his beard.

"How certain are you of this?" Master Torrence demanded.

Ben swallowed under the Masters' eyes and he could feel himself begin to sweat.

"Completely certain, Master," he said. "They were so concerned about it that they had the Sorcerer Andrew Barton teleport in a doctor from New York."

"What doctor?" Master Simons snapped.

Ben had assumed his news would be received well. He hadn't expected to be challenged.

"Uh," he stuttered. "I don't know, some Brit."

"Older man?" Simons demanded.

"Yes."

"Someone you know, Rupert?" Master Torrence asked.

"Ignatius Bell," the older man said. "He's Lockerby's landlord and a former doctor in the Royal Navy."

"So?" Torrence said.

"So, he was in the British Navy," Master Morrow jumped in, obviously understanding Simons' concern. "That means he's not just a doctor, he's a runewright."

The Masters exchanged meaningful looks, then all their eyes turned to Ben.

"Did you hear anything more?" Morrow asked Ben. "Any suggestion that they know about the spike?"

"I'm sorry, Master. I've told you all I know."

Master Torrance sneered and bared his teeth, but Simons put a restraining hand on the man's shoulder.

"Easy," he said. "If the spike is in place, the pile will be charging. We'll go check it as soon as our game is over."

"I'm starting to take a real dislike to your private detective,"

Torrance sneered back. "Between him, his girlfriend, and his landlord, he's becoming a problem. I thought you were going to have him eliminated, Lloyd."

That last was directed at Master Morrow.

"An attempt was made," Morrow said, "but it failed. From the report I got, it didn't even slow him down."

"We should make removing him a priority," Torrence growled.

"That might be unwise," Simons said, stroking his beard.

"What are you saying, Rupert?" Torrence scoffed. "He's interfered in major operations twice now, cost us dozens of assets and thousands of dollars. What are you waiting for, him to find his way in here?"

"No," Master Morrow cut in before Simons could respond. "Rupert is right. This Lockerby fellow must know about our existence. How else could he interfere so completely?"

"All the more reason to eliminate him."

"If we kill him, we'll never learn what he knows about us," Morrow countered.

"Or, more importantly," Simons added, "where he learned of us in the first place."

"What if they break the spike rune?" Torrence asked. "The guy's a detective who made his bones with a finding rune. He could use the spike and trace it back to us."

"Relax, Dale," Morrow said in a conciliatory voice. "Finding runes have a fairly limited range. Even if Mr. Lockerby is capable of unraveling the spike—"

"And he isn't," Simons said.

"Even if he is," Morrow continued, "he wouldn't be able to trace it to Washington from New York."

"So we're just going to let this private detective run wild and muck up our plans?" Torrence demanded.

"Of course not," Simons said, turning to look at Ben. "Young Ben here is going to use his talents to keep an eye on him."

Ben's blood went cold. He liked his cushy job keeping a Senator's calendar. Besides, Legion agents close to Alexander Lockerby tended to end up dead.

"T-thank you, Master," he managed, his voice a bit higher than normal.

"What about the spike?" Torrence said. "If this detective is so smart, he might figure it out."

"It's much more likely that he and the doctor will break the rune if they try to remove it," Morrow said.

"They won't do that," Simons said, chuckling to himself. "If that British doctor is any good at his craft at all, he's going to know that breaking the spike rune will kill Miss Kincaid. From where I sit, there's nothing they can do about it but watch as she gets weaker."

"Eventually, they'll get desperate and try something," Morrow said. "What then?"

"With any luck," Simons said, sliding his bishop across the board, "the rune will explode when they try, and we'll be rid of the entire problem. Checkmate."

Torrence growled as he examined the board.

"I think that will be all, Journeyman Robertson," Morrow said as the other two Masters began to reset the chessboard. "Why don't you get your affairs in order, and we'll get you set up with a new job and apartment in New York?"

"Thank you, Master," Ben said, not meaning it.

There was nothing in Ben's voice to indicate his displeasure, but Master Morrow seemed to sense it. He put his arm around Ben's shoulder and walked him back to the door.

"Don't worry, young Ben," he said. "This is one of the most important jobs we have at the moment. Keep your eyes open and send detailed reports. If you see something we can use, it may just be your ticket to Master."

Ben did like the sound of that, and he smiled in spite of himself.

"Thank you, Master," he repeated, meaning it this time.

By the time Alex trudged through the door of his office, he was tired, hungry, and footsore. He'd been all over the city, checking with every contact, crawling through every archive, and he'd come up empty. As far as he could tell, Felix Markle was a figment of the Legion's imagination. No record of someone with that name existed anywhere.

"Bad day, boss?" Sherry asked. She sat behind her desk going through her notepads, no doubt picking out new cases for him.

"You could say that," he growled. He'd been back in New York for a week and so far, the only useful thing he'd done was reinstalling his permanent vault door to the brownstone. Neither he nor Iggy had managed to learn anything about the Gordian rune leeching Sorsha's power, but at least she was recovering tolerably well.

He sighed, stuffing his anger down deep. None of this was Sherry's fault, and she didn't deserve to feel the effects of his mood.

"Anything new?" he asked.

"I put a couple of potential cases on your desk," she said. As she spoke, she stood up, and Alex noticed that she winced.

"What's the matter?" he asked.

"What?" she asked, looking up at him.

Alex's eyebrows dropped down over his eyes. He knew Sherry well, and she was lying to him. Deliberately. He fixed her with his most penetrating stare. When she stood, she'd used her left hand, pushing up on the desk as if the muscles of her back were weak.

Did she take a bad fall? Maybe a customer got physical.

That thought made Alex furious.

"Boss?" Sherry said, alarmed by what she read on his face.

"Let me see your back," he said. When she instantly blushed, he knew he was on the right track.

"Alex," she gasped in faux indignation. "That's hardly appropriate."

He crossed the distance between them in two steps, grabbing her left hand and pulling it up. With his free hand he pressed on her lower back, and she winced.

"Are you going to make me look for myself," he said, releasing her hand, "or are you going to come clean?"

Sherry gave him a hard look, then she sighed and turned around, pulling up her shirt to reveal a burn mark across her side with an oblong scar in the middle. The wound was clearly healing, but unless

Alex was very much mistaken, his secretary had been grazed by a bullet.

"Spill," he growled.

"I was in the wrong place at the wrong time," she said with a sigh.

"And where was that?" he demanded, not sure he believed her, especially since she began blushing immediately.

"It's none of your business, Alex," she said, not meeting his eyes. "I did something stupid, things happened, and I'm fine. I don't need you getting involved in my personal life."

Alex ground his teeth. Of course, Sherry was entitled to her privacy, but on the other hand, someone had taken a shot at her.

"Please, Alex," she said, giving him a stern look. "This isn't your business."

"All right," he said at last. "But if you get in trouble you tag me in immediately, got it?"

"Yes, boss," she said with a shy smile. She picked up a paper from her desk and held it out to him. "You have a message and there's a package for you."

Alex held her gaze for a moment, then took the paper.

"What is it?" he asked.

"Someone named Lyle Gundersen," Sherry said, heading for the coffee pot. "He says you have some pictures that he needs back."

Alex nodded, tucking the note into his shirt pocket. With all that had happened since Oak Ridge, he'd completely forgotten about the insurance photographs. They were currently sitting on the sideboard in his office. With his vault door in Washington D.C. closed, he'd have to send it down by courier.

"All right," he said. "Call a courier service to send a package of photographs to...to..."

"Boss?" Sherry asked.

"Photographs..." Alex said, his mind racing back to something he'd heard years ago. It was back when he'd first met Sorsha, when he'd first seen the runes from the Archimedean Monograph, but he didn't think that he'd be able to learn much because the pictures were made with a standard camera.

"Forget the courier," he told Sherry. "Get Billy Tasker on the phone and ask him if he has the kind of camera that can take pictures of active runes."

Sherry looked confused for a moment, then nodded and sat down.

"I'll be in my office," he said. "If Billy has one of those cameras, tell him to get it over here right away."

He left Sherry dialing the phone and made his way down the short back hall to his office. A stack of files sat on his desk, but he ignored them. He was too keyed up to worry about that. The biggest problem he had with the rune attached to Sorsha was getting a good enough look at it. If the camera worked, he'd at least have somewhere to start figuring it out.

As he paced back and forth in front of his desk, he noticed a small package wrapped in brown paper sitting to one side. Sherry had mentioned a package. With nothing to do but wait, he picked it up and tore it open. Inside was a folded white cloth with a note on top.

Alex,

I didn't hear back from you, so here's the pattern you asked for. Looks pretty weird to me.

The note was signed, Lewis Clayton, Alex's friend in the textile industry. Setting the note aside, Alex picked up the folded cloth. He'd forgotten that he'd asked Lewis to recreate the mysterious pattern from the Jacquard Loom.

The rune camera momentarily forgotten, he picked up the folded cloth and unfurled it like a flag. A moment later he almost dropped it as his hands started to shake. Laid out against the background of white was a blue pattern reproduced by a modern loom.

"What's that?" Sherry asked from his doorway.

"It's a shield rune," Alex said.

"Can you weave a rune?"

Alex shook his head slowly, then shrugged.

"You're not supposed to be able to," he said, then he realized it was Sherry at his door.

"What about that camera?"

She grinned at him and leaned against the doorframe.

"Billy says he'll be here in an hour with the camera," she said.

Alex closed his eyes and an enormous weight seemed to lift off him. Sorsha wasn't out of the woods, but this was the first real step in that direction.

"I'm going to go get Dr. Bell," he said, heading past her and pulling out his pocketwatch. "Call over to Sorsha's office and tell her we're coming to see her."

He pulled open his door, but looked back to see Sherry smiling at him.

"Will do, boss," she said. "And it's good to have you back."

THE END

You Know the Drill.

Thanks so much for reading my book, it really means a lot to me. This is the part where I ask you to please leave this book a review over on Amazon. It really helps me out since Amazon favors books with lots of reviews. That means I can share these books with more people, and that keeps me writing more books.

So leave a review by going to the Capital Murder book page on Amazon. It doesn't have to be anything fancy, just a quick note saying whether or not you liked the book.

Thanks so much. You Rock!

. . .

I love talking to my readers, so please drop me a line at dan@danwillisauthor.com — I read every one. Or join the discussion on the Arcane Casebook Facebook Group. Just search for Arcane Casebook and ask to join.

And Look for Alex's continuing adventures in Hostile Takeover, Arcane Casebook #8.

ALSO BY DAN WILLIS

Arcane Casebook Series:

Dead Letter - Prequel

Get Dead Letter free at www.danwillisauthor.com

Available on Amazon and Audible.

In Plain Sight - Book 1

Ghost of a Chance - Book 2

The Long Chain - Book 3

Mind Games - Book 4

Limelight - Book 5

Blood Relation - Book 6

Capital Murder - Book 7

Hostile Takeover - Book 8

Hidden Voices - Book 9

Dragons of the Confederacy Series:

A steampunk Civil War story with NYT Bestseller, Tracy Hickman.

These books are currently unavailable, but I will be putting them back on the market in 2022

Lincoln's Wizard

The Georgia Alchemist

Other books:

The Flux Engine

In a Steampunk Wild West, fifteen-year-old John Porter wants nothing more than to find his missing family. Unfortunately a legendary lawman, a talented thief, and a homicidal madman have other plans, and now John will need his wits, his pistol, and a lot of luck if he's going to survive.

Get The Flux Engine at Amazon.

ABOUT THE AUTHOR

Dan Willis wrote for the long-running DragonLance series. He is the author of the Arcane Casebook series and the Dragons of the Confederacy series.

For more information:
www.danwillisauthor.com
dan@danwillisauthor.com

facebook.com/danwillisauthor
twitter.com/WDanWillis
instagram.com/danwillisauthor
tiktok.com/@danwillisauthor

Printed in Great Britain
by Amazon